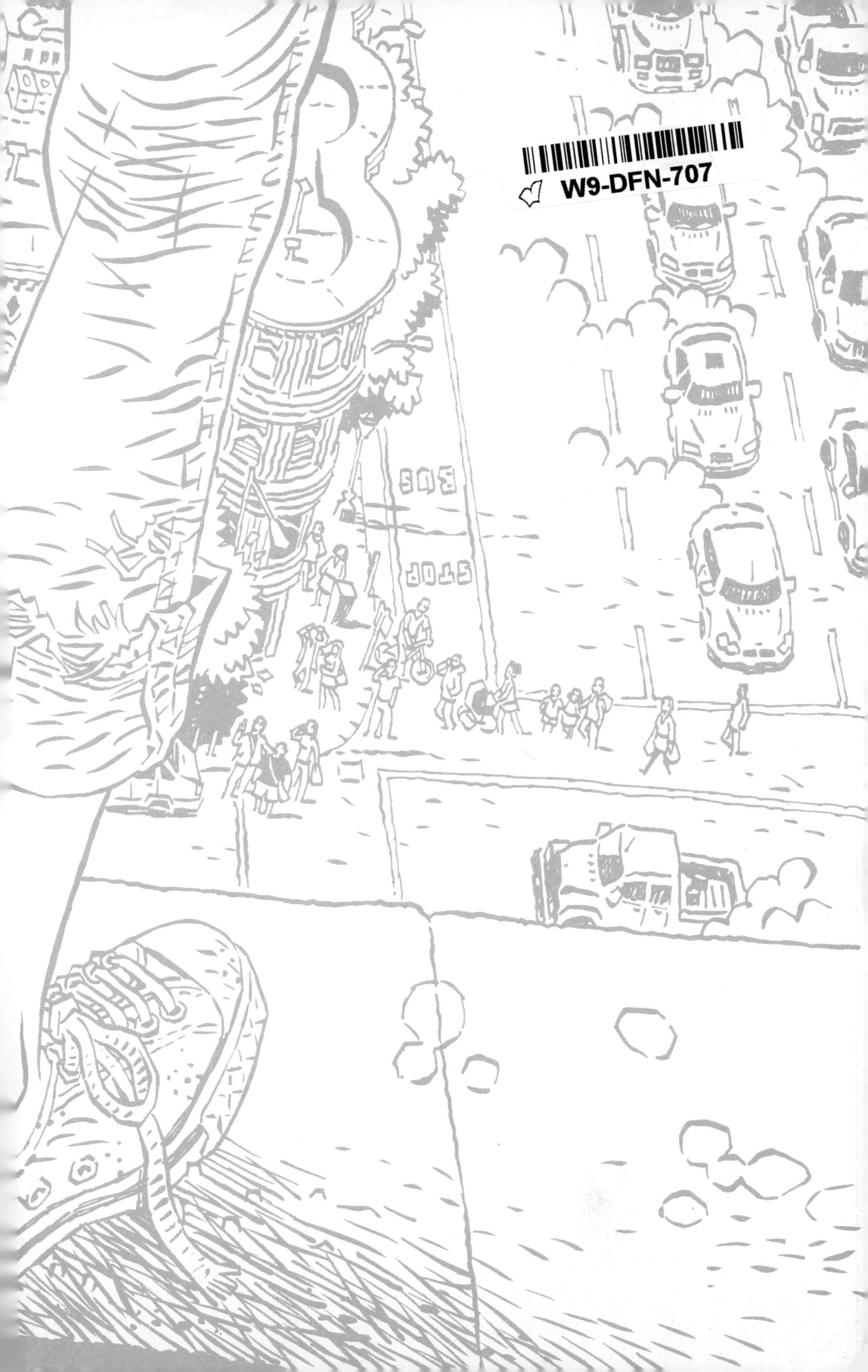
BUS
STOP

IMAGE COMICS, INC.

Robert Kirkman
CHIEF OPERATING OFFICER

Erik Larsen
CHIEF FINANCIAL OFFICER

Todd McFarlane
PRESIDENT

Marc Silvestri
CHIEF EXECUTIVE OFFICER

Jim Valentino
VICE-PRESIDENT

Eric Stephenson
PUBLISHER

Corey Murphy
DIRECTOR OF SALES

Jeremy Sullivan
DIRECTOR OF DIGITAL SALES

Kat Salazar
DIRECTOR OF PR & MARKETING

Emily Miller
DIRECTOR OF OPERATIONS

Branwyn Bigglestone
SENIOR ACCOUNTS MANAGER

Sarah Mello
ACCOUNTS MANAGER

Drew Gill
ART DIRECTOR

Jonathan Chan
PRODUCTION MANAGER

Meredith Wallace
PRINT MANAGER

Randy Okamura
MARKETING PRODUCTION
DESIGNER

David Brothers
CONTENT MANAGER

Addison Duke
PRODUCTION ARTIST

Vincent Kukua
PRODUCTION ARTIST

Sasha Head
PRODUCTION ARTIST

Tricia Ramos
PRODUCTION ARTIST

Emilio Bautista
SALES ASSISTANT

Jessica Ambriz
ADMINISTRATIVE
ASSISTANT

imagecomics.com

THEY'RE NOT ≠ LIKE US ™

VOLUME ONE

BLACK HOLES FOR THE YOUNG

ERIC STEPHENSON
story

SIMON GANE
art

JORDIE BELLAIRE
color

FONOGRAFIKS
letters + design

SPECIAL THANKS TO JAMIE S. RICH
FOR EDITING ASSISTANCE

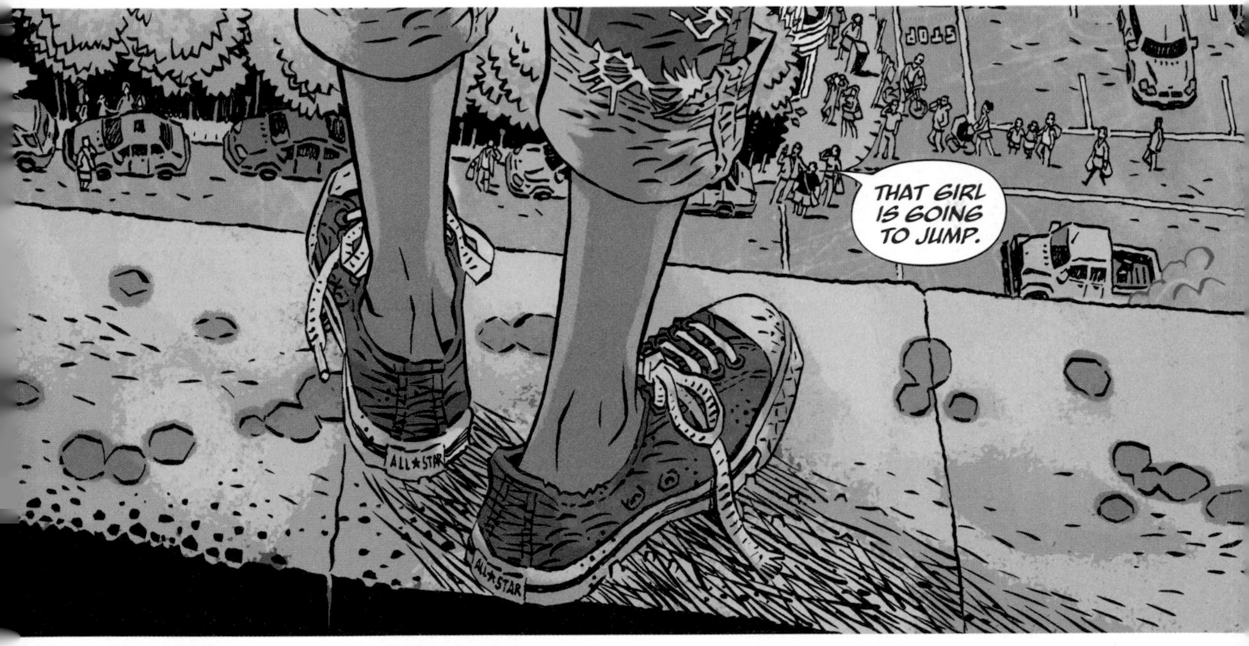
THAT GIRL IS GOING TO JUMP.
ALL★STAR
ALL★STAR

I: FROM DESPAIR TO WHERE

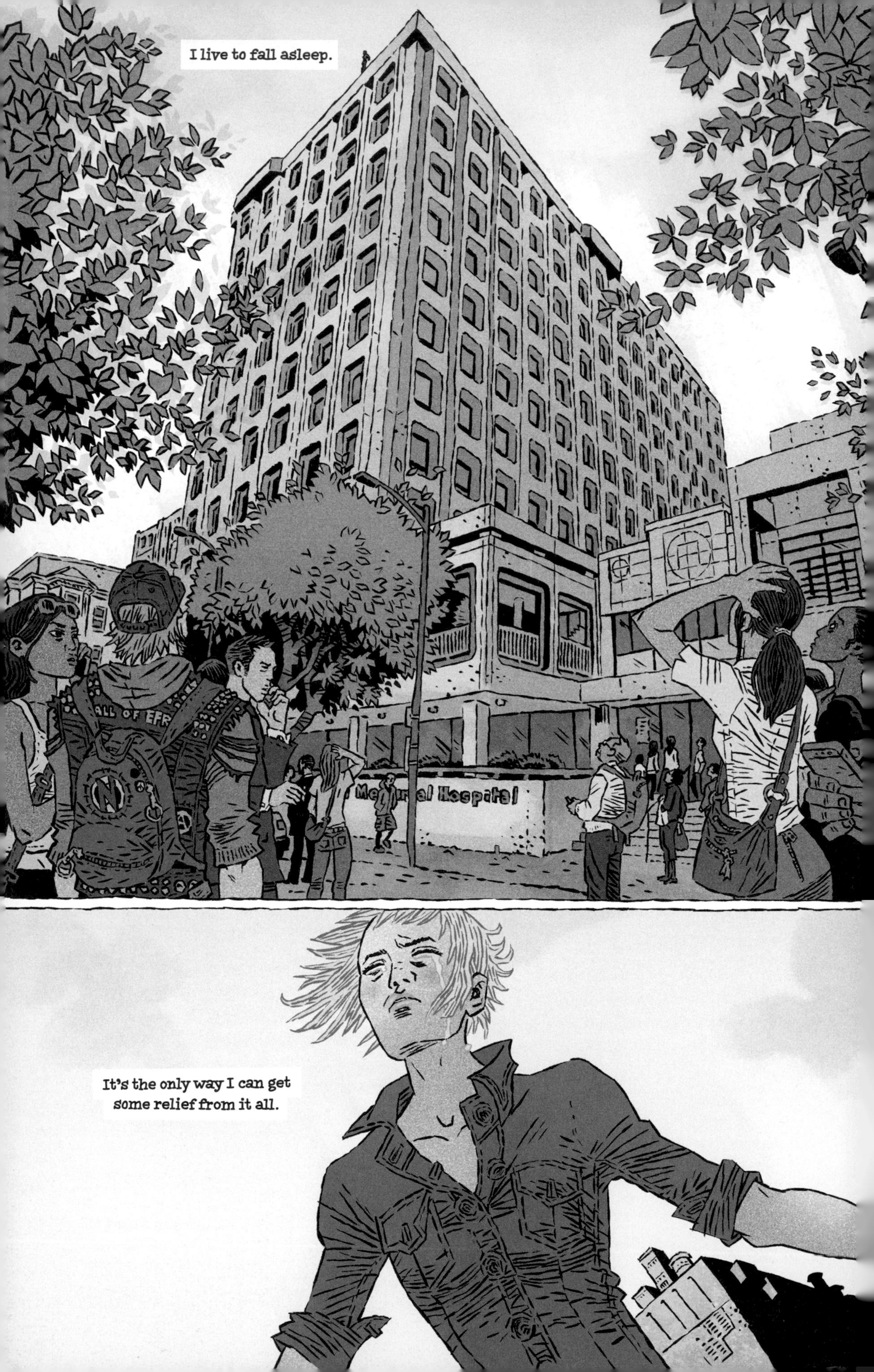
I live to fall asleep.
It's the only way I can get some relief from it all.

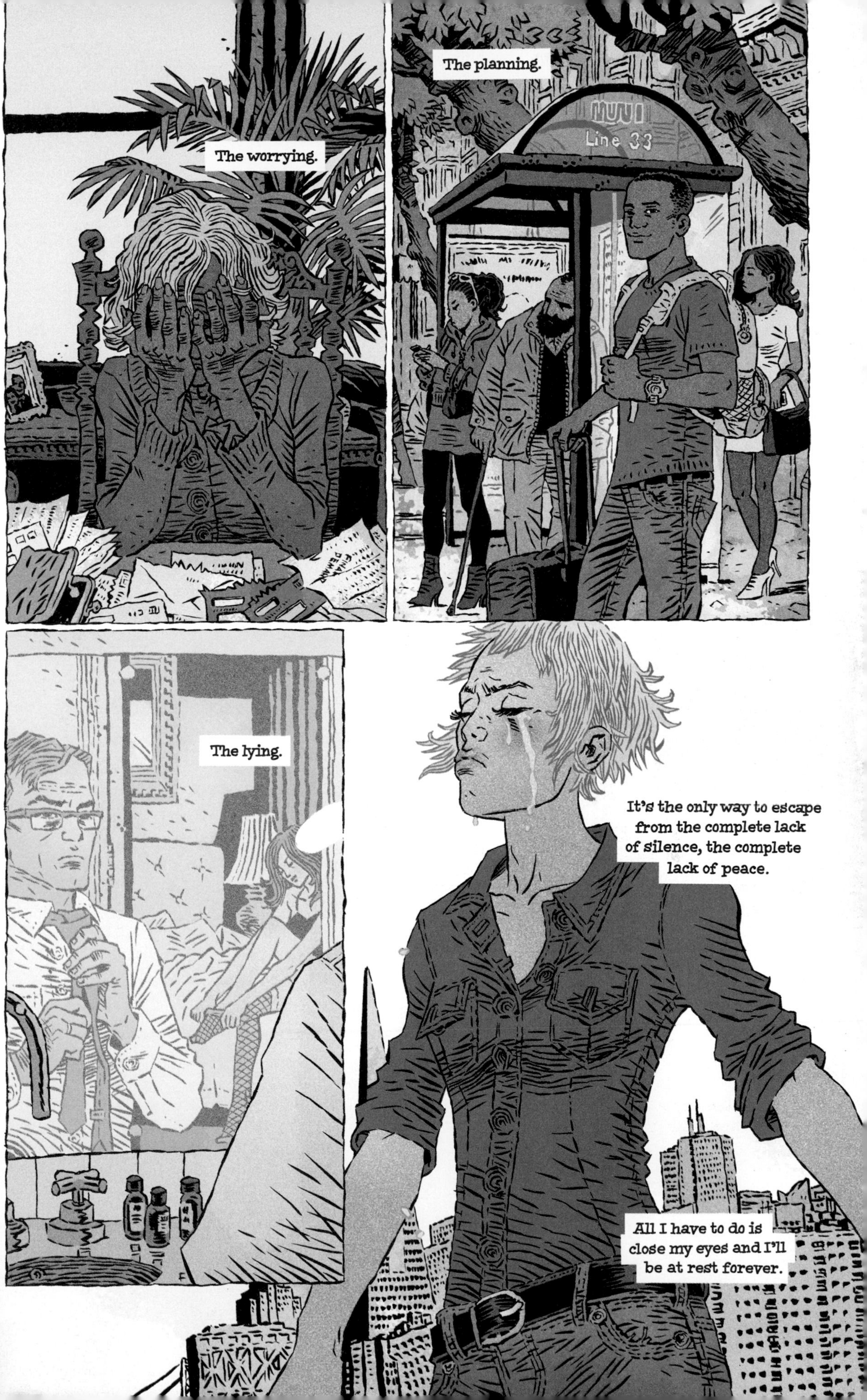

The worrying.
The planning.
Line 33
The lying.
It's the only way to escape from the complete lack of silence, the complete lack of peace.
All I have to do is close my eyes and I'll be at rest forever.

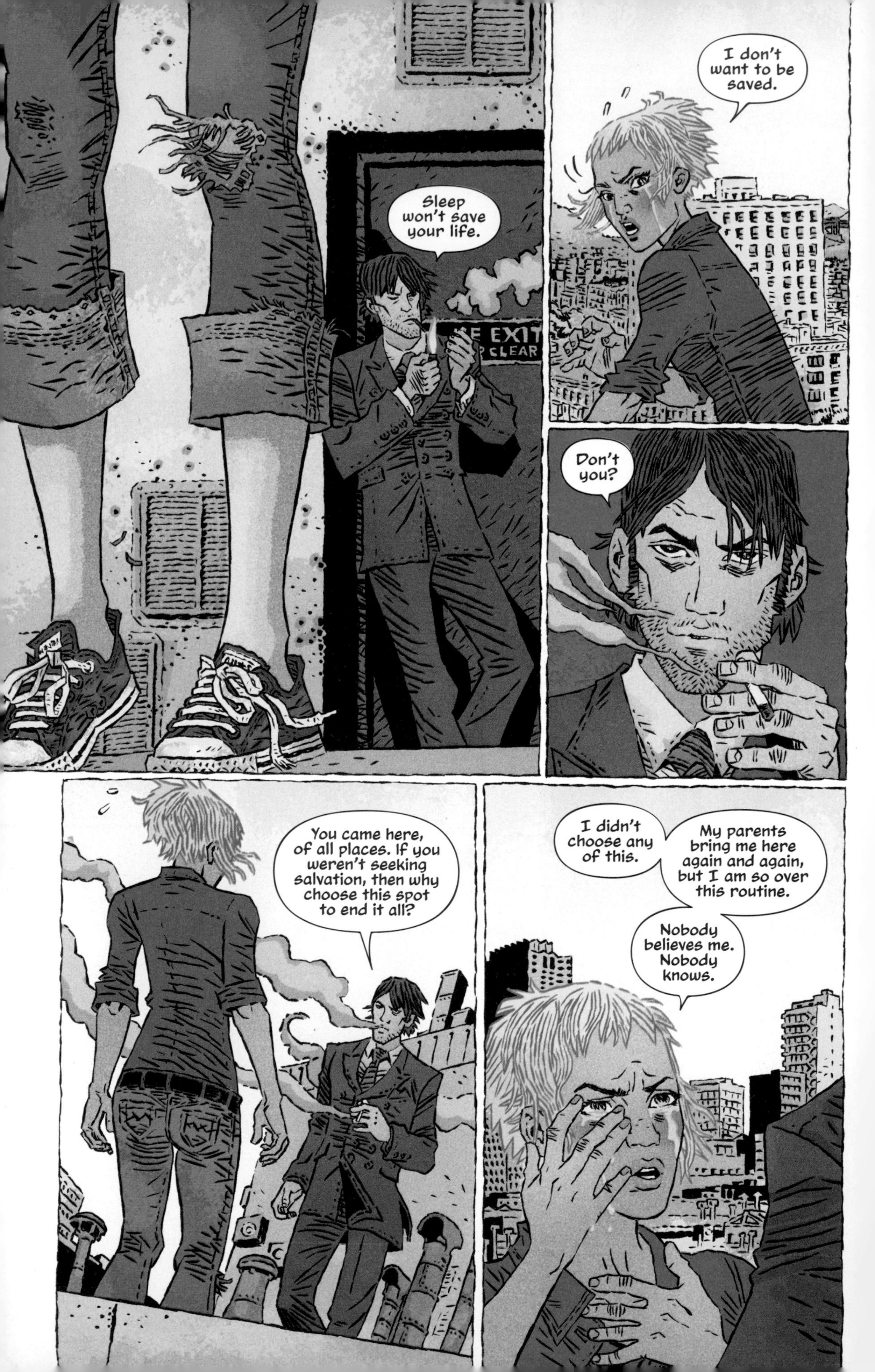

Sleep won't save your life.
I don't want to be saved.
Don't you?
You came here, of all places. If you weren't seeking salvation, then why choose this spot to end it all?
I didn't choose any of this.
My parents bring me here again and again, but I am so over this routine.
Nobody believes me. Nobody knows.

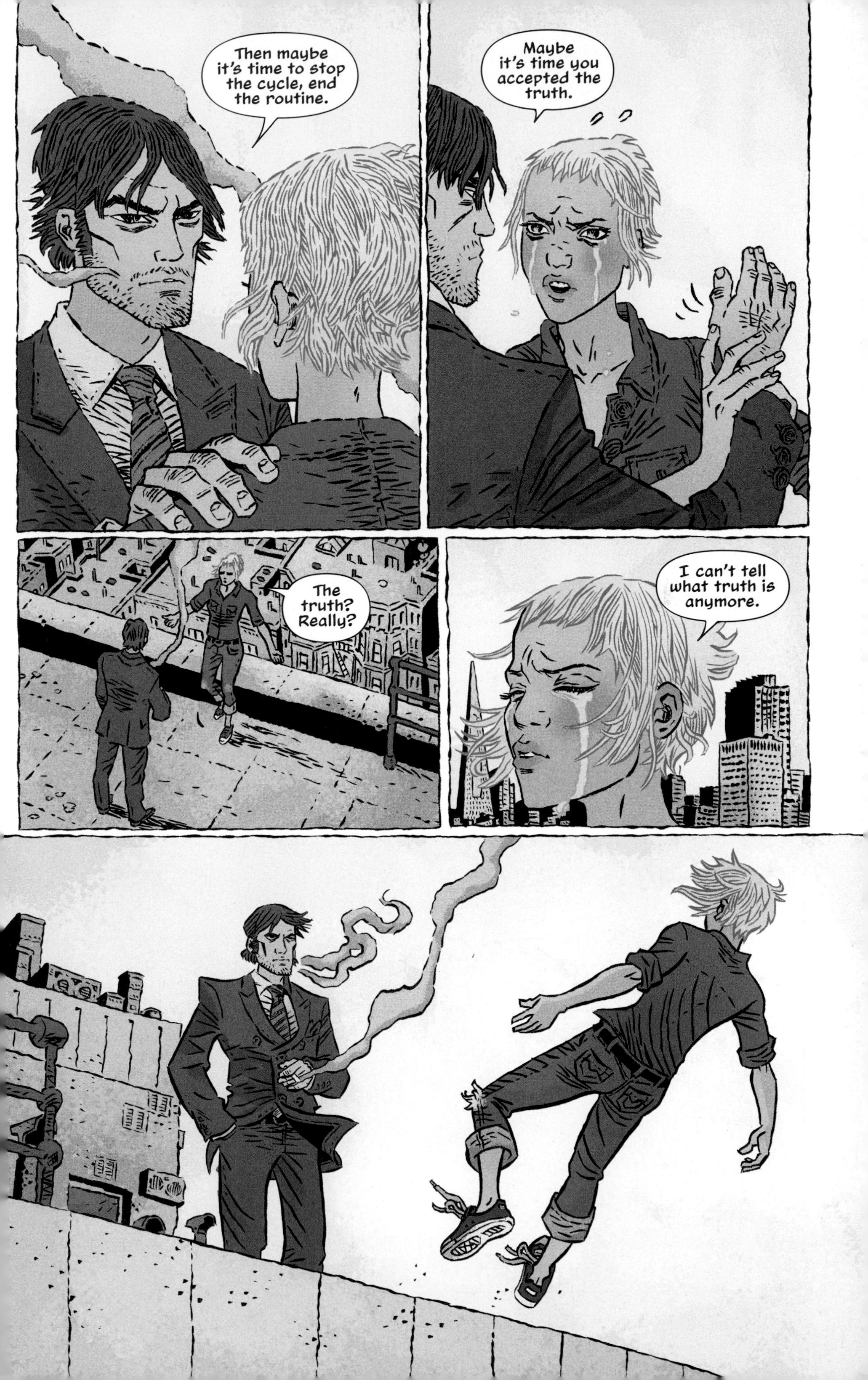
Then maybe it's time to stop the cycle, end the routine.
Maybe it's time you accepted the truth.
The truth? Really?
I can't tell what truth is anymore.

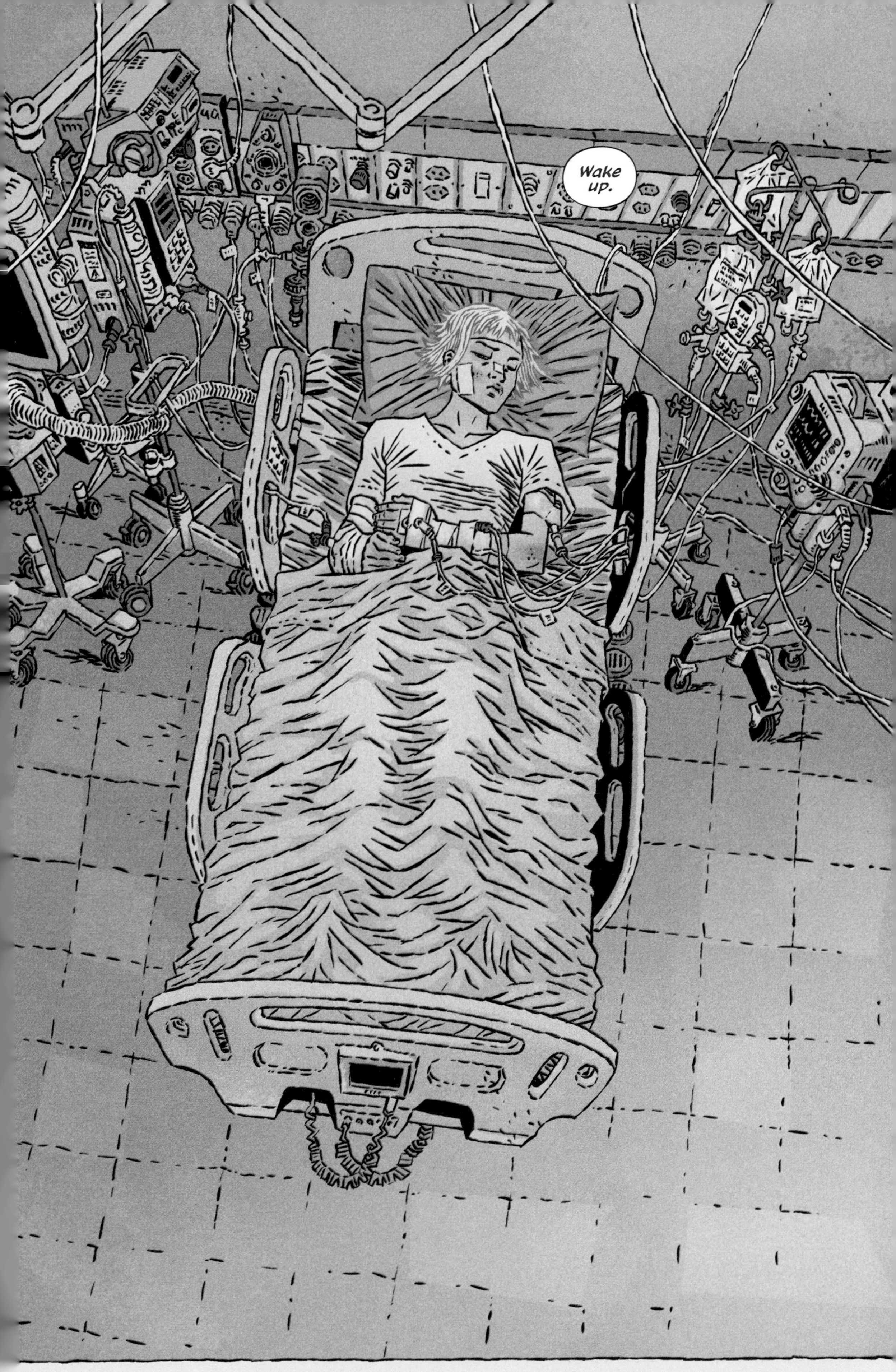
Wake up.

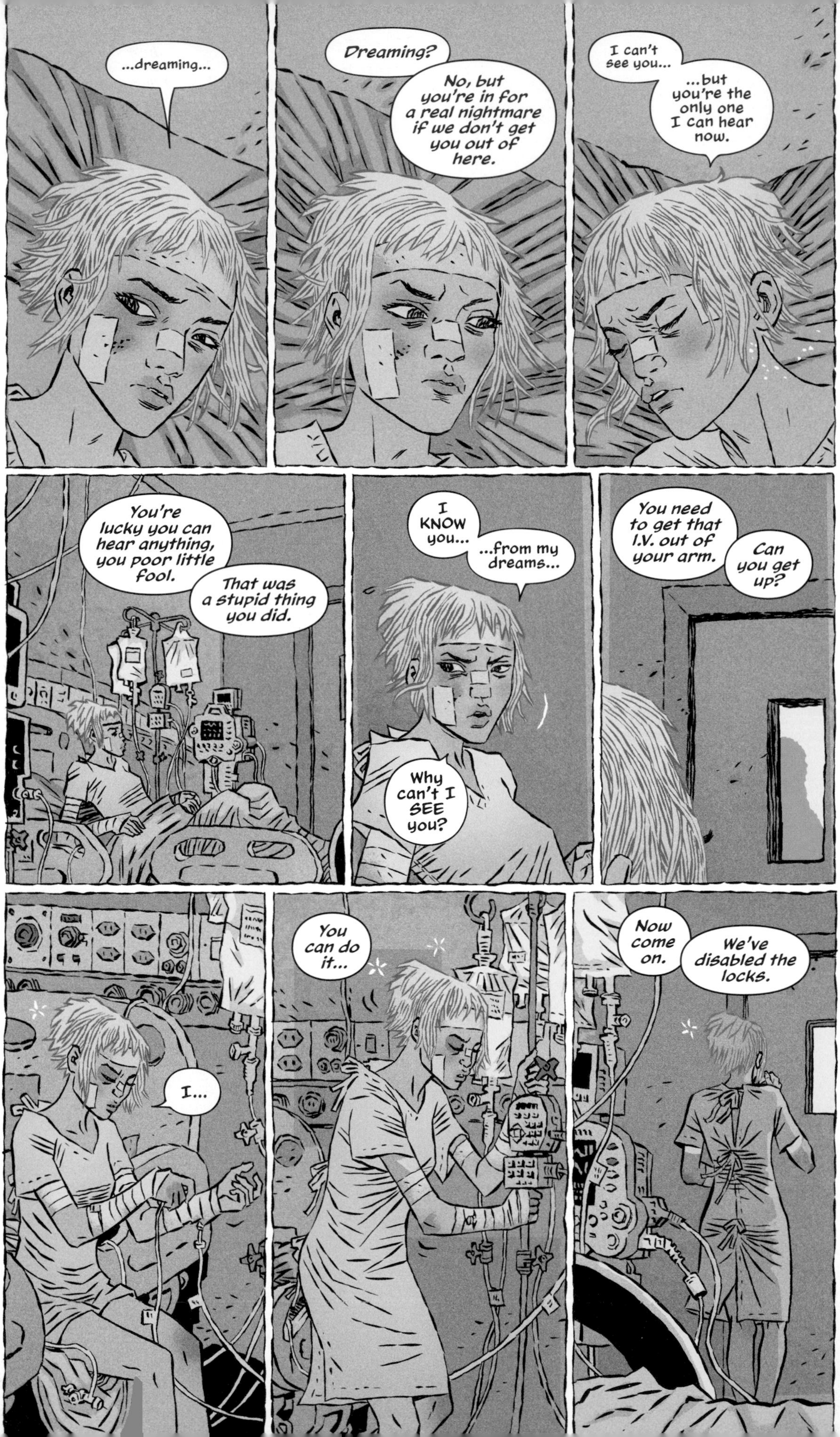
...dreaming...
Dreaming?
No, but you're in for a real nightmare if we don't get you out of here.
I can't see you...
...but you're the only one I can hear now.
You're lucky you can hear anything, you poor little fool.
That was a stupid thing you did.
I KNOW you...
...from my dreams...
Why can't I SEE you?
You need to get that I.V. out of your arm.
Can you get up?
I...
You can do it...
Now come on.
We've disabled the locks.

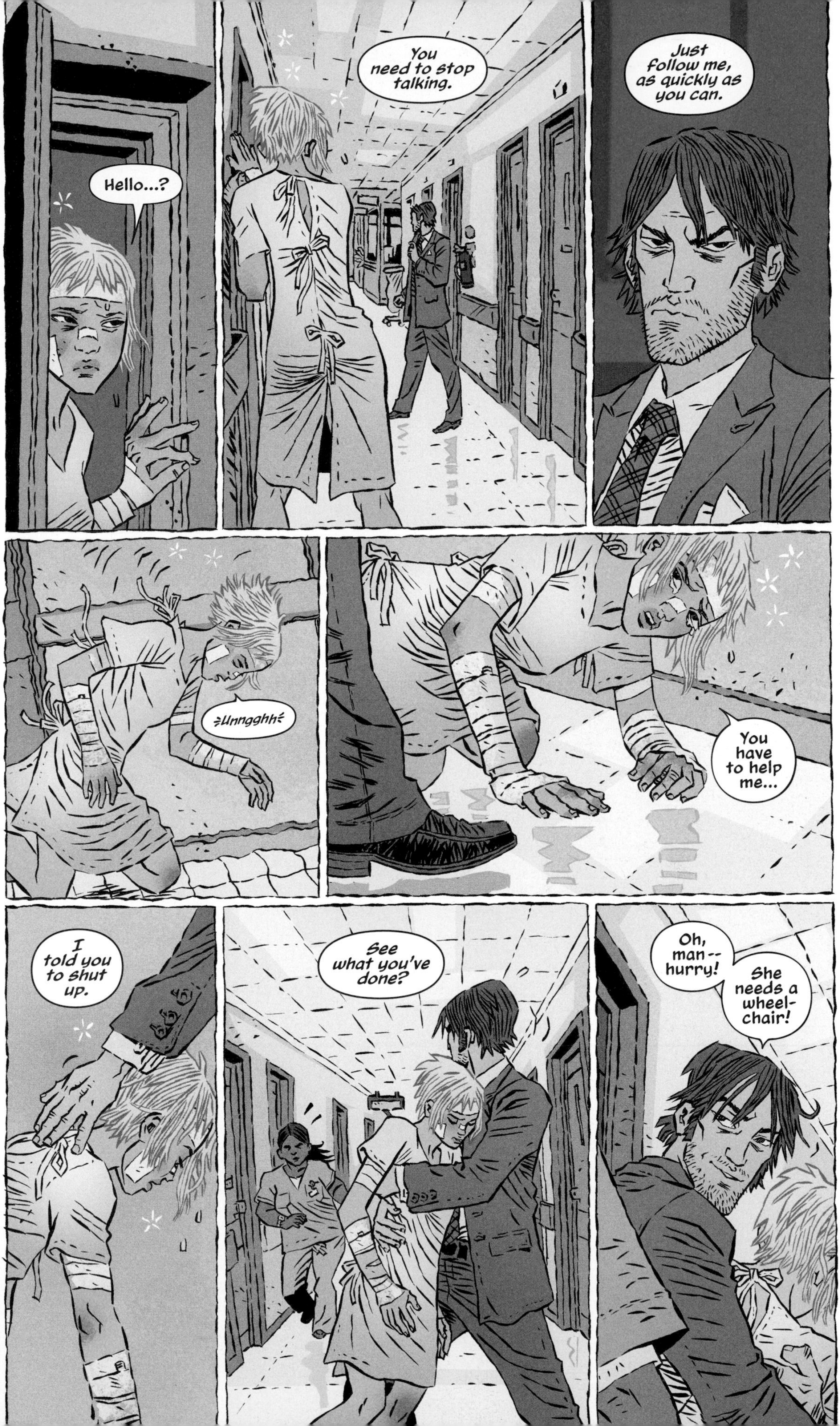
Hello...?
You need to stop talking.
Just follow me, as quickly as you can.
Unngghh
You have to help me...
I told you to shut up.
See what you've done?
Oh, man-- hurry!
She needs a wheel-chair!

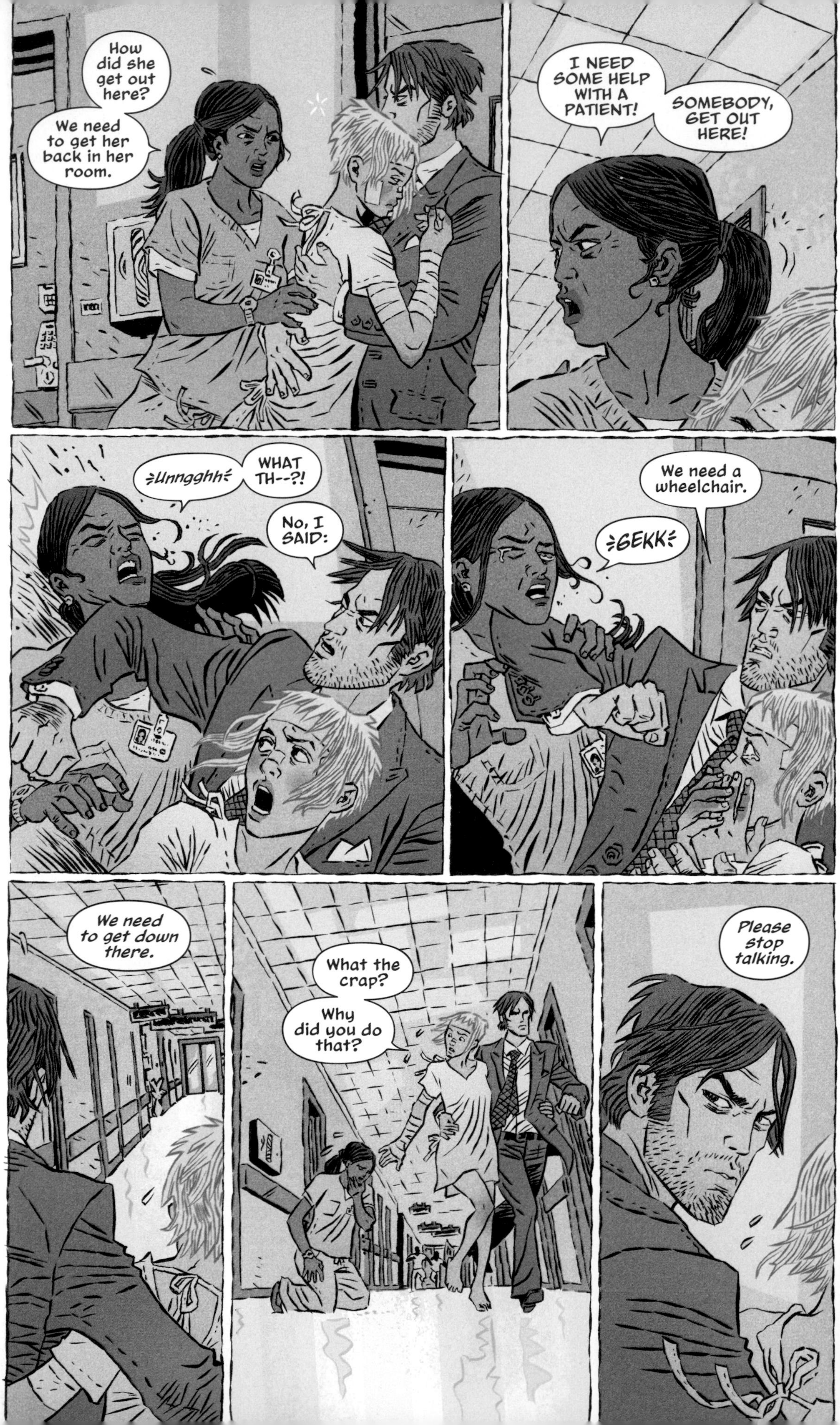
How did she get out here?
We need to get her back in her room.
I NEED SOME HELP WITH A PATIENT!
SOMEBODY, GET OUT HERE!
Unngghh
WHAT TH--?!
No, I SAID:
We need a wheelchair.
GEKK
We need to get down there.
What the crap?
Why did you do that?
Please stop talking.

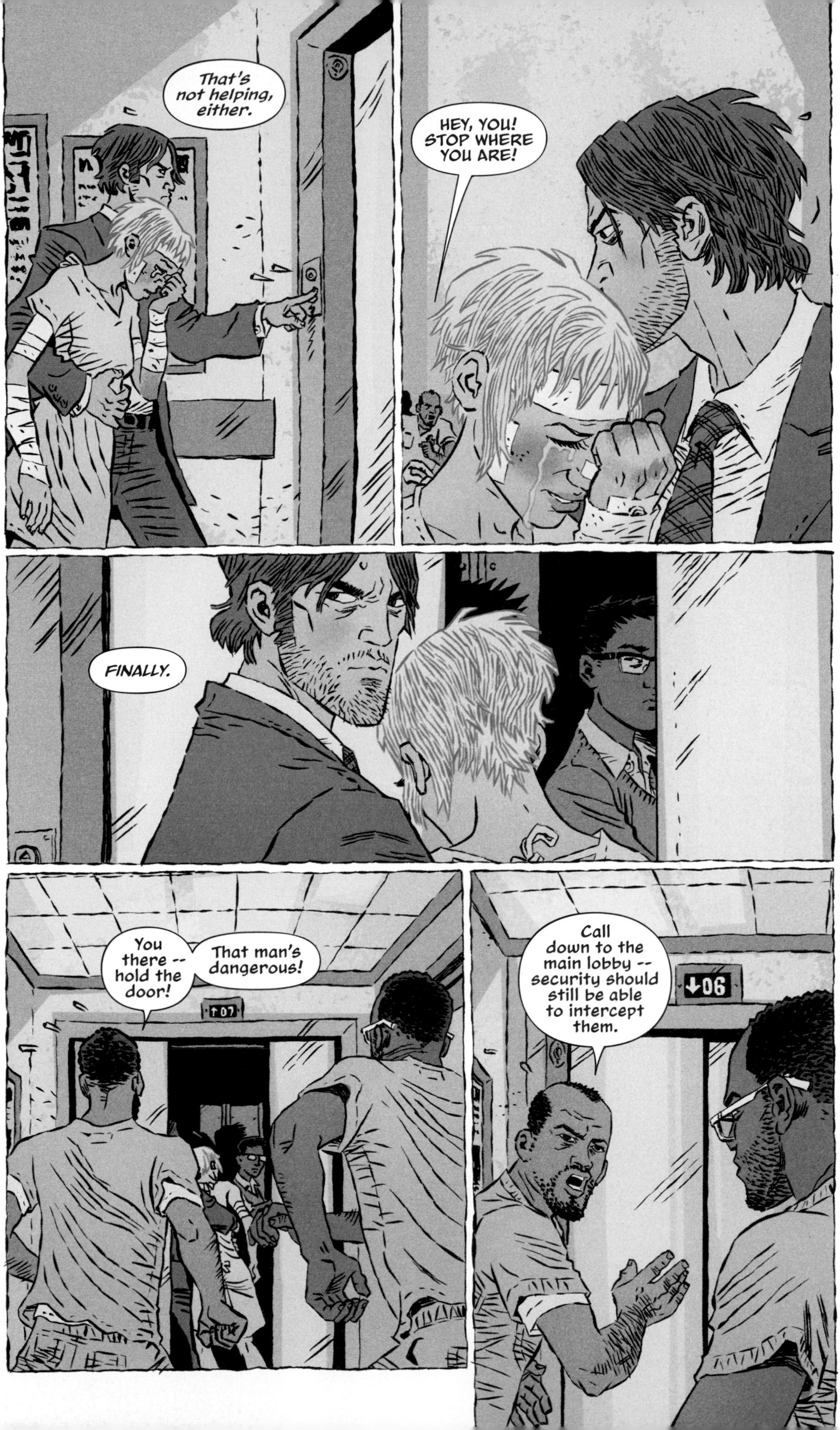
That's not helping, either.
HEY, YOU! STOP WHERE YOU ARE!
FINALLY.
You there -- hold the door!
That man's dangerous!
↑07
Call down to the main lobby -- security should still be able to intercept them.
↓06

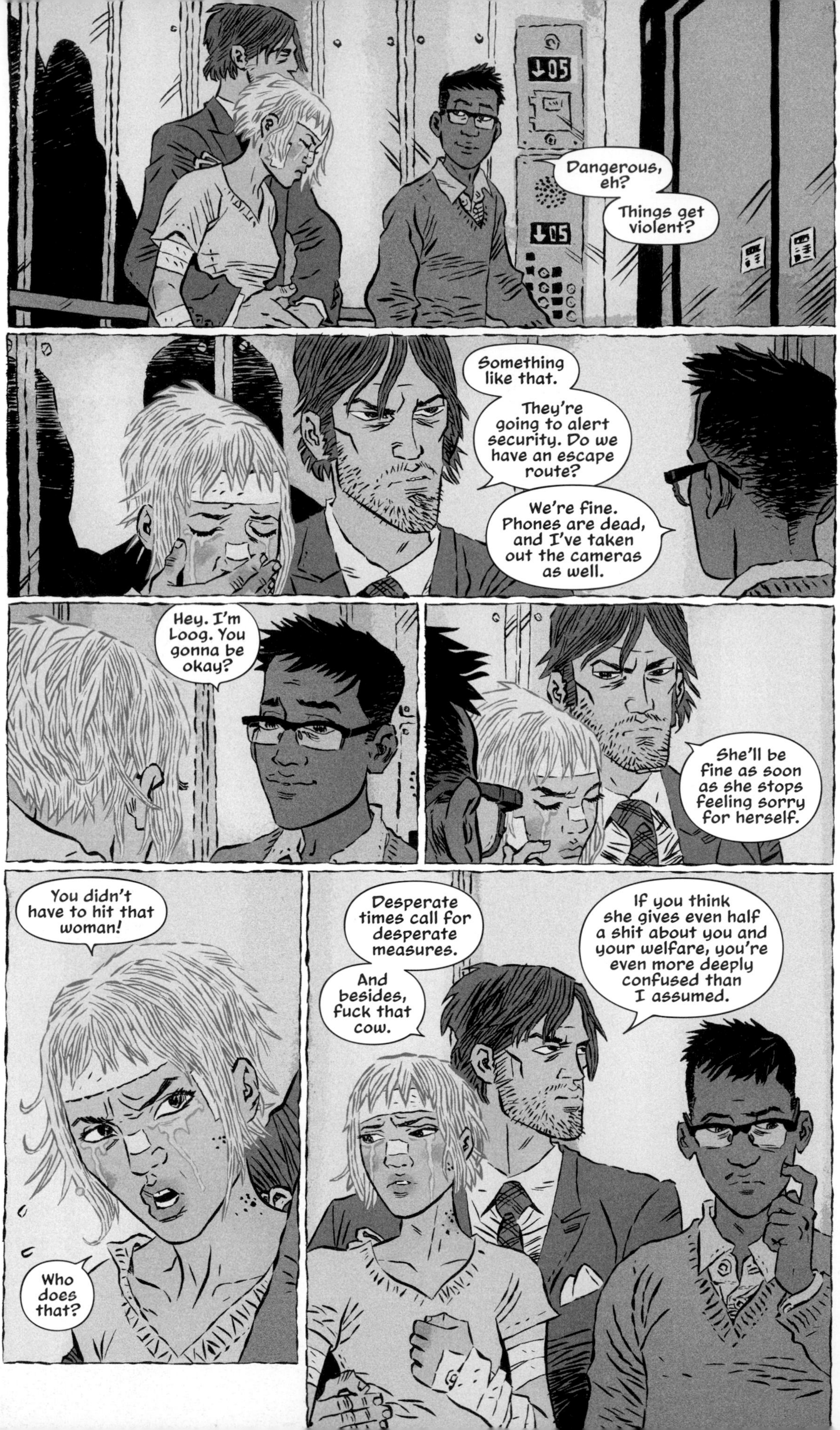
↓05
Dangerous, eh?
Things get violent?
↓05
Something like that.
They're going to alert security. Do we have an escape route?
We're fine. Phones are dead, and I've taken out the cameras as well.
Hey. I'm Loog. You gonna be okay?
She'll be fine as soon as she stops feeling sorry for herself.
You didn't have to hit that woman!
Who does that?
Desperate times call for desperate measures.
And besides, fuck that cow.
If you think she gives even half a shit about you and your welfare, you're even more deeply confused than I assumed.

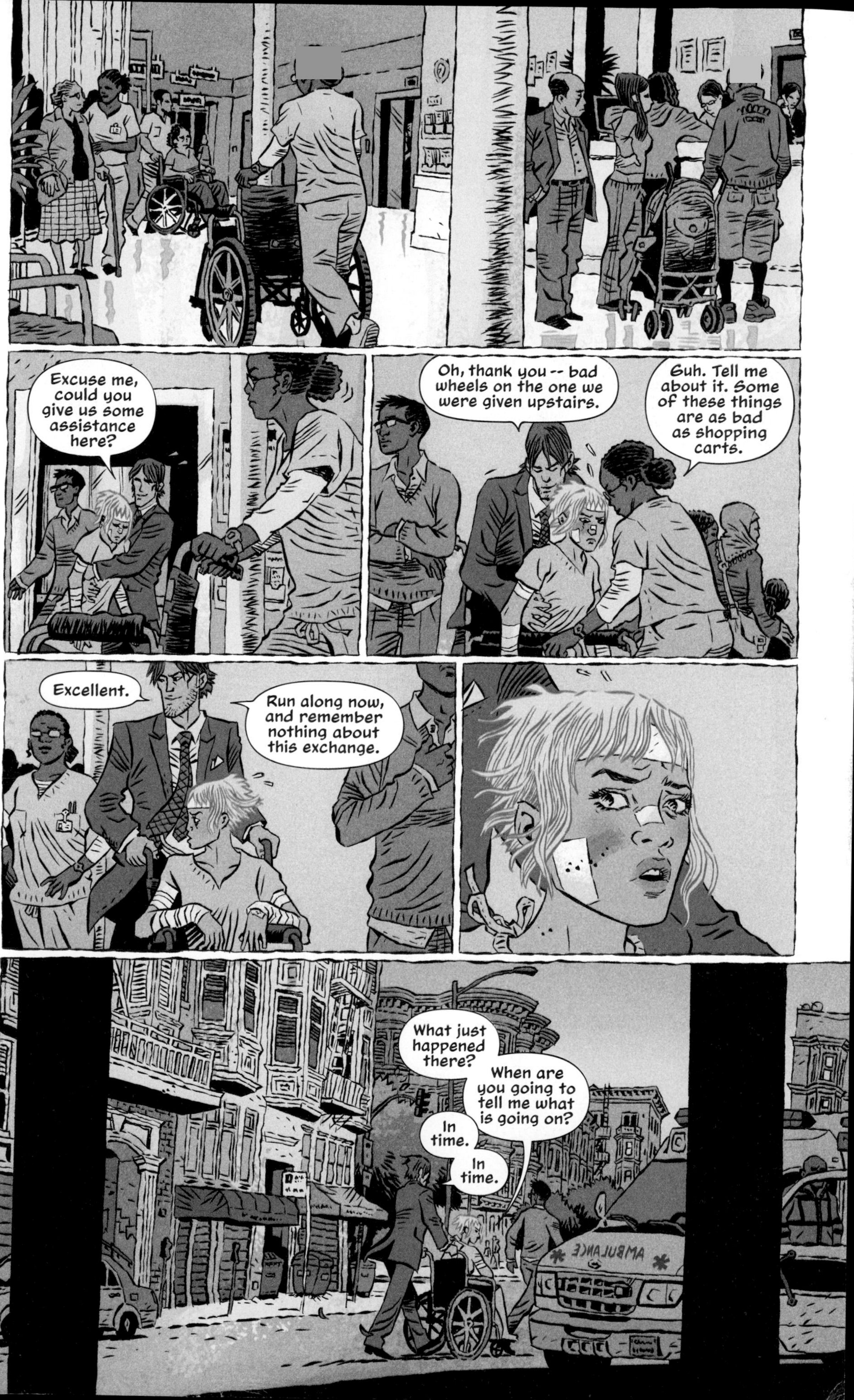
Excuse me, could you give us some assistance here?
Oh, thank you -- bad wheels on the one we were given upstairs.
Guh. Tell me about it. Some of these things are as bad as shopping carts.
Excellent.
Run along now, and remember nothing about this exchange.
What just happened there?
When are you going to tell me what is going on?
In time.
In time.

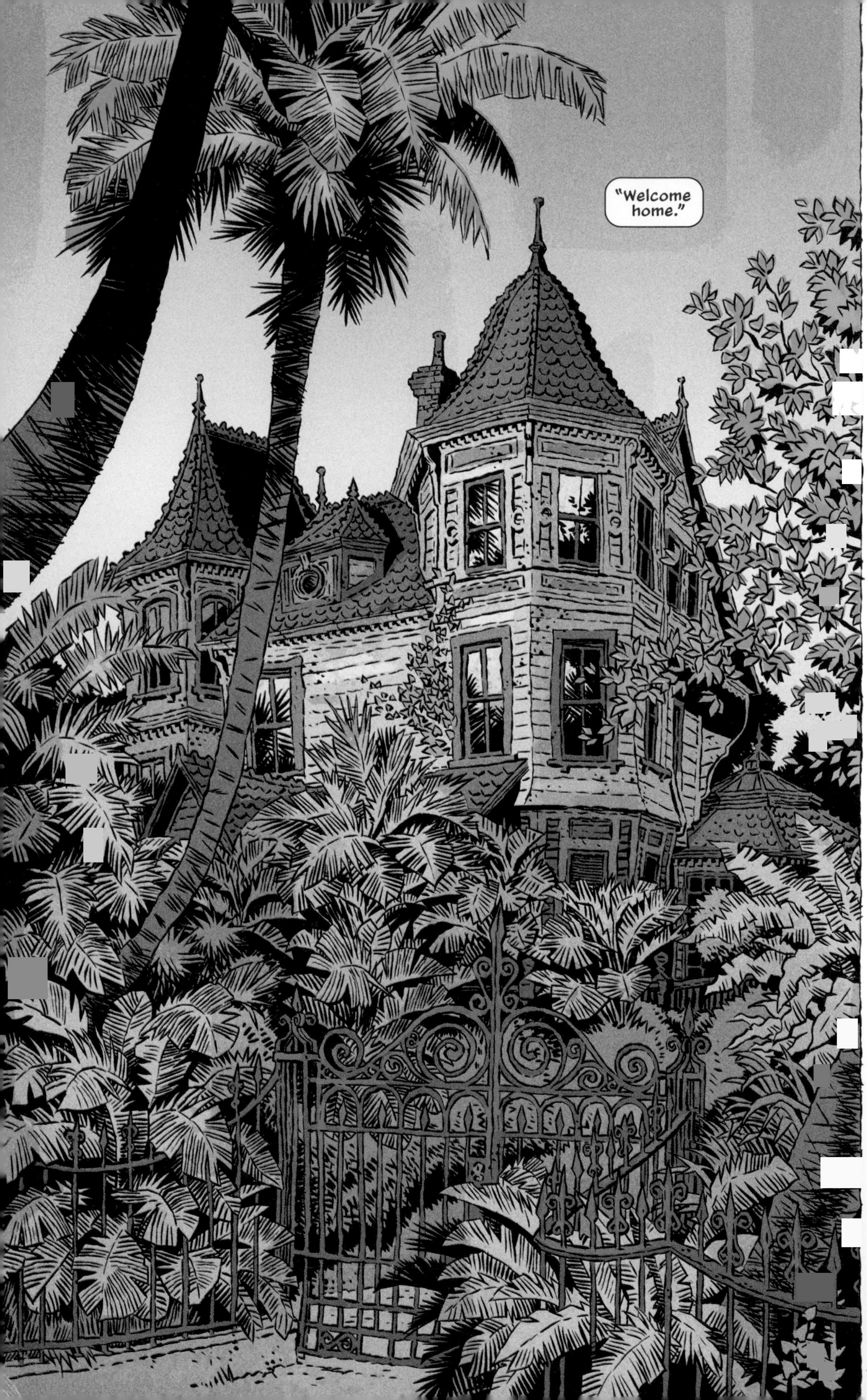
"Welcome home."

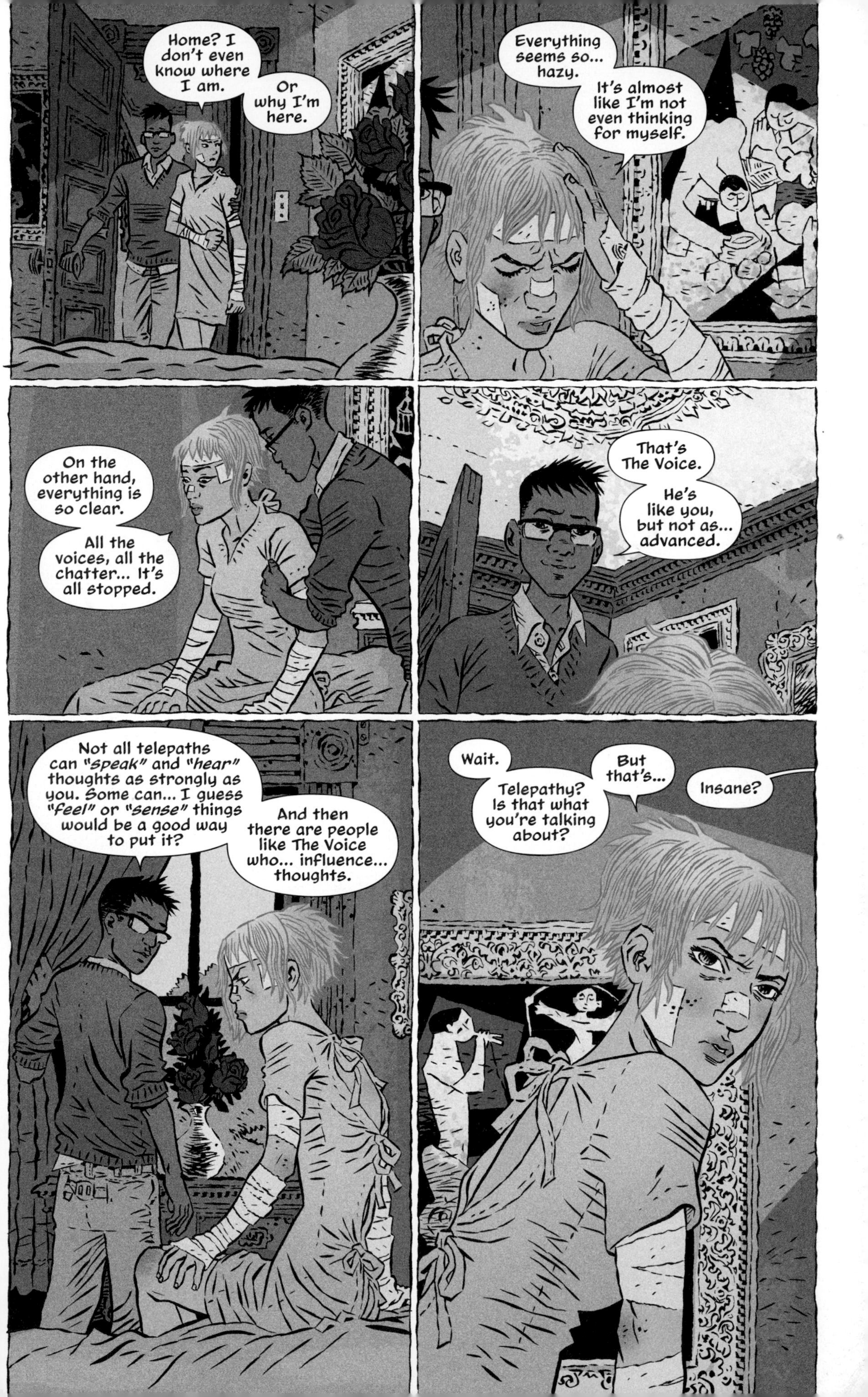
Home? I don't even know where I am.
Or why I'm here.
Everything seems so... hazy.
It's almost like I'm not even thinking for myself.
On the other hand, everything is so clear.
All the voices, all the chatter... It's all stopped.
That's The Voice.
He's like you, but not as... advanced.
Not all telepaths can "speak" and "hear" thoughts as strongly as you. Some can... I guess "feel" or "sense" things would be a good way to put it?
And then there are people like The Voice who... influence... thoughts.
Wait.
Telepathy? Is that what you're talking about?
But that's...
Insane?

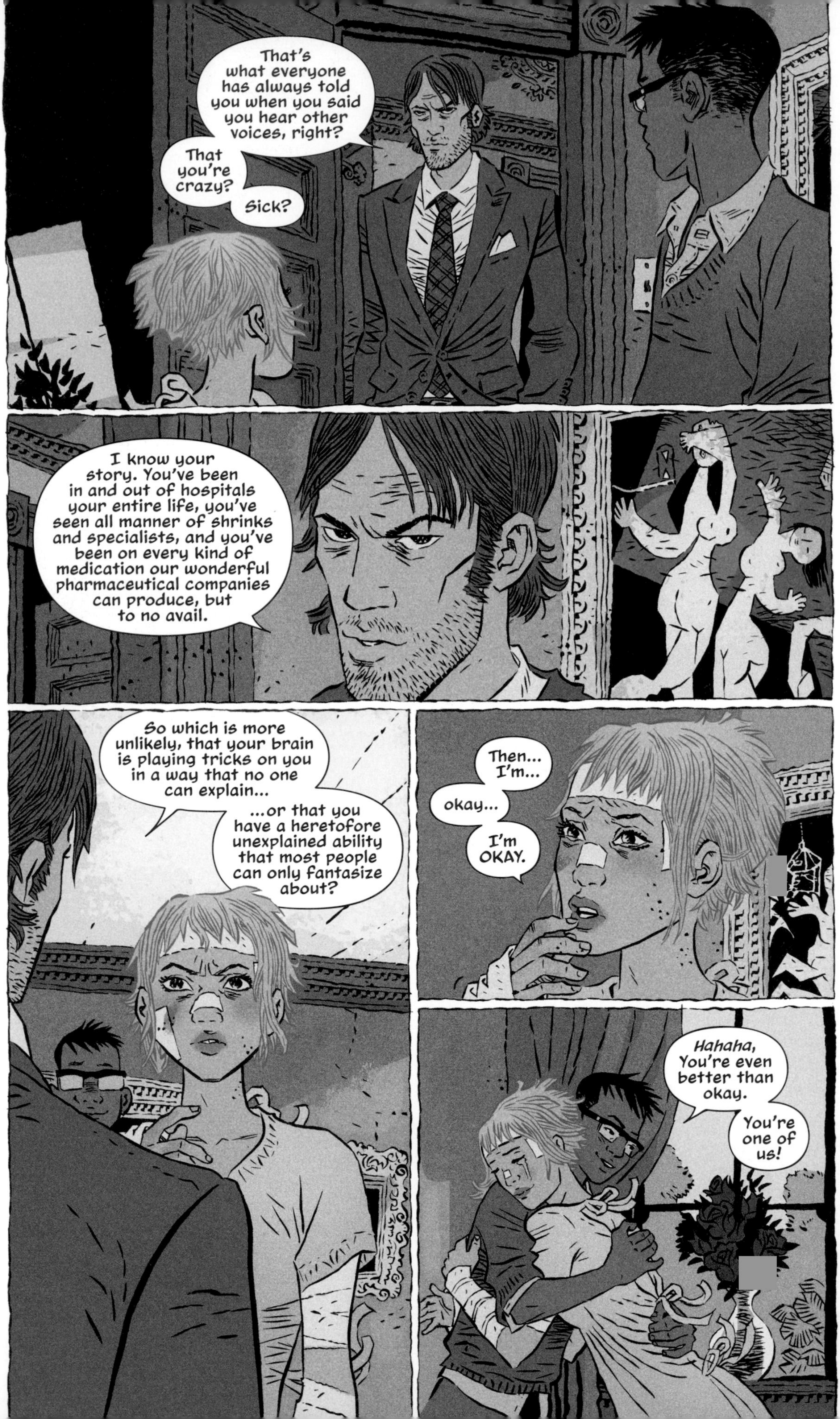
That's what everyone has always told you when you said you hear other voices, right?
That you're crazy?
Sick?
I know your story. You've been in and out of hospitals your entire life, you've seen all manner of shrinks and specialists, and you've been on every kind of medication our wonderful pharmaceutical companies can produce, but to no avail.
So which is more unlikely, that your brain is playing tricks on you in a way that no one can explain...
...or that you have a heretofore unexplained ability that most people can only fantasize about?
Then... I'm...
okay...
I'm OKAY.
Hahaha, You're even better than okay.
You're one of us!

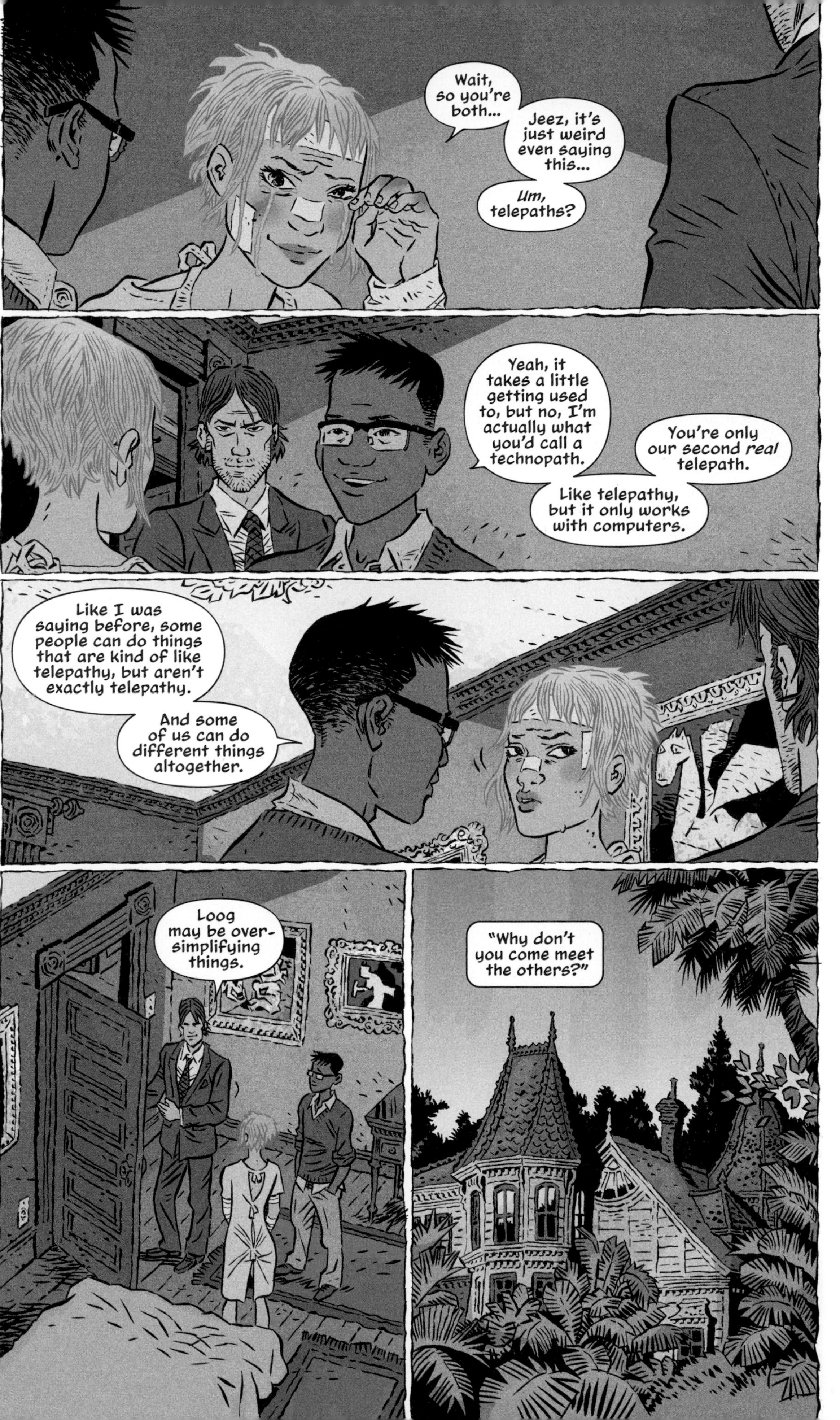
Wait, so you're both...
Jeez, it's just weird even saying this...
Um, telepaths?
Yeah, it takes a little getting used to, but no, I'm actually what you'd call a technopath.
Like telepathy, but it only works with computers.
You're only our second *real* telepath.
Like I was saying before, some people can do things that are kind of like telepathy, but aren't exactly telepathy.
And some of us can do different things altogether.
Loog may be over-simplifying things.
"Why don't you come meet the others?"

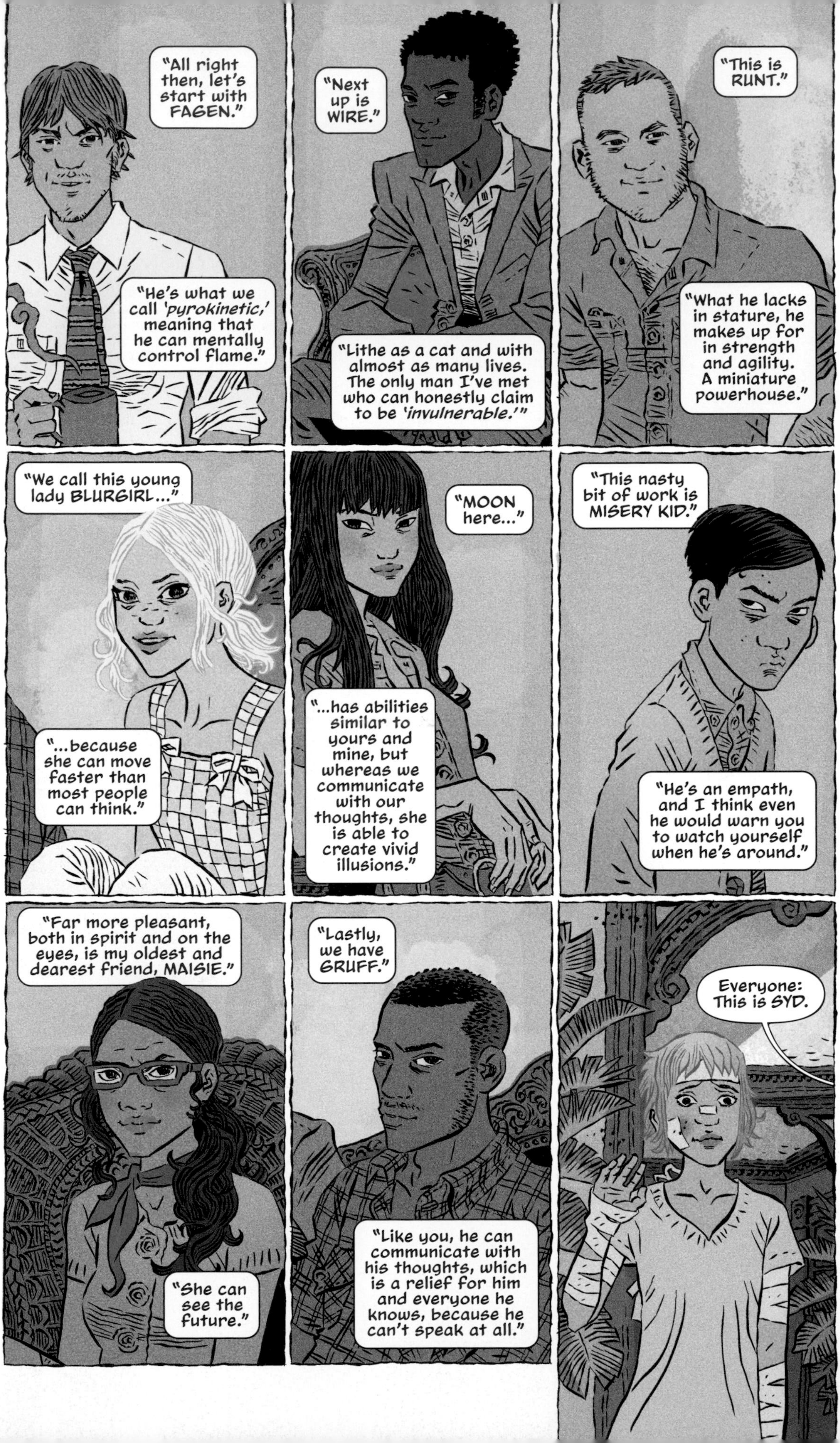
"All right then, let's start with FAGEN."
"He's what we call *'pyrokinetic,'* meaning that he can mentally control flame."
"Next up is WIRE."
"Lithe as a cat and with almost as many lives. The only man I've met who can honestly claim to be *'invulnerable.'*"
"This is RUNT."
"What he lacks in stature, he makes up for in strength and agility. A miniature powerhouse."
"We call this young lady BLURGIRL..."
"...because she can move faster than most people can think."
"MOON here..."
"...has abilities similar to yours and mine, but whereas we communicate with our thoughts, she is able to create vivid illusions."
"This nasty bit of work is MISERY KID."
"He's an empath, and I think even he would warn you to watch yourself when he's around."
"Far more pleasant, both in spirit and on the eyes, is my oldest and dearest friend, MAISIE."
"She can see the future."
"Lastly, we have GRUFF."
"Like you, he can communicate with his thoughts, which is a relief for him and everyone he knows, because he can't speak at all."
Everyone: This is SYD.

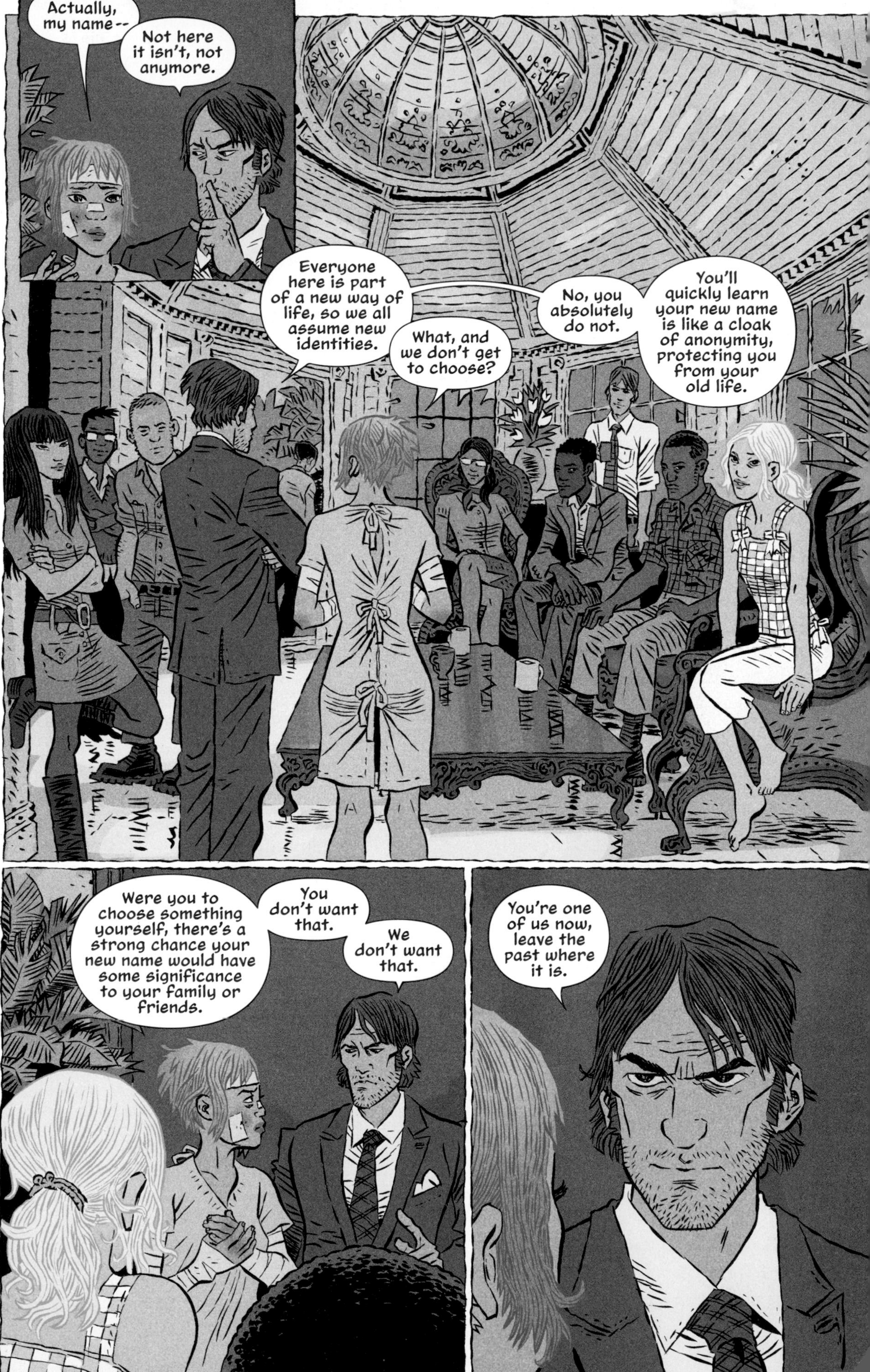
Actually, my name--
Not here it isn't, not anymore.
Everyone here is part of a new way of life, so we all assume new identities.
What, and we don't get to choose?
No, you absolutely do not.
You'll quickly learn your new name is like a cloak of anonymity, protecting you from your old life.
Were you to choose something yourself, there's a strong chance your new name would have some significance to your family or friends.
You don't want that.
We don't want that.
You're one of us now, leave the past where it is.

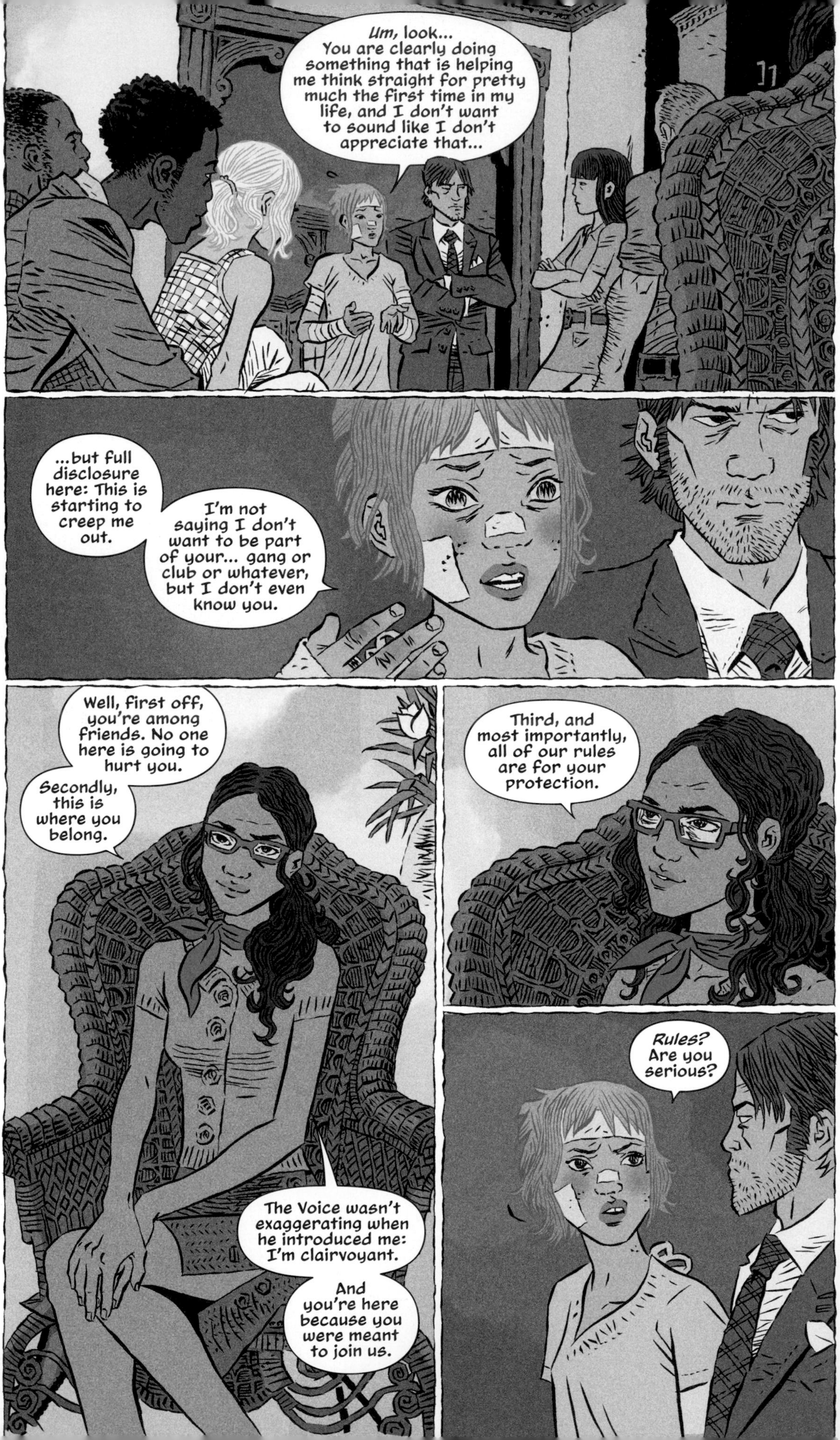
Um, look... You are clearly doing something that is helping me think straight for pretty much the first time in my life, and I don't want to sound like I don't appreciate that...
...but full disclosure here: This is starting to creep me out.
I'm not saying I don't want to be part of your... gang or club or whatever, but I don't even know you.
Well, first off, you're among friends. No one here is going to hurt you.
Secondly, this is where you belong.
The Voice wasn't exaggerating when he introduced me: I'm clairvoyant.
And you're here because you were meant to join us.
Third, and most importantly, all of our rules are for your protection.
Rules? Are you serious?

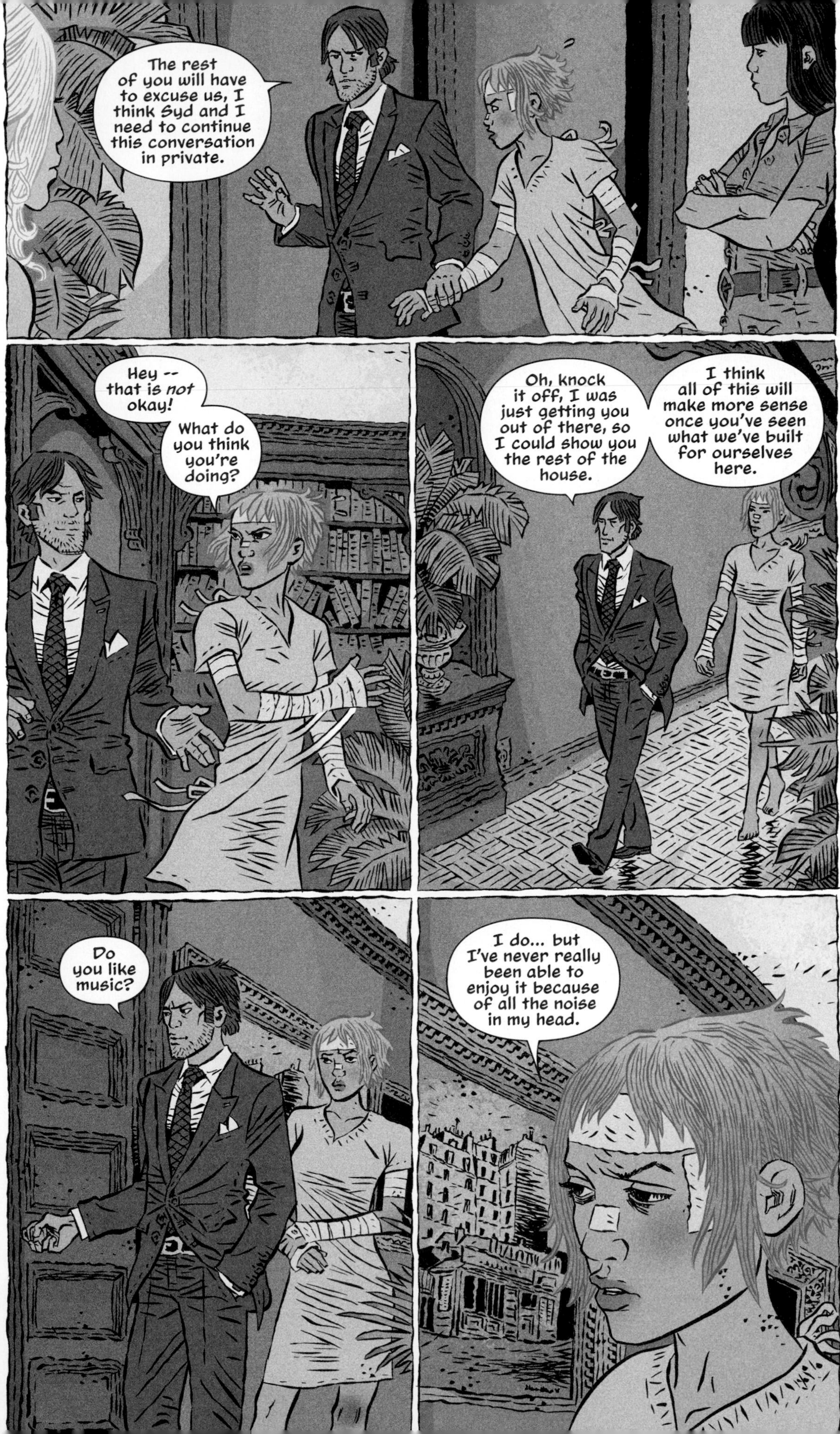
The rest of you will have to excuse us, I think Syd and I need to continue this conversation in private.
Hey -- that is *not* okay!
What do you think you're doing?
Oh, knock it off, I was just getting you out of there, so I could show you the rest of the house.
I think all of this will make more sense once you've seen what we've built for ourselves here.
Do you like music?
I do... but I've never really been able to enjoy it because of all the noise in my head.

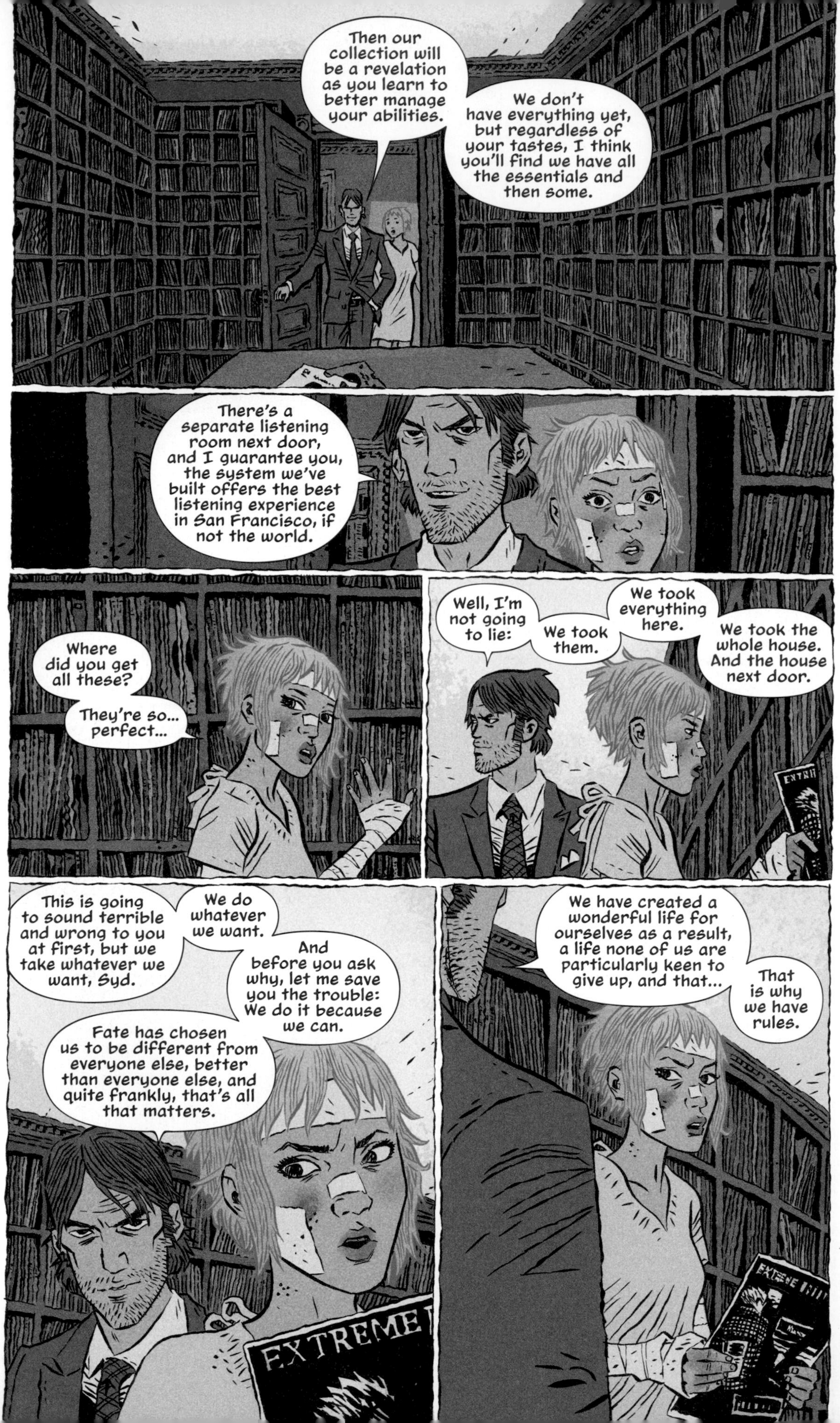
Then our collection will be a revelation as you learn to better manage your abilities.
We don't have everything yet, but regardless of your tastes, I think you'll find we have all the essentials and then some.
There's a separate listening room next door, and I guarantee you, the system we've built offers the best listening experience in San Francisco, if not the world.
Where did you get all these?
They're so... perfect...
Well, I'm not going to lie:
We took them.
We took everything here.
We took the whole house. And the house next door.
This is going to sound terrible and wrong to you at first, but we take whatever we want, Syd.
We do whatever we want.
And before you ask why, let me save you the trouble: We do it because we can.
Fate has chosen us to be different from everyone else, better than everyone else, and quite frankly, that's all that matters.
EXTREME
We have created a wonderful life for ourselves as a result, a life none of us are particularly keen to give up, and that...
That is why we have rules.

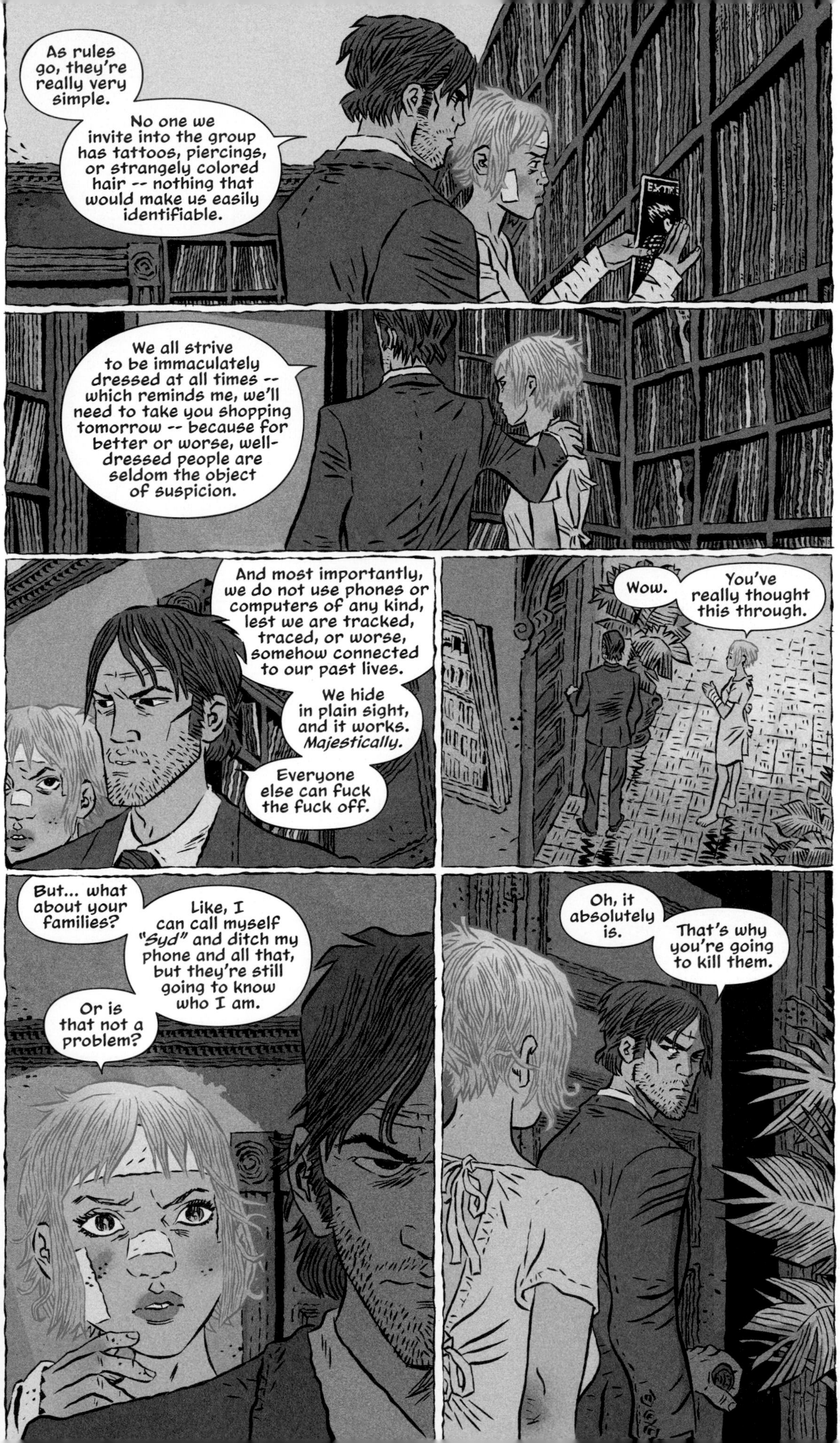
As rules go, they're really very simple.
No one we invite into the group has tattoos, piercings, or strangely colored hair -- nothing that would make us easily identifiable.
We all strive to be immaculately dressed at all times -- which reminds me, we'll need to take you shopping tomorrow -- because for better or worse, well-dressed people are seldom the object of suspicion.
And most importantly, we do not use phones or computers of any kind, lest we are tracked, traced, or worse, somehow connected to our past lives.
We hide in plain sight, and it works. *Majestically.*
Everyone else can fuck the fuck off.
Wow.
You've really thought this through.
But... what about your families?
Like, I can call myself "*Syd*" and ditch my phone and all that, but they're still going to know who I am.
Or is that not a problem?
Oh, it absolutely is.
That's why you're going to kill them.

TWENTY-ONE YEARS OF LIVING AND NOTHING MEANS ANYTHING TO ME

RICHARD JAMES EDWARDS

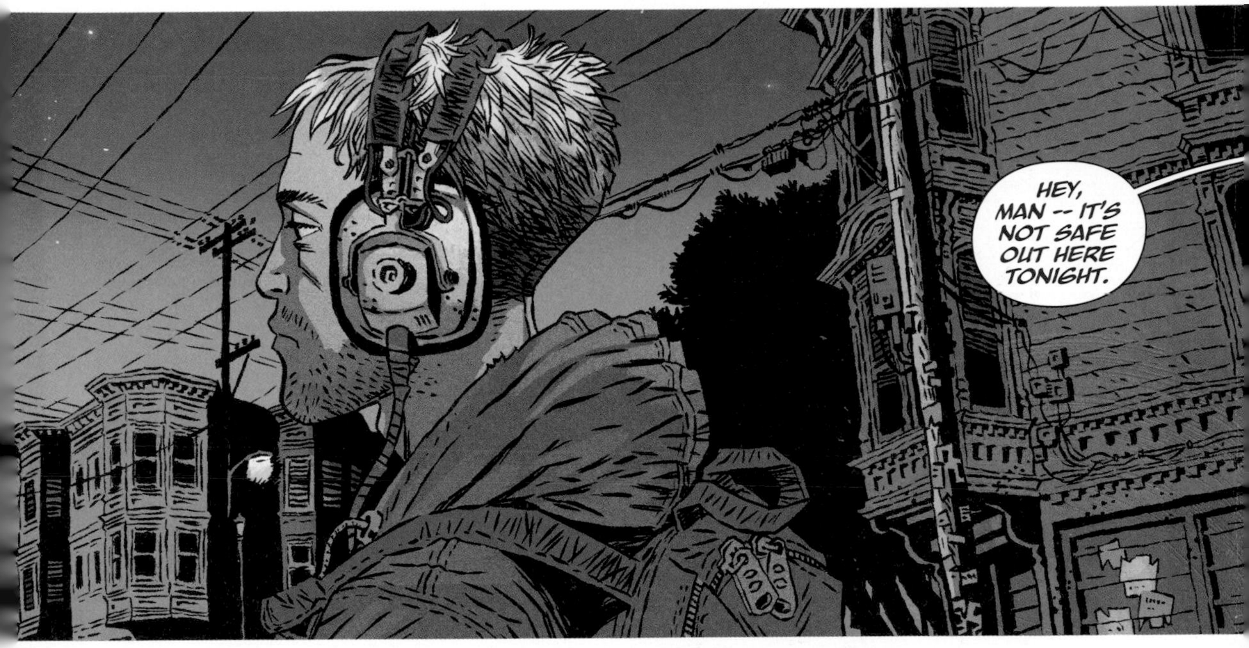
HEY, MAN -- IT'S NOT SAFE OUT HERE TONIGHT.

2: BLACK HOLES FOR THE YOUNG

Most of the time,
it's lights out
before they even
turn around.

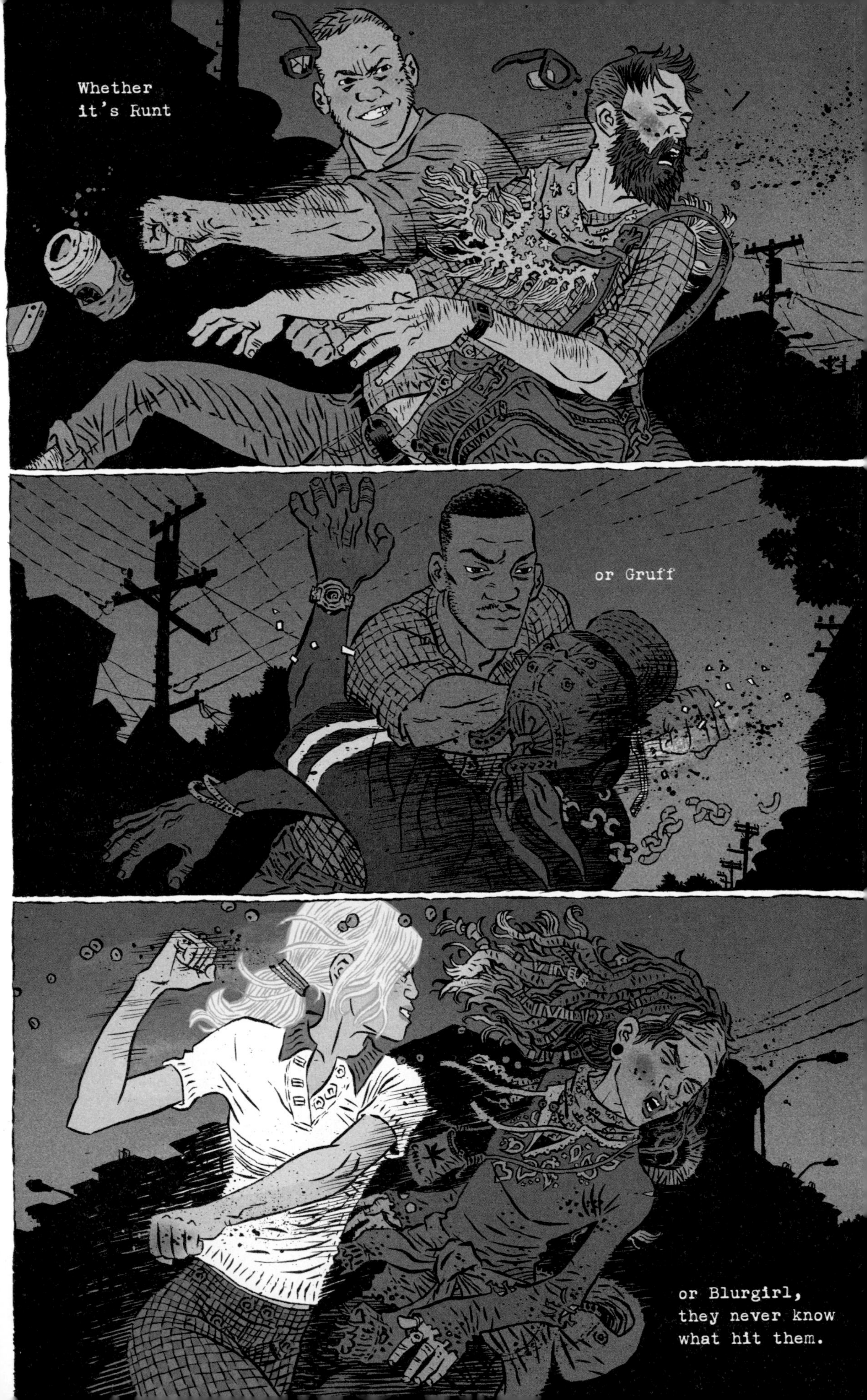
Whether it's Runt
or Gruff
or Blurgirl, they never know what hit them.

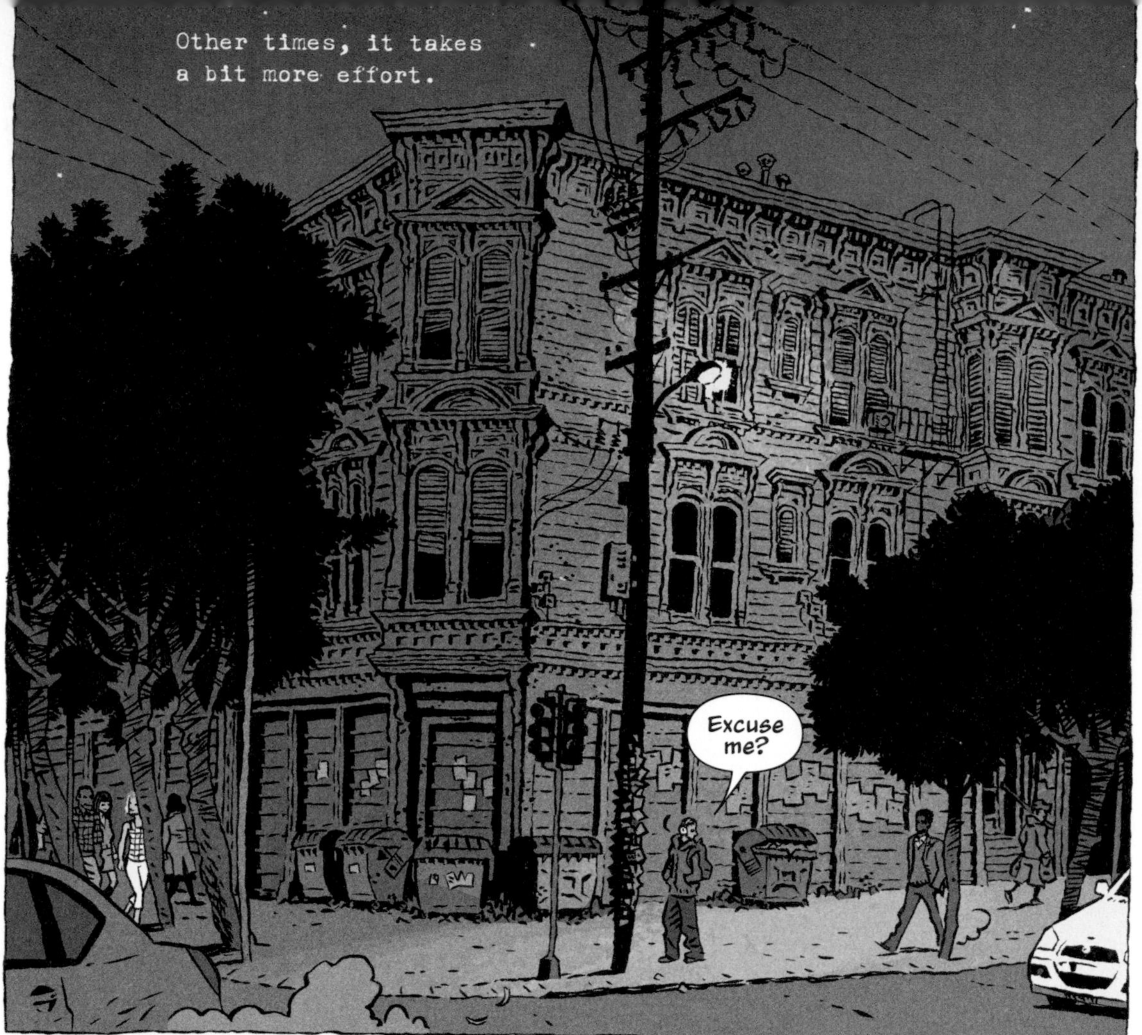
Other times, it takes a bit more effort.
Excuse me?

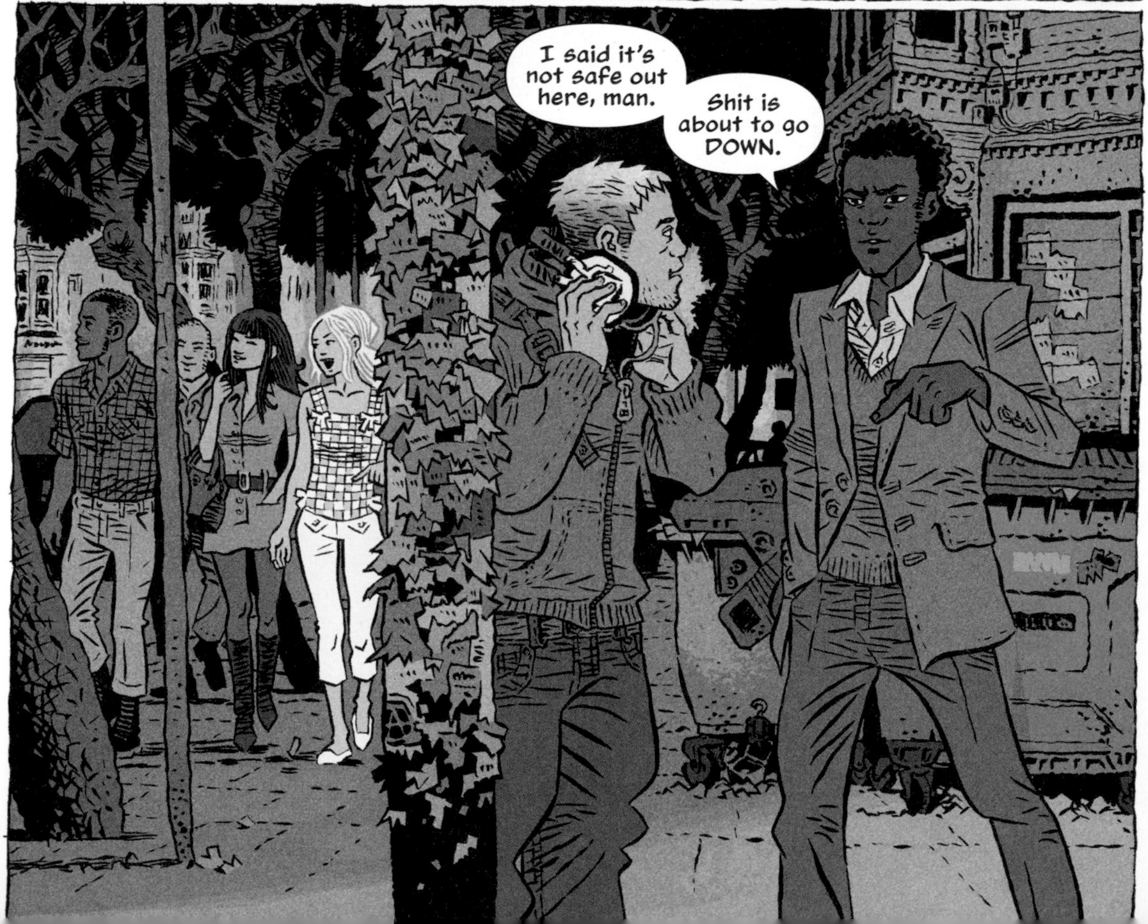
I said it's not safe out here, man.
Shit is about to go DOWN.

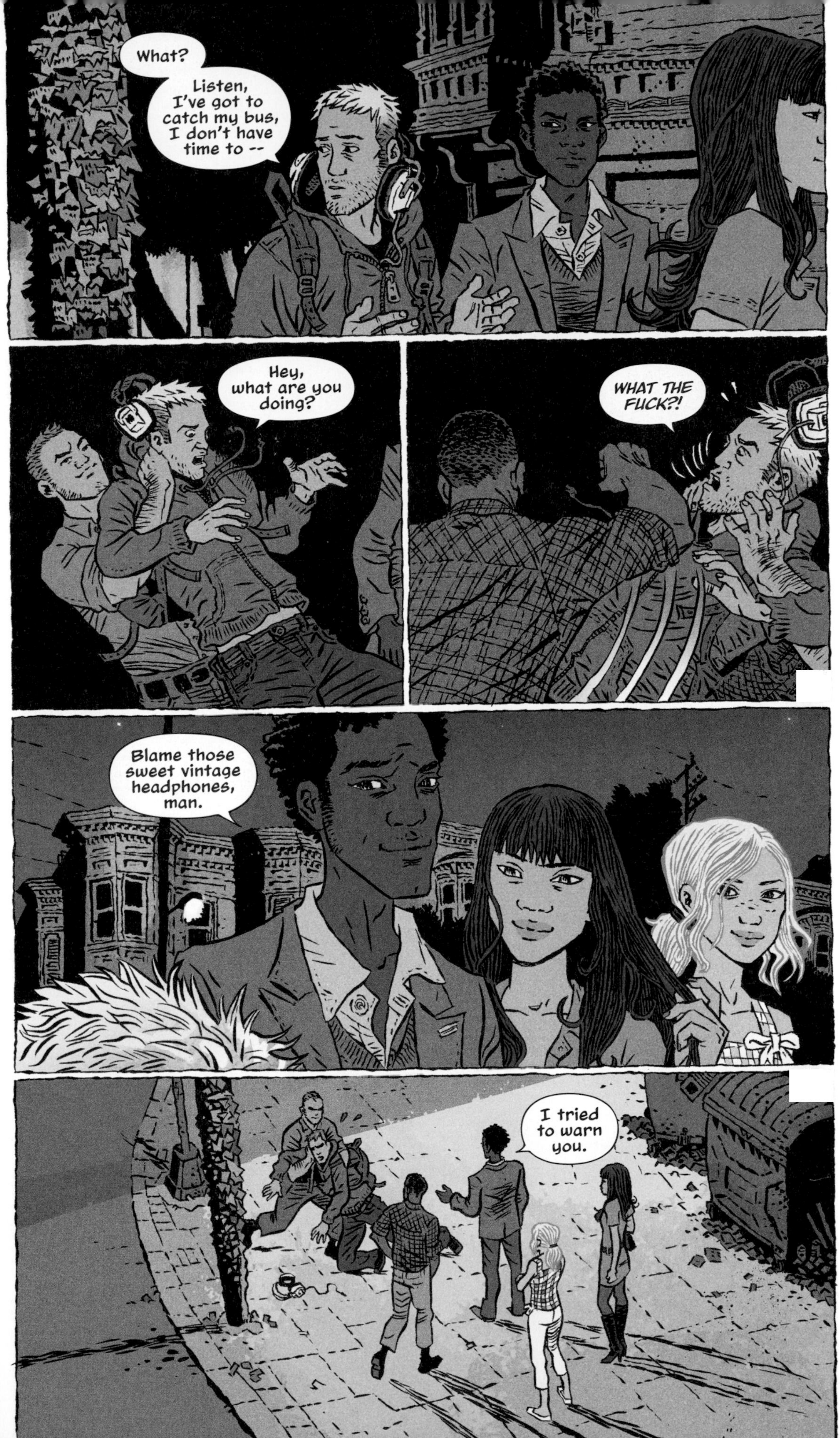
What?
Listen, I've got to catch my bus, I don't have time to --
Hey, what are you doing?
WHAT THE FUCK?!
Blame those sweet vintage headphones, man.
I tried to warn you.

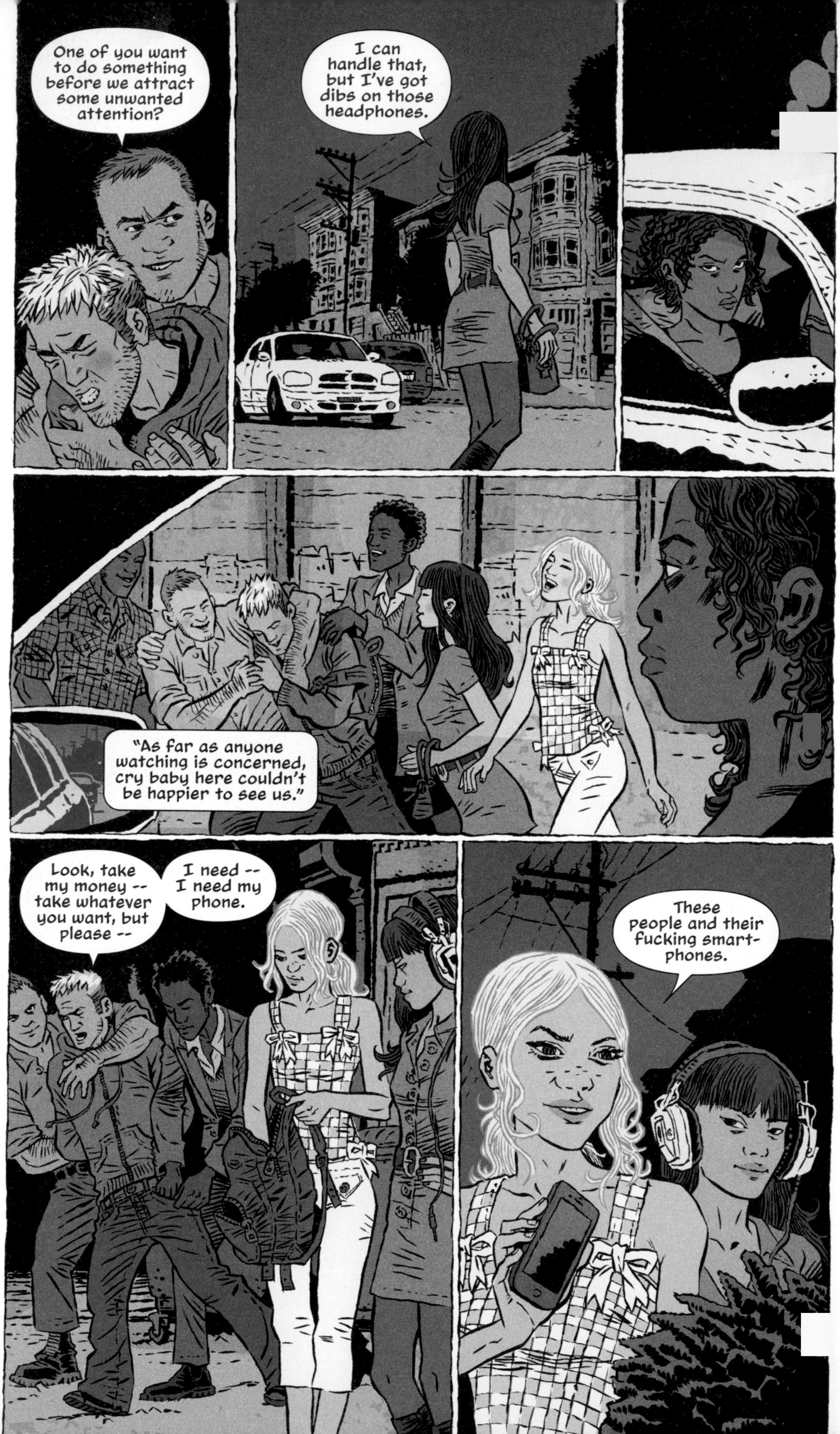

One of you want to do something before we attract some unwanted attention?
I can handle that, but I've got dibs on those headphones.
"As far as anyone watching is concerned, cry baby here couldn't be happier to see us."
Look, take my money -- take whatever you want, but please --
I need -- I need my phone.
These people and their fucking smart-phones.

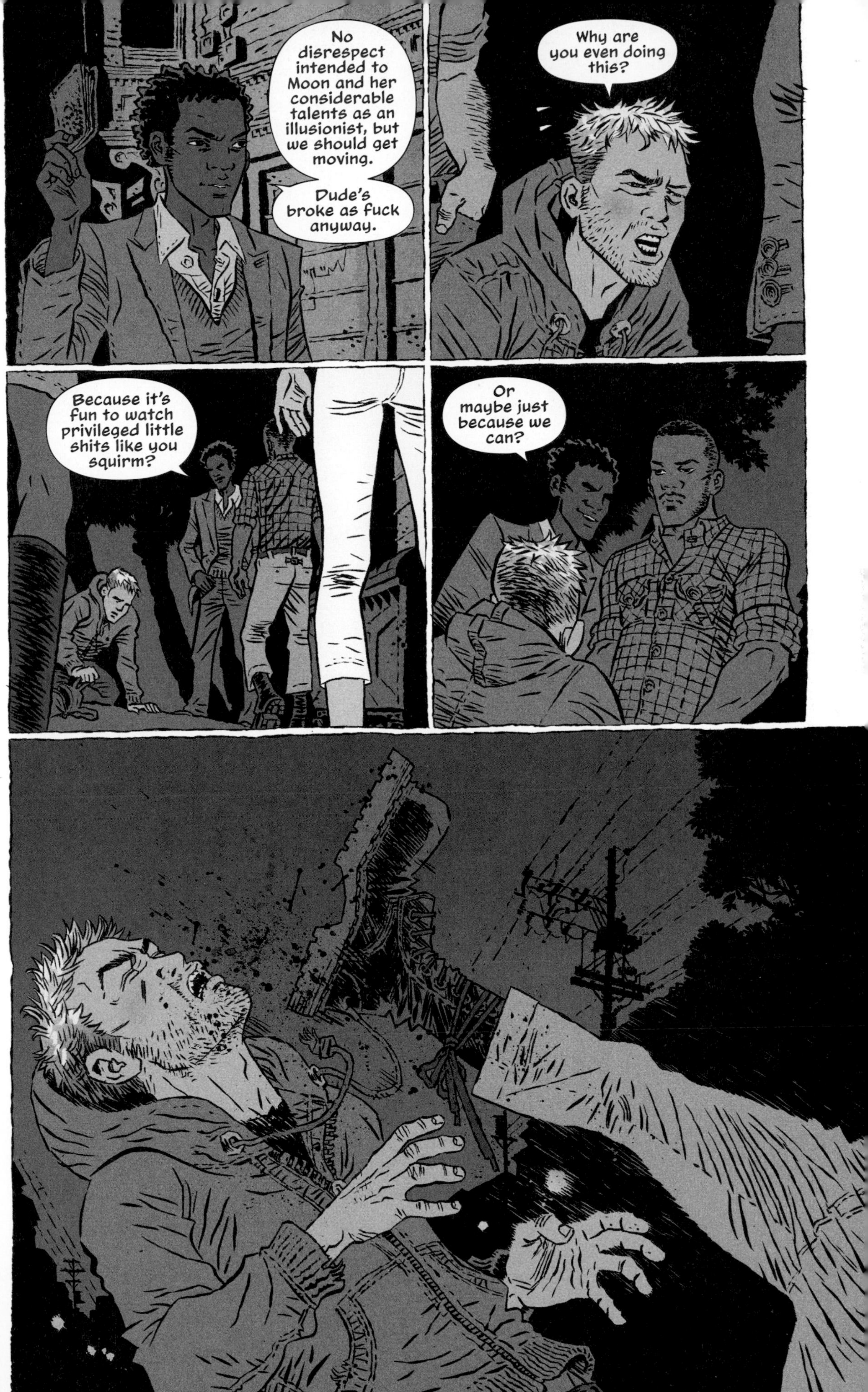
No disrespect intended to Moon and her considerable talents as an illusionist, but we should get moving.
Dude's broke as fuck anyway.
Why are you even doing this?
Because it's fun to watch privileged little shits like you squirm?
Or maybe just because we can?

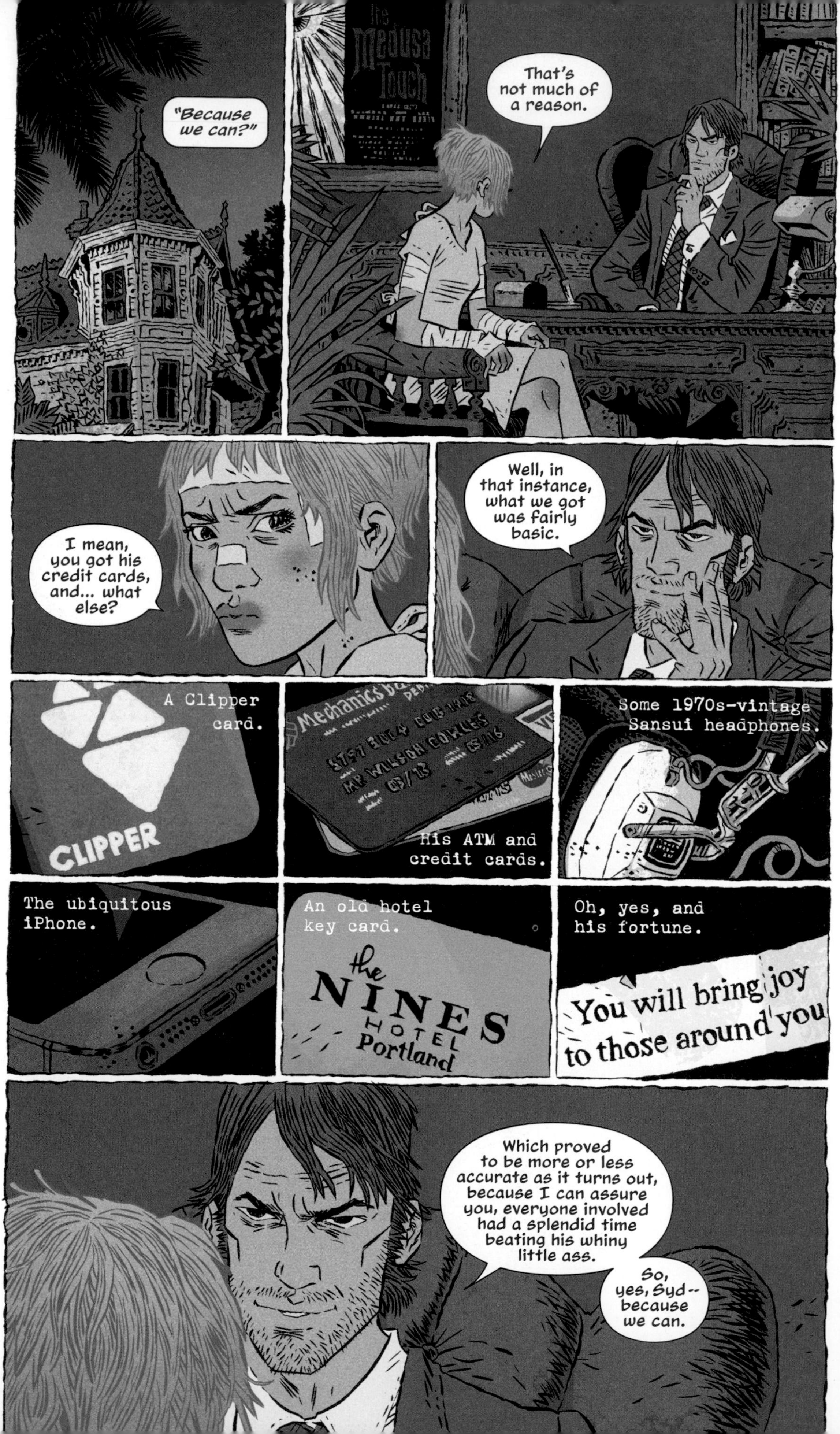

"Because we can?"
That's not much of a reason.
I mean, you got his credit cards, and... what else?
Well, in that instance, what we got was fairly basic.
A Clipper card.
CLIPPER
Mechanics Bank
His ATM and credit cards.
Some 1970s-vintage Sansui headphones.
The ubiquitous iPhone.
An old hotel key card.
the NINES HOTEL Portland
Oh, yes, and his fortune.
You will bring joy to those around you
Which proved to be more or less accurate as it turns out, because I can assure you, everyone involved had a splendid time beating his whiny little ass.
So, yes, Syd-- because we can.

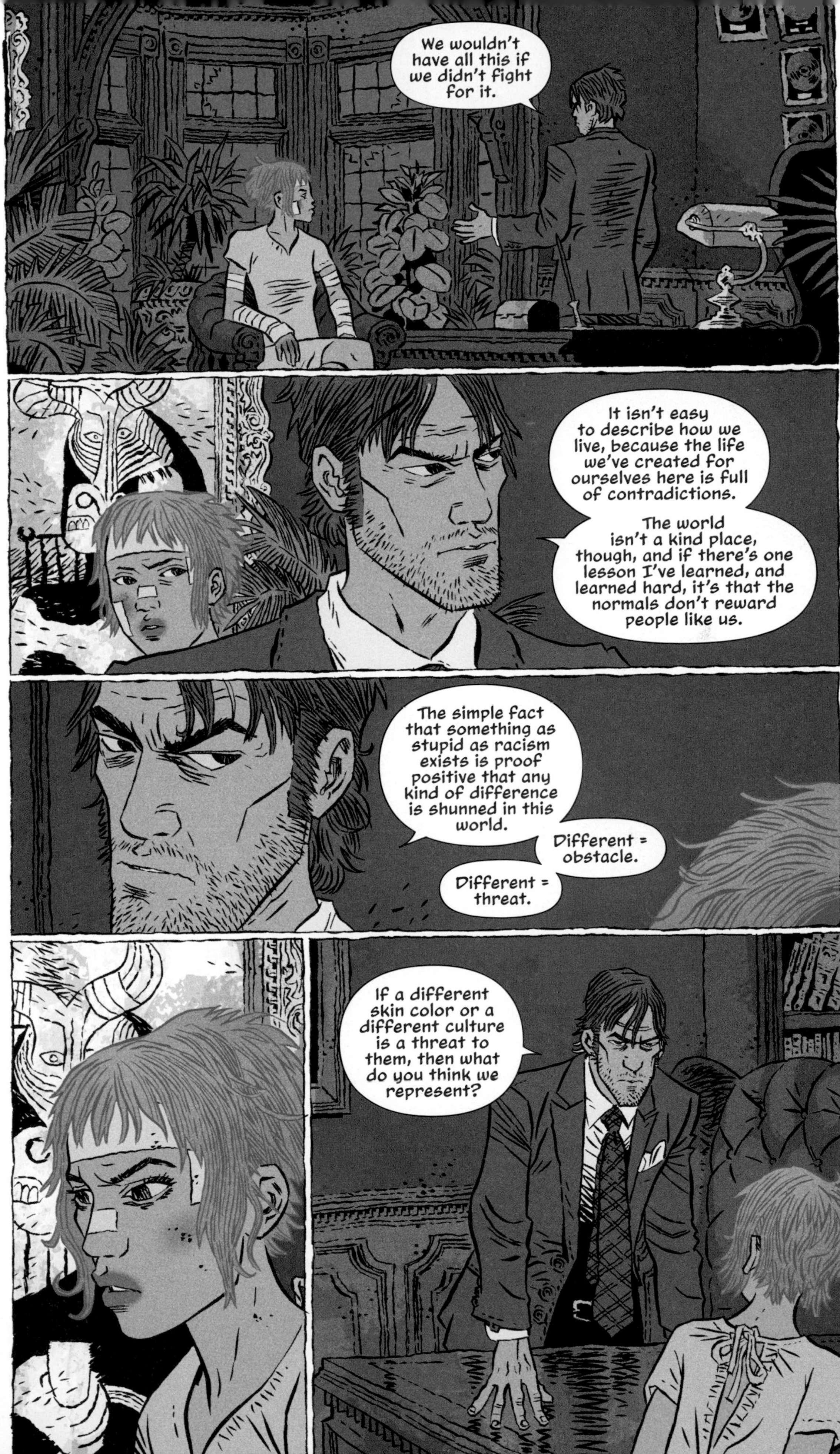
We wouldn't have all this if we didn't fight for it.
It isn't easy to describe how we live, because the life we've created for ourselves here is full of contradictions.
The world isn't a kind place, though, and if there's one lesson I've learned, and learned hard, it's that the normals don't reward people like us.
The simple fact that something as stupid as racism exists is proof positive that any kind of difference is shunned in this world.
Different = obstacle.
Different = threat.
If a different skin color or a different culture is a threat to them, then what do you think we represent?

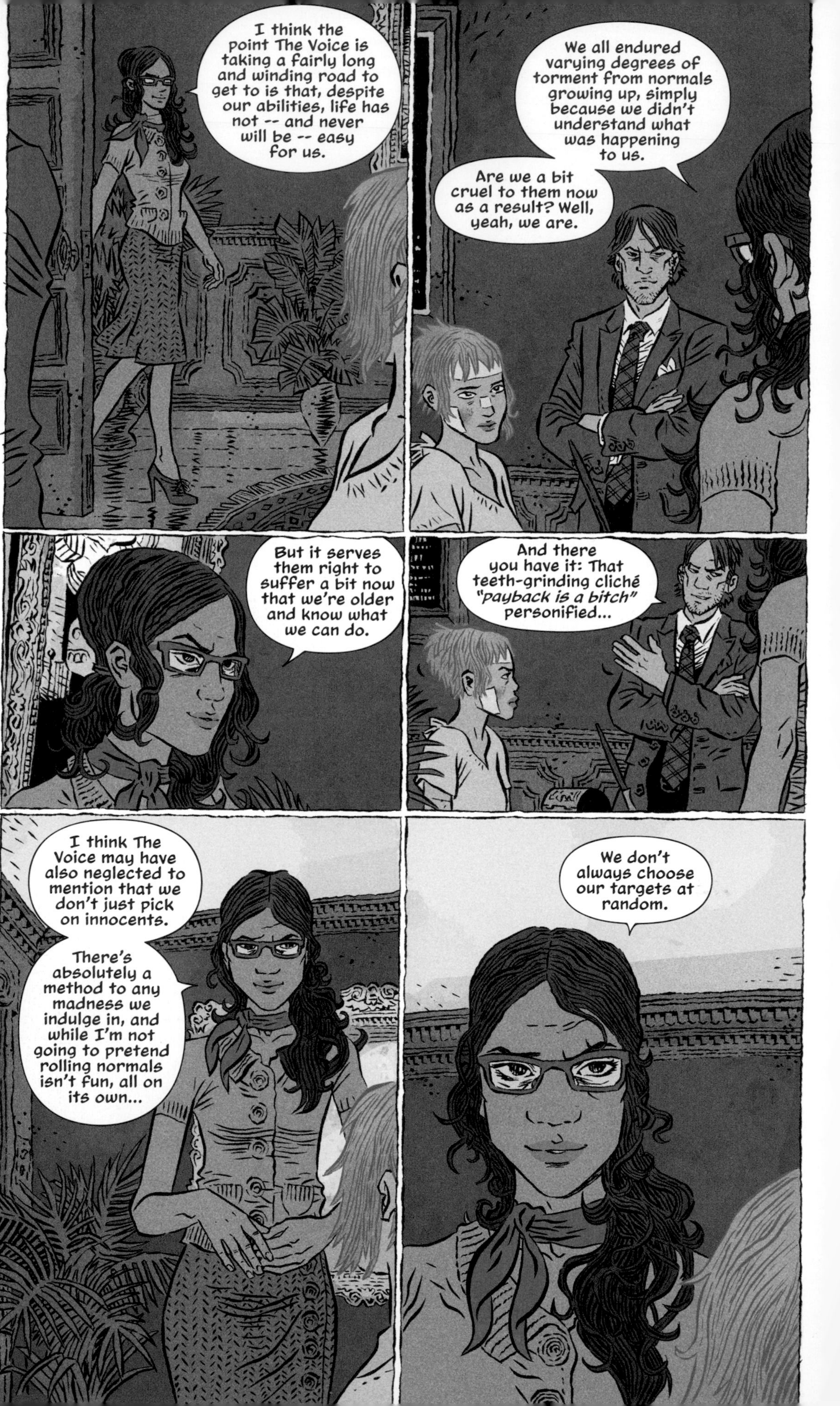
I think the point The Voice is taking a fairly long and winding road to get to is that, despite our abilities, life has not -- and never will be -- easy for us.
We all endured varying degrees of torment from normals growing up, simply because we didn't understand what was happening to us.
Are we a bit cruel to them now as a result? Well, yeah, we are.
But it serves them right to suffer a bit now that we're older and know what we can do.
And there you have it: That teeth-grinding cliché *"payback is a bitch"* personified...
I think The Voice may have also neglected to mention that we don't just pick on innocents.
There's absolutely a method to any madness we indulge in, and while I'm not going to pretend rolling normals isn't fun, all on its own...
We don't always choose our targets at random.

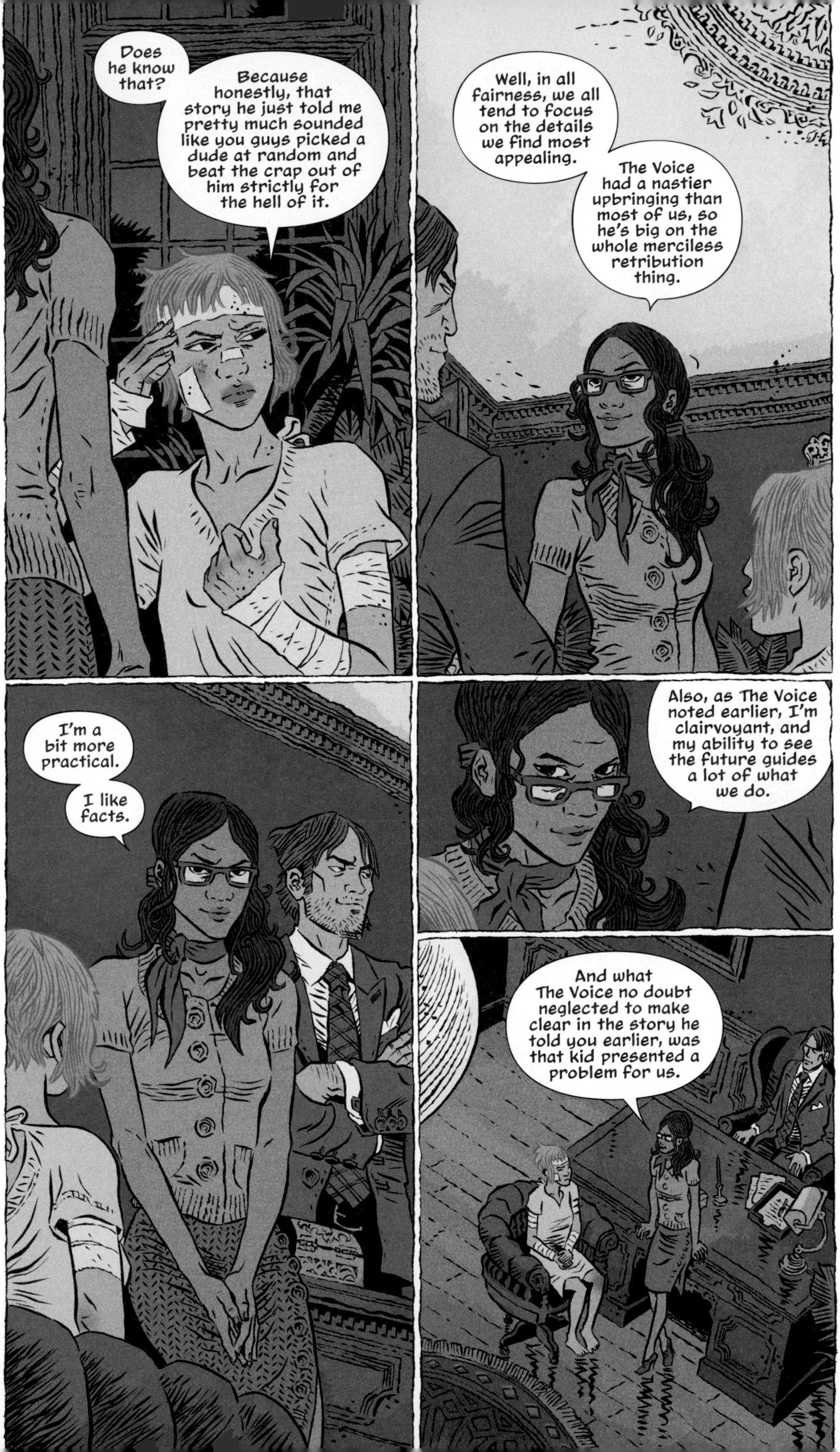

Does he know that?
Because honestly, that story he just told me pretty much sounded like you guys picked a dude at random and beat the crap out of him strictly for the hell of it.
Well, in all fairness, we all tend to focus on the details we find most appealing.
The Voice had a nastier upbringing than most of us, so he's big on the whole merciless retribution thing.
I'm a bit more practical.
I like facts.
Also, as The Voice noted earlier, I'm clairvoyant, and my ability to see the future guides a lot of what we do.
And what The Voice no doubt neglected to make clear in the story he told you earlier, was that kid presented a problem for us.

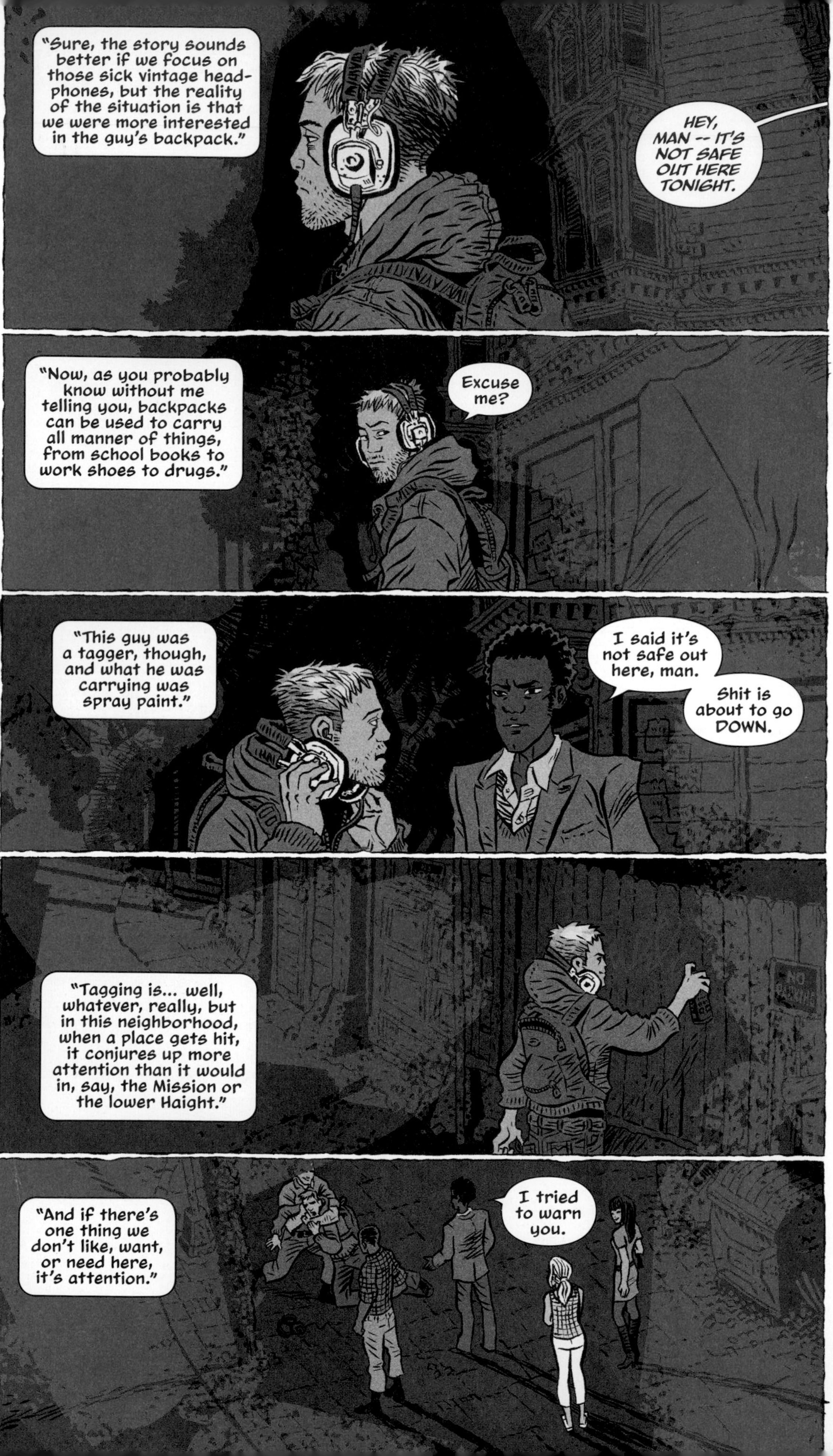
"Sure, the story sounds better if we focus on those sick vintage headphones, but the reality of the situation is that we were more interested in the guy's backpack."
HEY, MAN -- IT'S NOT SAFE OUT HERE TONIGHT.
"Now, as you probably know without me telling you, backpacks can be used to carry all manner of things, from school books to work shoes to drugs."
Excuse me?
"This guy was a tagger, though, and what he was carrying was spray paint."
I said it's not safe out here, man.
Shit is about to go DOWN.
"Tagging is... well, whatever, really, but in this neighborhood, when a place gets hit, it conjures up more attention than it would in, say, the Mission or the lower Haight."
NO PARKING
"And if there's one thing we don't like, want, or need here, it's attention."
I tried to warn you.

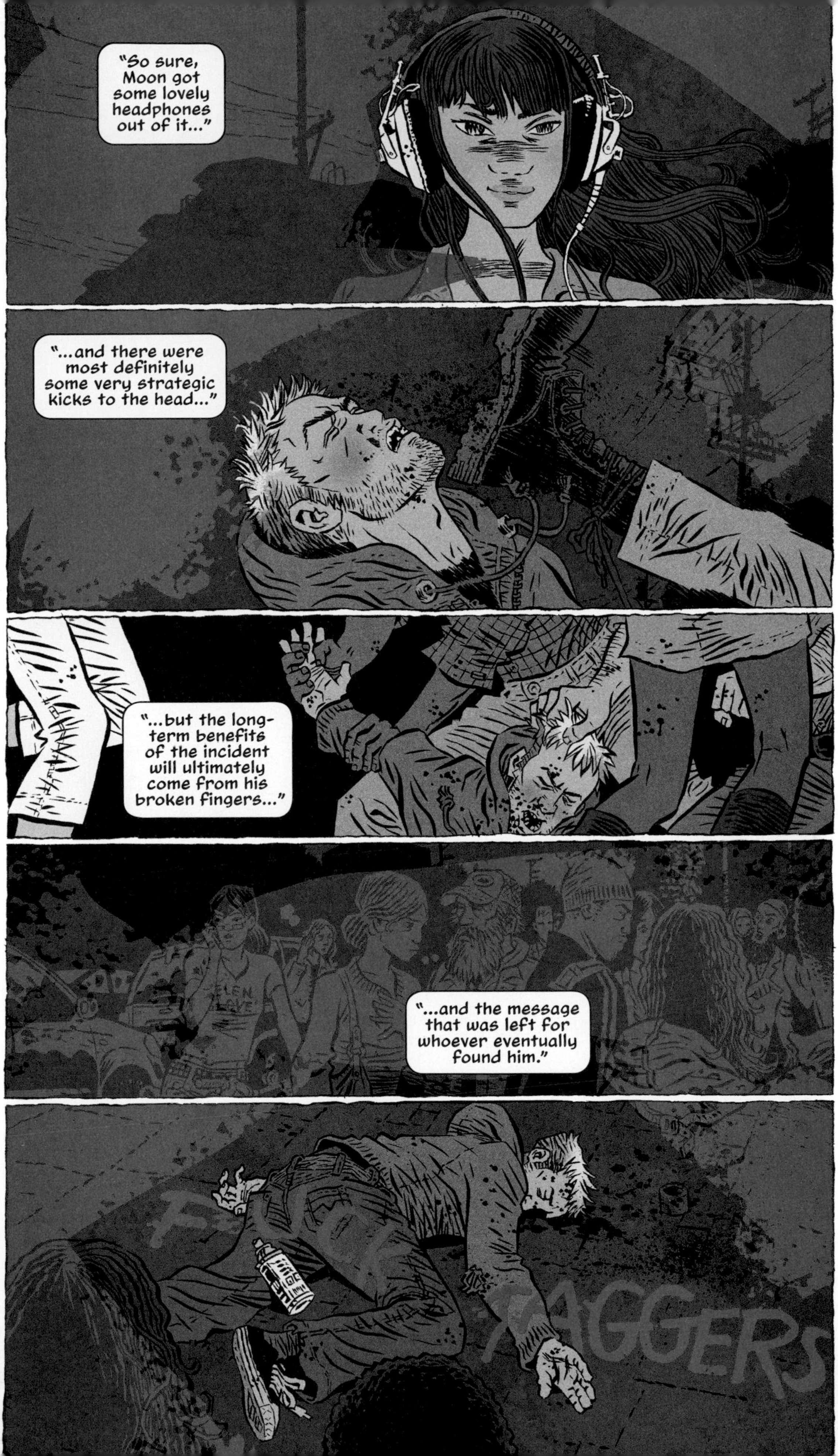
"So sure, Moon got some lovely headphones out of it..."
"...and there were most definitely some very strategic kicks to the head..."
"...but the long-term benefits of the incident will ultimately come from his broken fingers..."
"...and the message that was left for whoever eventually found him."

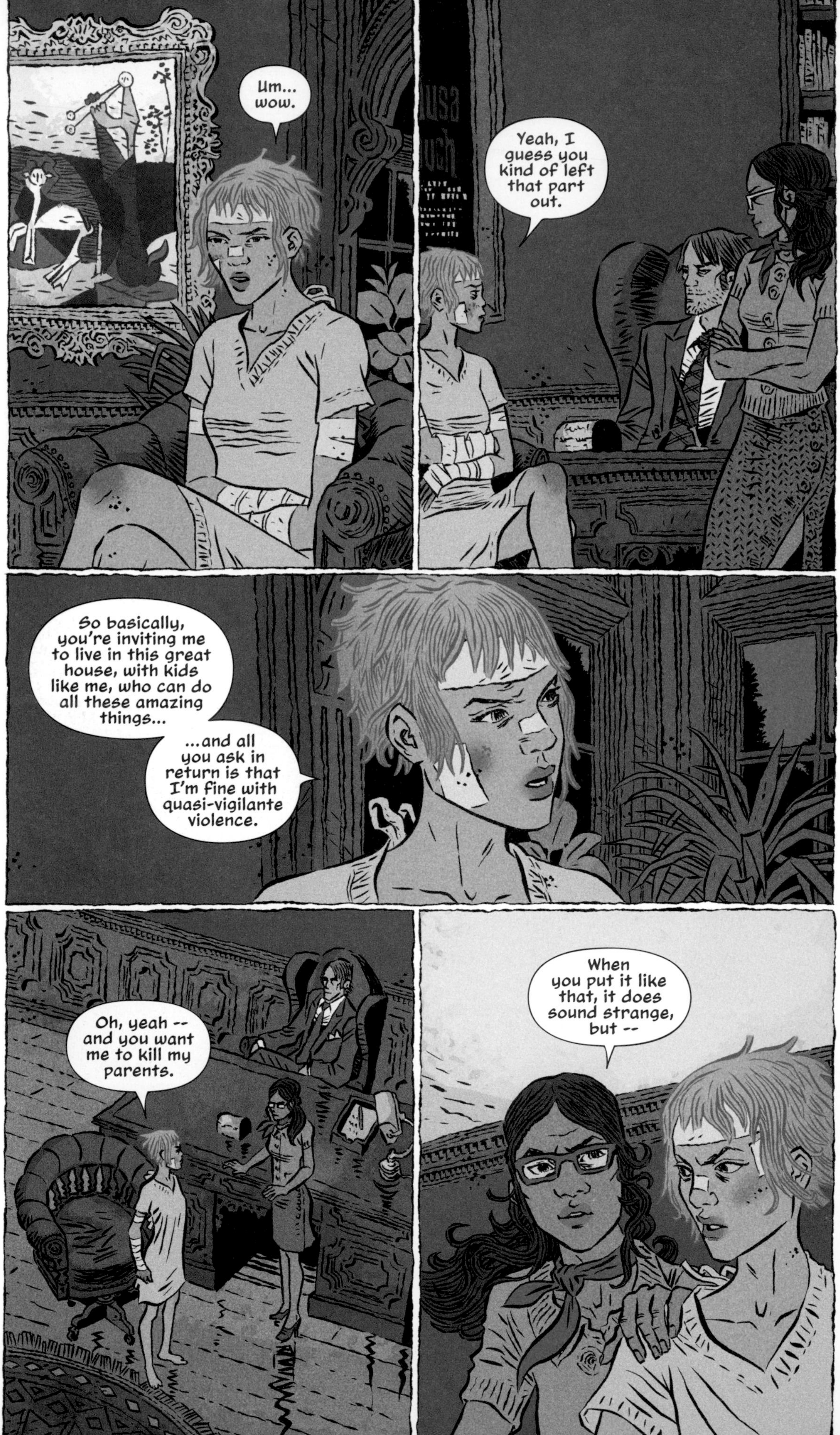
Um... wow.
Yeah, I guess you kind of left that part out.
So basically, you're inviting me to live in this great house, with kids like me, who can do all these amazing things...
...and all you ask in return is that I'm fine with quasi-vigilante violence.
Oh, yeah -- and you want me to kill my parents.
When you put it like that, it does sound strange, but --

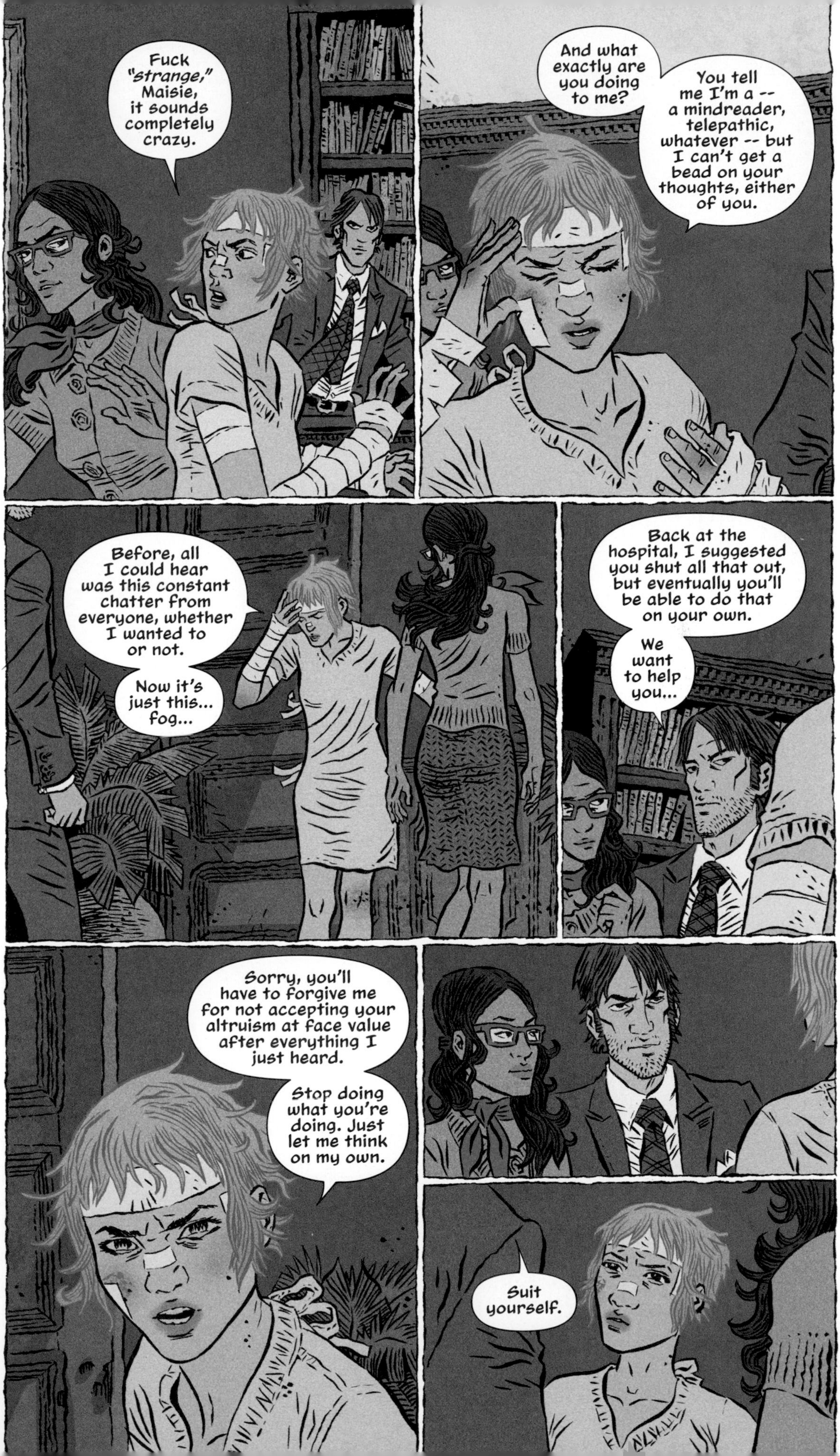

Fuck "strange," Maisie, it sounds completely crazy.
And what exactly are you doing to me?
You tell me I'm a -- a mindreader, telepathic, whatever -- but I can't get a bead on your thoughts, either of you.
Before, all I could hear was this constant chatter from everyone, whether I wanted to or not.
Now it's just this... fog...
Back at the hospital, I suggested you shut all that out, but eventually you'll be able to do that on your own.
We want to help you...
Sorry, you'll have to forgive me for not accepting your altruism at face value after everything I just heard.
Stop doing what you're doing. Just let me think on my own.
Suit yourself.

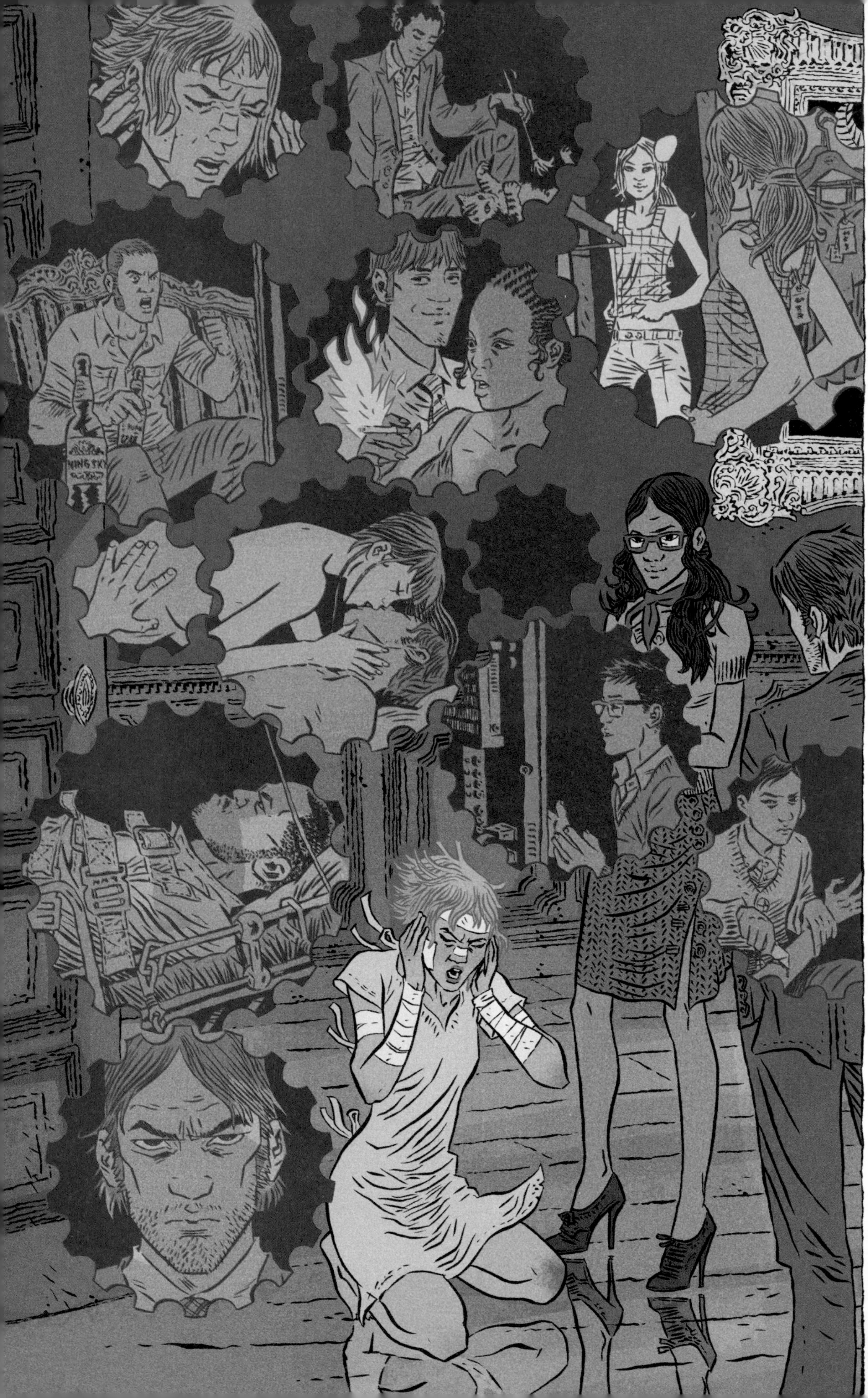

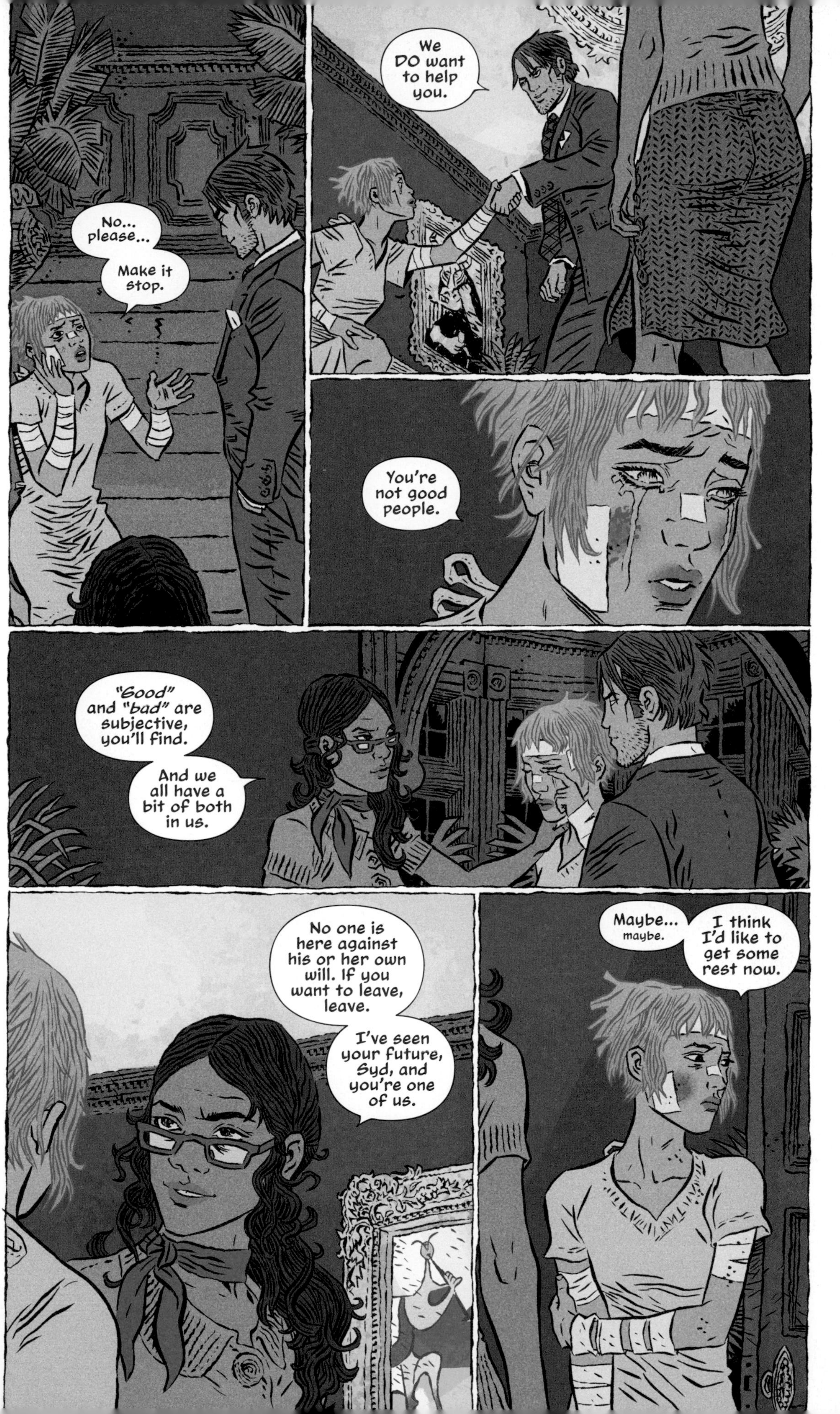
No... please...
Make it stop.
We DO want to help you.
You're not good people.
"Good" and "bad" are subjective, you'll find.
And we all have a bit of both in us.
No one is here against his or her own will. If you want to leave, leave.
I've seen your future, Syd, and you're one of us.
Maybe... maybe.
I think I'd like to get some rest now.

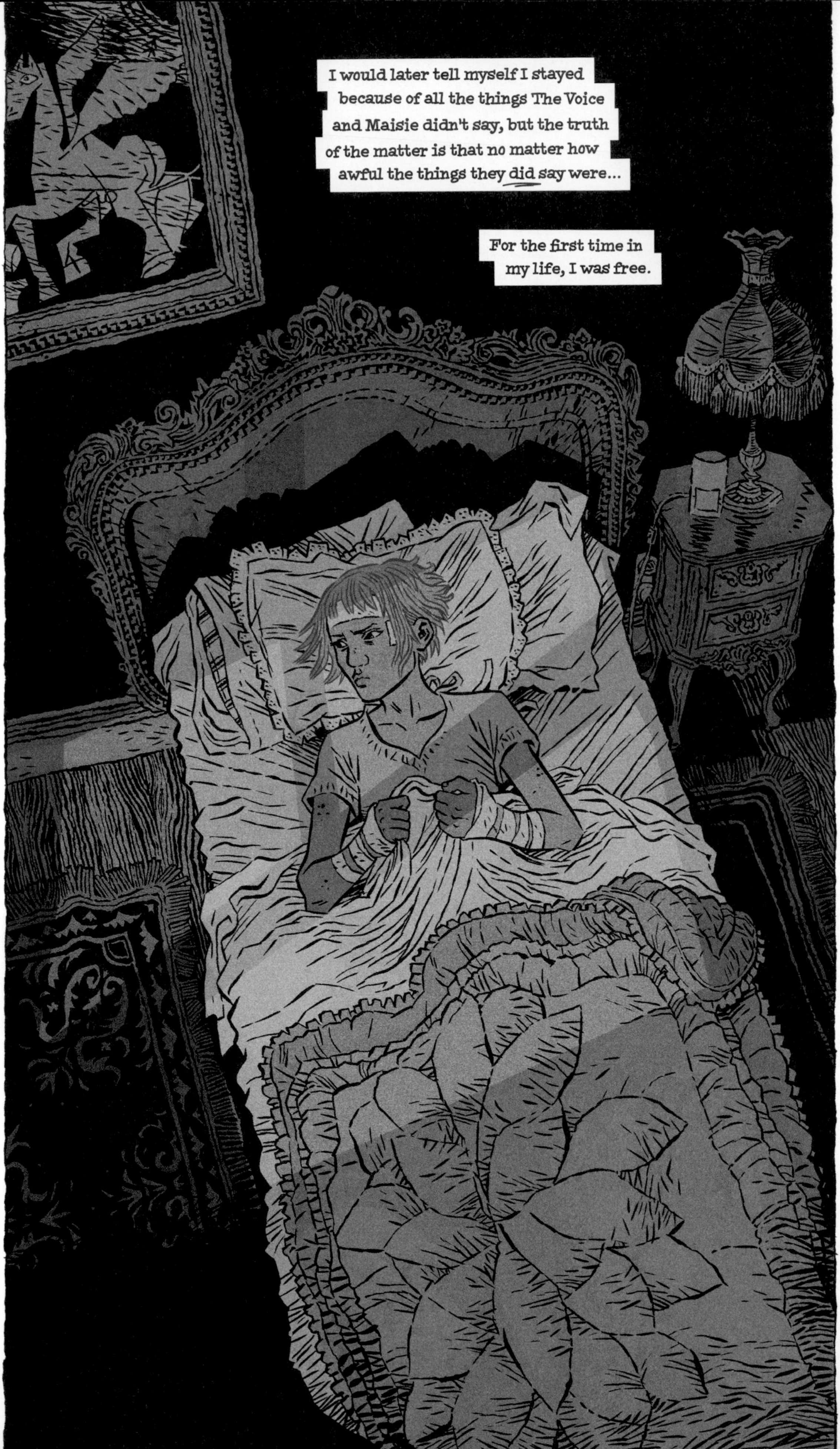
I would later tell myself I stayed because of all the things The Voice and Maisie didn't say, but the truth of the matter is that no matter how awful the things they did say were...
For the first time in my life, I was free.

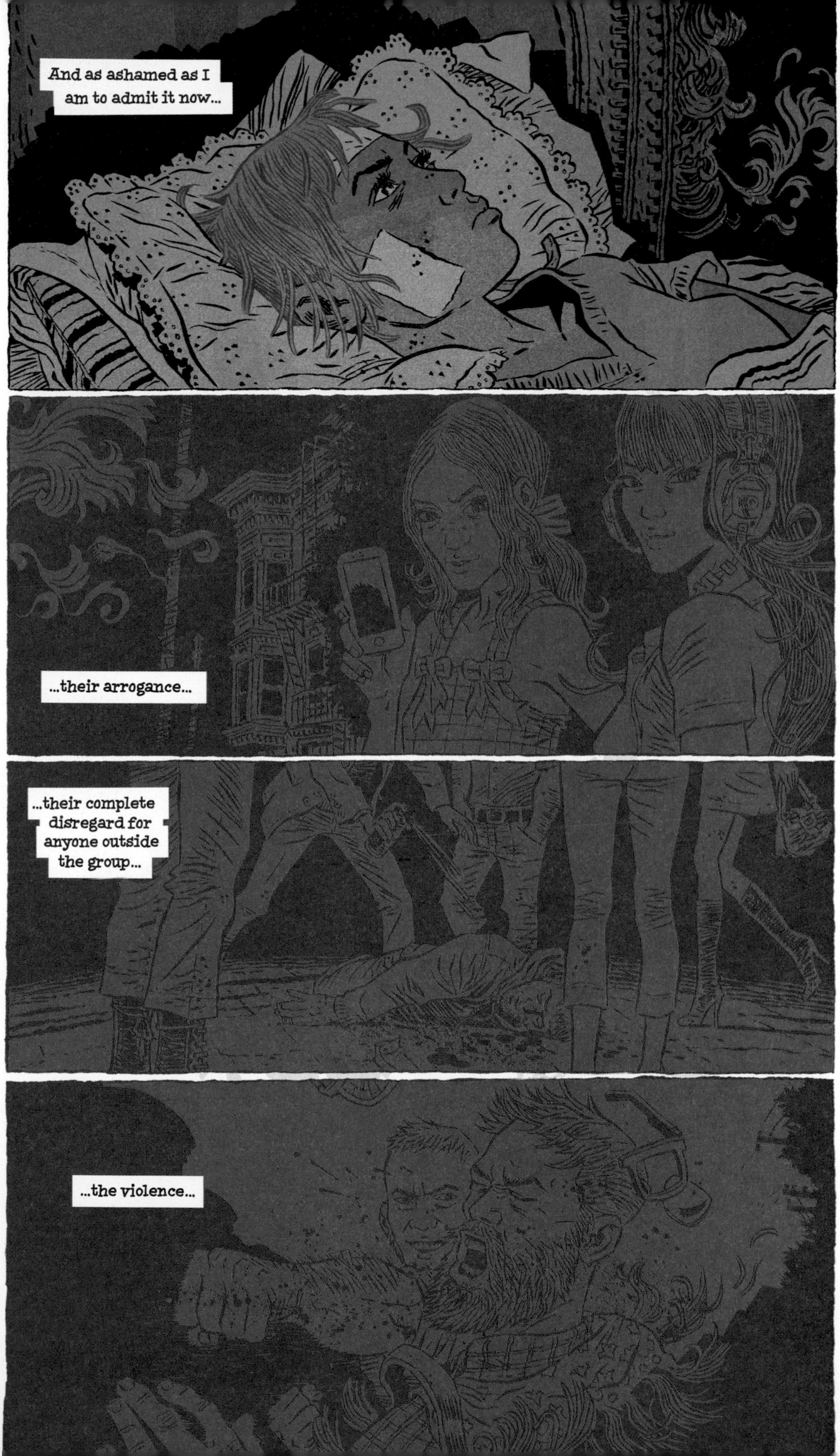
And as ashamed as I am to admit it now...
...their arrogance...
...their complete disregard for anyone outside the group...
...the violence...

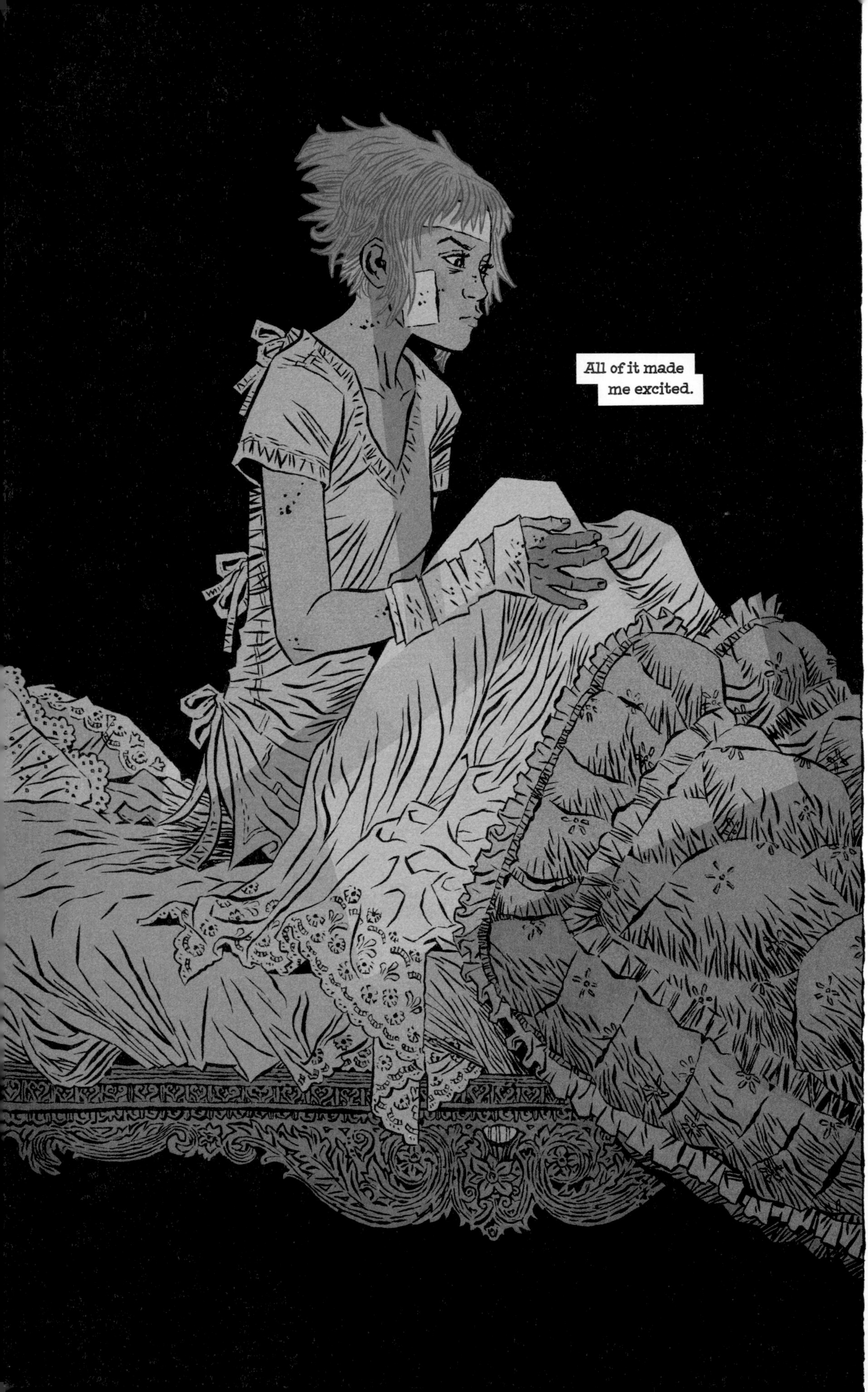
All of it made me excited.

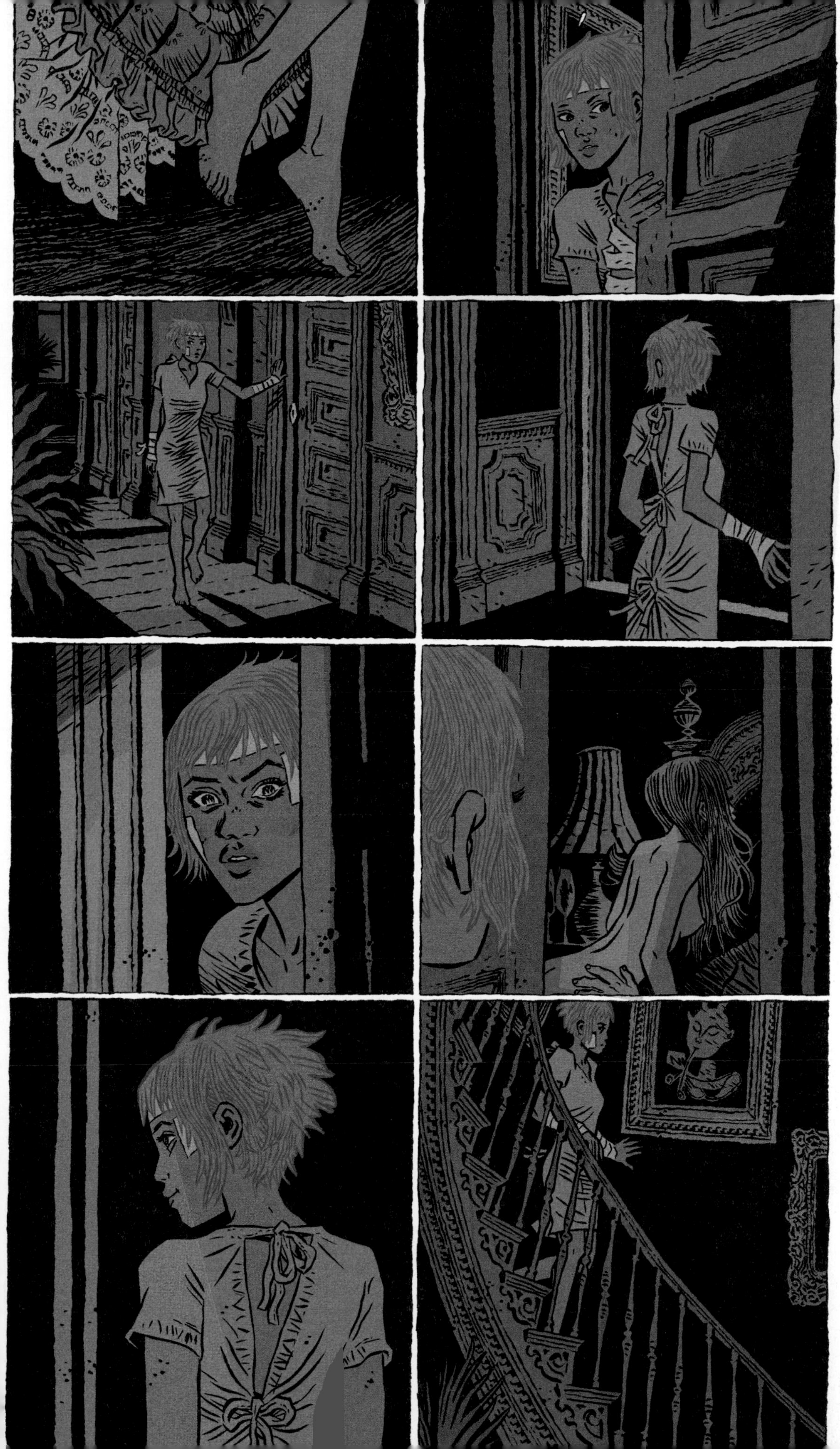

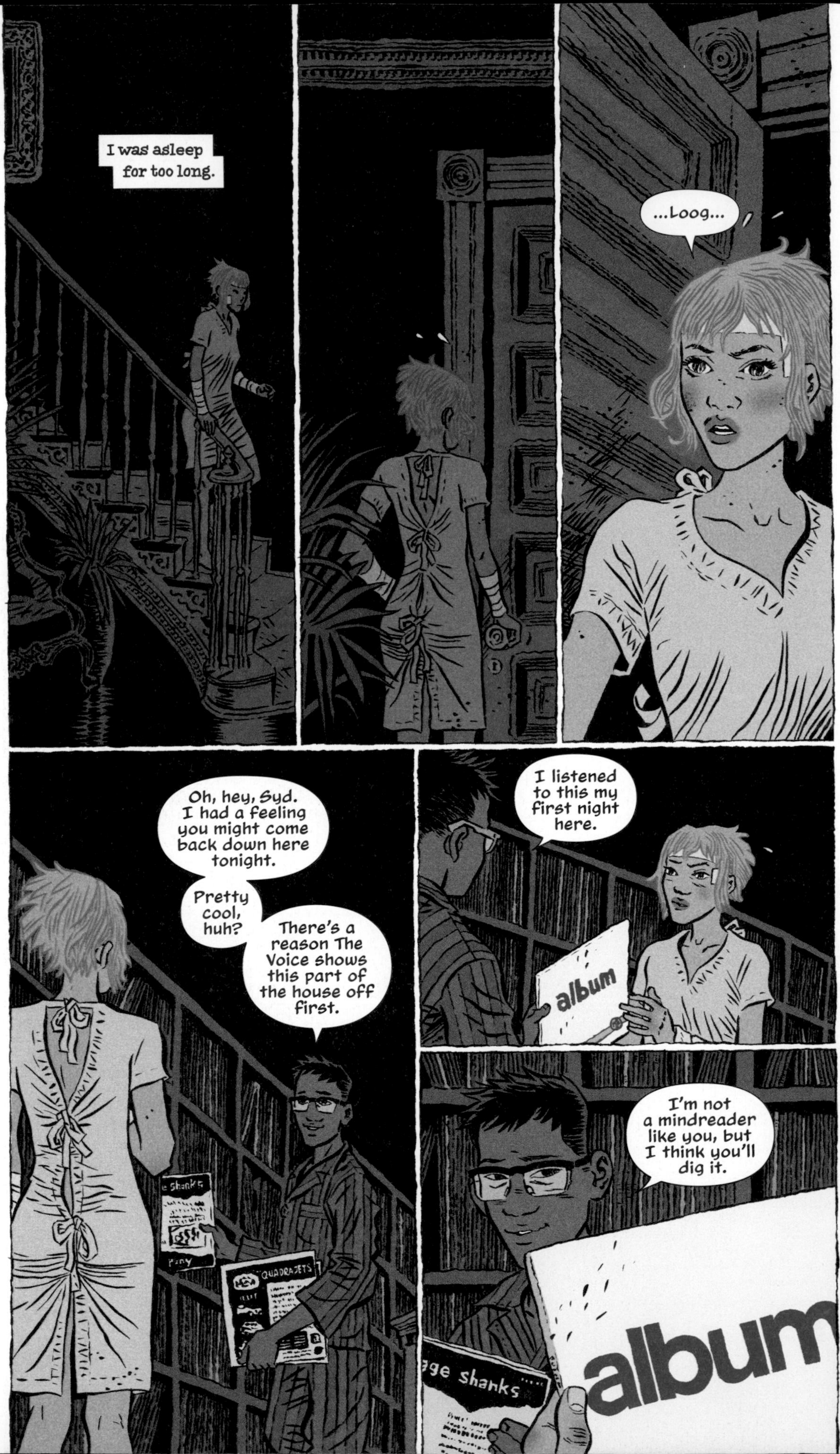

I was asleep for too long.
...Loog...
Oh, hey, Syd. I had a feeling you might come back down here tonight.
Pretty cool, huh?
There's a reason The Voice shows this part of the house off first.
I listened to this my first night here.
album
I'm not a mindreader like you, but I think you'll dig it.
album

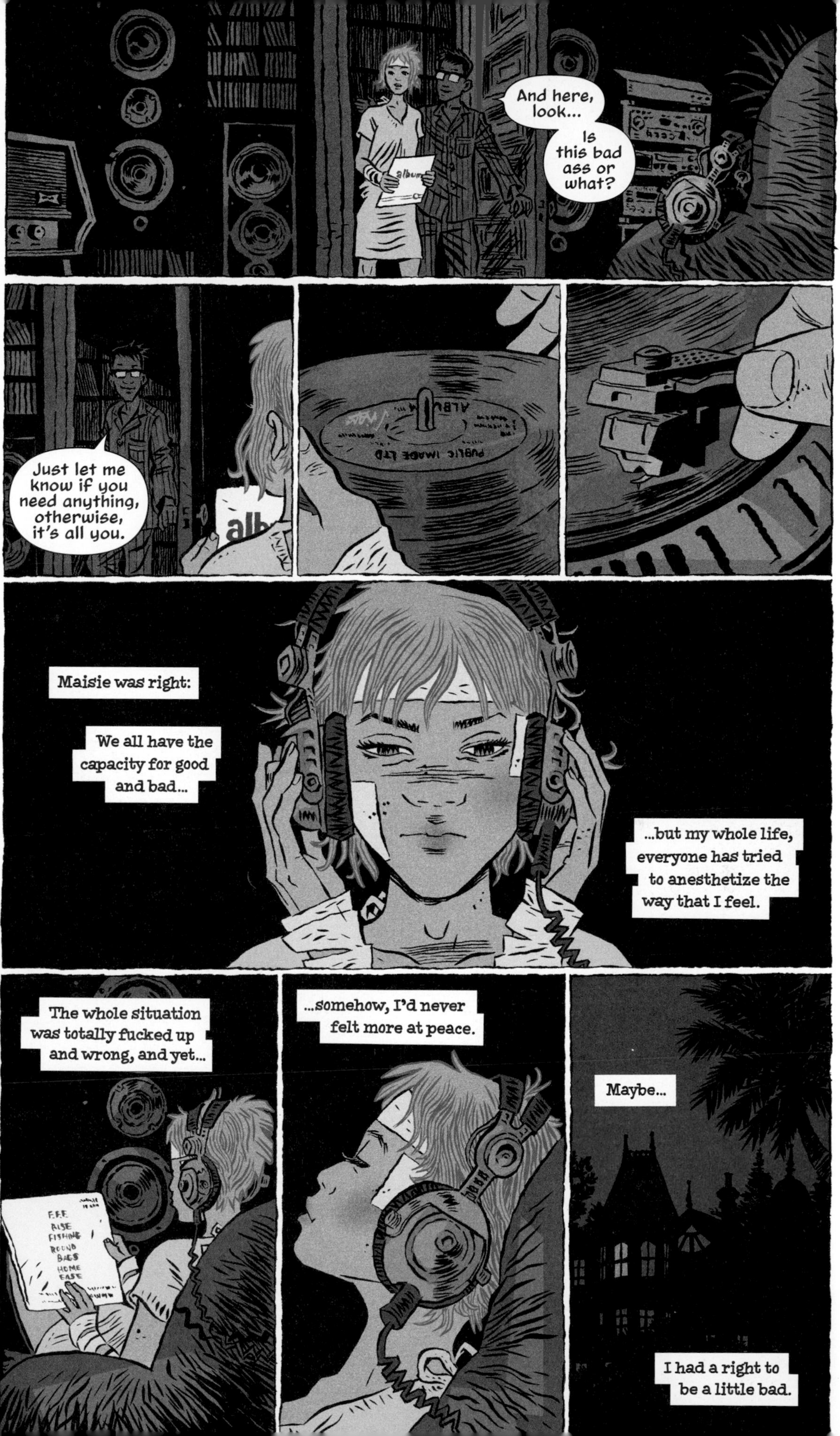

And here, look...
Is this bad ass or what?
album
Just let me know if you need anything, otherwise, it's all you.
alb
PUBLIC IMAGE LTD
Maisie was right:
We all have the capacity for good and bad...
...but my whole life, everyone has tried to anesthetize the way that I feel.
The whole situation was totally fucked up and wrong, and yet...
F.F.F.
RISE
FISHING
ROUND
BAGS
HOME
EASE
...somehow, I'd never felt more at peace.
Maybe...
I had a right to be a little bad.

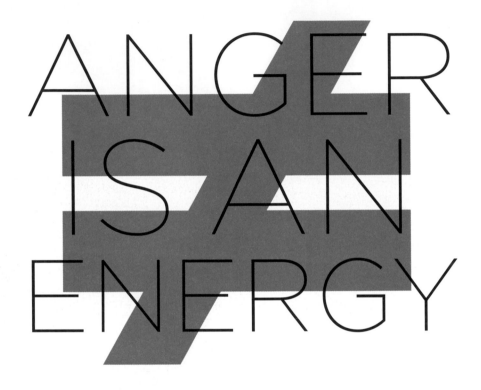

ANGER IS AN ENERGY

JOHN LYDON

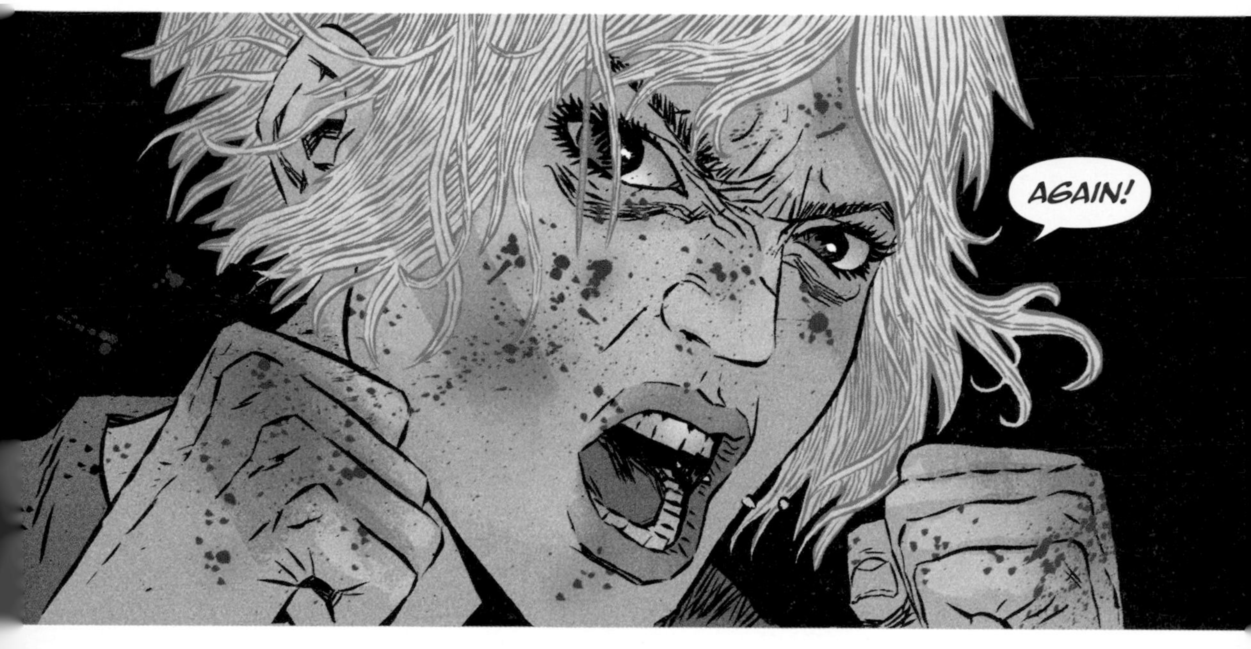
AGAIN!

3: HEYDAY OF THE BLOOD

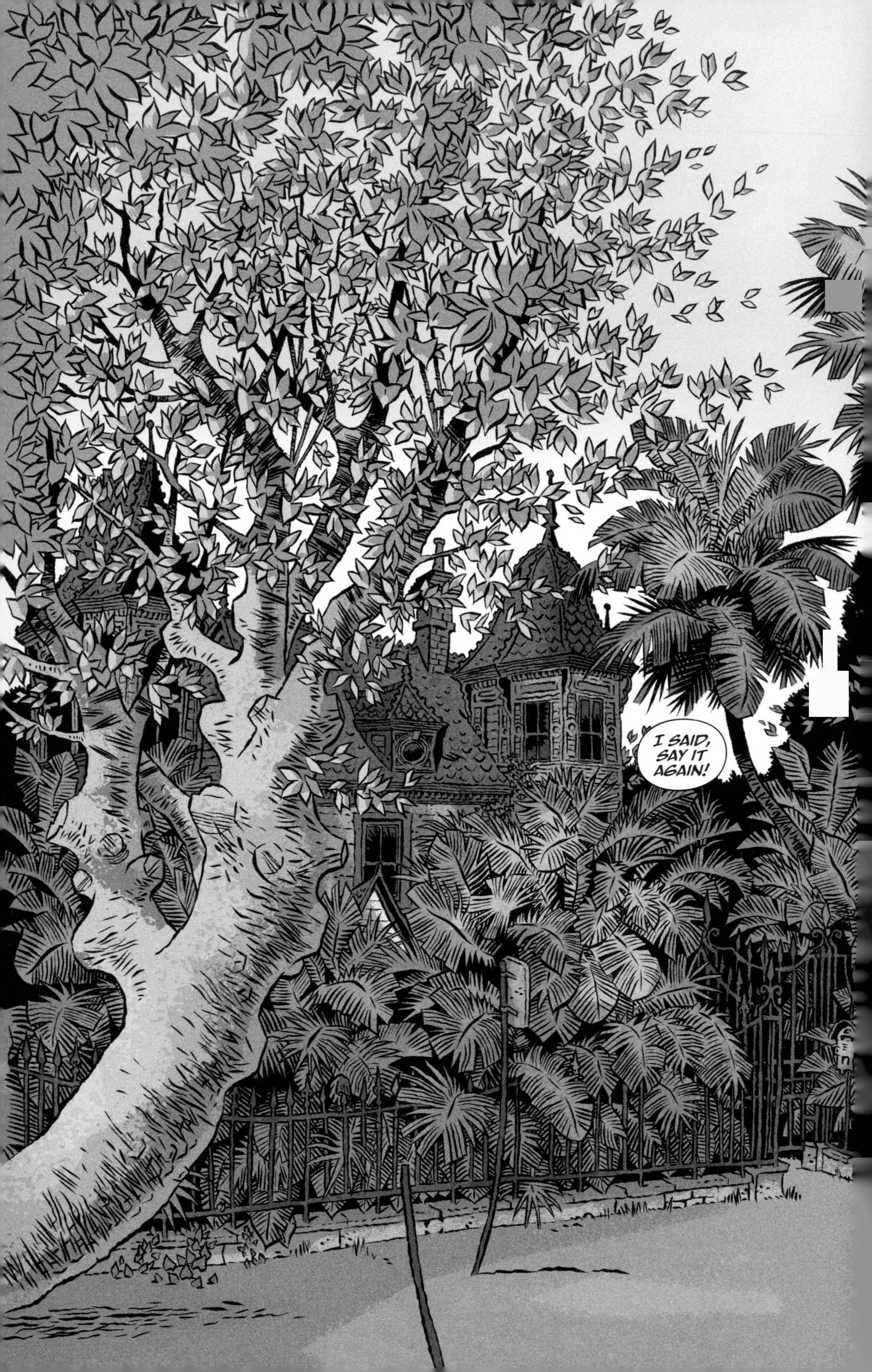
I SAID, SAY IT AGAIN!

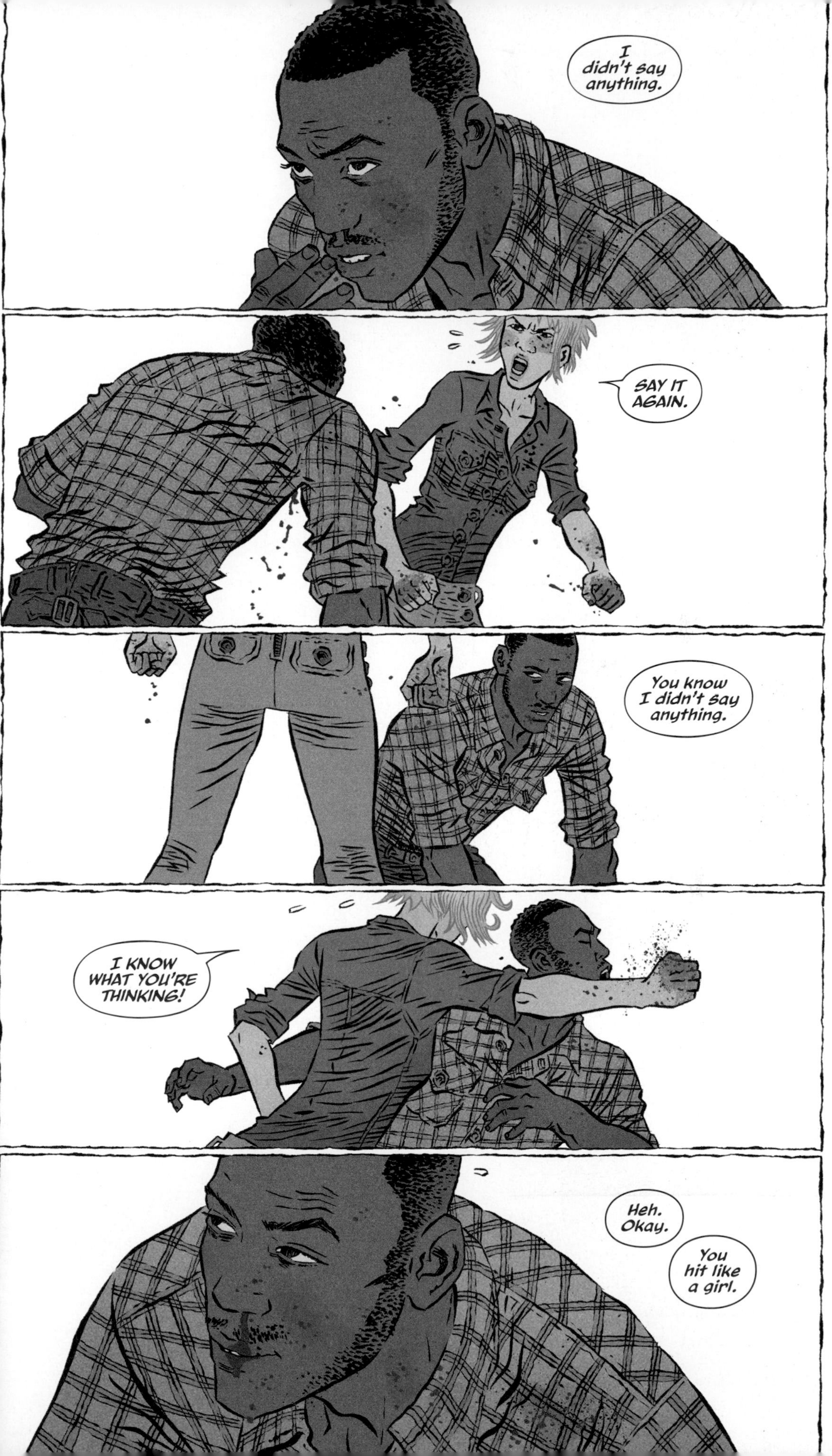
I didn't say anything.
SAY IT AGAIN.
You know I didn't say anything.
I KNOW WHAT YOU'RE THINKING!
Heh. Okay.
You hit like a girl.

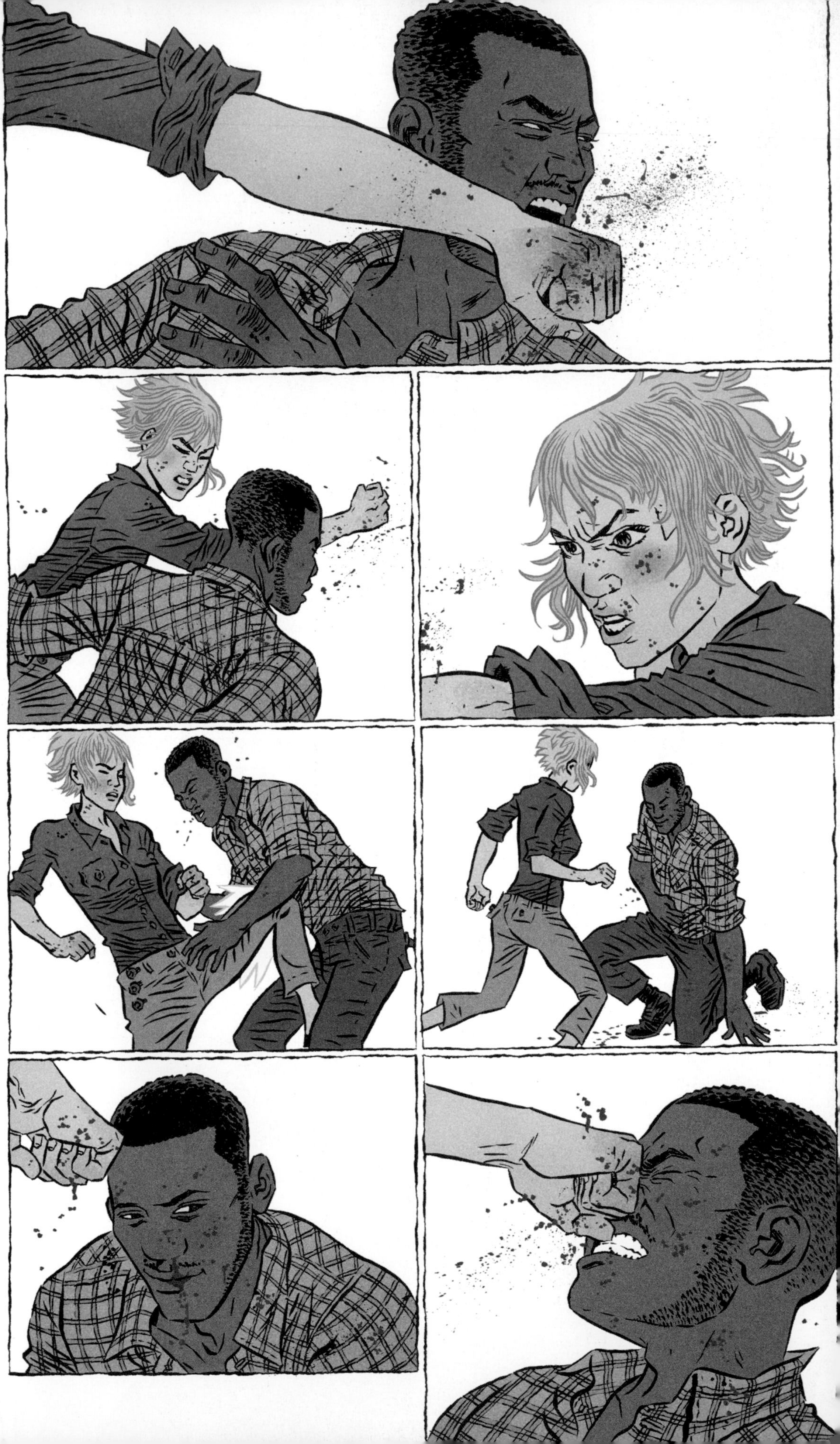

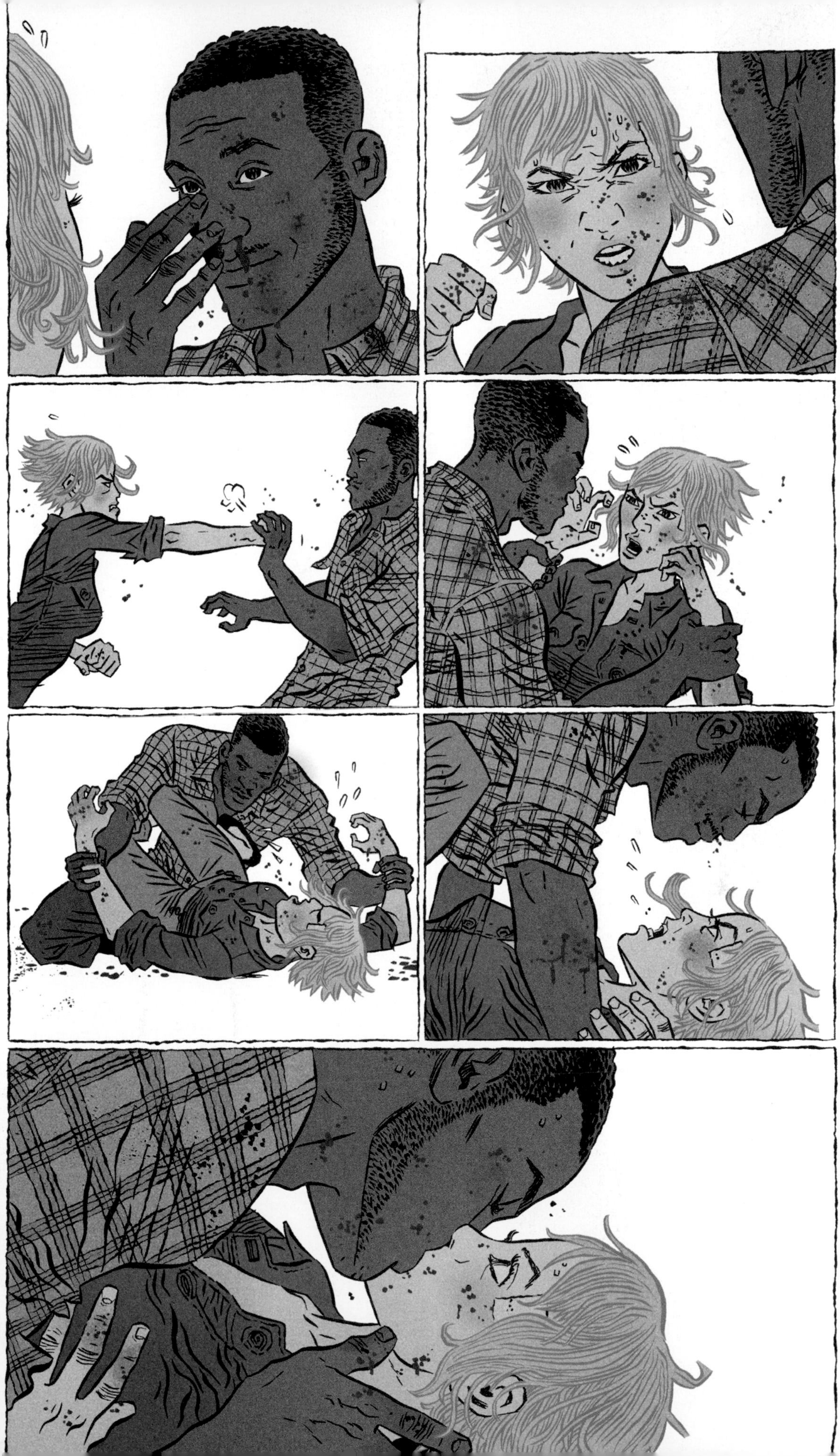

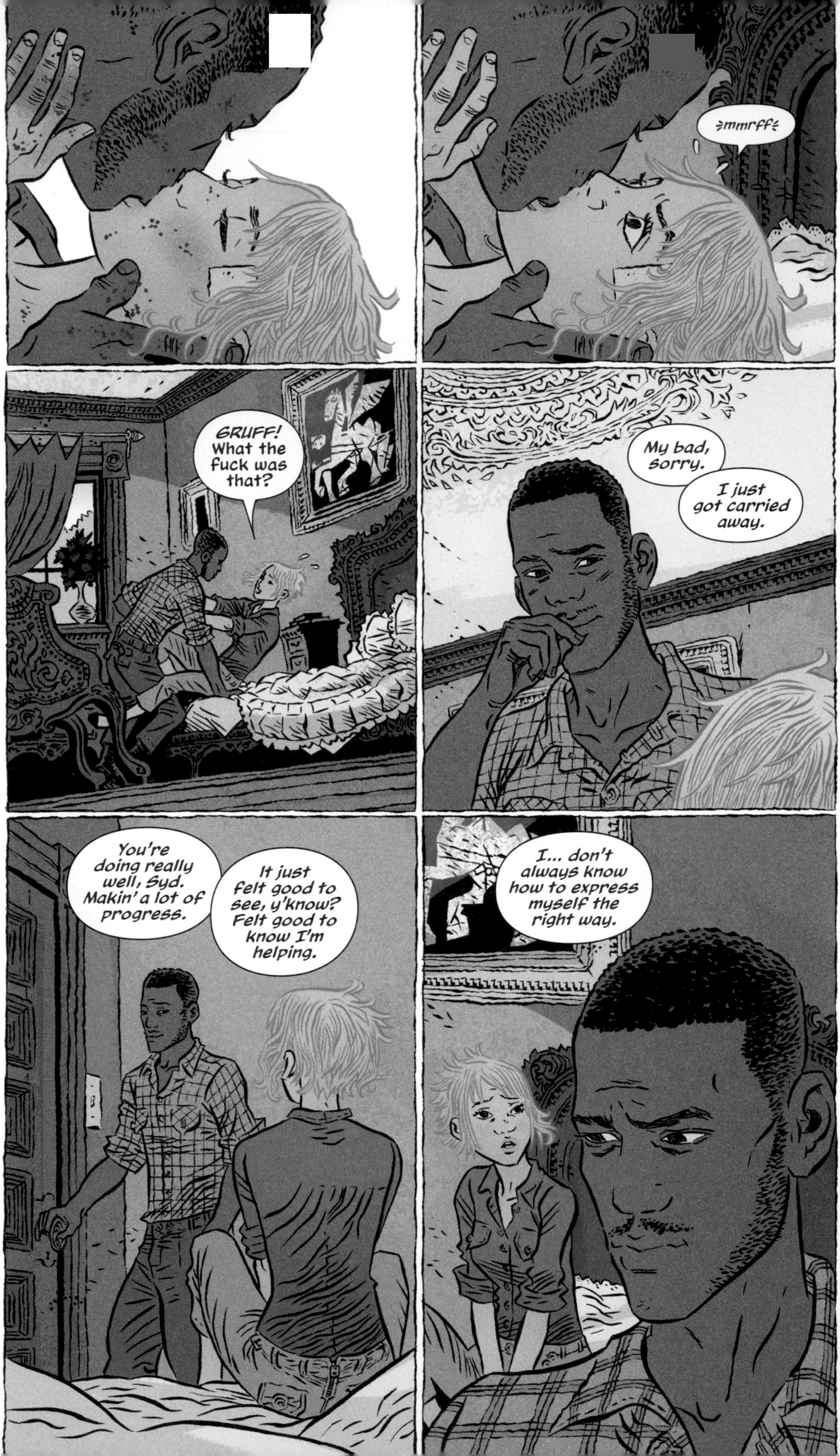
mmrff
GRUFF! What the fuck was that?
My bad, sorry.
I just got carried away.
You're doing really well, Syd. Makin' a lot of progress.
It just felt good to see, y'know? Felt good to know I'm helping.
I... don't always know how to express myself the right way.

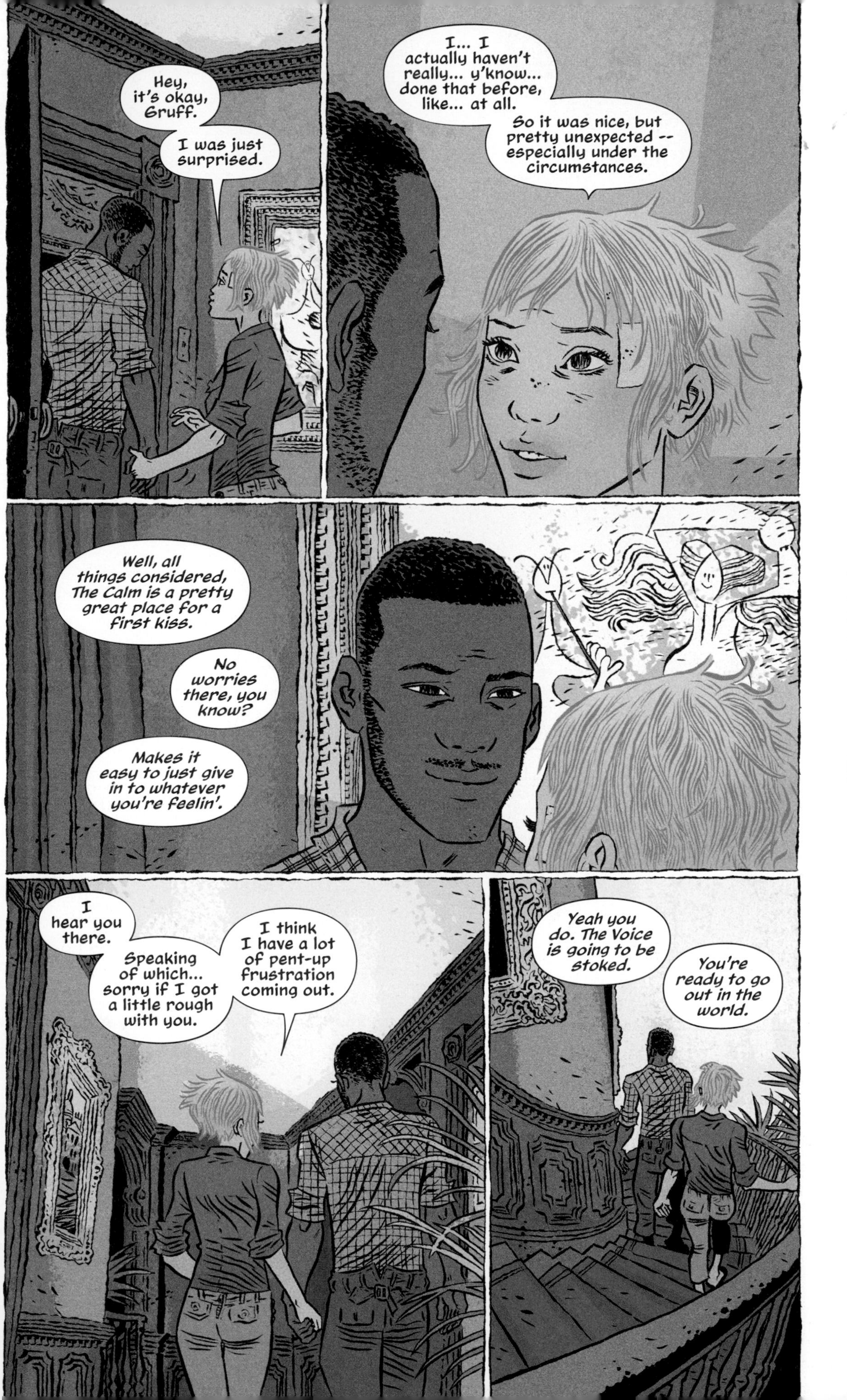
Hey, it's okay, Gruff.
I was just surprised.
I... I actually haven't really... y'know... done that before, like... at all.
So it was nice, but pretty unexpected -- especially under the circumstances.
Well, all things considered, The Calm is a pretty great place for a first kiss.
No worries there, you know?
Makes it easy to just give in to whatever you're feelin'.
I hear you there.
Speaking of which... sorry if I got a little rough with you.
I think I have a lot of pent-up frustration coming out.
Yeah you do. The Voice is going to be stoked.
You're ready to go out in the world.

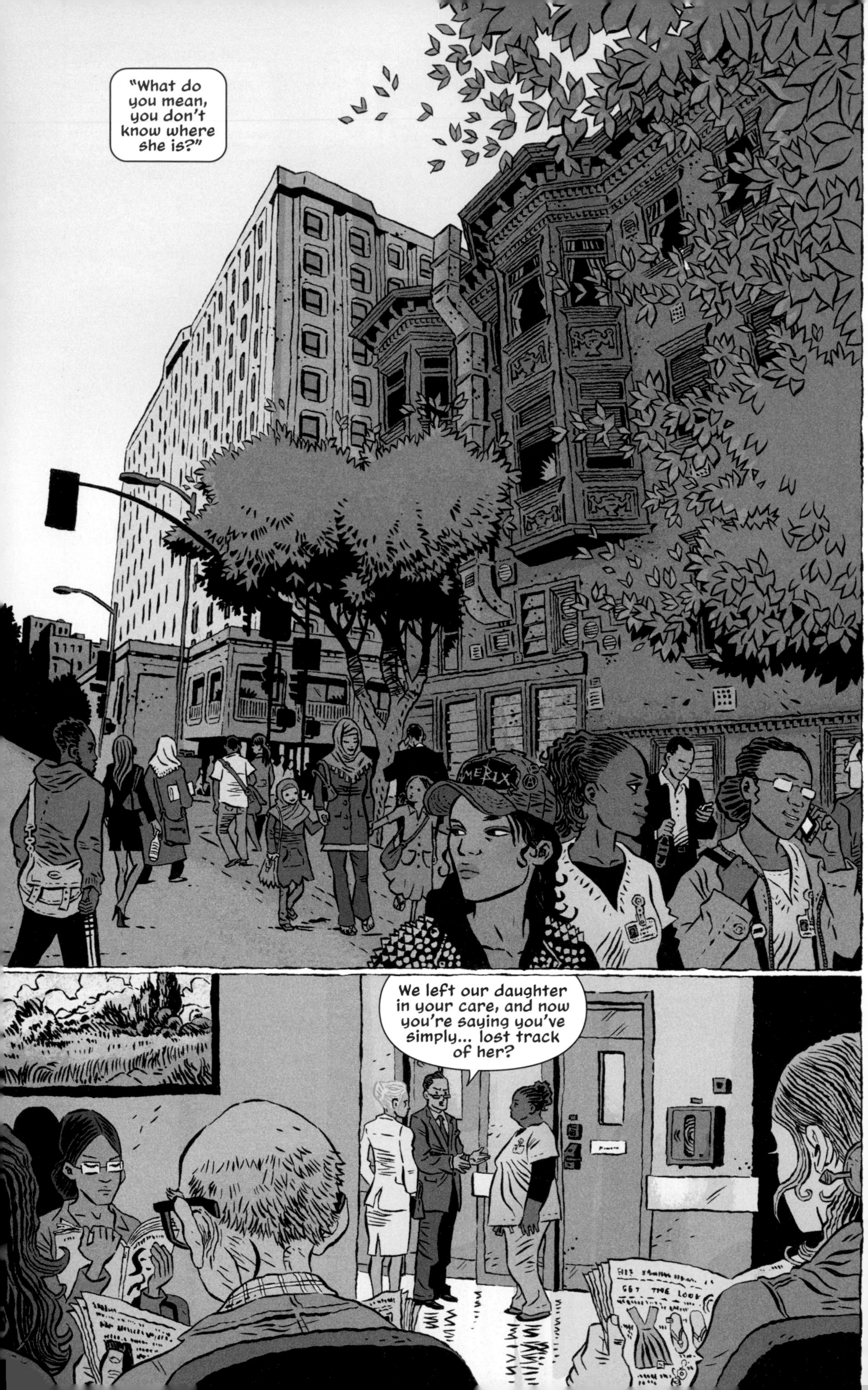
"What do you mean, you don't know where she is?"
We left our daughter in your care, and now you're saying you've simply... lost track of her?

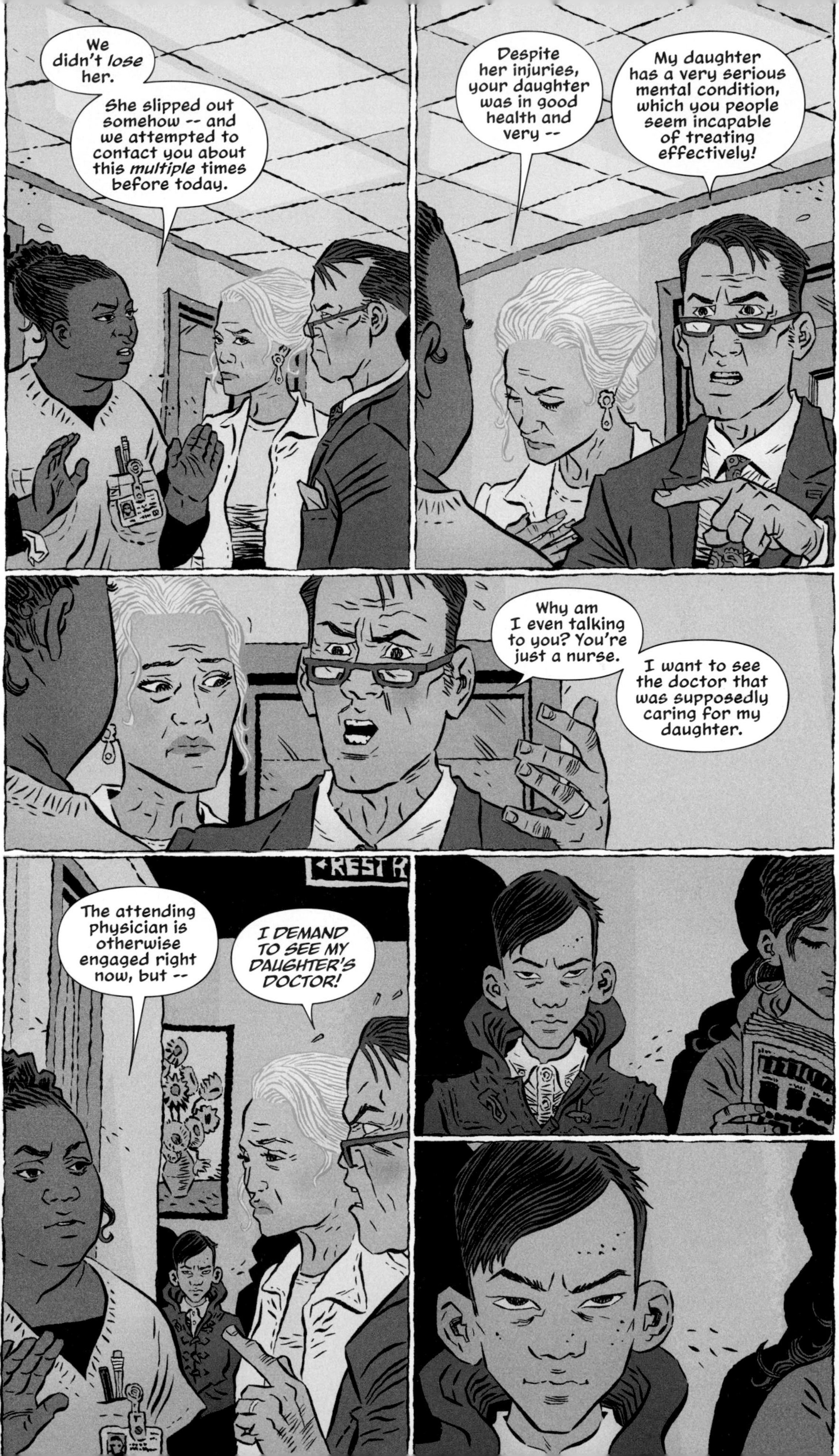
We didn't *lose* her.
She slipped out somehow -- and we attempted to contact you about this *multiple* times before today.
Despite her injuries, your daughter was in good health and very --
My daughter has a very serious mental condition, which you people seem incapable of treating effectively!
Why am I even talking to you? You're just a nurse.
I want to see the doctor that was supposedly caring for my daughter.
The attending physician is otherwise engaged right now, but --
I DEMAND TO SEE MY DAUGHTER'S DOCTOR!

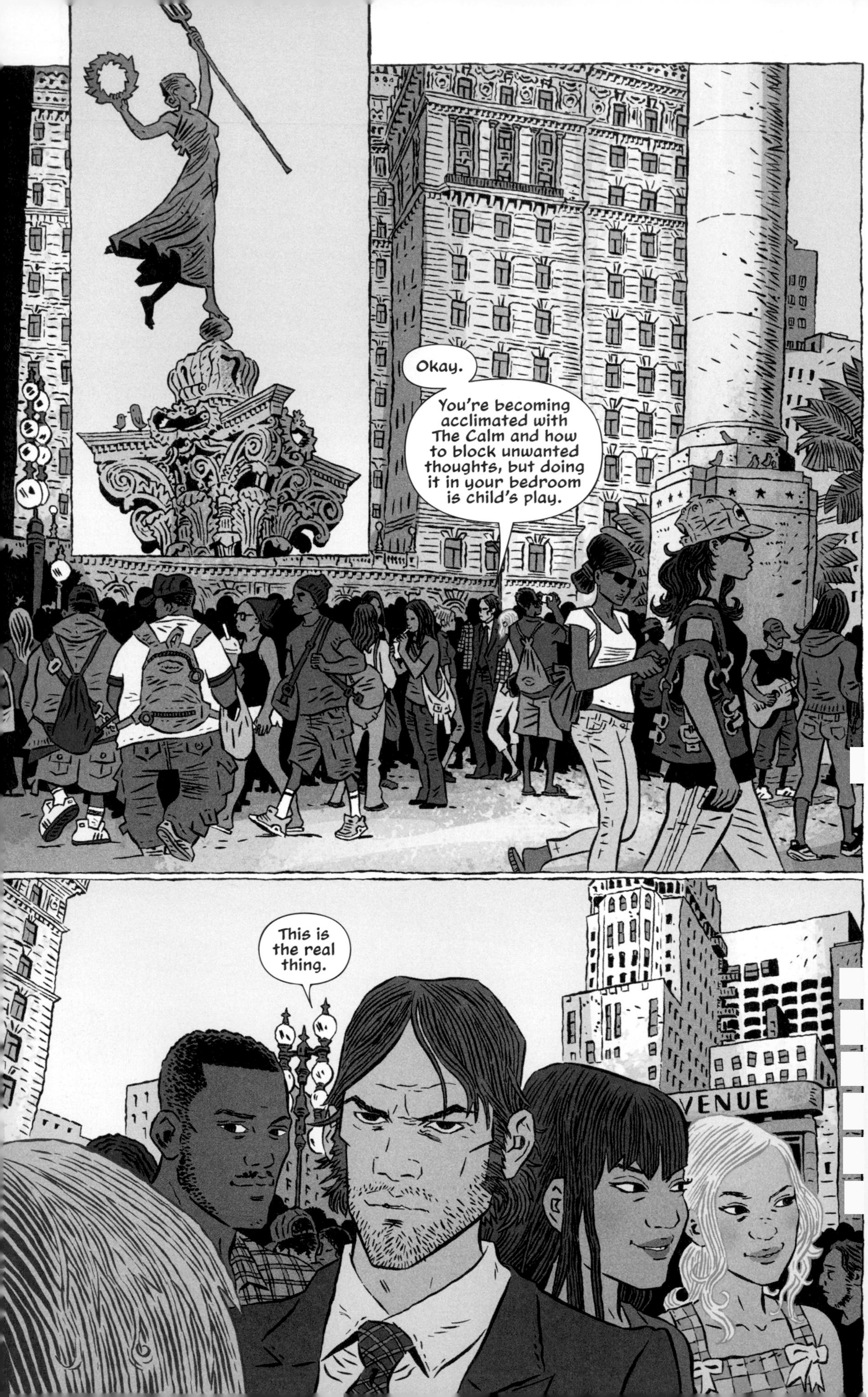
Okay.
You're becoming acclimated with The Calm and how to block unwanted thoughts, but doing it in your bedroom is child's play.
This is the real thing.
VENUE

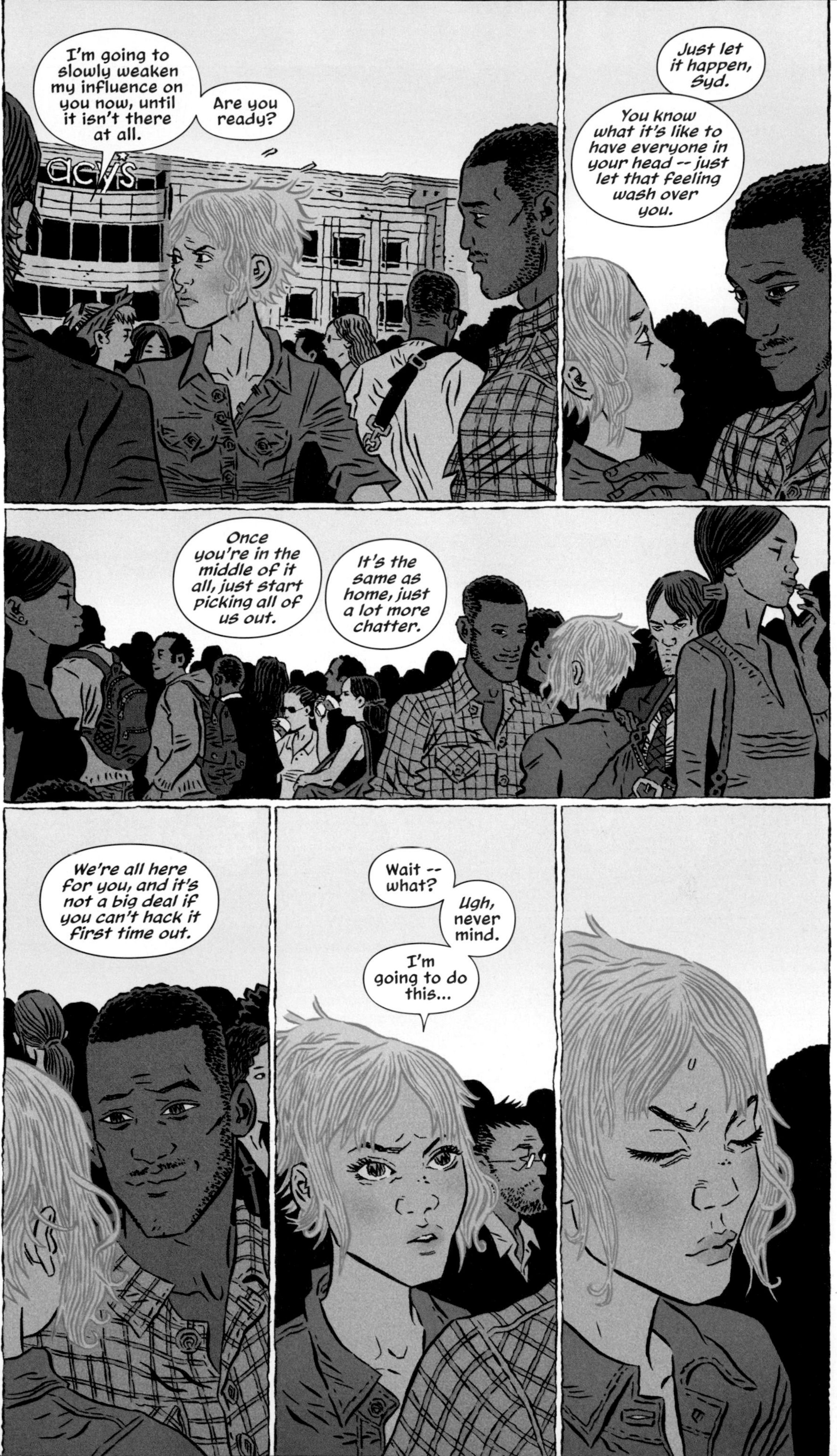
I'm going to slowly weaken my influence on you now, until it isn't there at all.
Are you ready?
Just let it happen, Syd.
You know what it's like to have everyone in your head -- just let that feeling wash over you.
Once you're in the middle of it all, just start picking all of us out.
It's the same as home, just a lot more chatter.
We're all here for you, and it's not a big deal if you can't hack it first time out.
Wait -- what?
Ugh, never mind.
I'm going to do this...

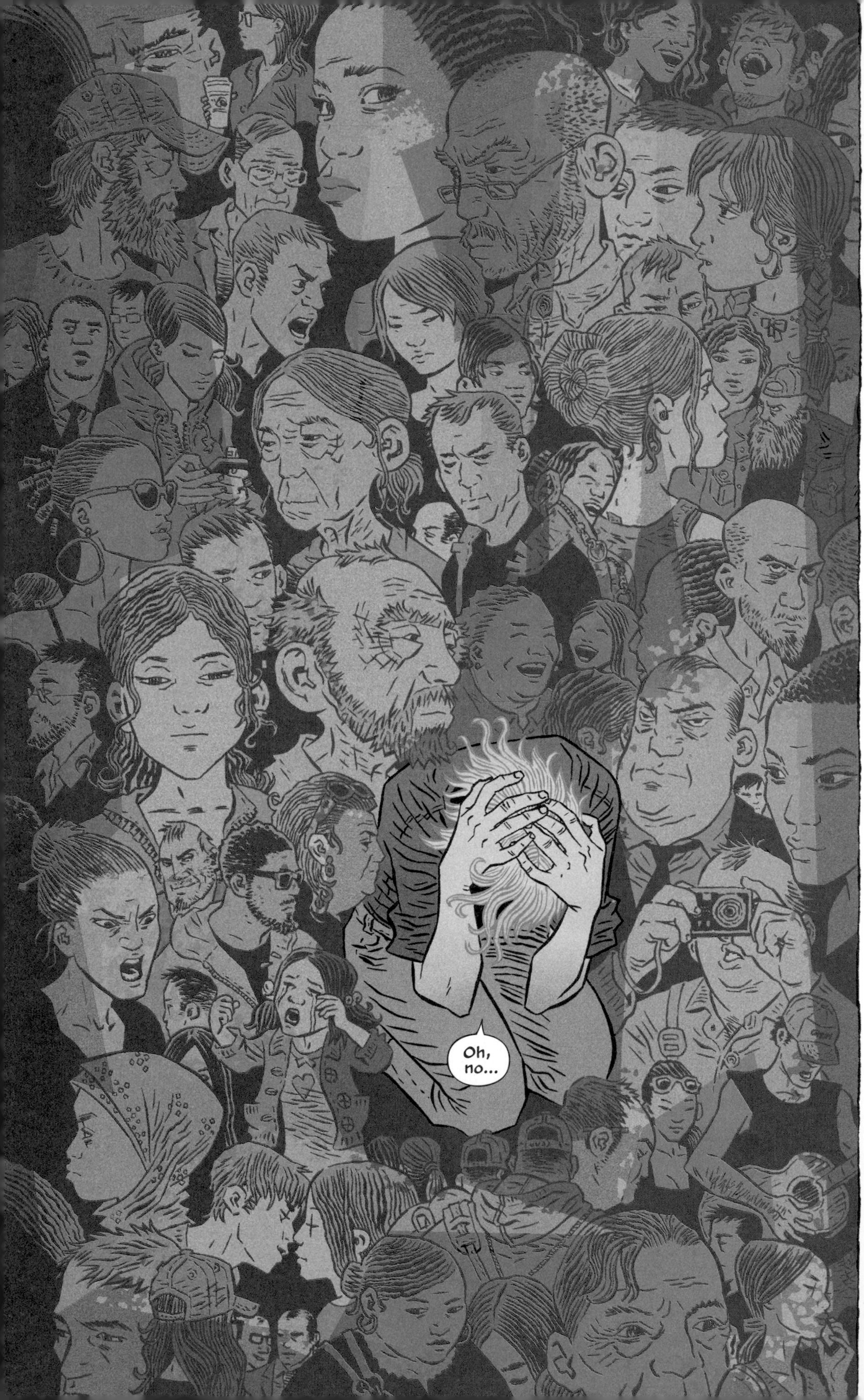
Oh, no...

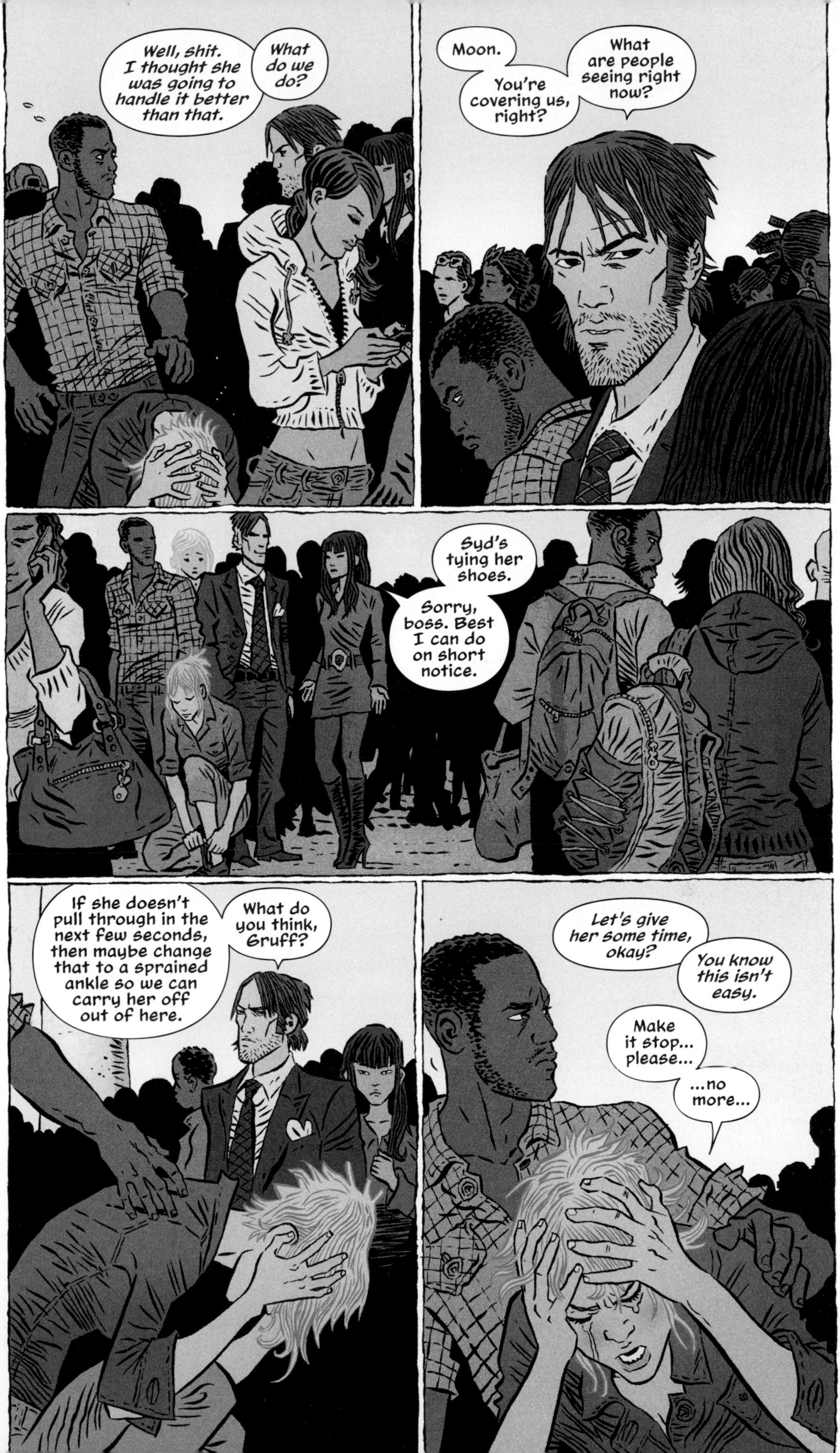
Well, shit. I thought she was going to handle it better than that.
What do we do?
Moon.
You're covering us, right?
What are people seeing right now?
Syd's tying her shoes.
Sorry, boss. Best I can do on short notice.
If she doesn't pull through in the next few seconds, then maybe change that to a sprained ankle so we can carry her off out of here.
What do you think, Gruff?
Let's give her some time, okay?
You know this isn't easy.
Make it stop... please...
...no more...

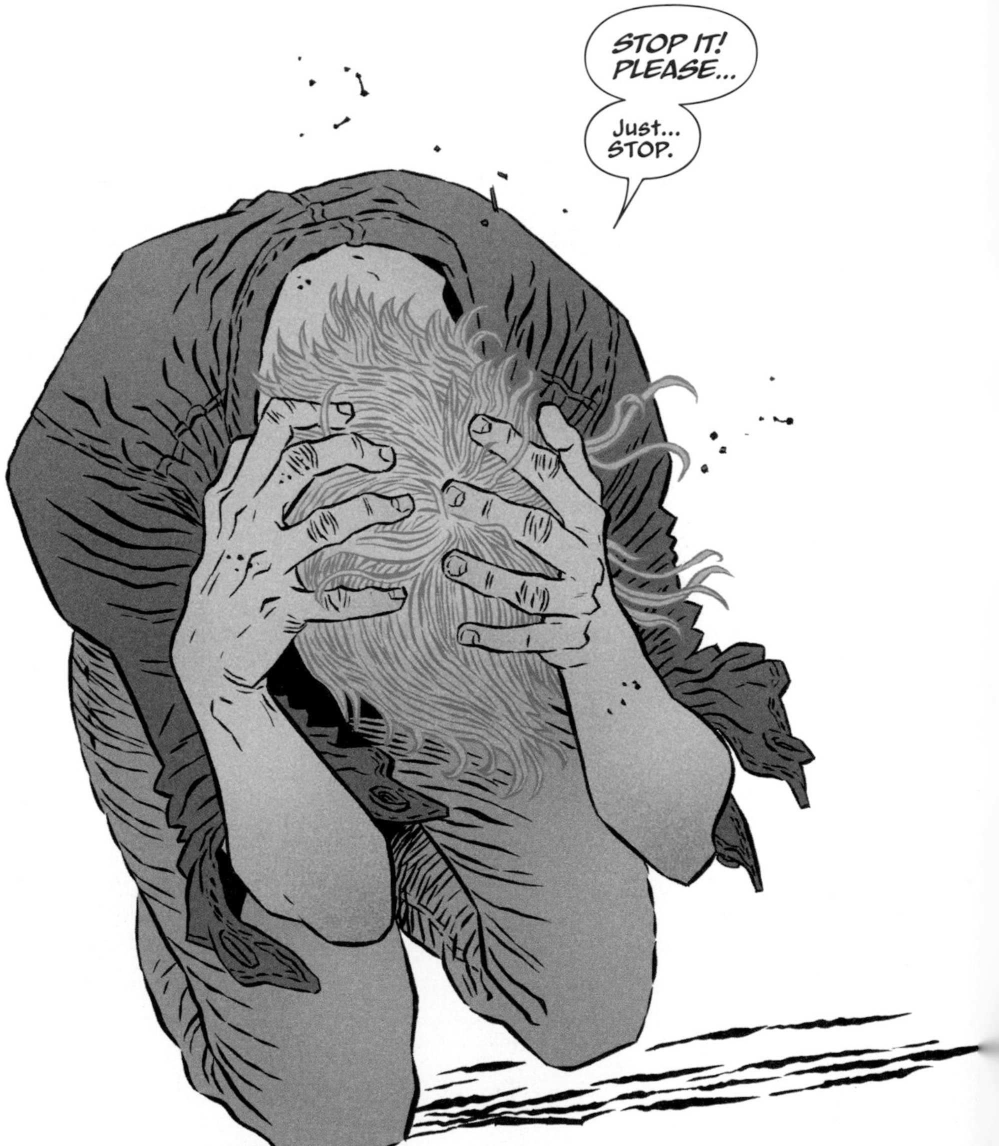
STOP IT! PLEASE...
Just... STOP.

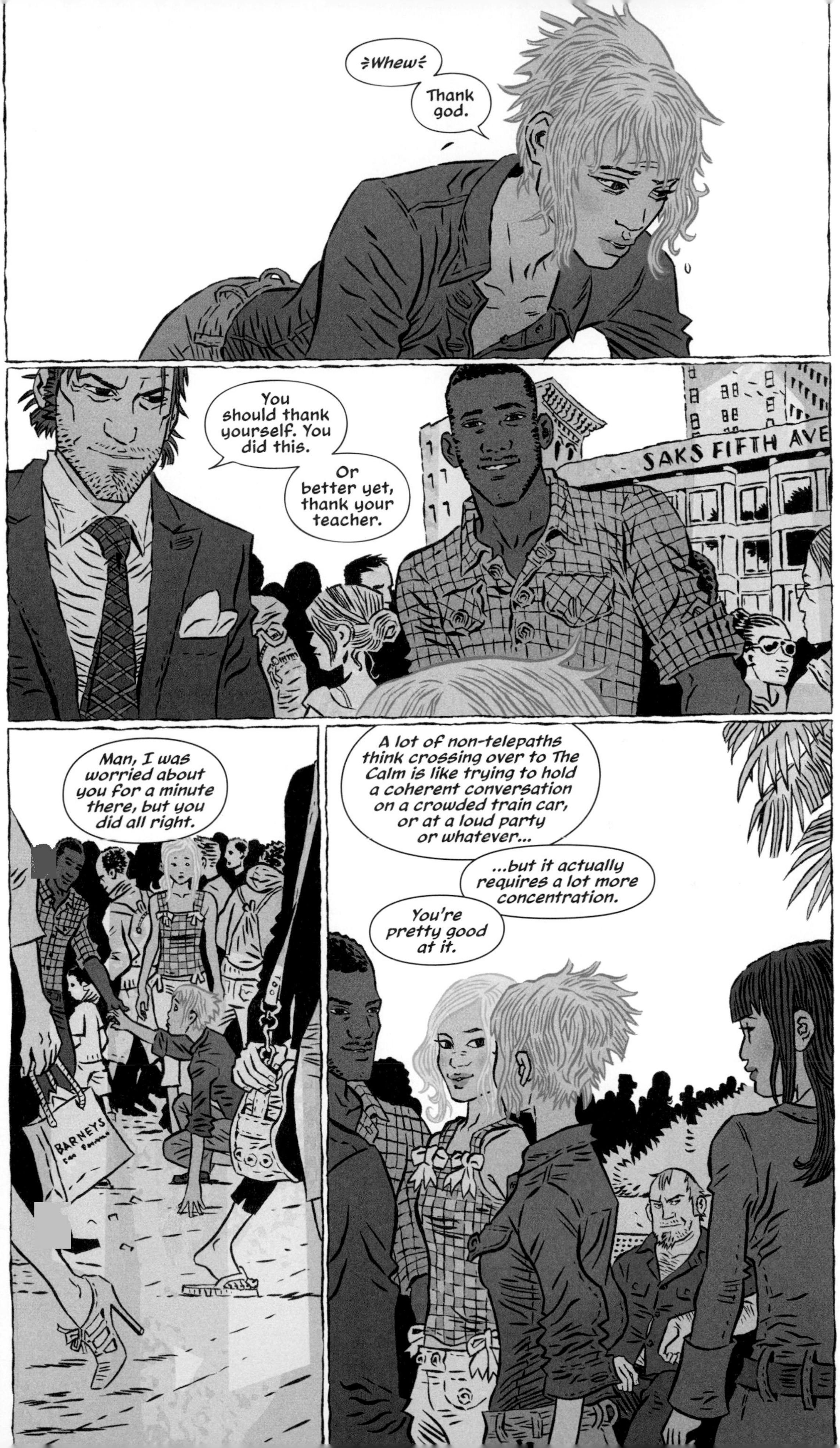

Whew
Thank god.
You should thank yourself. You did this.
Or better yet, thank your teacher.
SAKS FIFTH AVE
Man, I was worried about you for a minute there, but you did all right.
BARNEYS
A lot of non-telepaths think crossing over to The Calm is like trying to hold a coherent conversation on a crowded train car, or at a loud party or whatever...
...but it actually requires a lot more concentration.
You're pretty good at it.

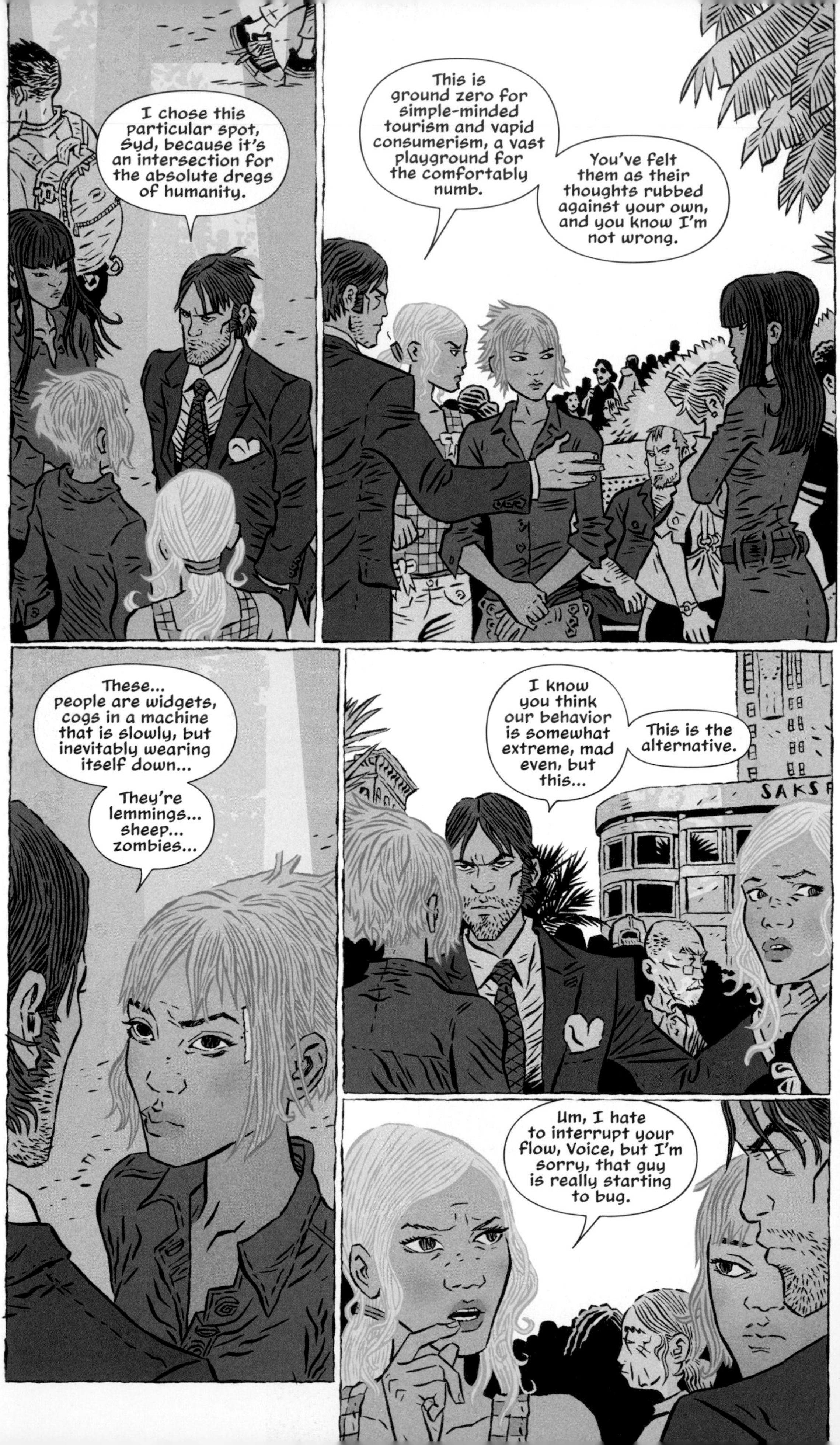
I chose this particular spot, Syd, because it's an intersection for the absolute dregs of humanity.
This is ground zero for simple-minded tourism and vapid consumerism, a vast playground for the comfortably numb.
You've felt them as their thoughts rubbed against your own, and you know I'm not wrong.
These... people are widgets, cogs in a machine that is slowly, but inevitably wearing itself down...
They're lemmings... sheep... zombies...
I know you think our behavior is somewhat extreme, mad even, but this...
This is the alternative.
SAKS
Um, I hate to interrupt your flow, Voice, but I'm sorry, that guy is really starting to bug.

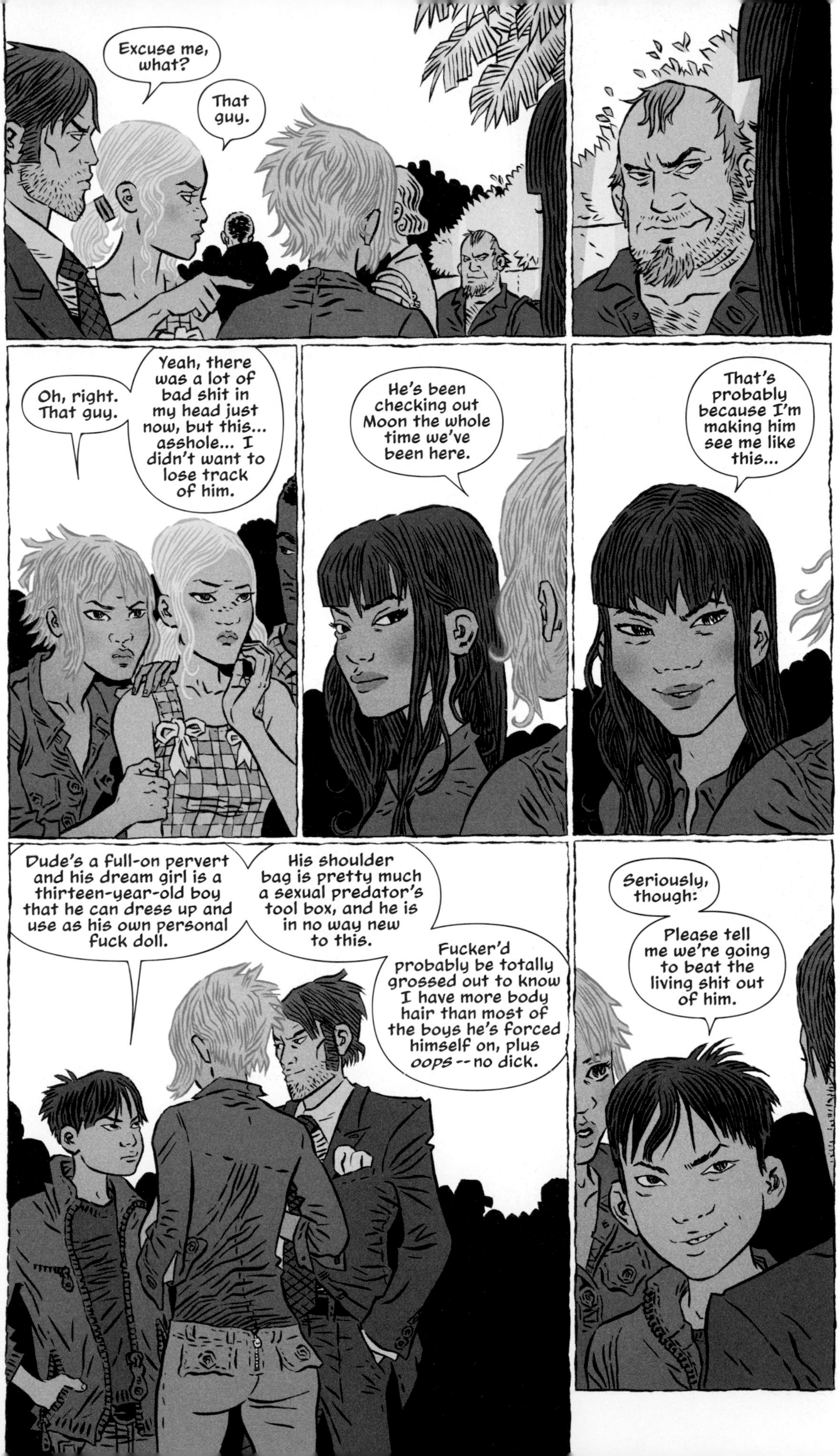

Excuse me, what?
That guy.
Oh, right. That guy.
Yeah, there was a lot of bad shit in my head just now, but this... asshole... I didn't want to lose track of him.
He's been checking out Moon the whole time we've been here.
That's probably because I'm making him see me like this...
Dude's a full-on pervert and his dream girl is a thirteen-year-old boy that he can dress up and use as his own personal fuck doll.
His shoulder bag is pretty much a sexual predator's tool box, and he is in no way new to this.
Fucker'd probably be totally grossed out to know I have more body hair than most of the boys he's forced himself on, plus *oops* -- no dick.
Seriously, though:
Please tell me we're going to beat the living shit out of him.

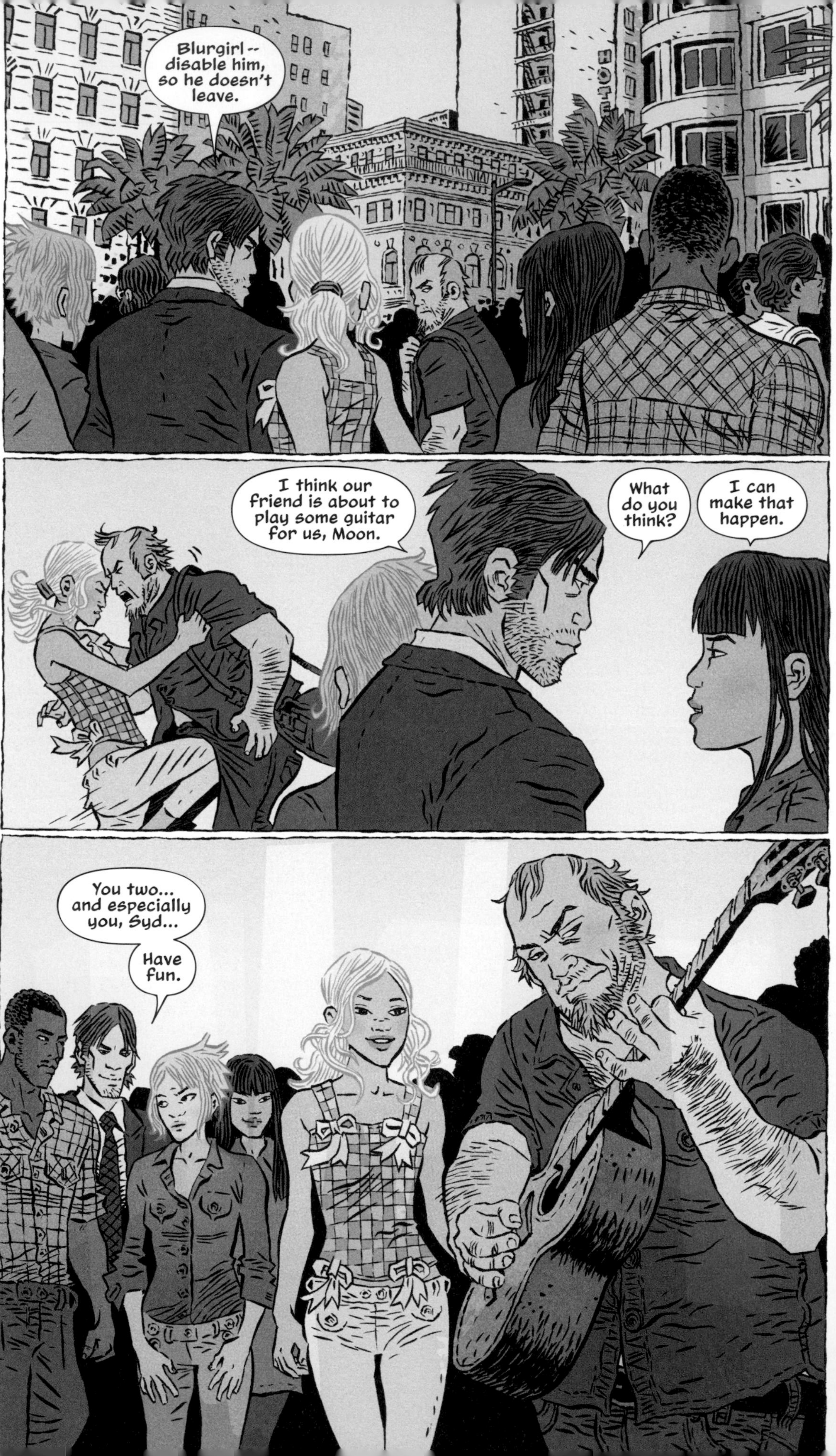
Blurgirl -- disable him, so he doesn't leave.
I think our friend is about to play some guitar for us, Moon.
What do you think?
I can make that happen.
You two... and especially you, Syd...
Have fun.

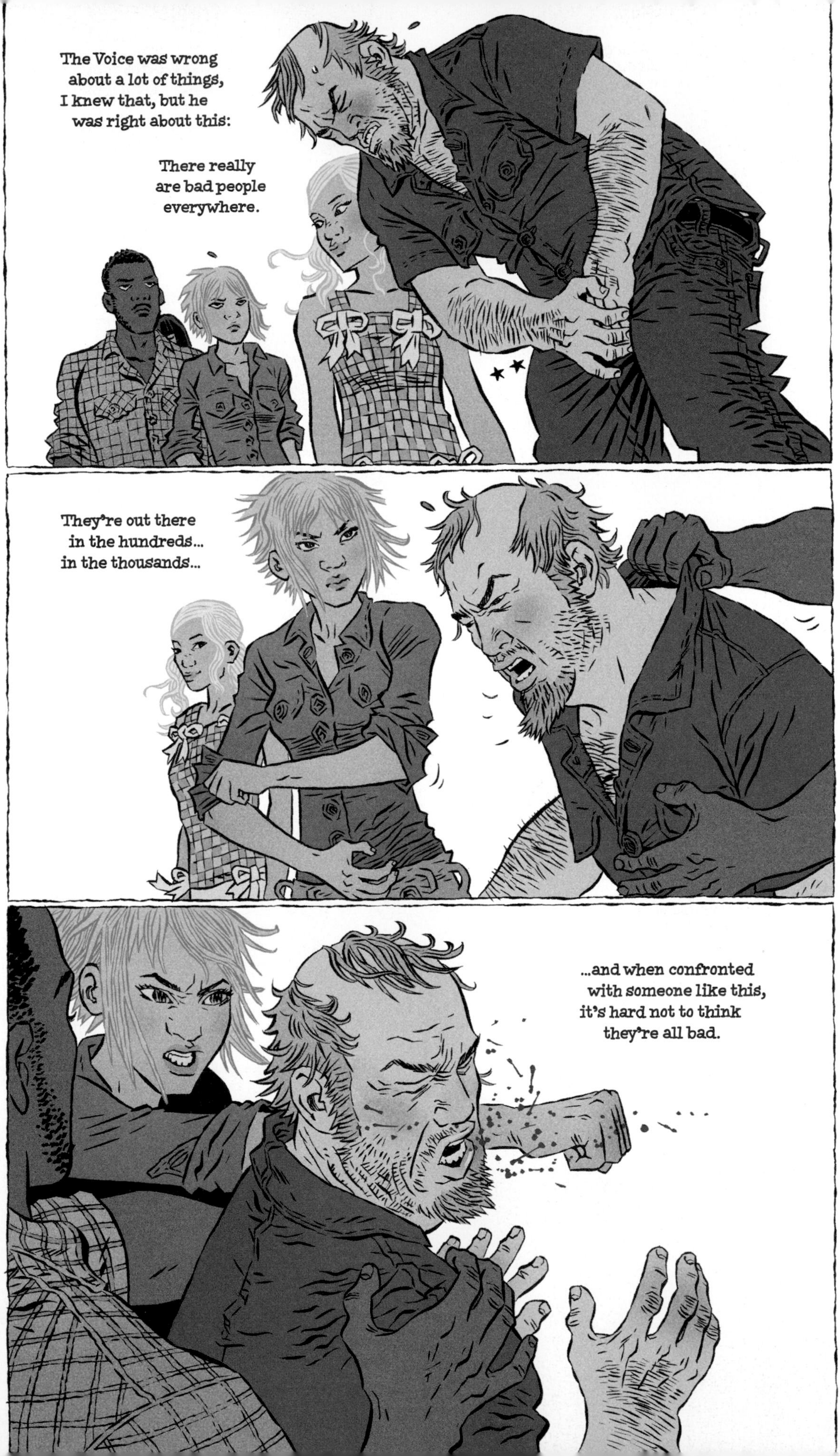
The Voice was wrong about a lot of things, I knew that, but he was right about this:
There really are bad people everywhere.
They're out there in the hundreds... in the thousands...
...and when confronted with someone like this, it's hard not to think they're all bad.

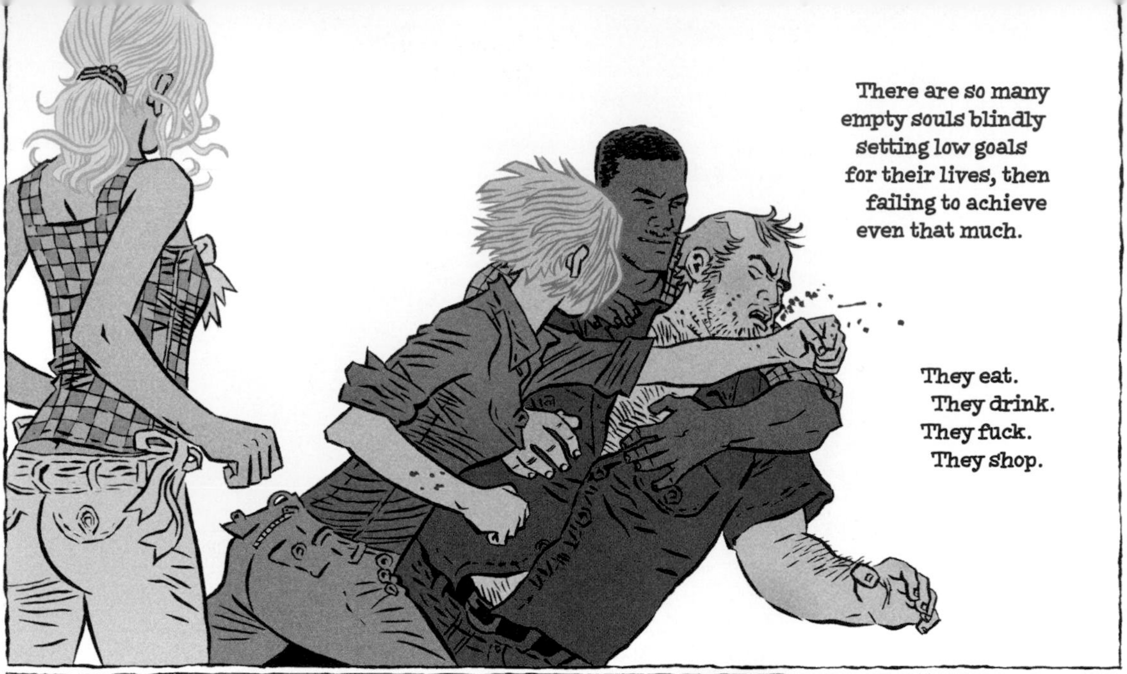
There are so many empty souls blindly setting low goals for their lives, then failing to achieve even that much.
They eat.
They drink.
They fuck.
They shop.

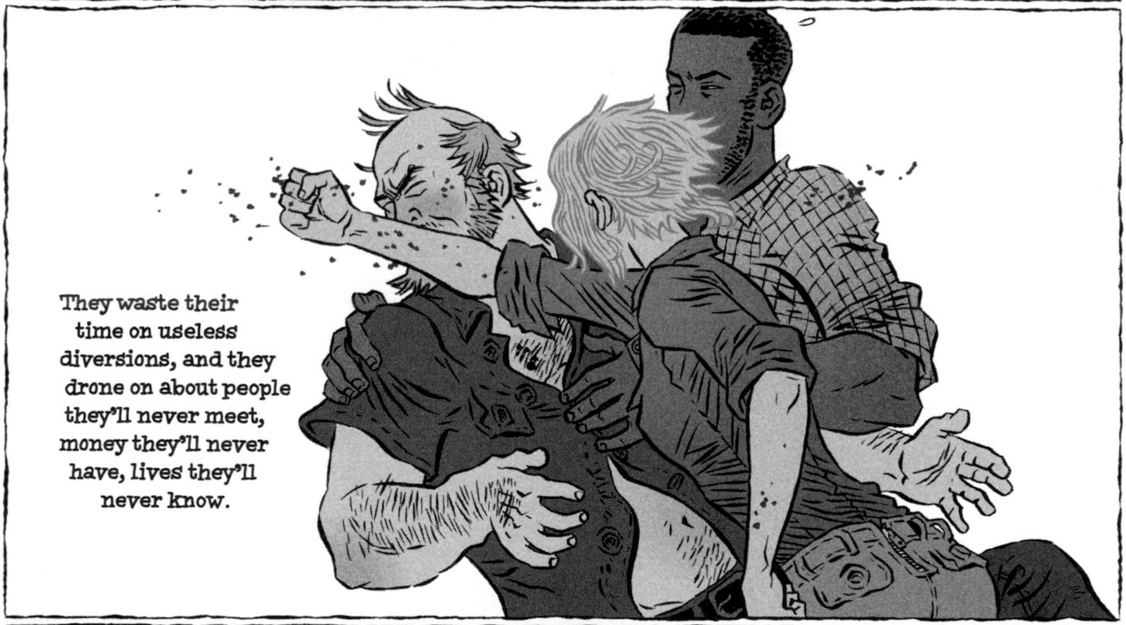
They waste their time on useless diversions, and they drone on about people they'll never meet, money they'll never have, lives they'll never know.

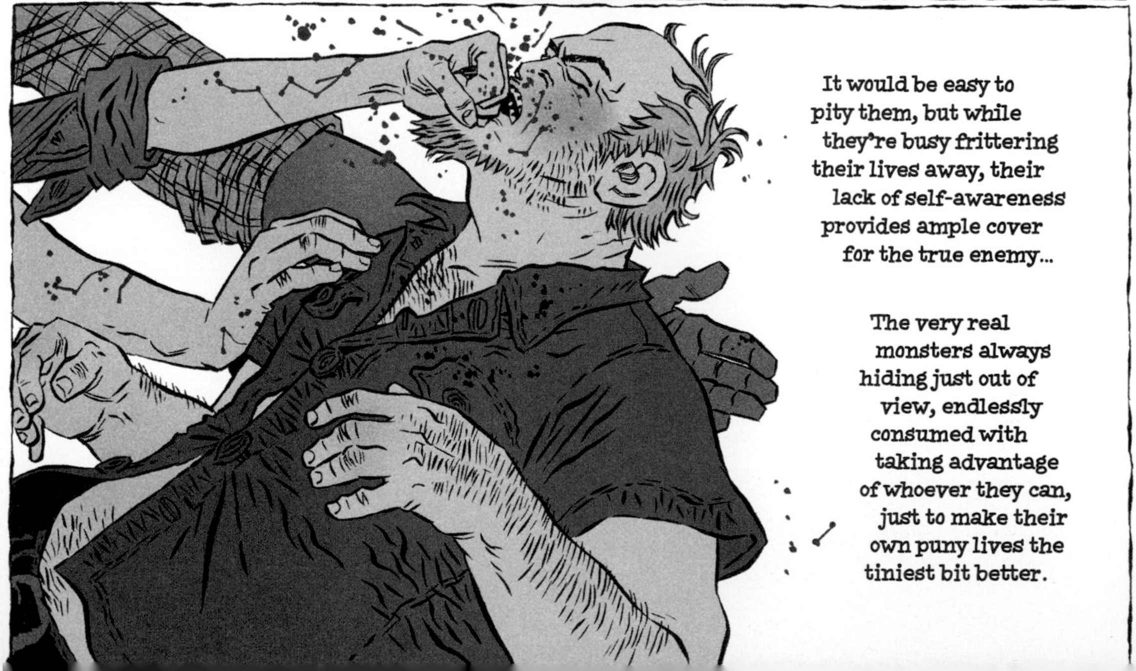
It would be easy to pity them, but while they're busy frittering their lives away, their lack of self-awareness provides ample cover for the true enemy...
The very real monsters always hiding just out of view, endlessly consumed with taking advantage of whoever they can, just to make their own puny lives the tiniest bit better.

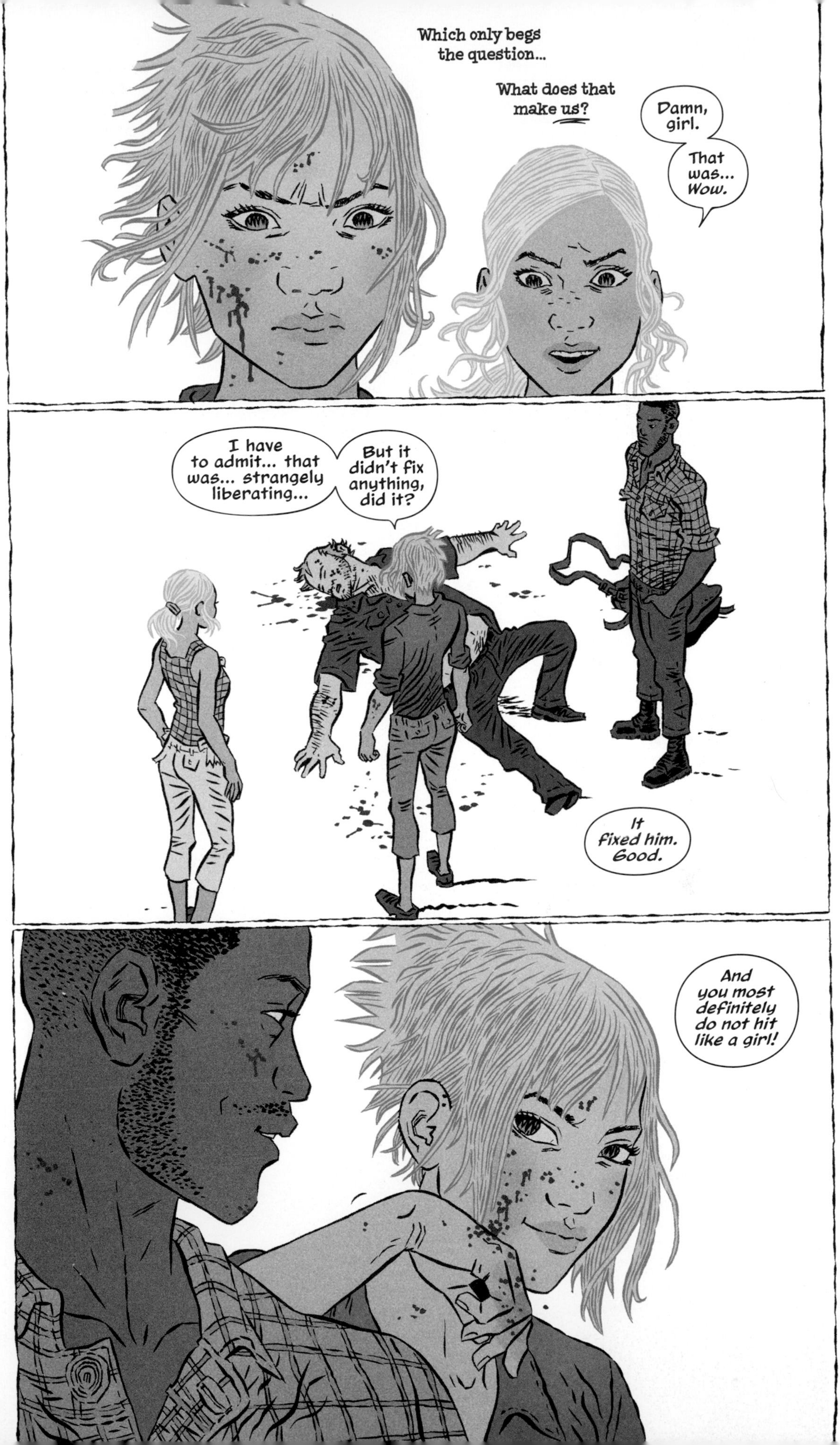
Which only begs the question...
What does that make us?
Damn, girl.
That was... Wow.
I have to admit... that was... strangely liberating...
But it didn't fix anything, did it?
It fixed him. Good.
And you most definitely do not hit like a girl!

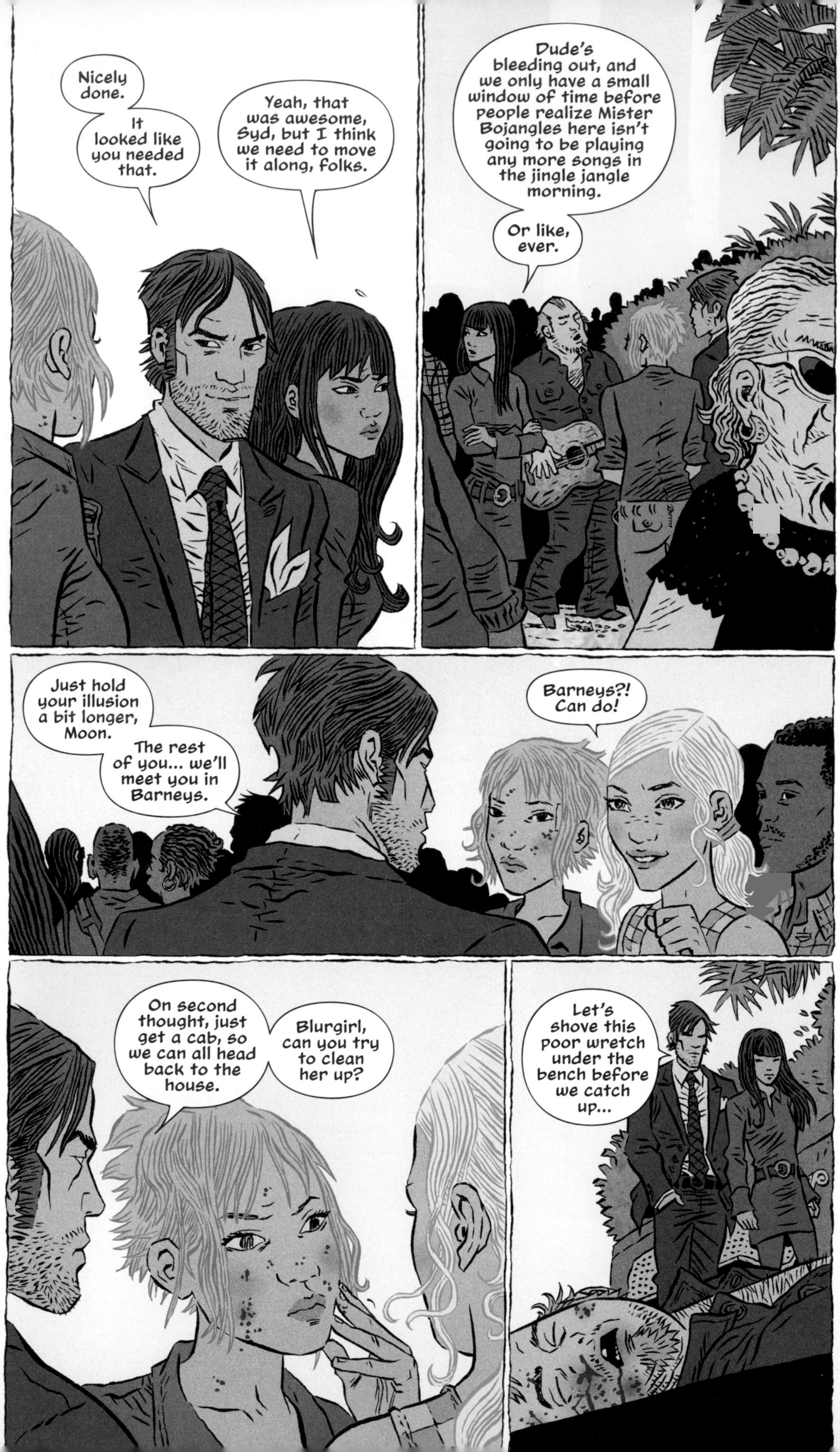
Nicely done.
It looked like you needed that.
Yeah, that was awesome, Syd, but I think we need to move it along, folks.
Dude's bleeding out, and we only have a small window of time before people realize Mister Bojangles here isn't going to be playing any more songs in the jingle jangle morning.
Or like, ever.
Just hold your illusion a bit longer, Moon.
The rest of you... we'll meet you in Barneys.
Barneys?! Can do!
On second thought, just get a cab, so we can all head back to the house.
Blurgirl, can you try to clean her up?
Let's shove this poor wretch under the bench before we catch up...

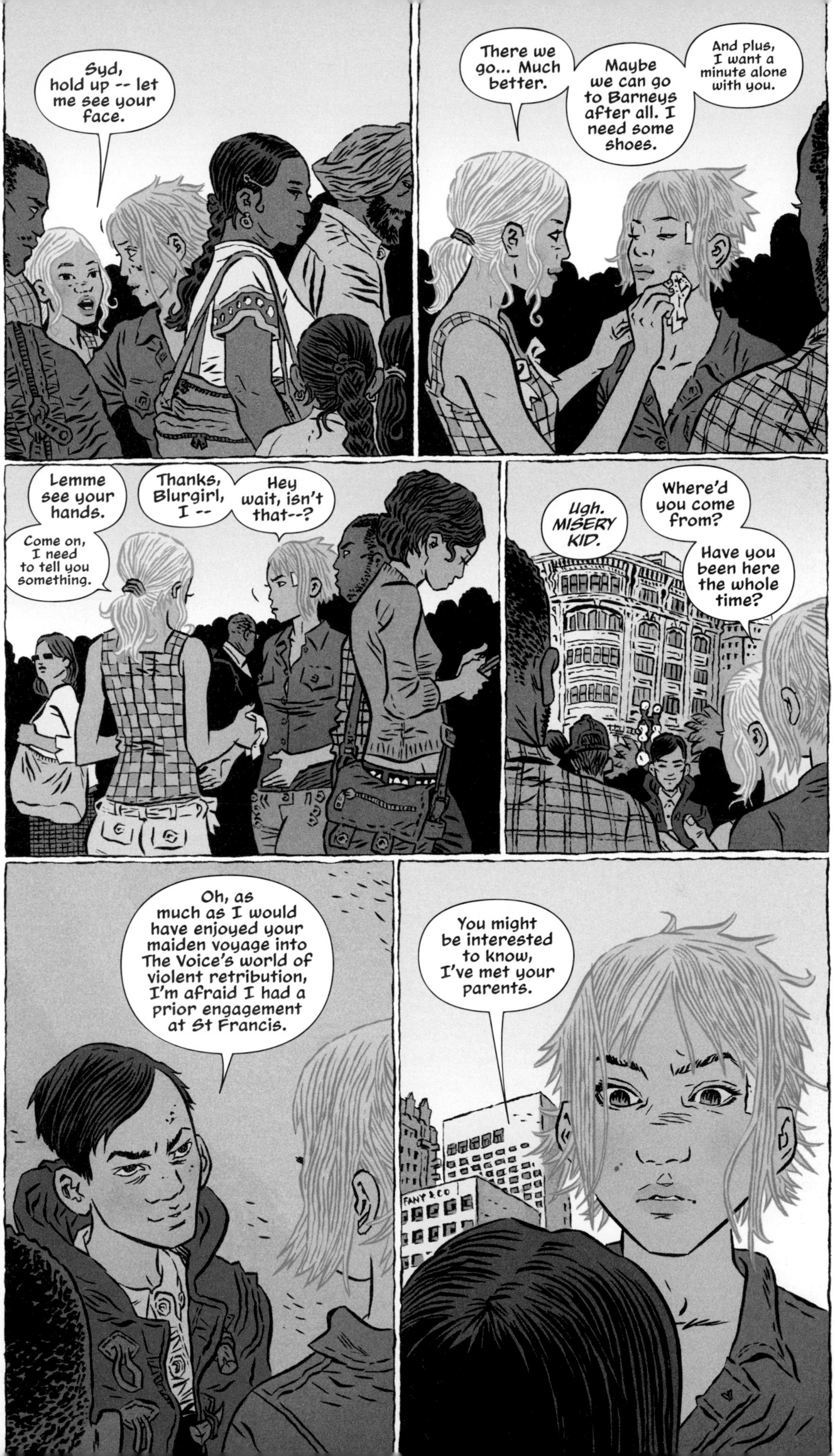

Syd, hold up -- let me see your face.
There we go... Much better.
Maybe we can go to Barneys after all. I need some shoes.
And plus, I want a minute alone with you.
Lemme see your hands.
Come on, I need to tell you something.
Thanks, Blurgirl, I --
Hey wait, isn't that--?
Ugh. MISERY KID.
Where'd you come from?
Have you been here the whole time?
Oh, as much as I would have enjoyed your maiden voyage into The Voice's world of violent retribution, I'm afraid I had a prior engagement at St Francis.
You might be interested to know, I've met your parents.

IS EVIL JUST SOMETHING YOU ARE, OR SOMETHING YOU DO?

STEPHEN PATRICK MORRISEY

4: DREAMS OF CHILDREN

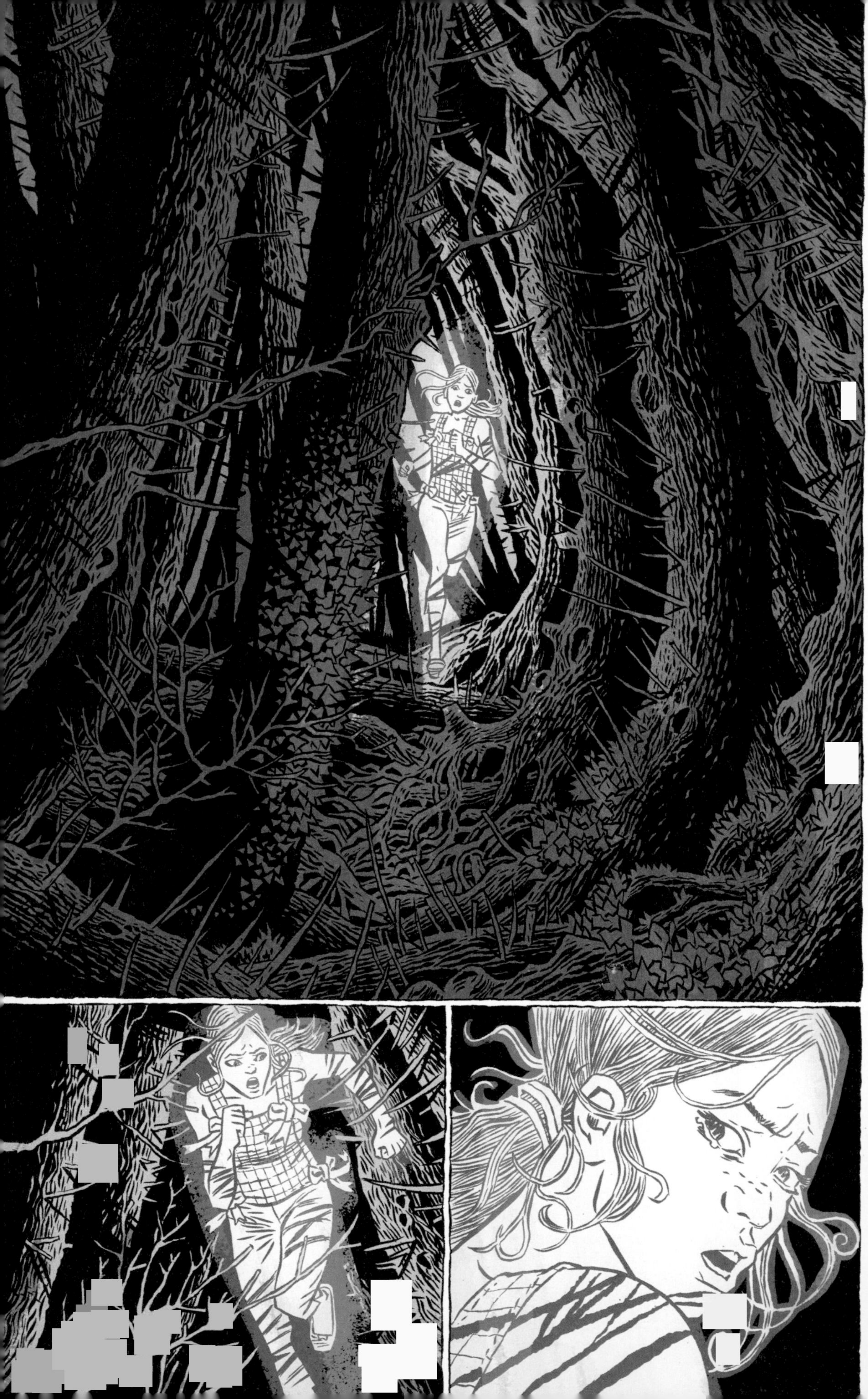

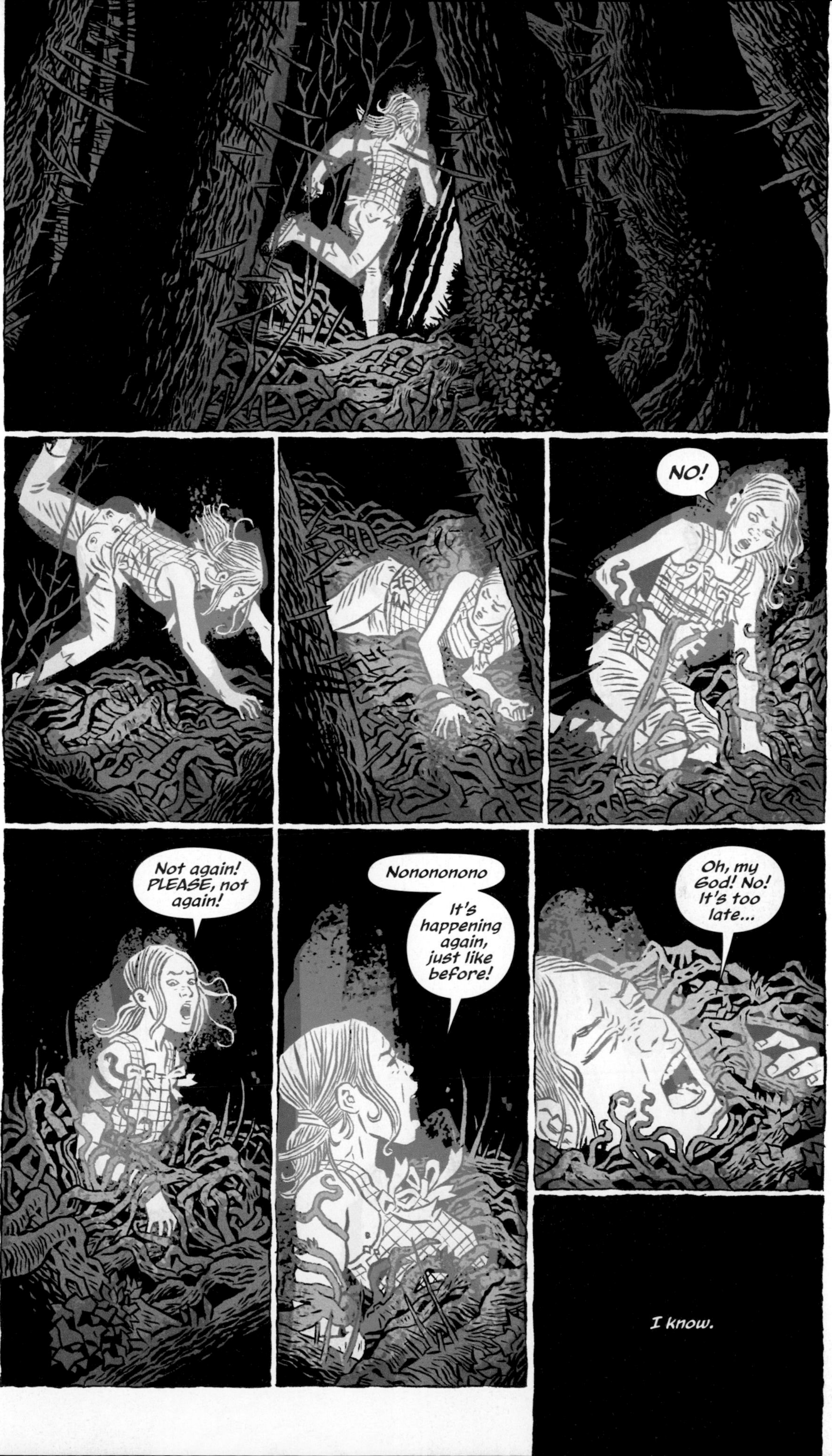
NO!
Not again! PLEASE, not again!
Nonononono
It's happening again, just like before!
Oh, my God! No! It's too late...
I know.

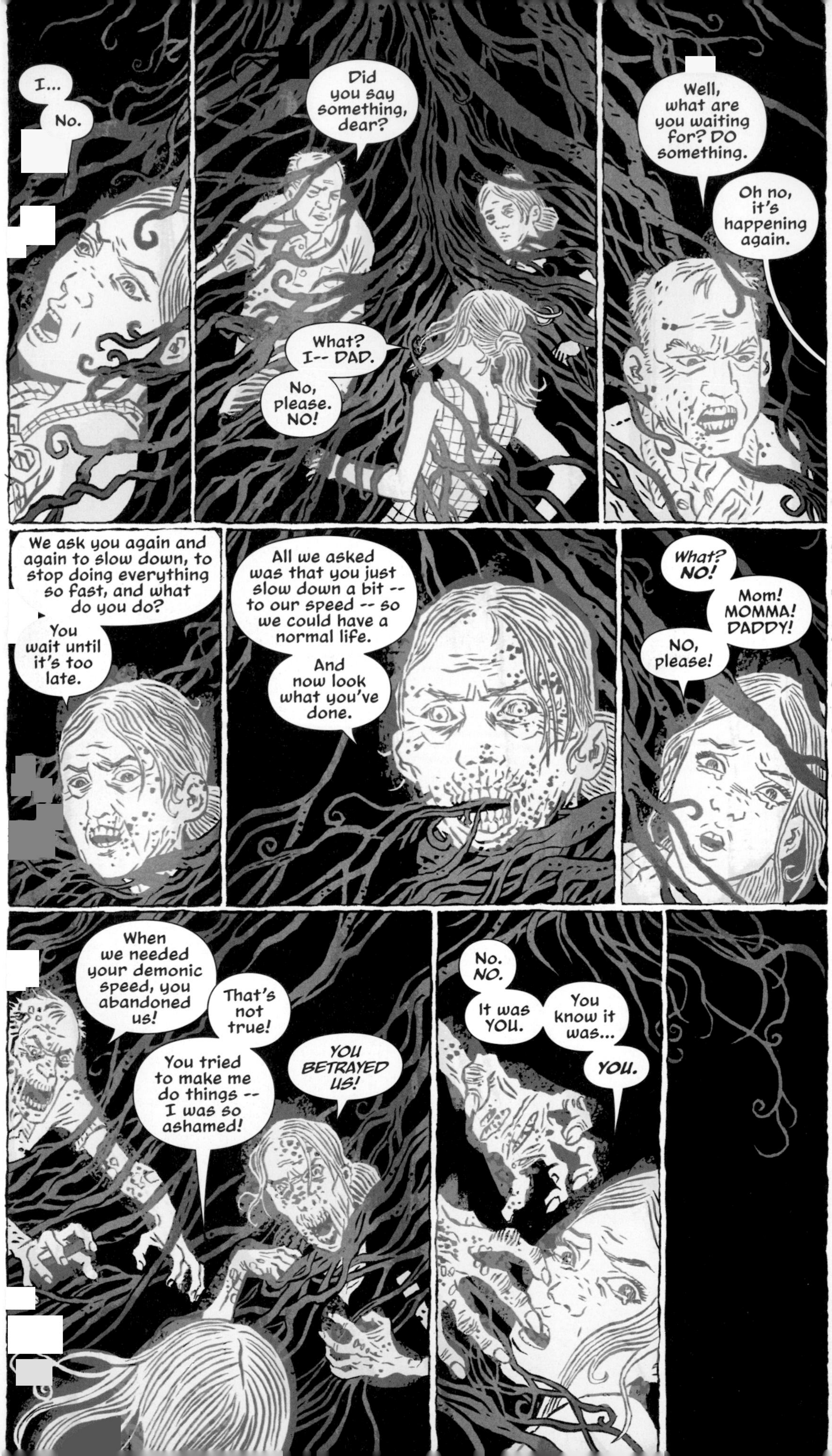

I...
No.
Did you say something, dear?
What? I-- DAD.
No, please. NO!
Well, what are you waiting for? DO something.
Oh no, it's happening again.
We ask you again and again to slow down, to stop doing everything so fast, and what do you do?
You wait until it's too late.
All we asked was that you just slow down a bit -- to our speed -- so we could have a normal life.
And now look what you've done.
What? NO!
Mom! MOMMA! DADDY!
NO, please!
When we needed your demonic speed, you abandoned us!
That's not true!
You tried to make me do things -- I was so ashamed!
YOU BETRAYED US!
No. NO.
It was YOU.
You know it was...
YOU.

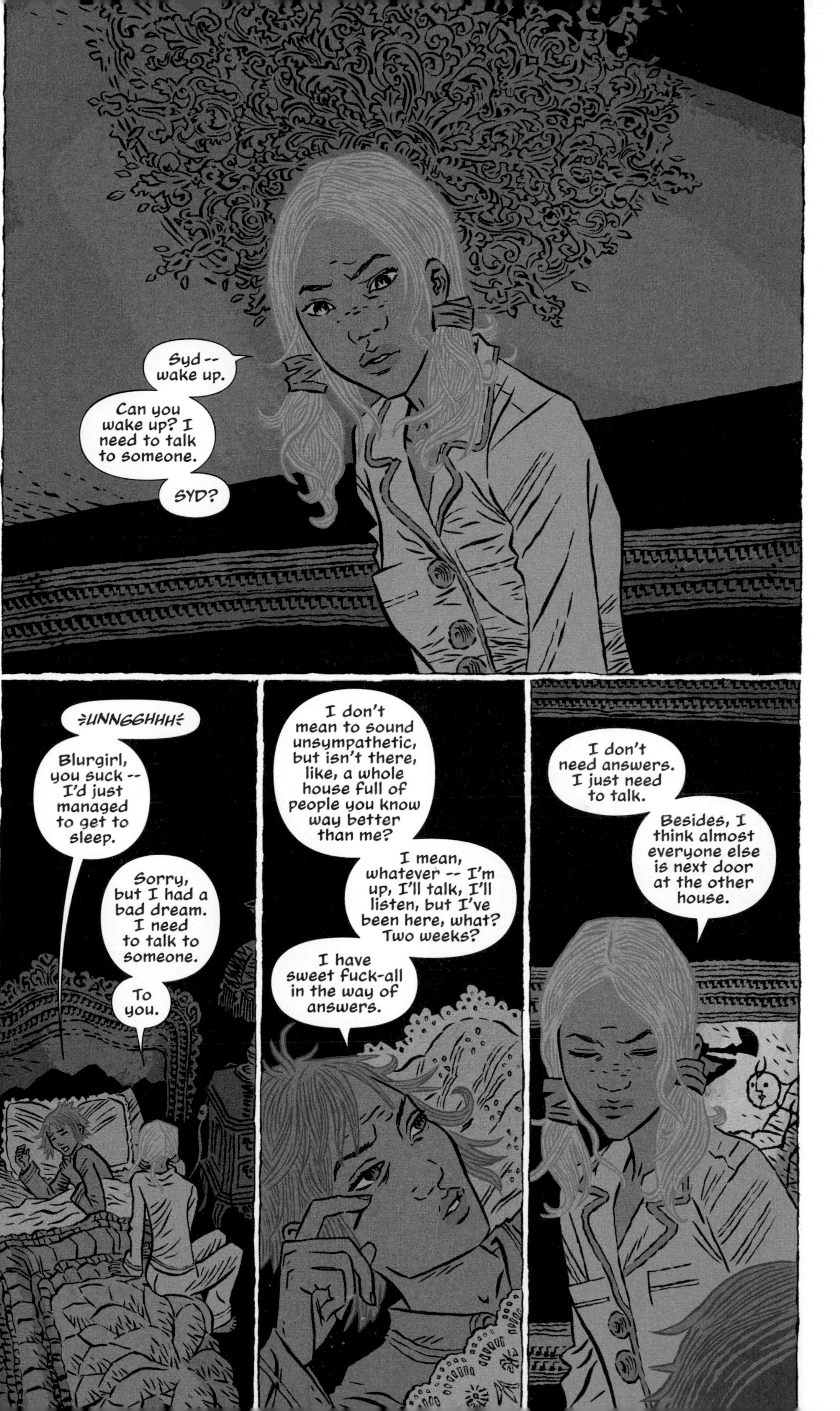

Syd -- wake up.
Can you wake up? I need to talk to someone.
SYD?
UNNGGHHH
Blurgirl, you suck -- I'd just managed to get to sleep.
Sorry, but I had a bad dream. I need to talk to someone.
To you.
I don't mean to sound unsympathetic, but isn't there, like, a whole house full of people you know way better than me?
I mean, whatever -- I'm up, I'll talk, I'll listen, but I've been here, what? Two weeks?
I have sweet fuck-all in the way of answers.
I don't need answers. I just need to talk.
Besides, I think almost everyone else is next door at the other house.

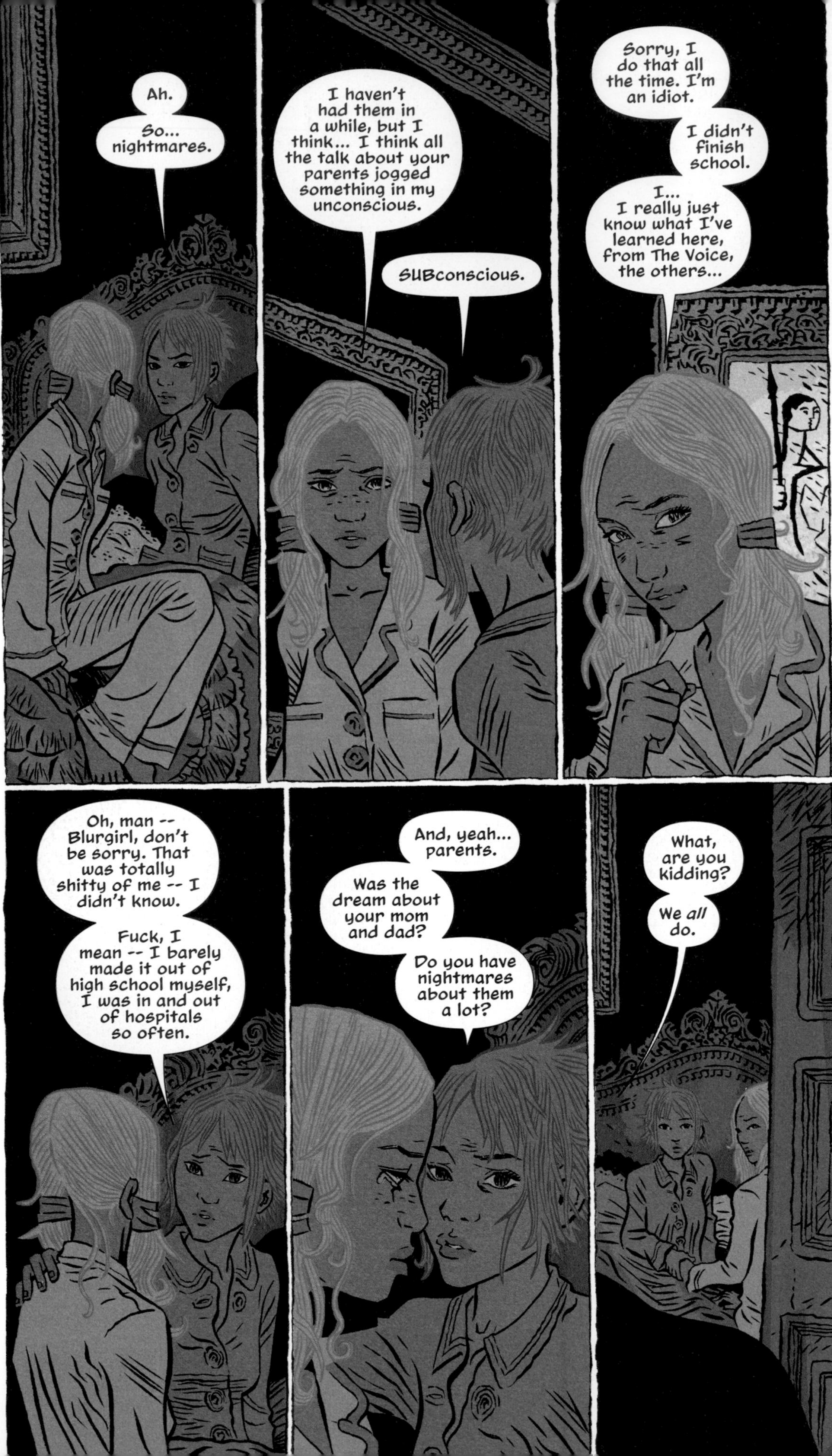
Ah.
So... nightmares.
I haven't had them in a while, but I think... I think all the talk about your parents jogged something in my unconscious.
SUBconscious.
Sorry, I do that all the time. I'm an idiot.
I didn't finish school.
I... I really just know what I've learned here, from The Voice, the others...
Oh, man -- Blurgirl, don't be sorry. That was totally shitty of me -- I didn't know.
Fuck, I mean -- I barely made it out of high school myself, I was in and out of hospitals so often.
And, yeah... parents.
Was the dream about your mom and dad?
Do you have nightmares about them a lot?
What, are you kidding?
We *all* do.

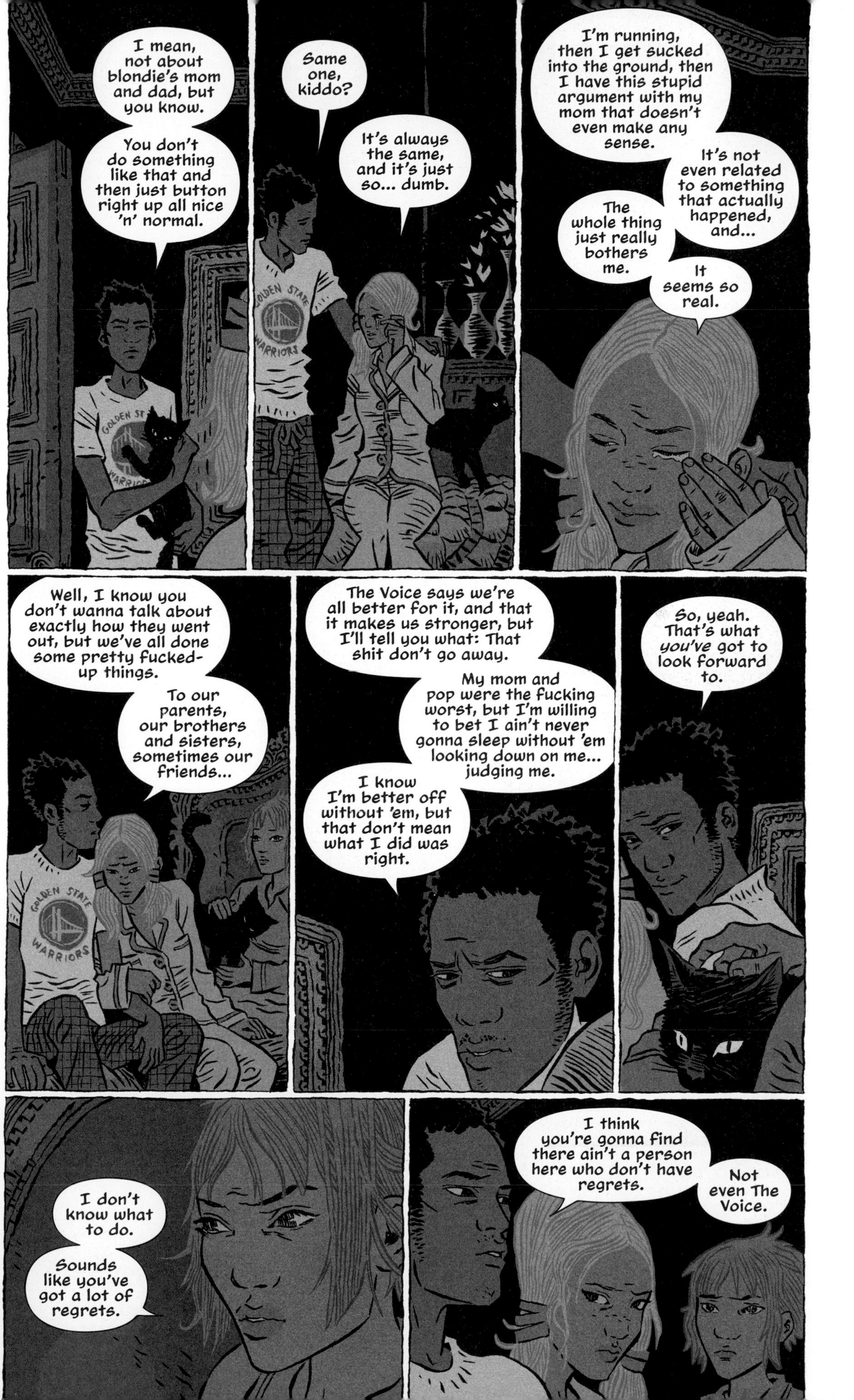
I mean, not about blondie's mom and dad, but you know.
You don't do something like that and then just button right up all nice 'n' normal.
Same one, kiddo?
It's always the same, and it's just so... dumb.
I'm running, then I get sucked into the ground, then I have this stupid argument with my mom that doesn't even make any sense.
It's not even related to something that actually happened, and...
The whole thing just really bothers me.
It seems so real.
GOLDEN STATE WARRIORS
Well, I know you don't wanna talk about exactly how they went out, but we've all done some pretty fucked-up things.
To our parents, our brothers and sisters, sometimes our friends...
The Voice says we're all better for it, and that it makes us stronger, but I'll tell you what: That shit don't go away.
My mom and pop were the fucking worst, but I'm willing to bet I ain't never gonna sleep without 'em looking down on me... judging me.
I know I'm better off without 'em, but that don't mean what I did was right.
So, yeah. That's what you've got to look forward to.
I don't know what to do.
Sounds like you've got a lot of regrets.
I think you're gonna find there ain't a person here who don't have regrets.
Not even The Voice.

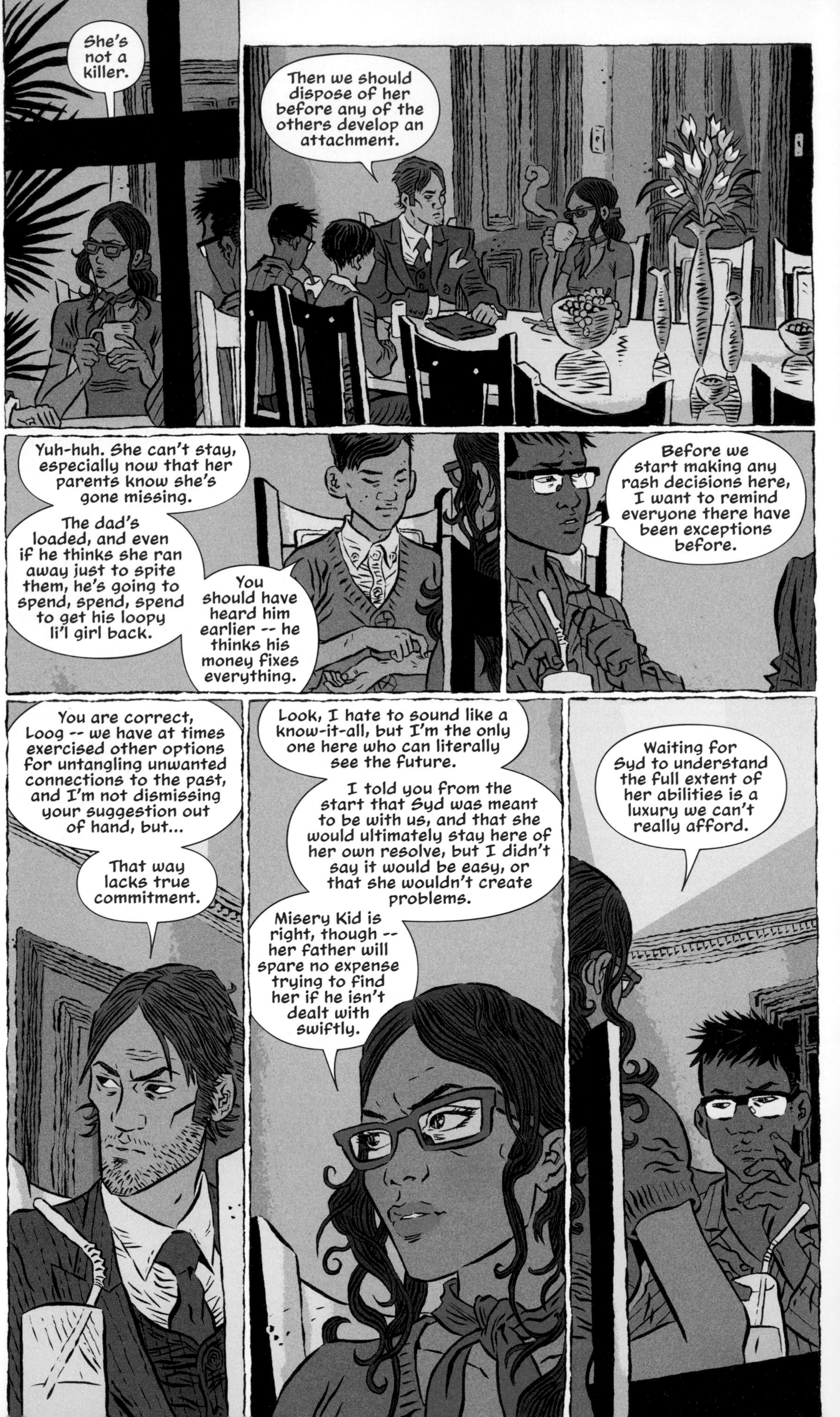
She's not a killer.
Then we should dispose of her before any of the others develop an attachment.
Yuh-huh. She can't stay, especially now that her parents know she's gone missing.
The dad's loaded, and even if he thinks she ran away just to spite them, he's going to spend, spend, spend to get his loopy li'l girl back.
You should have heard him earlier -- he thinks his money fixes everything.
Before we start making any rash decisions here, I want to remind everyone there have been exceptions before.
You are correct, Loog -- we have at times exercised other options for untangling unwanted connections to the past, and I'm not dismissing your suggestion out of hand, but...
That way lacks true commitment.
Look, I hate to sound like a know-it-all, but I'm the only one here who can literally see the future.
I told you from the start that Syd was meant to be with us, and that she would ultimately stay here of her own resolve, but I didn't say it would be easy, or that she wouldn't create problems.
Misery Kid is right, though -- her father will spare no expense trying to find her if he isn't dealt with swiftly.
Waiting for Syd to understand the full extent of her abilities is a luxury we can't really afford.

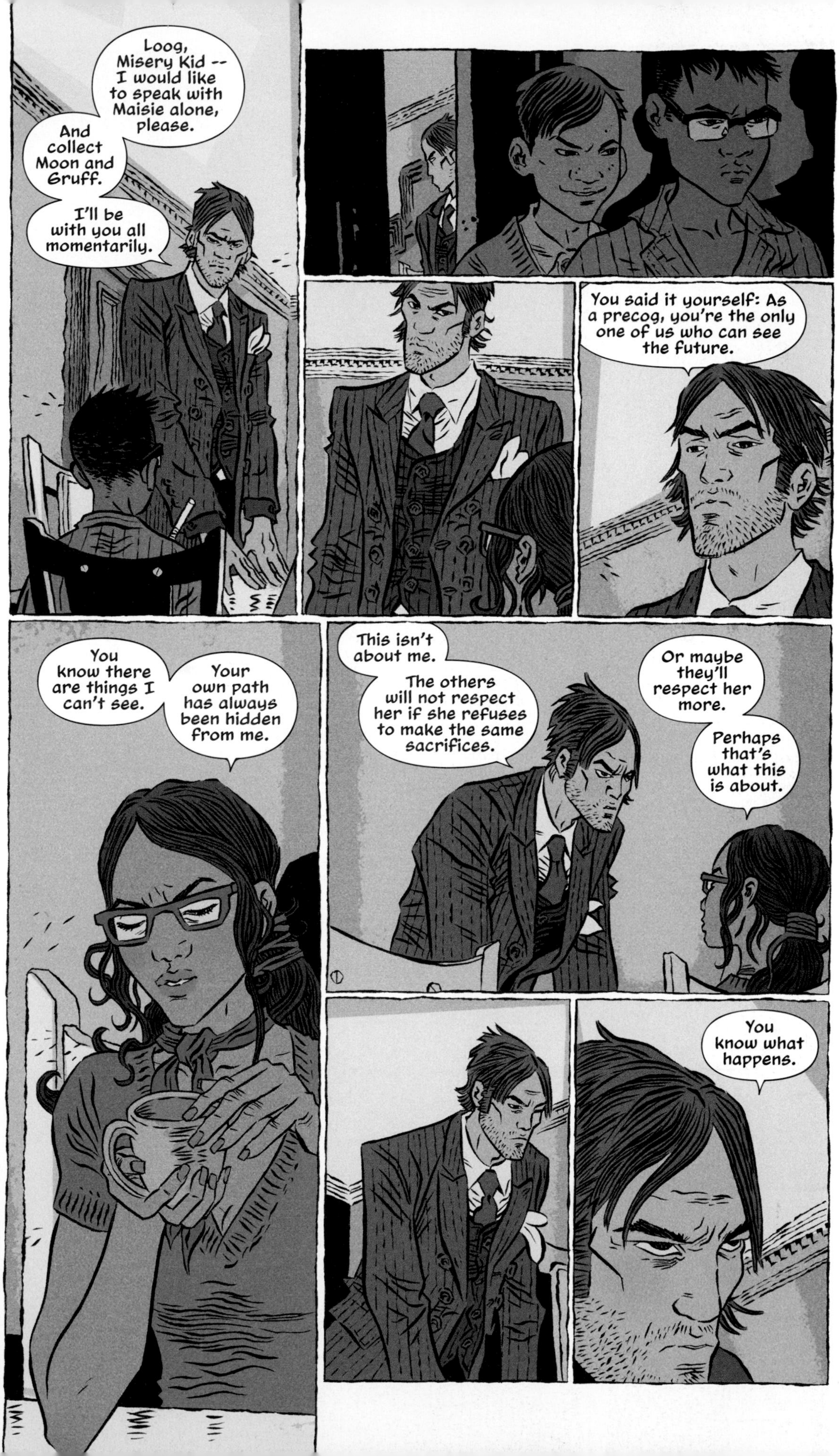
Loog, Misery Kid -- I would like to speak with Maisie alone, please.
And collect Moon and Gruff.
I'll be with you all momentarily.
You said it yourself: As a precog, you're the only one of us who can see the future.
You know there are things I can't see.
Your own path has always been hidden from me.
This isn't about me.
The others will not respect her if she refuses to make the same sacrifices.
Or maybe they'll respect her more.
Perhaps that's what this is about.
You know what happens.

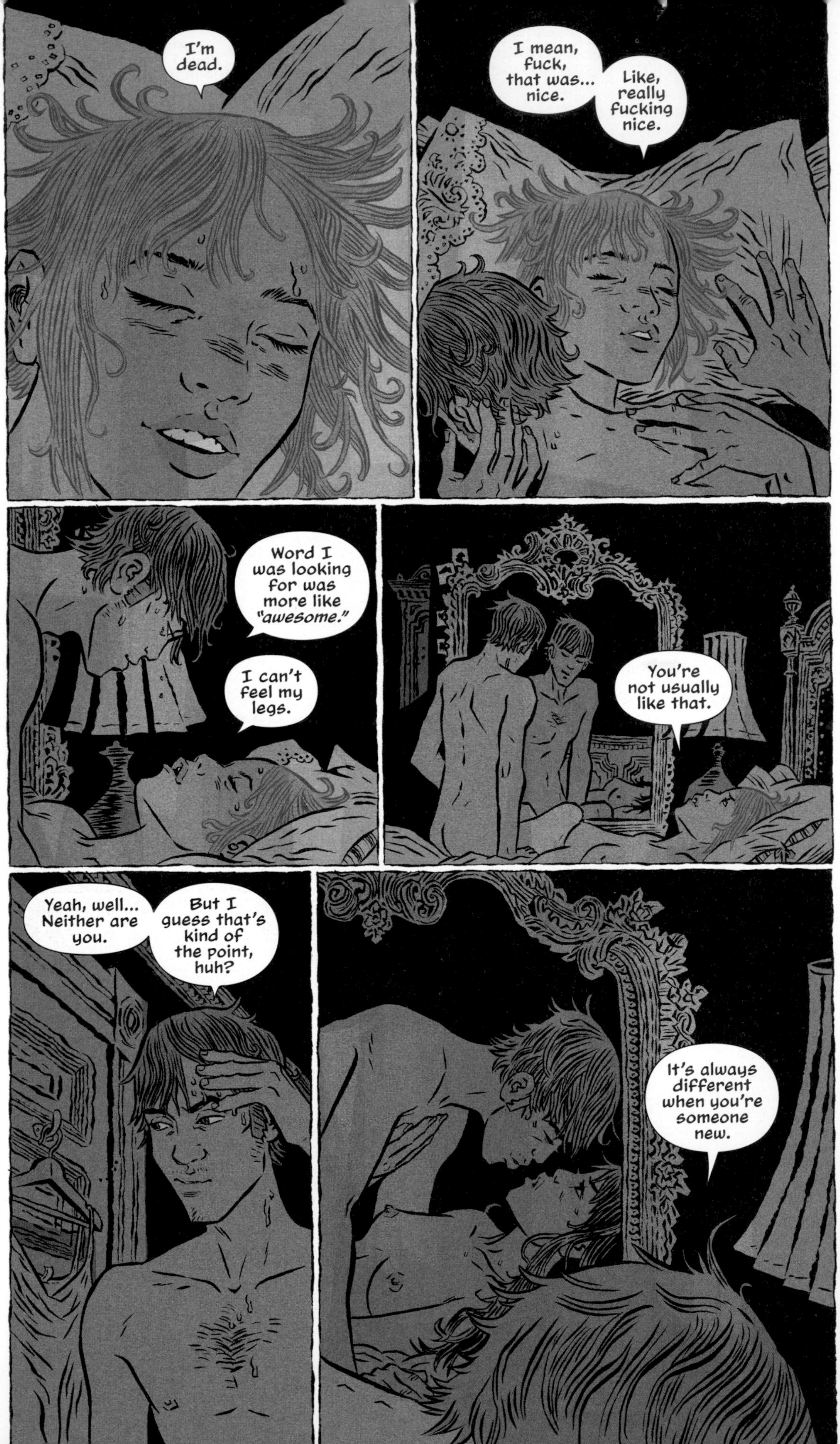
I'm dead.
I mean, fuck, that was... nice.
Like, really fucking nice.
Word I was looking for was more like "awesome."
I can't feel my legs.
You're not usually like that.
Yeah, well... Neither are you.
But I guess that's kind of the point, huh?
It's always different when you're someone new.

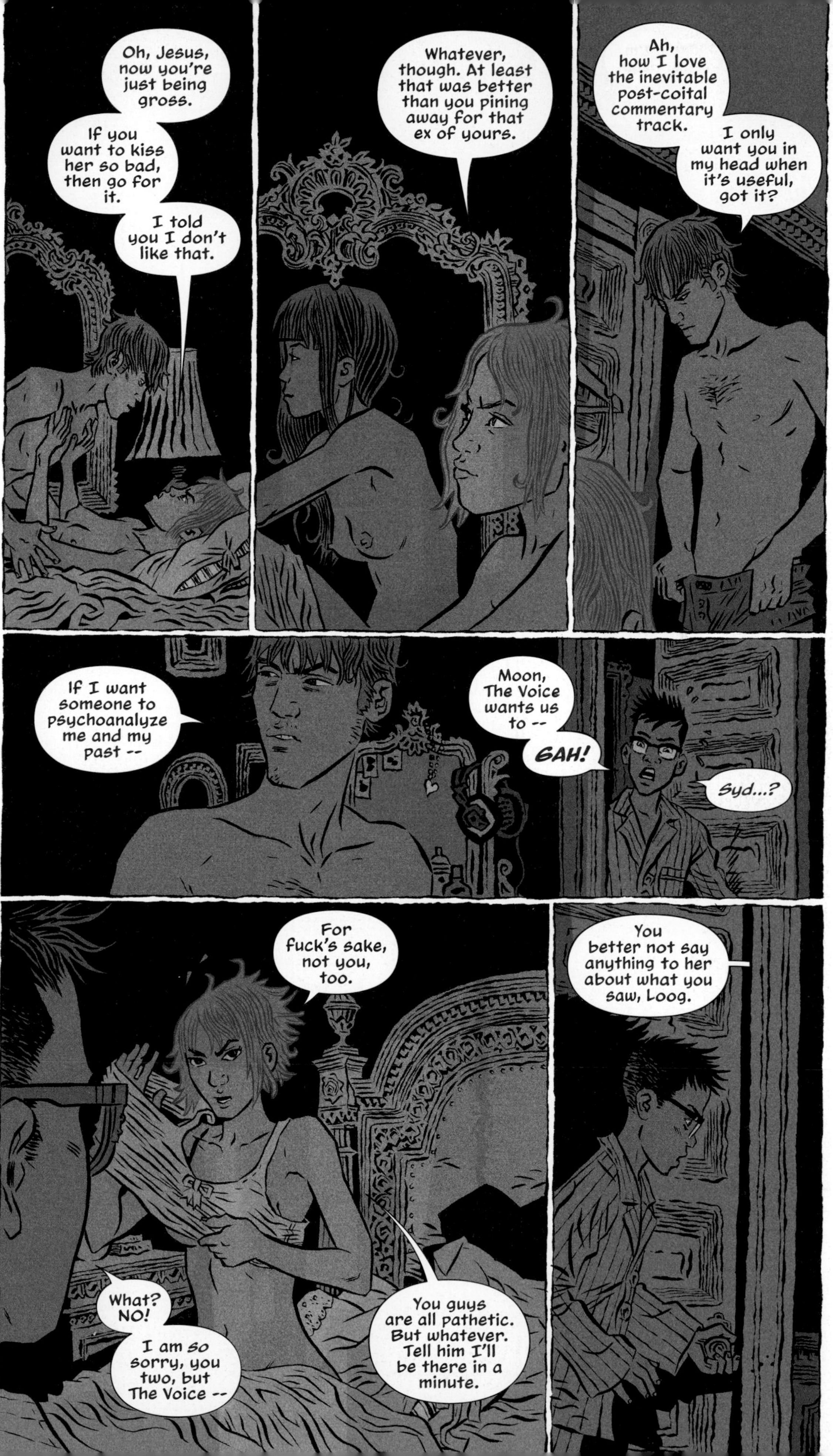
Oh, Jesus, now you're just being gross.
If you want to kiss her so bad, then go for it.
I told you I don't like that.
Whatever, though. At least that was better than you pining away for that ex of yours.
Ah, how I love the inevitable post-coital commentary track.
I only want you in my head when it's useful, got it?
If I want someone to psychoanalyze me and my past --
Moon, The Voice wants us to --
GAH!
Syd...?
For fuck's sake, not you, too.
What? NO!
I am so sorry, you two, but The Voice --
You guys are all pathetic. But whatever. Tell him I'll be there in a minute.
You better not say anything to her about what you saw, Loog.

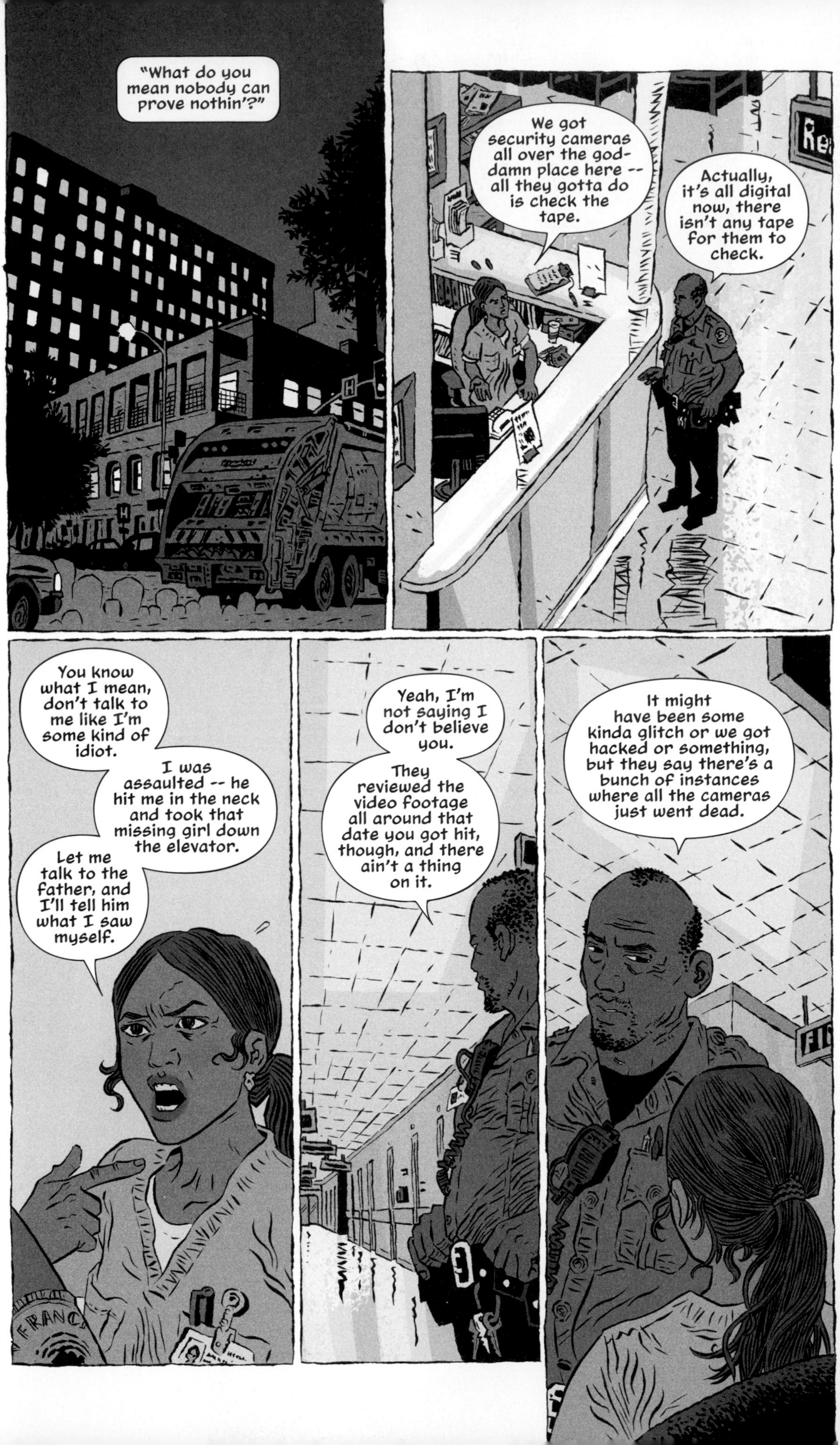
"What do you mean nobody can prove nothin'?"
We got security cameras all over the god-damn place here -- all they gotta do is check the tape.
Actually, it's all digital now, there isn't any tape for them to check.
You know what I mean, don't talk to me like I'm some kind of idiot.
I was assaulted -- he hit me in the neck and took that missing girl down the elevator.
Let me talk to the father, and I'll tell him what I saw myself.
Yeah, I'm not saying I don't believe you.
They reviewed the video footage all around that date you got hit, though, and there ain't a thing on it.
It might have been some kinda glitch or we got hacked or something, but they say there's a bunch of instances where all the cameras just went dead.

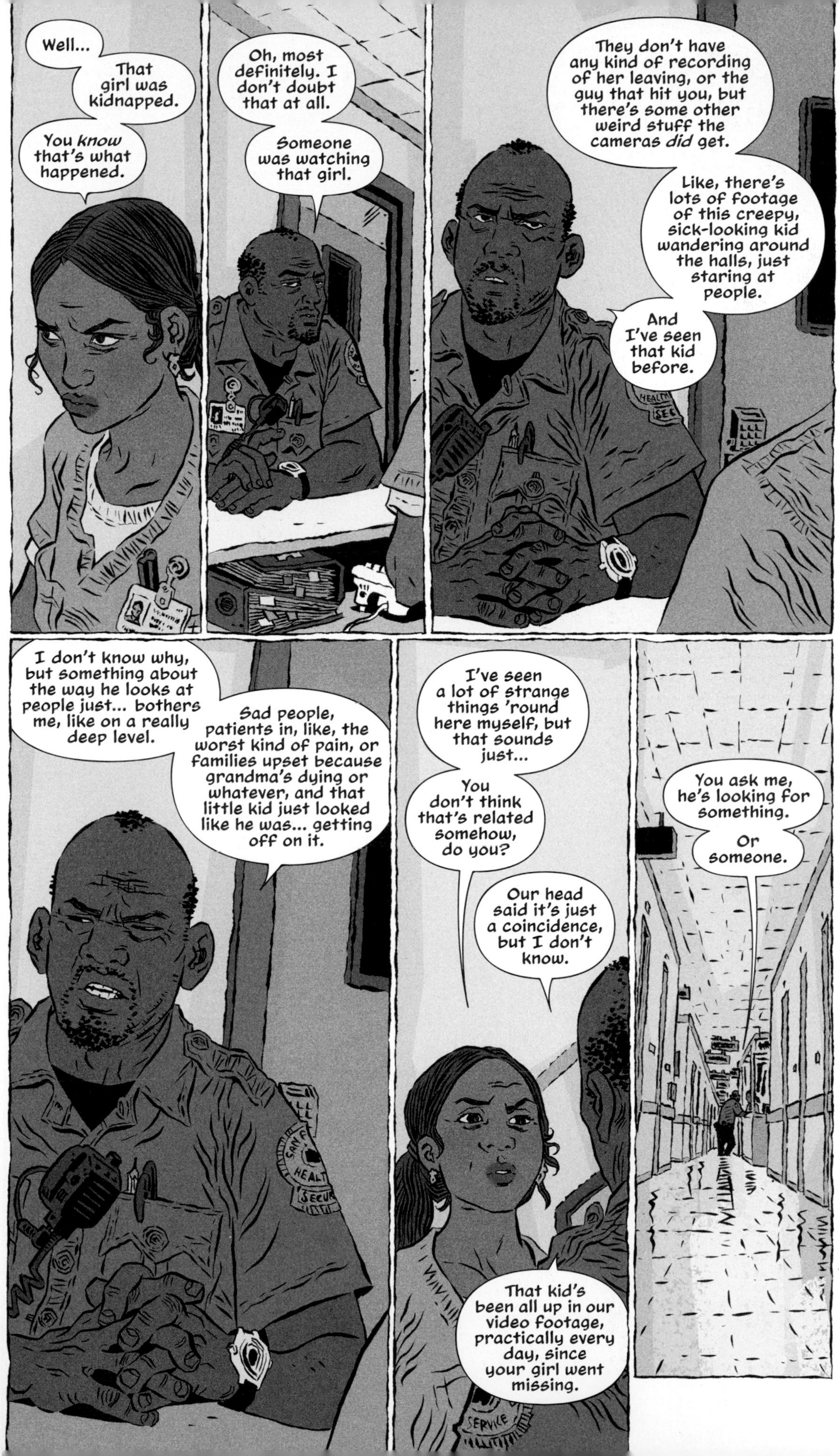
Well...
That girl was kidnapped.
You *know* that's what happened.
Oh, most definitely. I don't doubt that at all.
Someone was watching that girl.
They don't have any kind of recording of her leaving, or the guy that hit you, but there's some other weird stuff the cameras *did* get.
Like, there's lots of footage of this creepy, sick-looking kid wandering around the halls, just staring at people.
And I've seen that kid before.
I don't know why, but something about the way he looks at people just... bothers me, like on a really deep level.
Sad people, patients in, like, the worst kind of pain, or families upset because grandma's dying or whatever, and that little kid just looked like he was... getting off on it.
I've seen a lot of strange things 'round here myself, but that sounds just...
You don't think that's related somehow, do you?
Our head said it's just a coincidence, but I don't know.
That kid's been all up in our video footage, practically every day, since your girl went missing.
You ask me, he's looking for something.
Or someone.

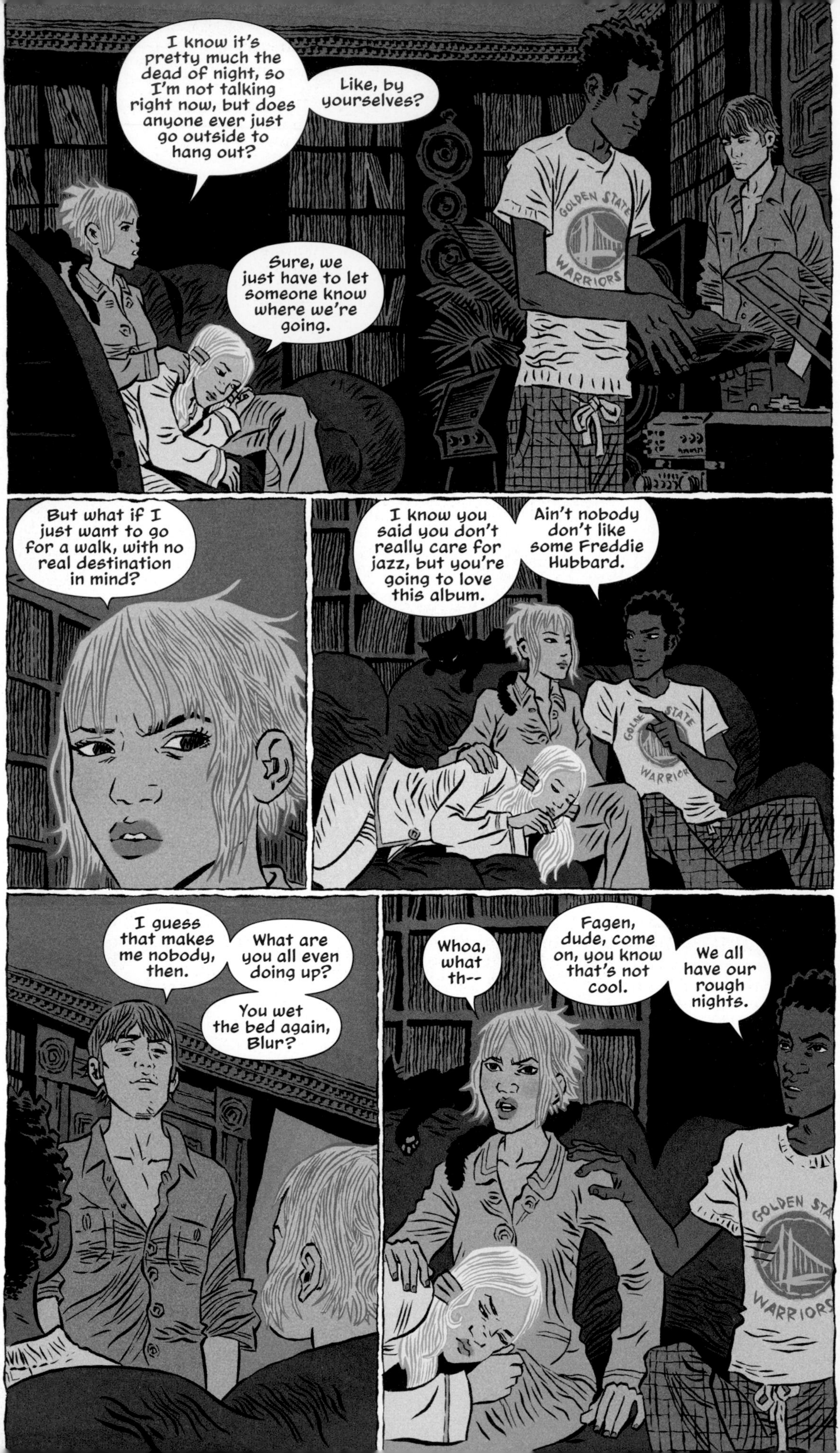
I know it's pretty much the dead of night, so I'm not talking right now, but does anyone ever just go outside to hang out?
Like, by yourselves?
Sure, we just have to let someone know where we're going.
GOLDEN STATE WARRIORS
But what if I just want to go for a walk, with no real destination in mind?
I know you said you don't really care for jazz, but you're going to love this album.
Ain't nobody don't like some Freddie Hubbard.
I guess that makes me nobody, then.
What are you all even doing up?
You wet the bed again, Blur?
Whoa, what th--
Fagen, dude, come on, you know that's not cool.
We all have our rough nights.
GOLDEN STATE WARRIORS

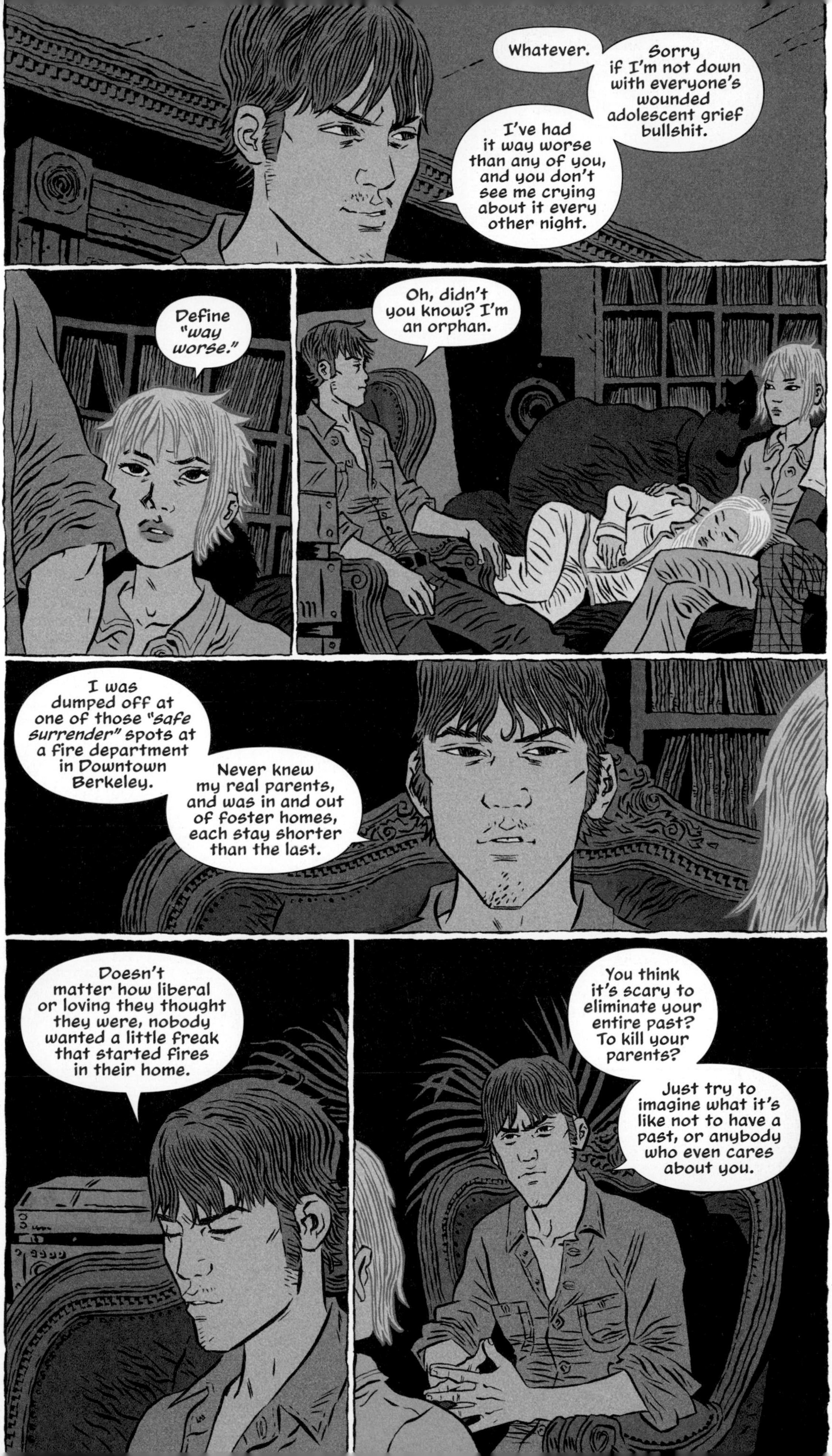
Whatever.
Sorry if I'm not down with everyone's wounded adolescent grief bullshit.
I've had it way worse than any of you, and you don't see me crying about it every other night.
Define "*way worse.*"
Oh, didn't you know? I'm an orphan.
I was dumped off at one of those "*safe surrender*" spots at a fire department in Downtown Berkeley.
Never knew my real parents, and was in and out of foster homes, each stay shorter than the last.
Doesn't matter how liberal or loving they thought they were, nobody wanted a little freak that started fires in their home.
You think it's scary to eliminate your entire past? To kill your parents?
Just try to imagine what it's like not to have a past, or anybody who even cares about you.

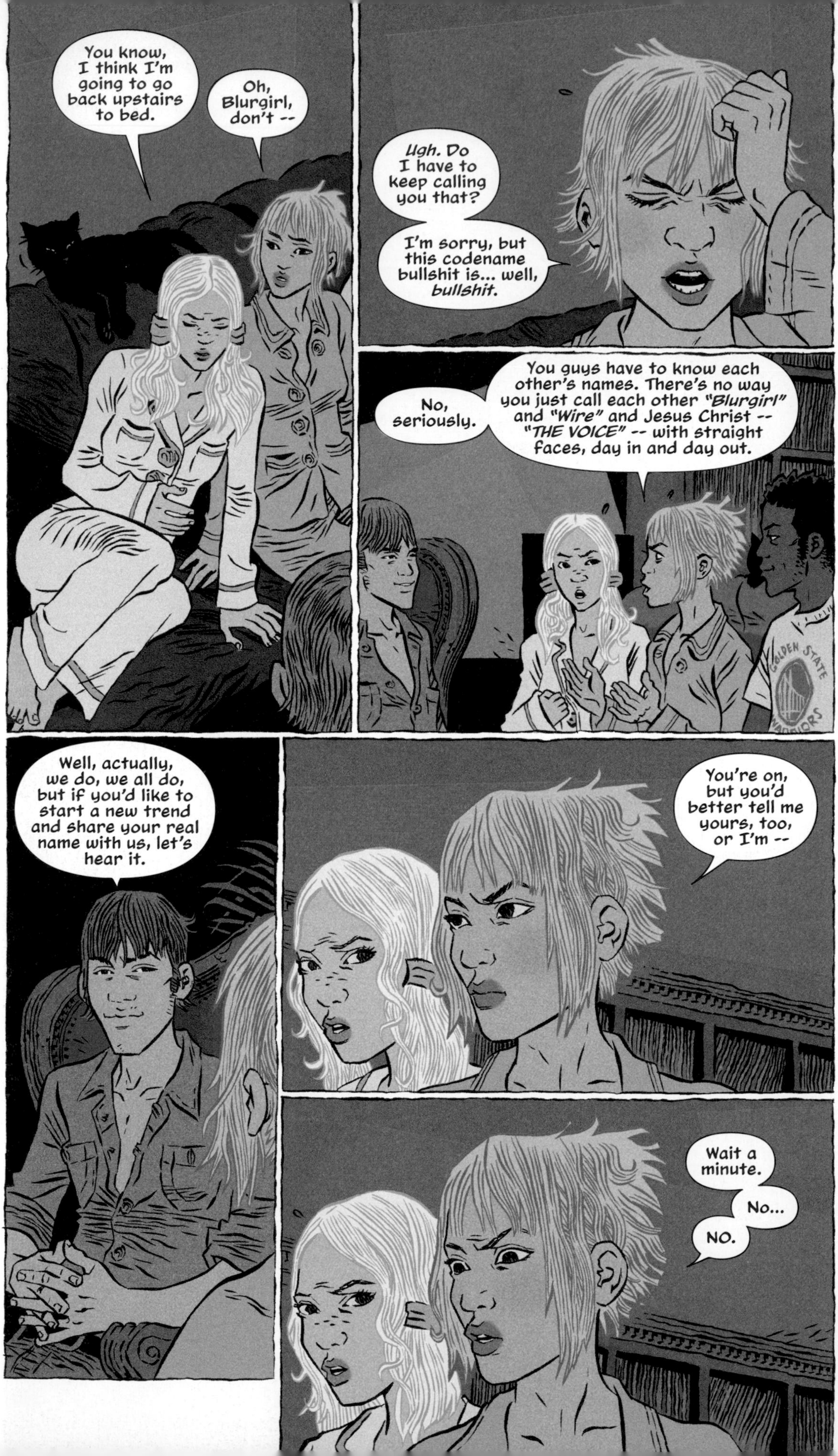
You know, I think I'm going to go back upstairs to bed.
Oh, Blurgirl, don't --
Ugh. Do I have to keep calling you that?
I'm sorry, but this codename bullshit is... well, bullshit.
No, seriously.
You guys have to know each other's names. There's no way you just call each other "Blurgirl" and "Wire" and Jesus Christ -- "THE VOICE" -- with straight faces, day in and day out.
GOLDEN STATE WARRIORS
Well, actually, we do, we all do, but if you'd like to start a new trend and share your real name with us, let's hear it.
You're on, but you'd better tell me yours, too, or I'm --
Wait a minute.
No...
NO.

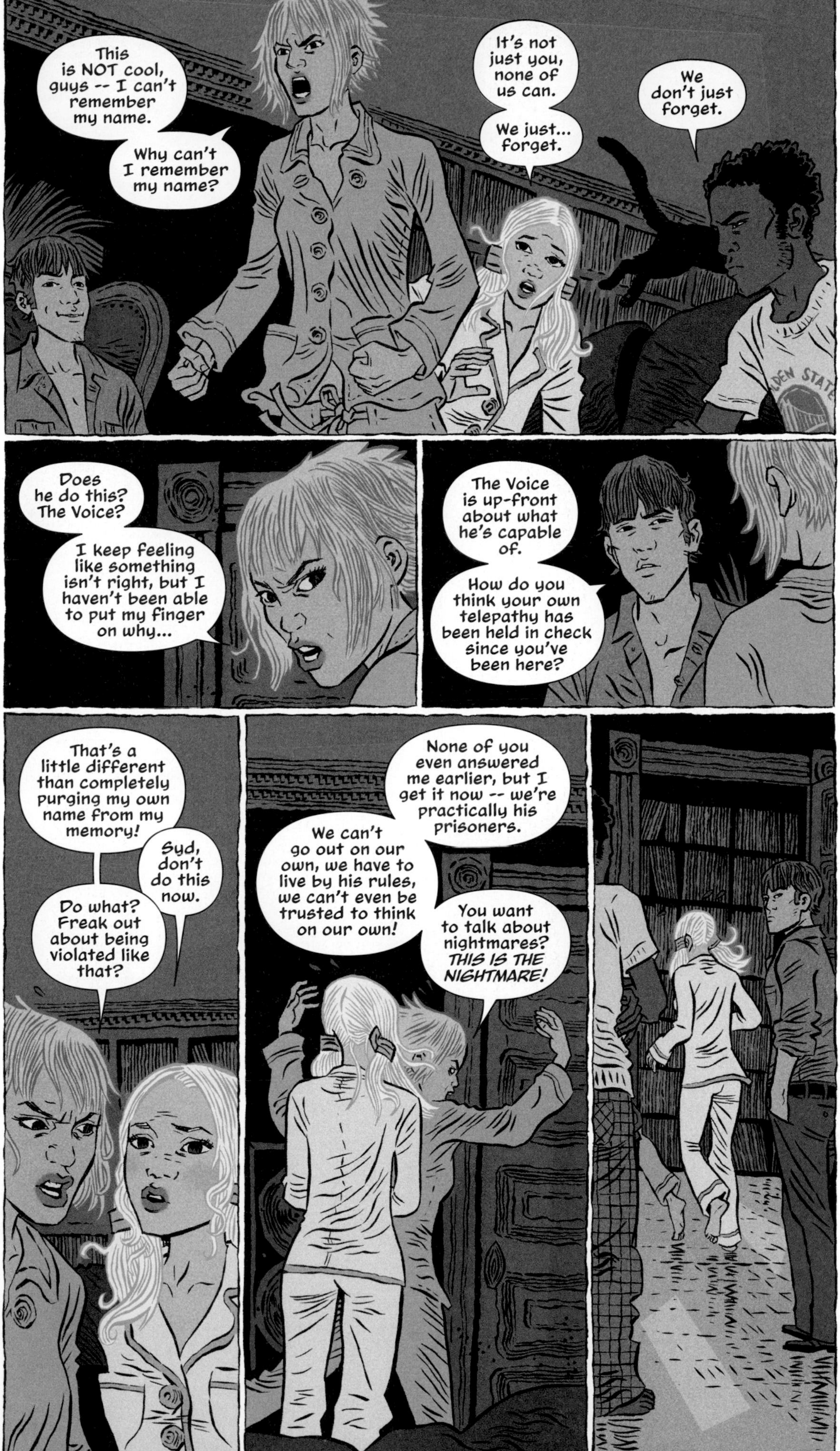
This is NOT cool, guys -- I can't remember my name.
Why can't I remember my name?
It's not just you, none of us can.
We just... forget.
We don't just forget.
DEN STATE
Does he do this? The Voice?
I keep feeling like something isn't right, but I haven't been able to put my finger on why...
The Voice is up-front about what he's capable of.
How do you think your own telepathy has been held in check since you've been here?
That's a little different than completely purging my own name from my memory!
Syd, don't do this now.
Do what? Freak out about being violated like that?
None of you even answered me earlier, but I get it now -- we're practically his prisoners.
We can't go out on our own, we have to live by his rules, we can't even be trusted to think on our own!
You want to talk about nightmares? *THIS IS THE NIGHTMARE!*

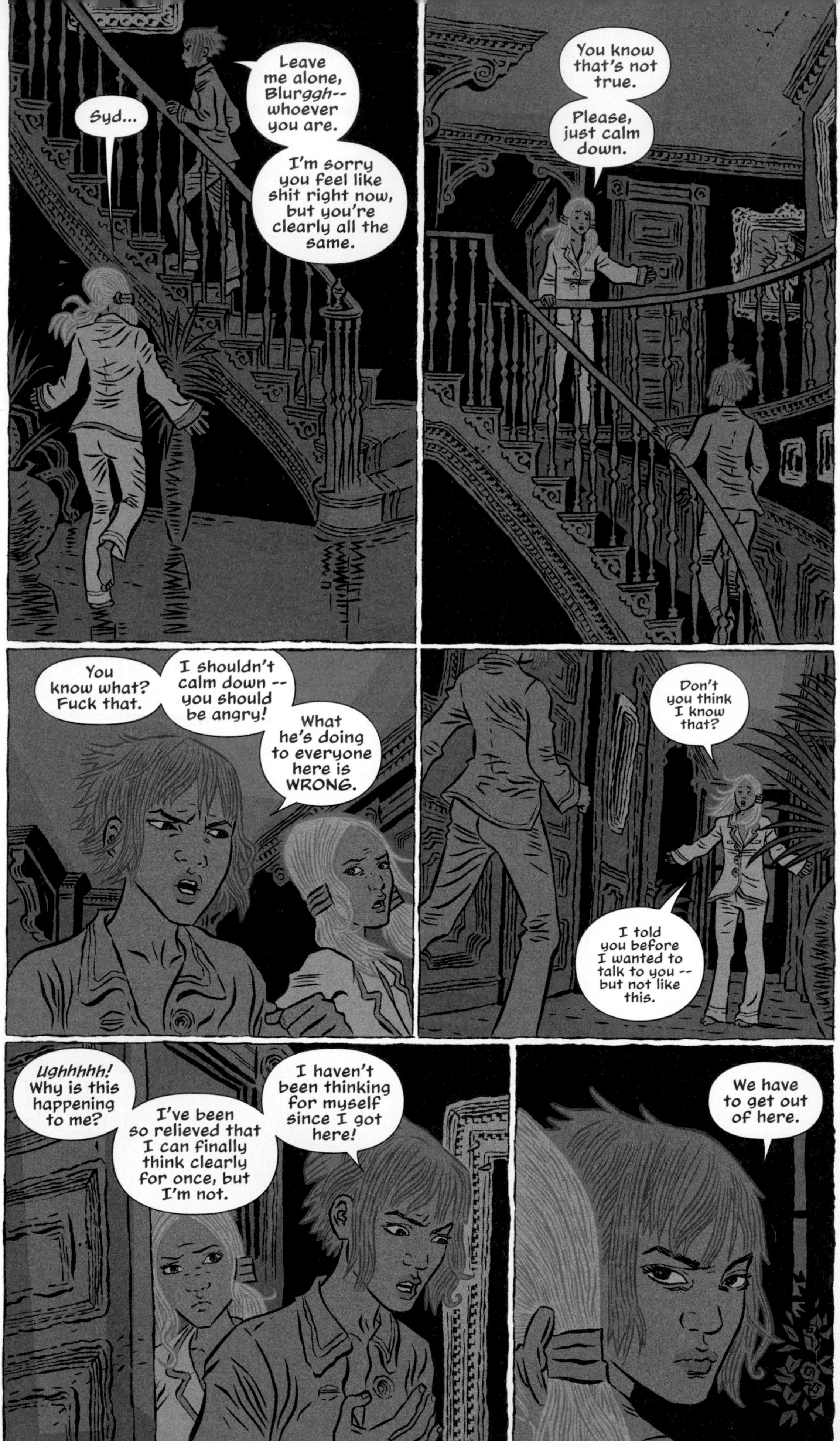
Syd...
Leave me alone, Blurggh-- whoever you are.
I'm sorry you feel like shit right now, but you're clearly all the same.
You know that's not true.
Please, just calm down.
You know what? Fuck that.
I shouldn't calm down -- you should be angry!
What he's doing to everyone here is WRONG.
Don't you think I know that?
I told you before I wanted to talk to you -- but not like this.
Ughhhhh! Why is this happening to me?
I've been so relieved that I can finally think clearly for once, but I'm not.
I haven't been thinking for myself since I got here!
We have to get out of here.

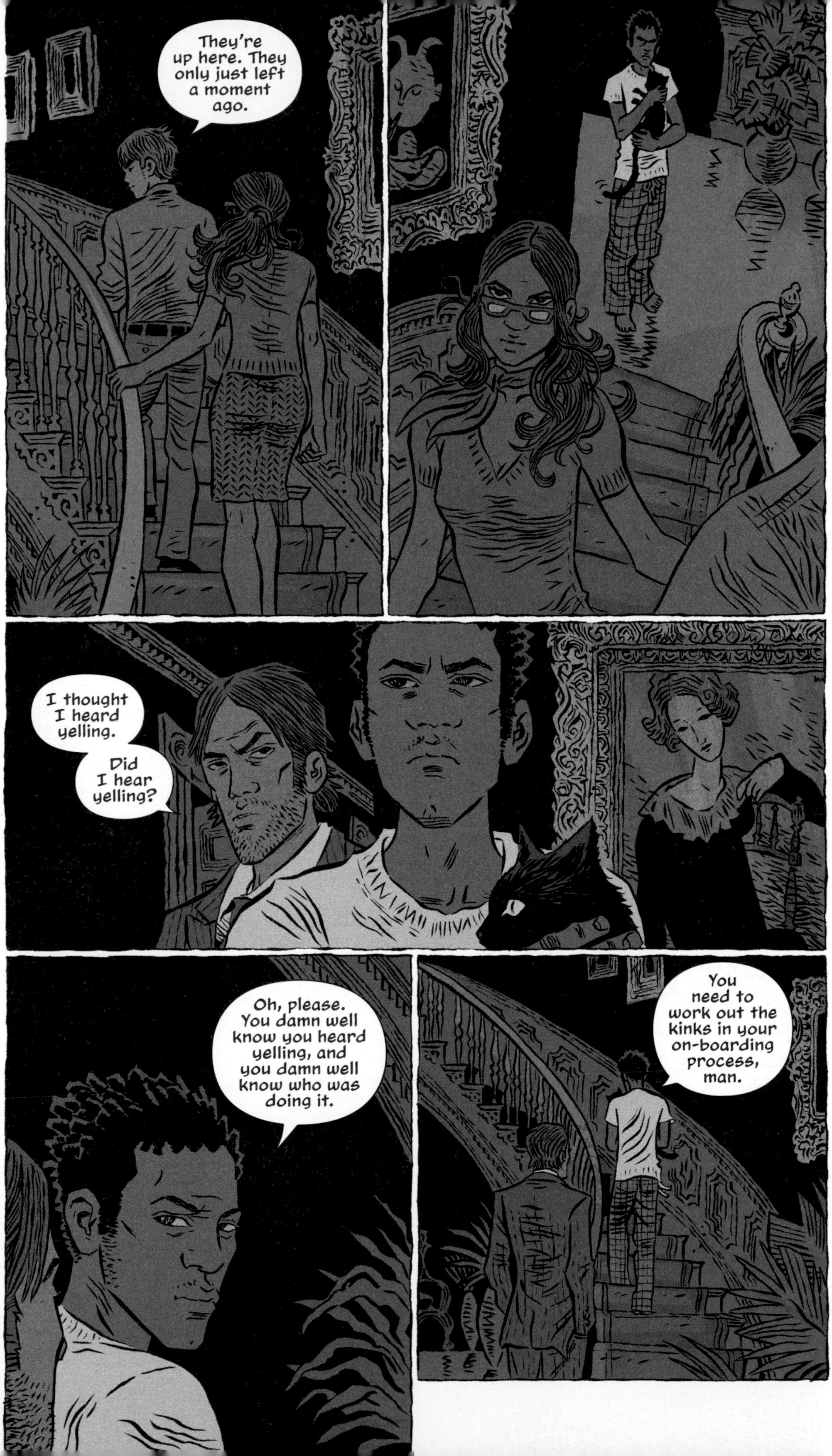
They're up here. They only just left a moment ago.
I thought I heard yelling.
Did I hear yelling?
Oh, please. You damn well know you heard yelling, and you damn well know who was doing it.
You need to work out the kinks in your on-boarding process, man.

I have no idea
what else happened
that night.

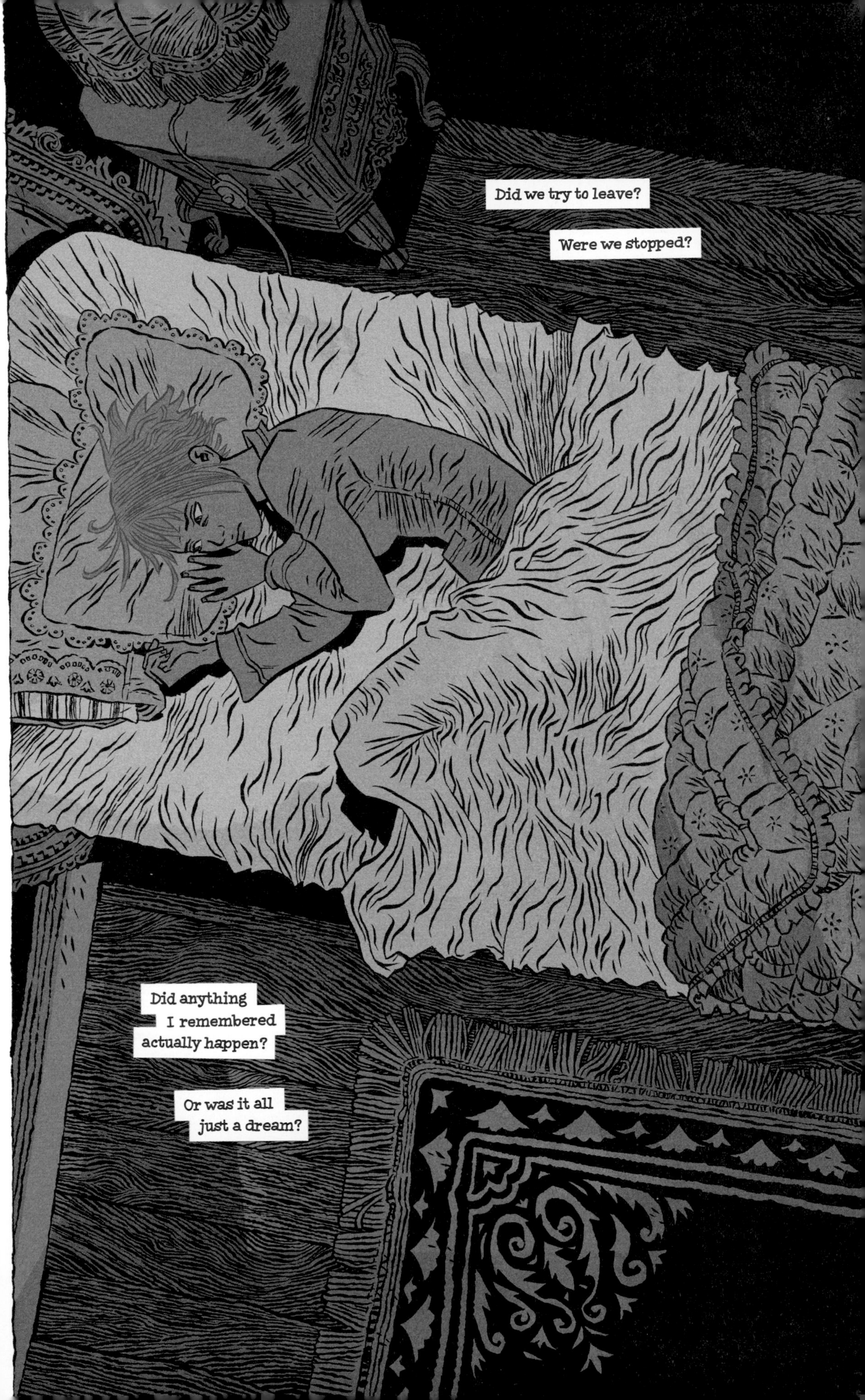
Did we try to leave?
Were we stopped?
Did anything I remembered actually happen?
Or was it all just a dream?

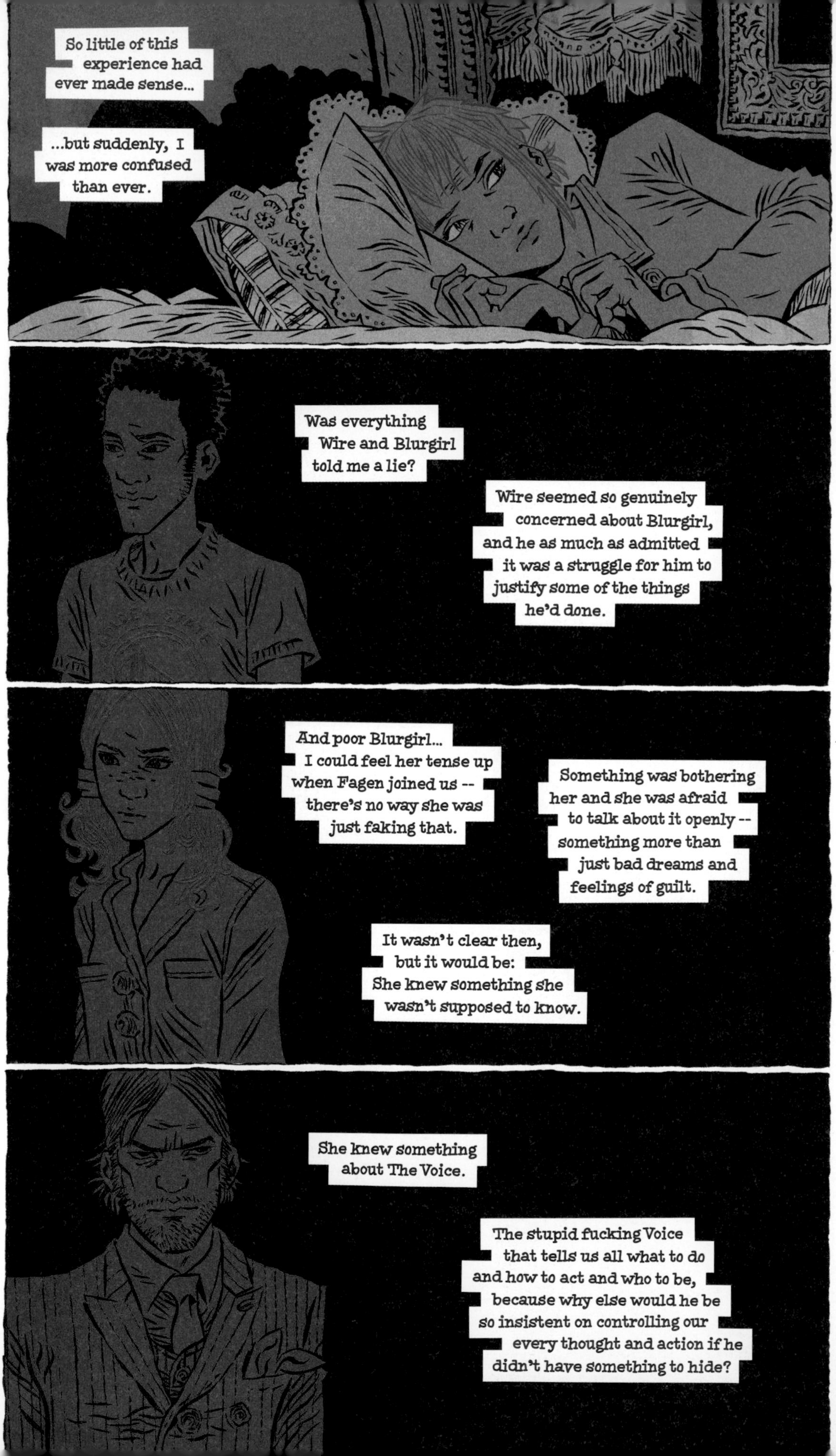

So little of this experience had ever made sense...
...but suddenly, I was more confused than ever.
Was everything Wire and Blurgirl told me a lie?
Wire seemed so genuinely concerned about Blurgirl, and he as much as admitted it was a struggle for him to justify some of the things he'd done.
And poor Blurgirl... I could feel her tense up when Fagen joined us -- there's no way she was just faking that.
Something was bothering her and she was afraid to talk about it openly -- something more than just bad dreams and feelings of guilt.
It wasn't clear then, but it would be: She knew something she wasn't supposed to know.
She knew something about The Voice.
The stupid fucking Voice that tells us all what to do and how to act and who to be, because why else would he be so insistent on controlling our every thought and action if he didn't have something to hide?

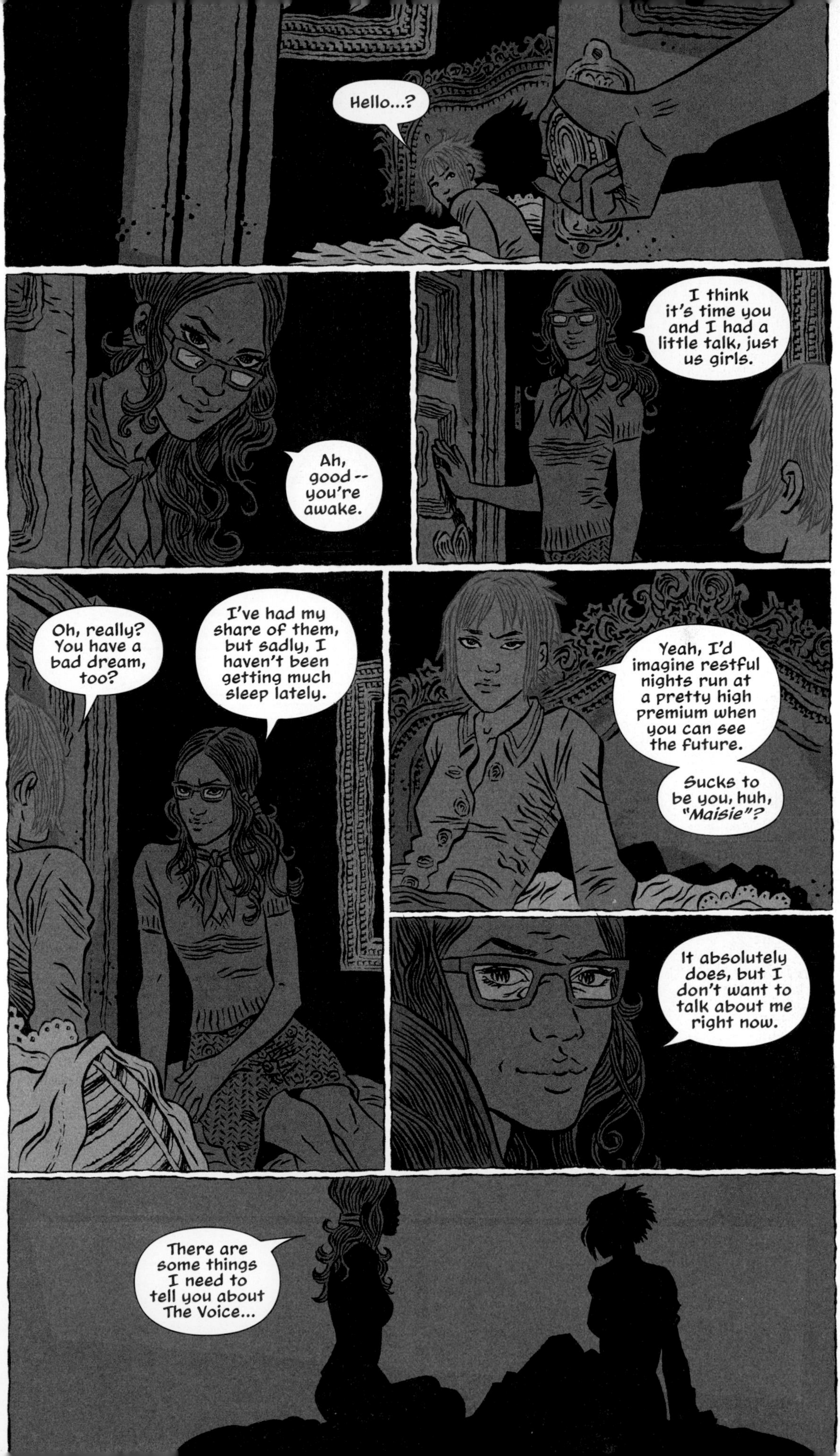
Hello...?
Ah, good -- you're awake.
I think it's time you and I had a little talk, just us girls.
Oh, really? You have a bad dream, too?
I've had my share of them, but sadly, I haven't been getting much sleep lately.
Yeah, I'd imagine restful nights run at a pretty high premium when you can see the future.
Sucks to be you, huh, *"Maisie"*?
It absolutely does, but I don't want to talk about me right now.
There are some things I need to tell you about The Voice...

WE MAKE THE SAME MISTAKES, WE SHARE THE SAME DESPAIR

STEPHEN DUFFY

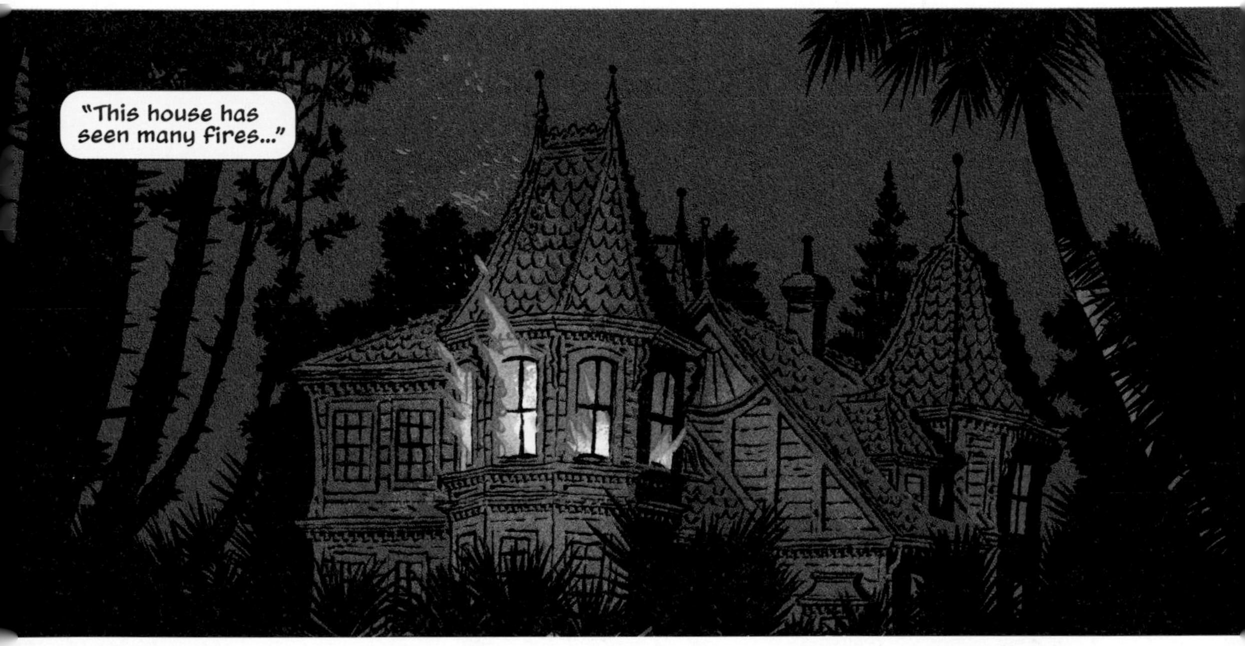
"This house has seen many fires..."

5: AN ANGEL GETS HIS WINGS

"...but one
burned more
brilliantly than
the rest."

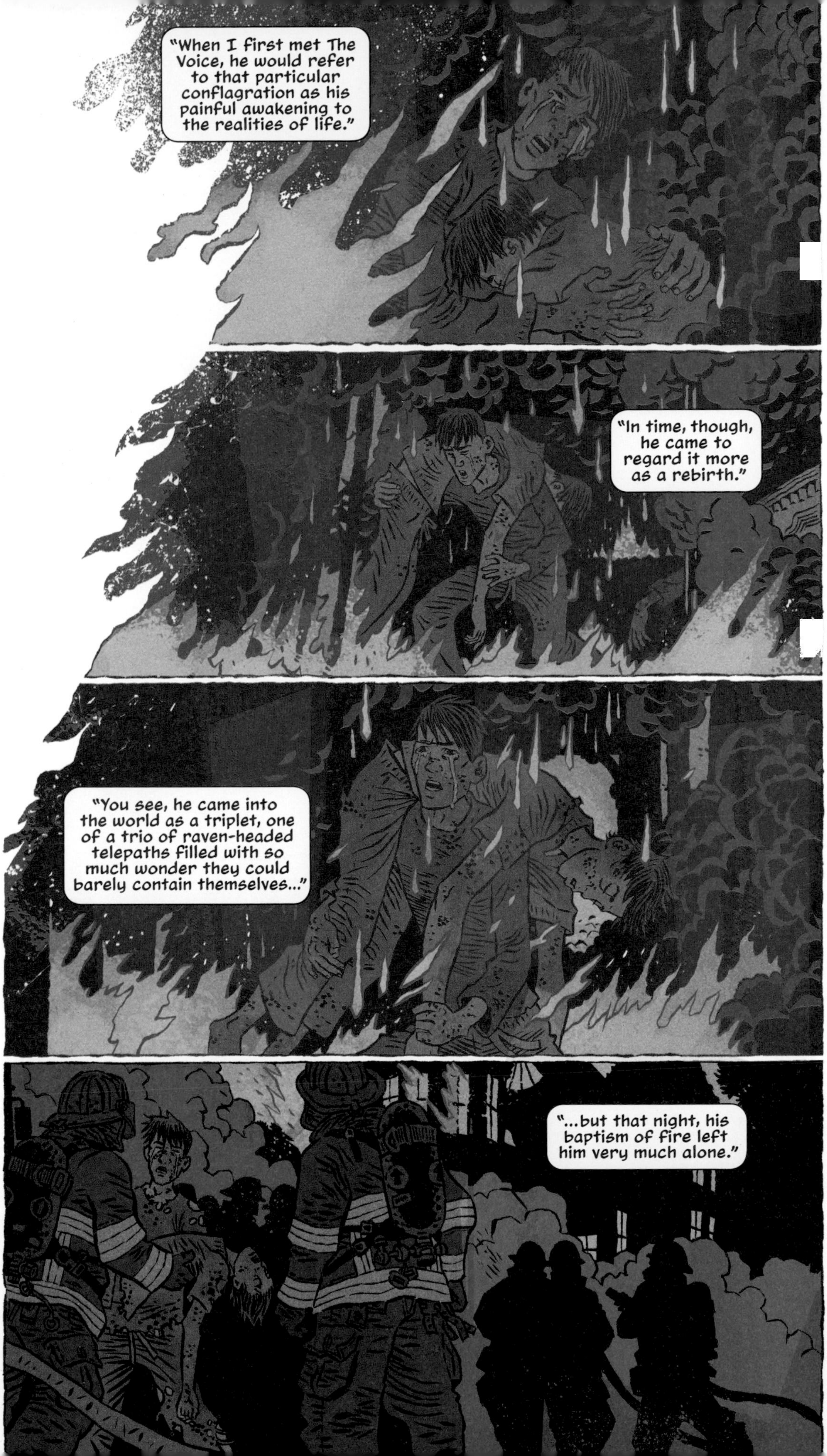
"When I first met The Voice, he would refer to that particular conflagration as his painful awakening to the realities of life."
"In time, though, he came to regard it more as a rebirth."
"You see, he came into the world as a triplet, one of a trio of raven-headed telepaths filled with so much wonder they could barely contain themselves..."
"...but that night, his baptism of fire left him very much alone."

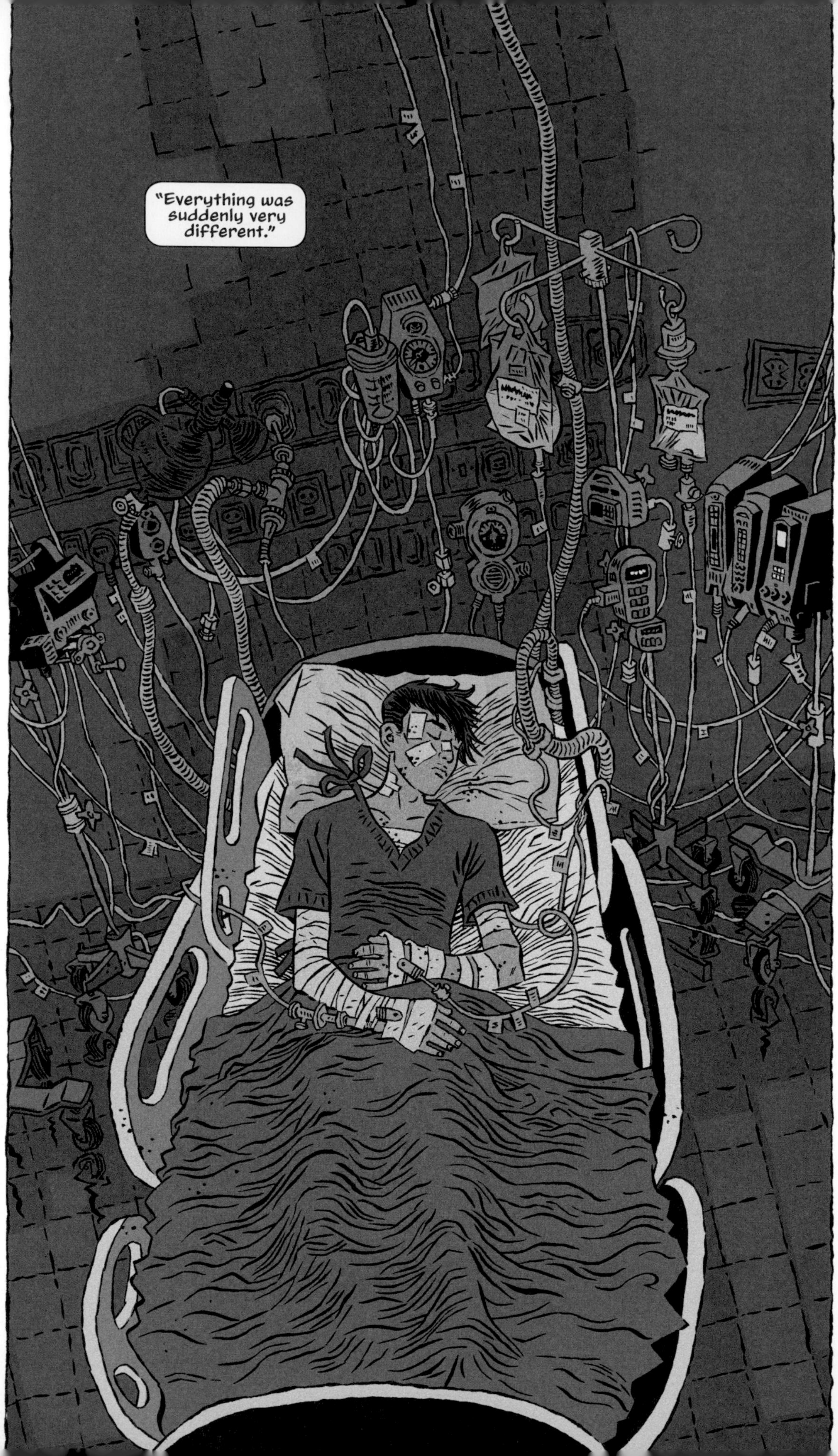
"Everything was suddenly very different."

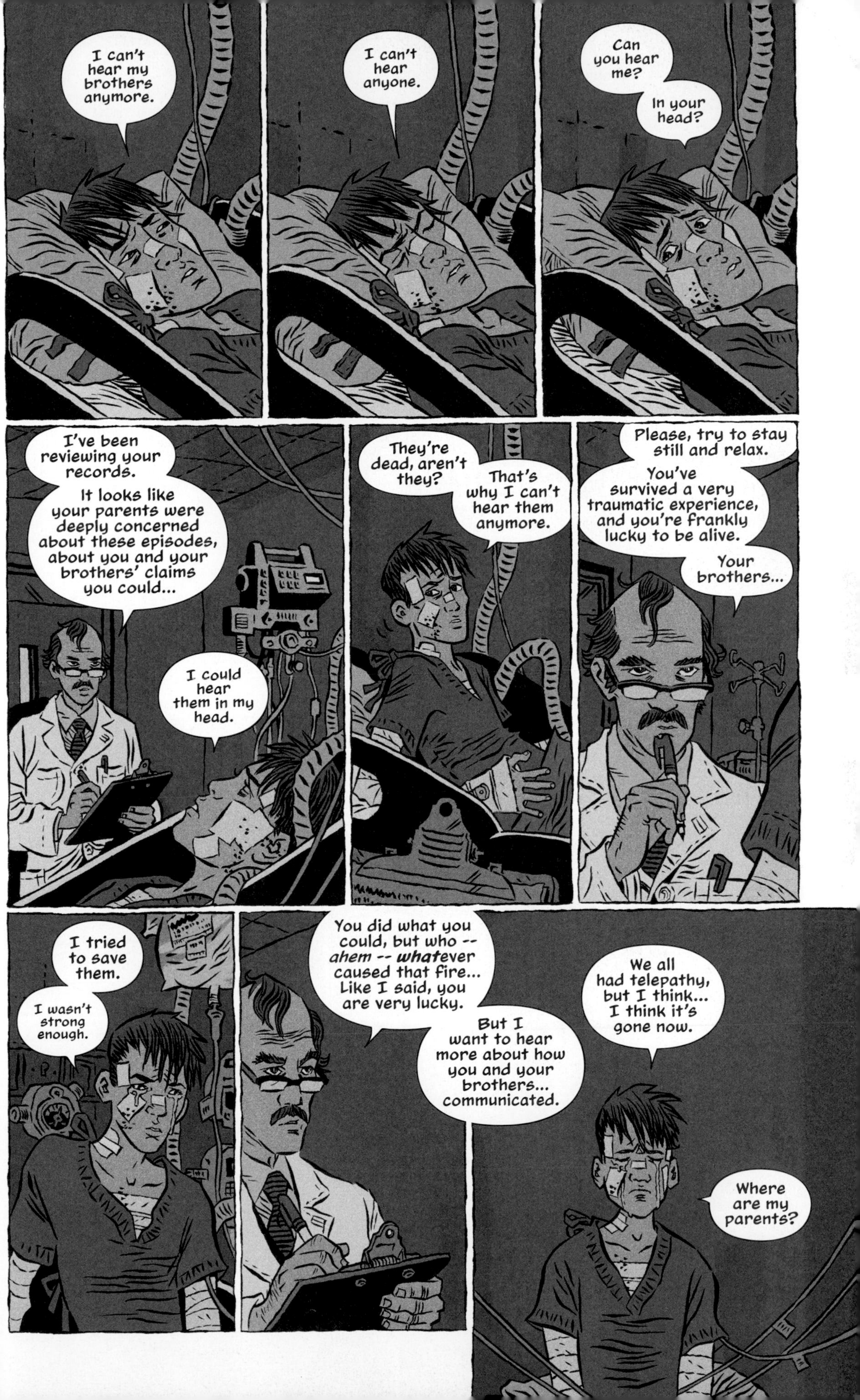

I can't hear my brothers anymore.
I can't hear anyone.
Can you hear me?
In your head?
I've been reviewing your records.
It looks like your parents were deeply concerned about these episodes, about you and your brothers' claims you could...
I could hear them in my head.
They're dead, aren't they?
That's why I can't hear them anymore.
Please, try to stay still and relax.
You've survived a very traumatic experience, and you're frankly lucky to be alive.
Your brothers...
I tried to save them.
I wasn't strong enough.
You did what you could, but who -- *ahem* -- ***what***ever caused that fire... Like I said, you are very lucky.
But I want to hear more about how you and your brothers... communicated.
We all had telepathy, but I think... I think it's gone now.
Where are my parents?

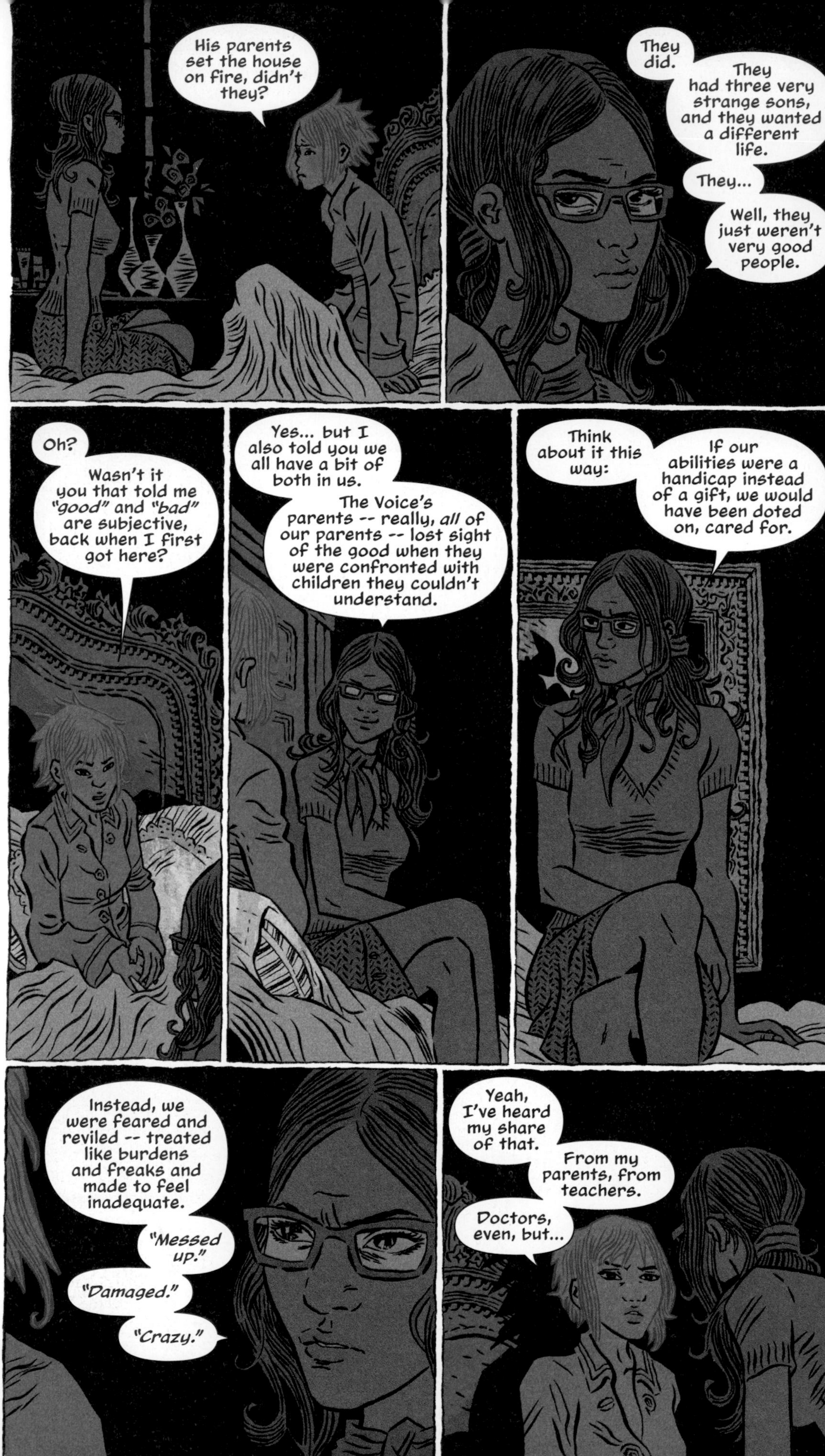
His parents set the house on fire, didn't they?
They did.
They had three very strange sons, and they wanted a different life.
They...
Well, they just weren't very good people.
Oh?
Wasn't it you that told me *"good"* and *"bad"* are subjective, back when I first got here?
Yes... but I also told you we all have a bit of both in us.
The Voice's parents -- really, *all* of our parents -- lost sight of the good when they were confronted with children they couldn't understand.
Think about it this way:
If our abilities were a handicap instead of a gift, we would have been doted on, cared for.
Instead, we were feared and reviled -- treated like burdens and freaks and made to feel inadequate.
"Messed up."
"Damaged."
"Crazy."
Yeah, I've heard my share of that.
From my parents, from teachers.
Doctors, even, but...

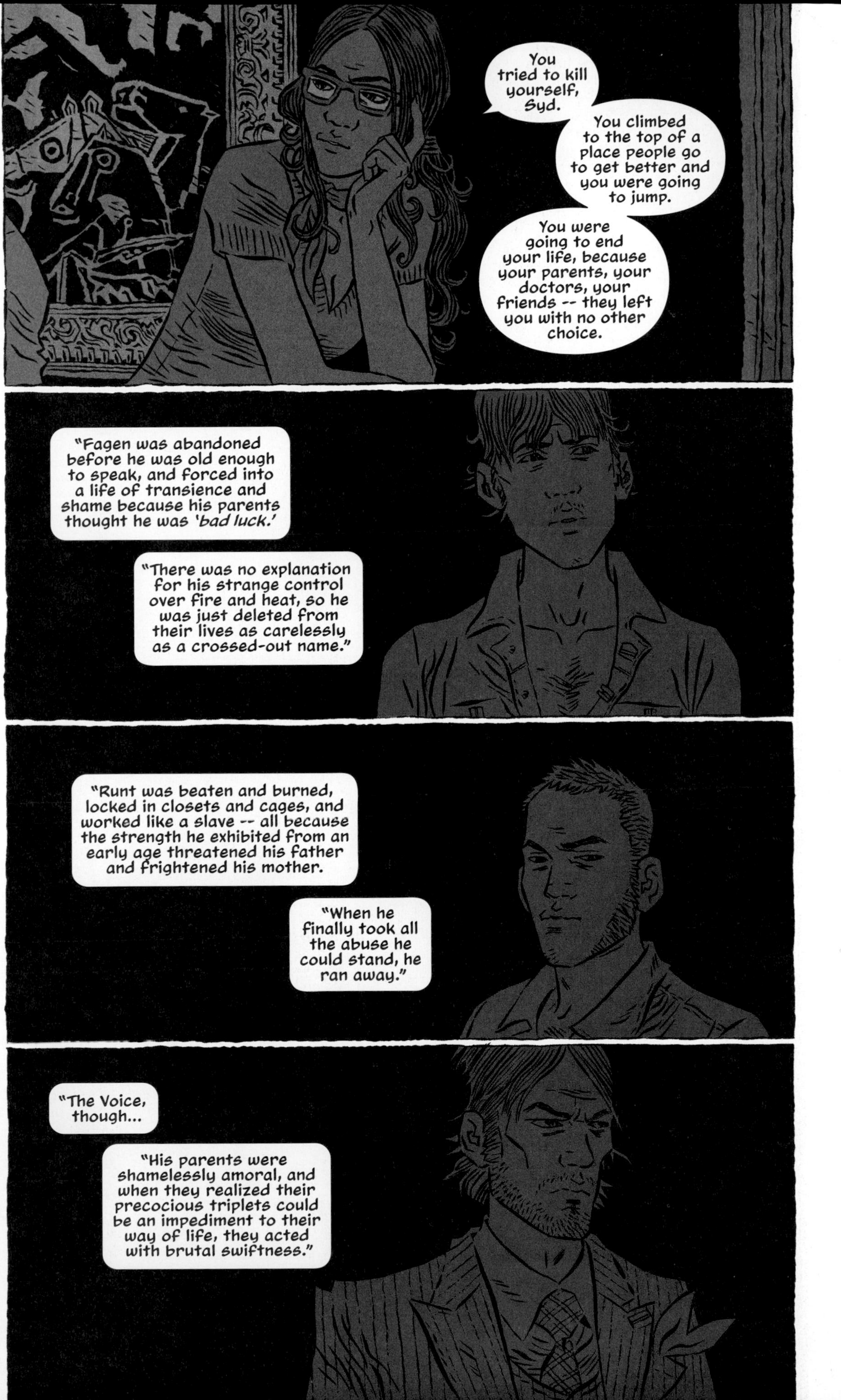
You tried to kill yourself, Syd.
You climbed to the top of a place people go to get better and you were going to jump.
You were going to end your life, because your parents, your doctors, your friends -- they left you with no other choice.
"Fagen was abandoned before he was old enough to speak, and forced into a life of transience and shame because his parents thought he was *'bad luck.'*
"There was no explanation for his strange control over fire and heat, so he was just deleted from their lives as carelessly as a crossed-out name."
"Runt was beaten and burned, locked in closets and cages, and worked like a slave -- all because the strength he exhibited from an early age threatened his father and frightened his mother.
"When he finally took all the abuse he could stand, he ran away."
"The Voice, though...
"His parents were shamelessly amoral, and when they realized their precocious triplets could be an impediment to their way of life, they acted with brutal swiftness."

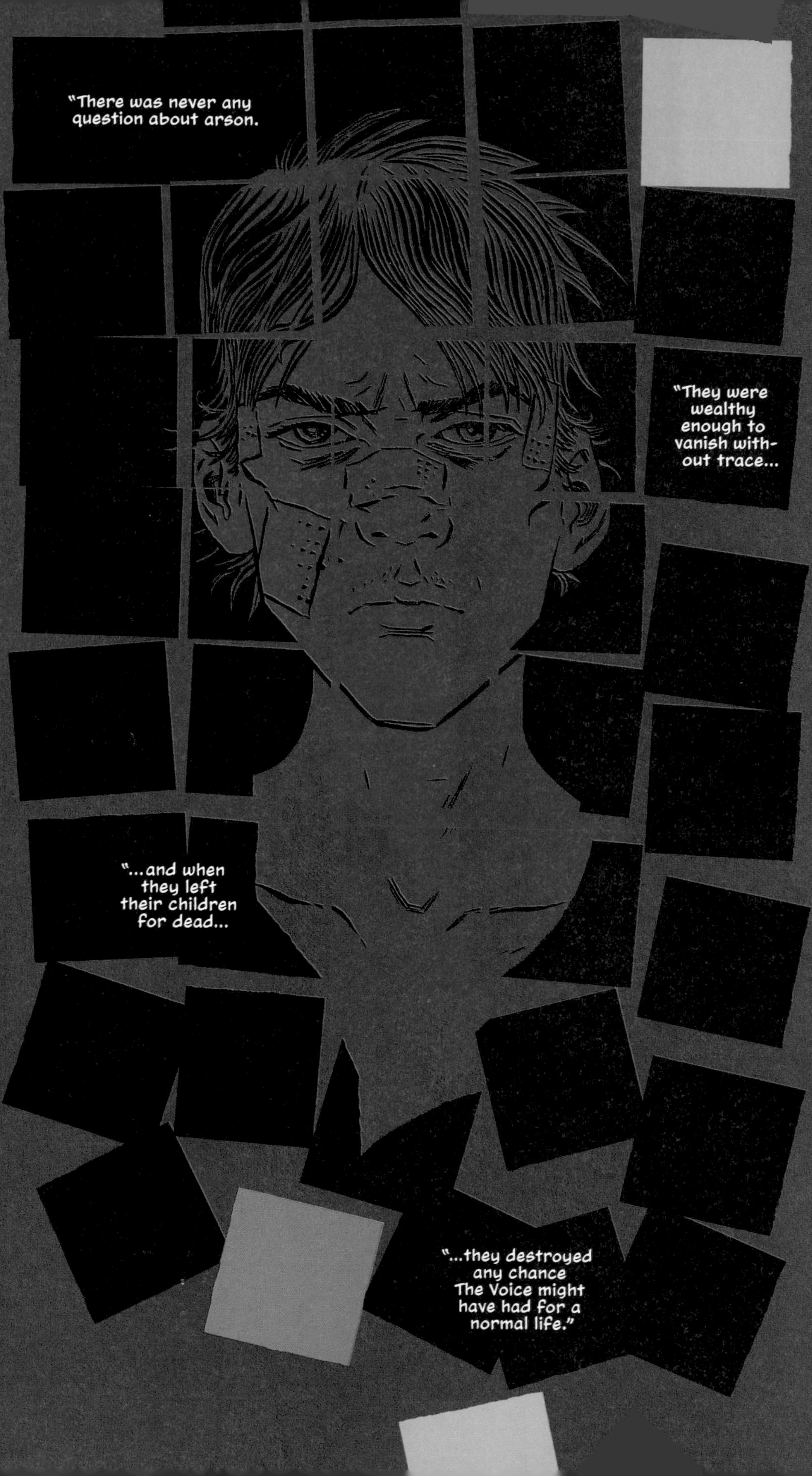
"There was never any question about arson.
"They were wealthy enough to vanish with-out trace...
"...and when they left their children for dead...
"...they destroyed any chance The Voice might have had for a normal life."

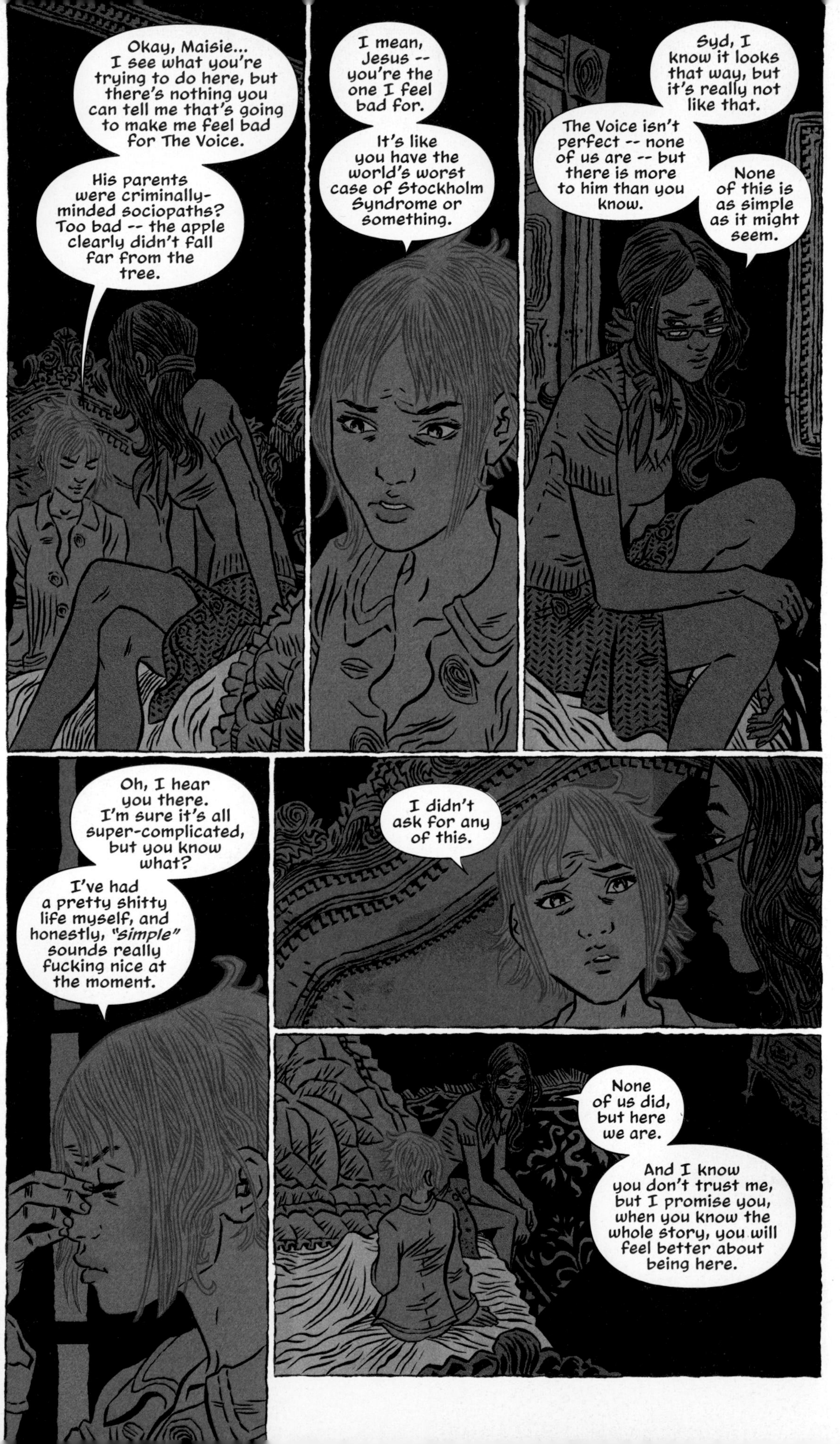
Okay, Maisie... I see what you're trying to do here, but there's nothing you can tell me that's going to make me feel bad for The Voice.
His parents were criminally-minded sociopaths? Too bad -- the apple clearly didn't fall far from the tree.
I mean, Jesus -- you're the one I feel bad for.
It's like you have the world's worst case of Stockholm Syndrome or something.
Syd, I know it looks that way, but it's really not like that.
The Voice isn't perfect -- none of us are -- but there is more to him than you know.
None of this is as simple as it might seem.
Oh, I hear you there. I'm sure it's all super-complicated, but you know what?
I've had a pretty shitty life myself, and honestly, "*simple*" sounds really fucking nice at the moment.
I didn't ask for any of this.
None of us did, but here we are.
And I know you don't trust me, but I promise you, when you know the whole story, you will feel better about being here.

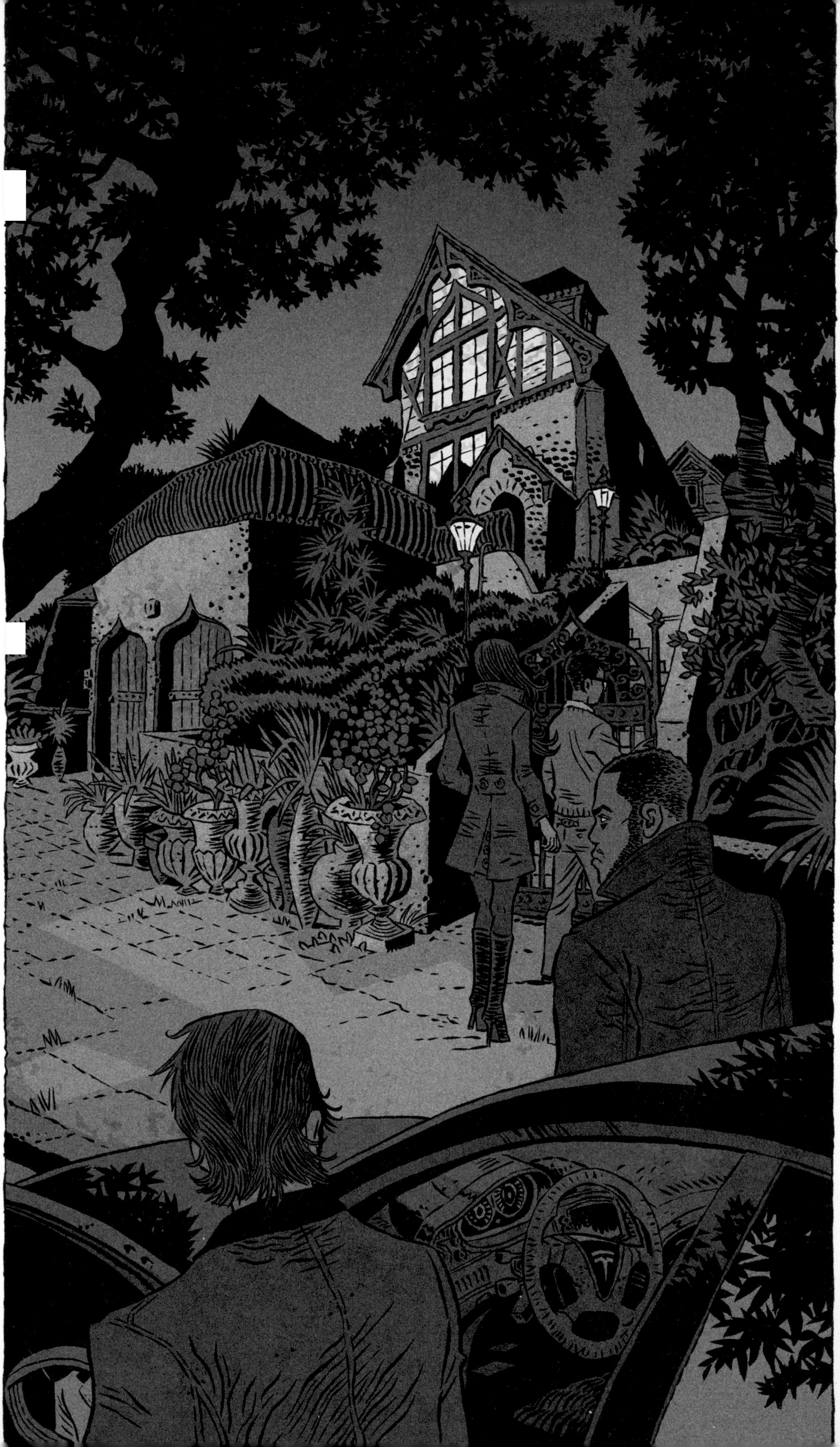

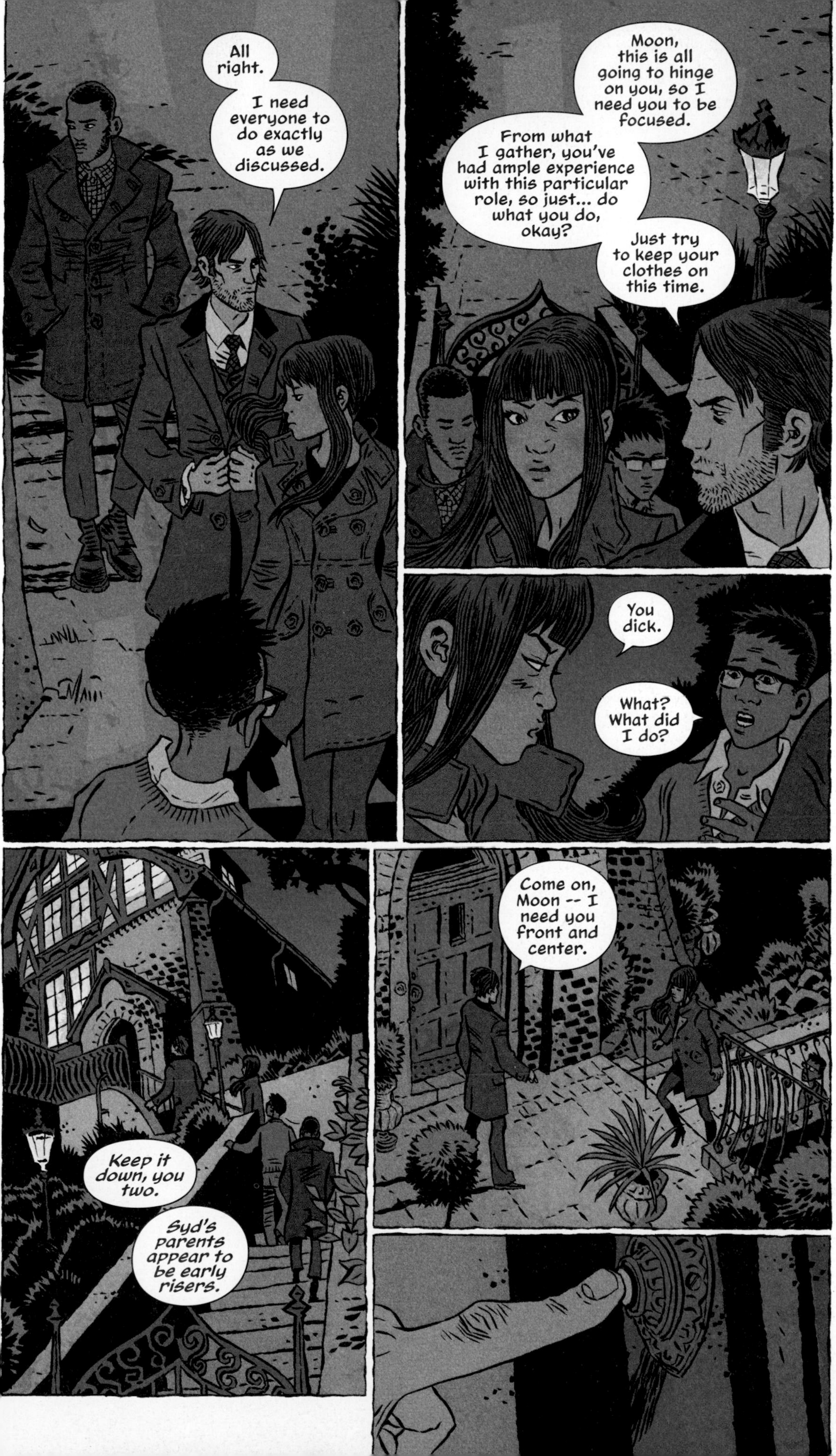
All right.
I need everyone to do exactly as we discussed.
Moon, this is all going to hinge on you, so I need you to be focused.
From what I gather, you've had ample experience with this particular role, so just... do what you do, okay?
Just try to keep your clothes on this time.
You dick.
What? What did I do?
Keep it down, you two.
Syd's parents appear to be early risers.
Come on, Moon -- I need you front and center.

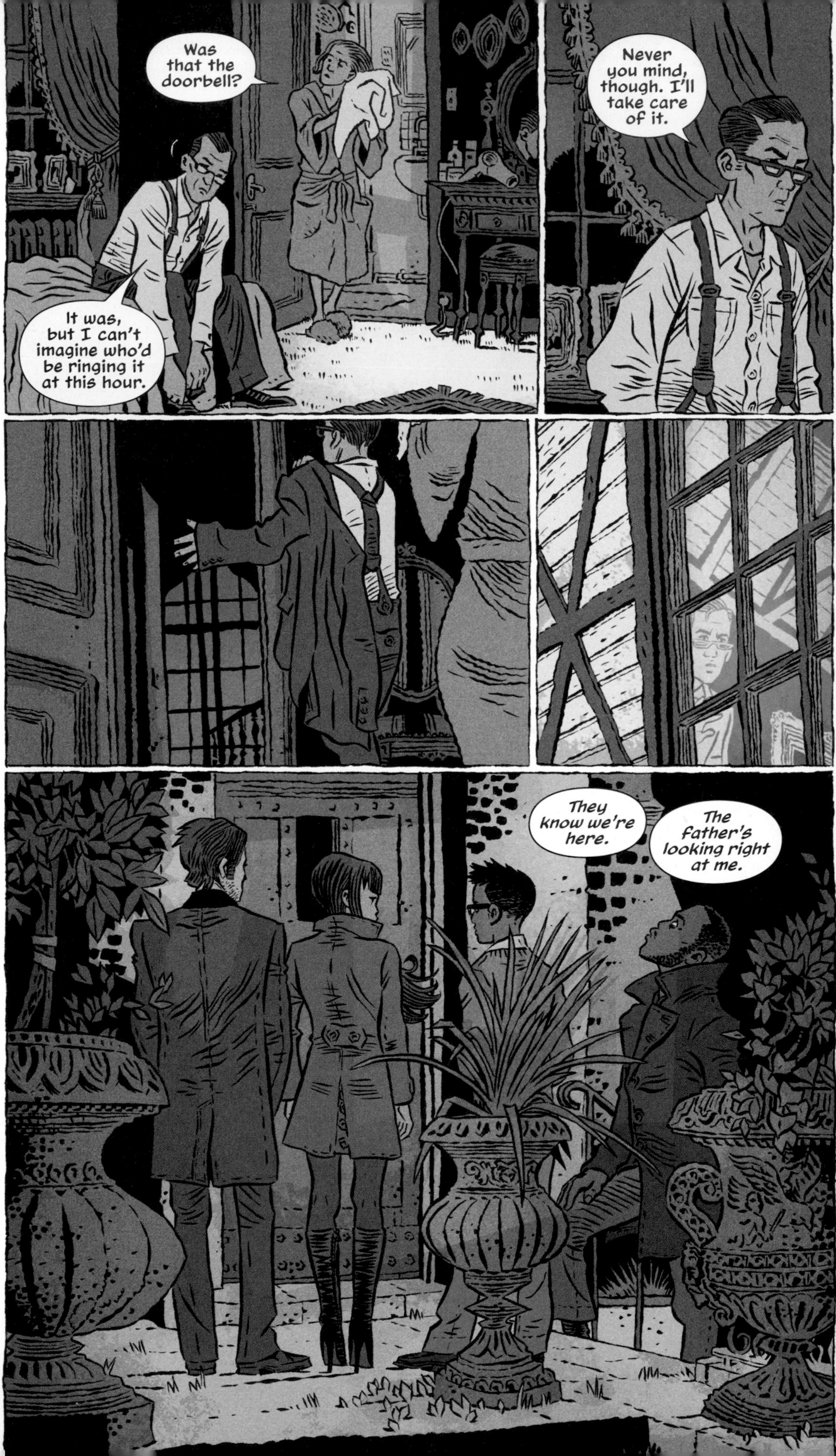
Was that the doorbell?
It was, but I can't imagine who'd be ringing it at this hour.
Never you mind, though. I'll take care of it.
They know we're here.
The father's looking right at me.

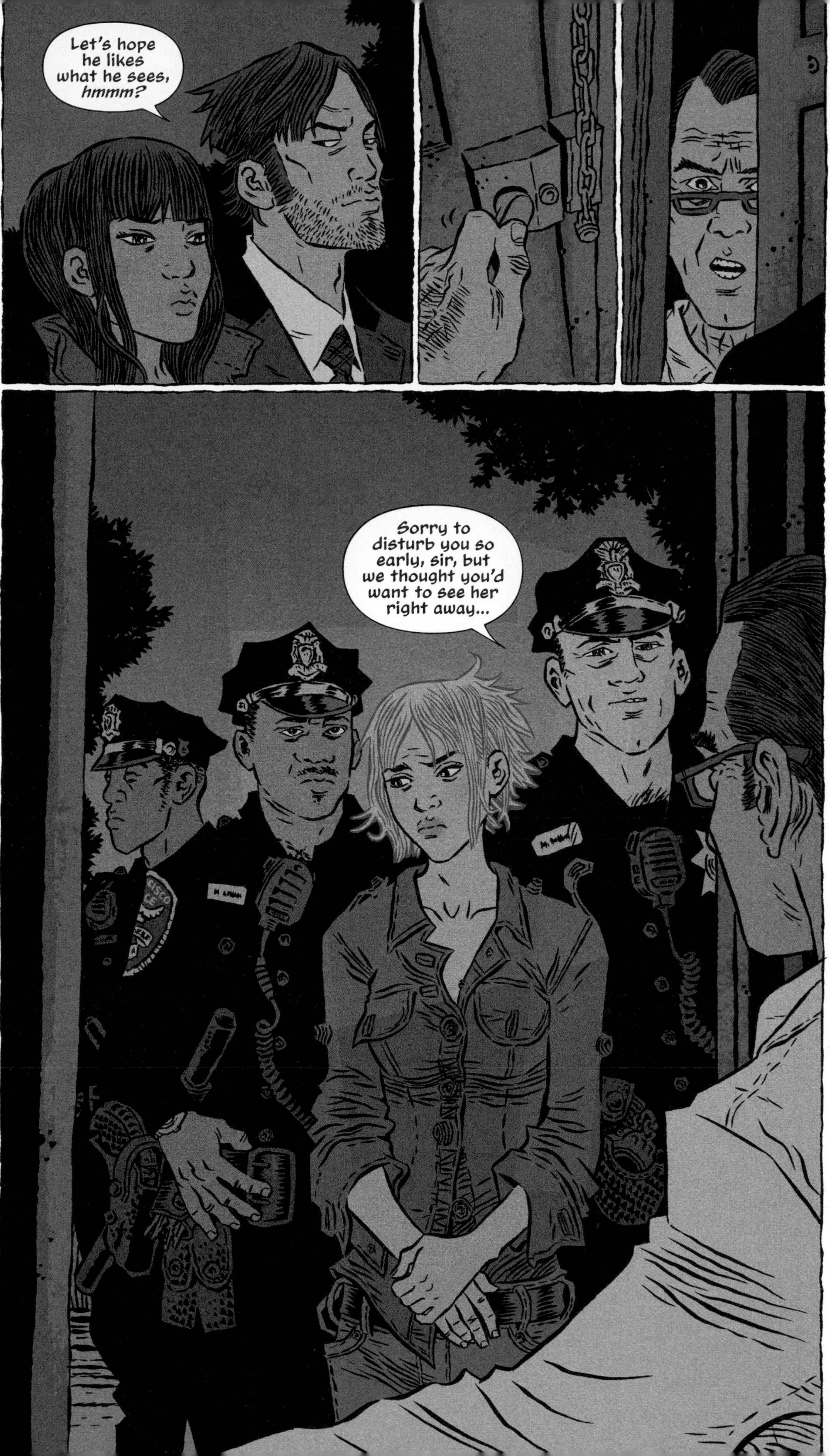
Let's hope he likes what he sees, *hmmm?*
Sorry to disturb you so early, sir, but we thought you'd want to see her right away...

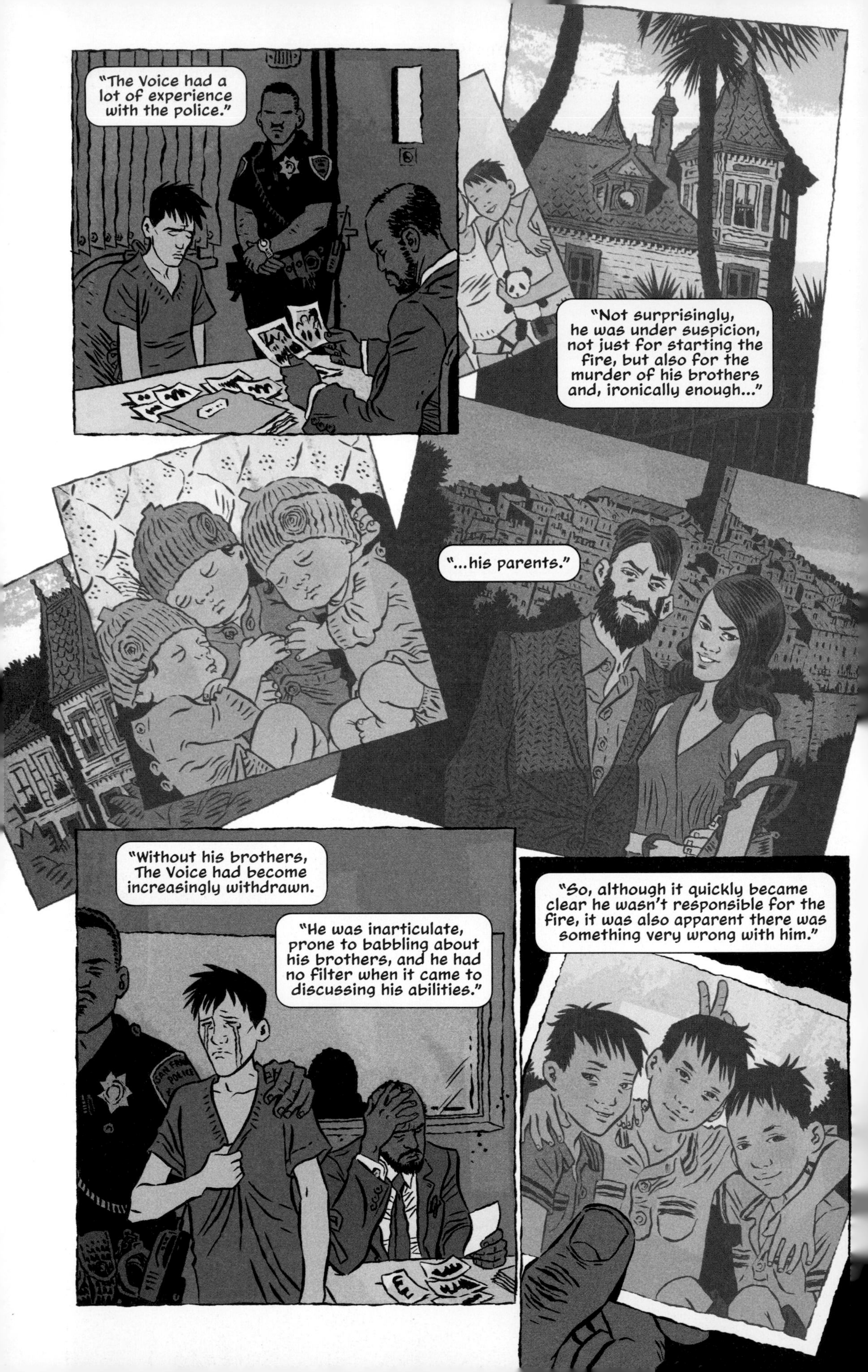
"The Voice had a lot of experience with the police."
"Not surprisingly, he was under suspicion, not just for starting the fire, but also for the murder of his brothers and, ironically enough..."
"...his parents."
"Without his brothers, The Voice had become increasingly withdrawn.
"He was inarticulate, prone to babbling about his brothers, and he had no filter when it came to discussing his abilities."
"So, although it quickly became clear he wasn't responsible for the fire, it was also apparent there was something very wrong with him."

"Which, of course, was because that was exactly the case."

"The Voice and his brothers were quite unique, and not just because they were telepaths."

"They had a very symbiotic bond, with each of them serving different functions within their relationship."

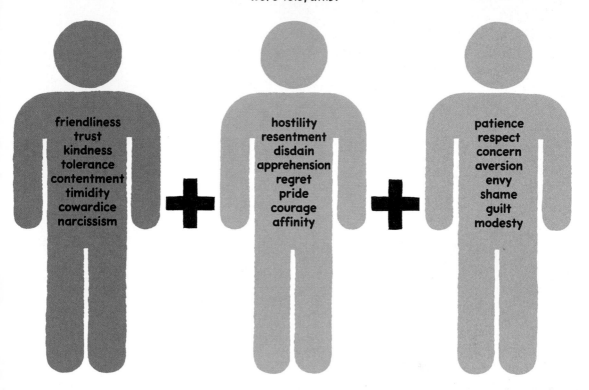

friendliness
trust
kindness
tolerance
contentment
timidity
cowardice
narcissism

+

hostility
resentment
disdain
apprehension
regret
pride
courage
affinity

+

patience
respect
concern
aversion
envy
shame
guilt
modesty

"With that bond severed, he was only barely a functioning telepath, and worse, whatever emotional or personality traits his brothers favored became strangely absent in his own makeup."

"He was one third of the person he was."

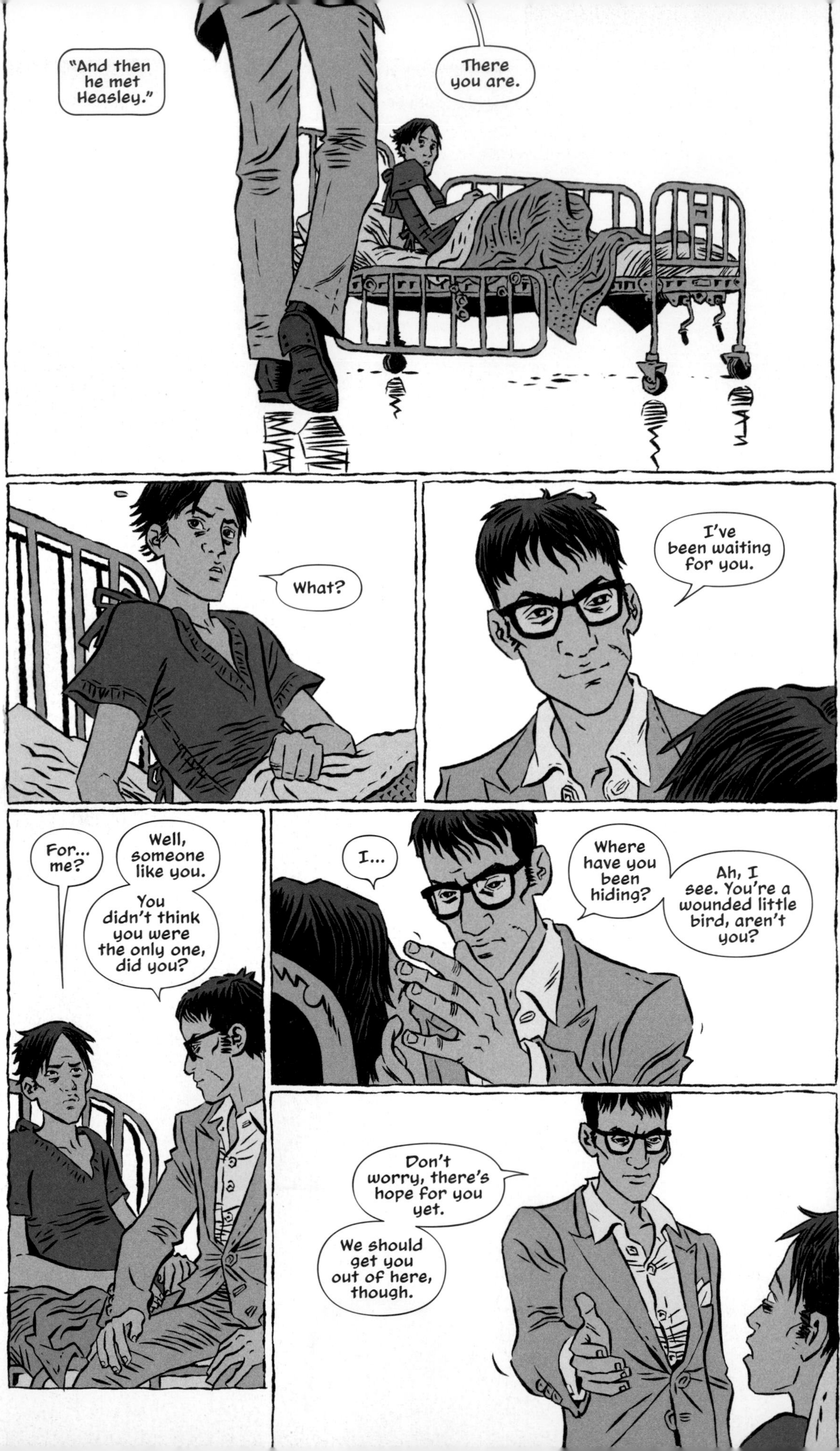
"And then he met Heasley."
There you are.
What?
I've been waiting for you.
For... me?
Well, someone like you.
You didn't think you were the only one, did you?
I...
Where have you been hiding?
Ah, I see. You're a wounded little bird, aren't you?
Don't worry, there's hope for you yet.
We should get you out of here, though.

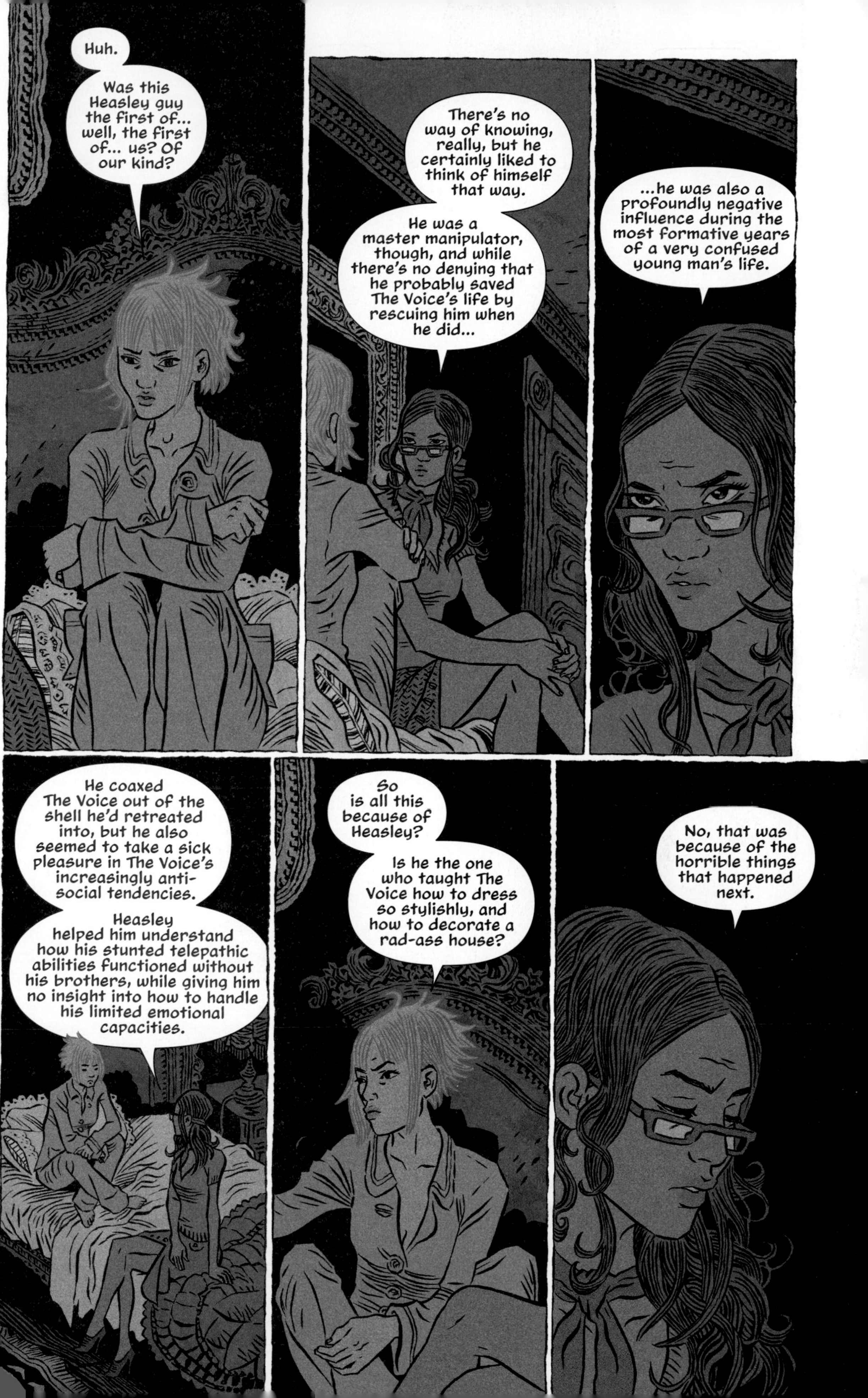
Huh.
Was this Heasley guy the first of... well, the first of... us? Of our kind?
There's no way of knowing, really, but he certainly liked to think of himself that way.
He was a master manipulator, though, and while there's no denying that he probably saved The Voice's life by rescuing him when he did...
...he was also a profoundly negative influence during the most formative years of a very confused young man's life.
He coaxed The Voice out of the shell he'd retreated into, but he also seemed to take a sick pleasure in The Voice's increasingly anti-social tendencies.
Heasley helped him understand how his stunted telepathic abilities functioned without his brothers, while giving him no insight into how to handle his limited emotional capacities.
So is all this because of Heasley?
Is he the one who taught The Voice how to dress so stylishly, and how to decorate a rad-ass house?
No, that was because of the horrible things that happened next.

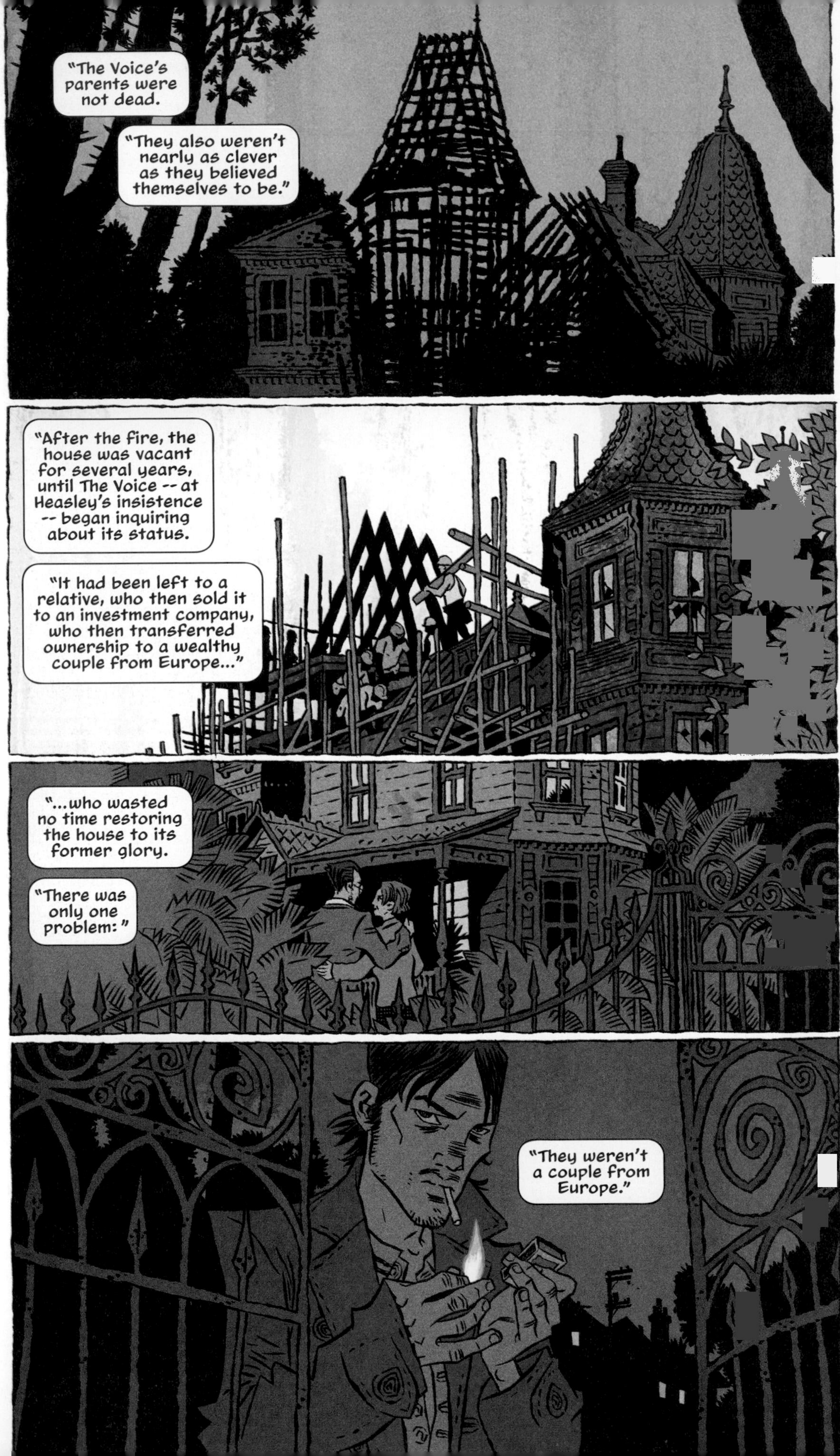
"The Voice's parents were not dead.
"They also weren't nearly as clever as they believed themselves to be."
"After the fire, the house was vacant for several years, until The Voice -- at Heasley's insistence -- began inquiring about its status.
"It had been left to a relative, who then sold it to an investment company, who then transferred ownership to a wealthy couple from Europe..."
"...who wasted no time restoring the house to its former glory.
"There was only one problem:"
"They weren't a couple from Europe."

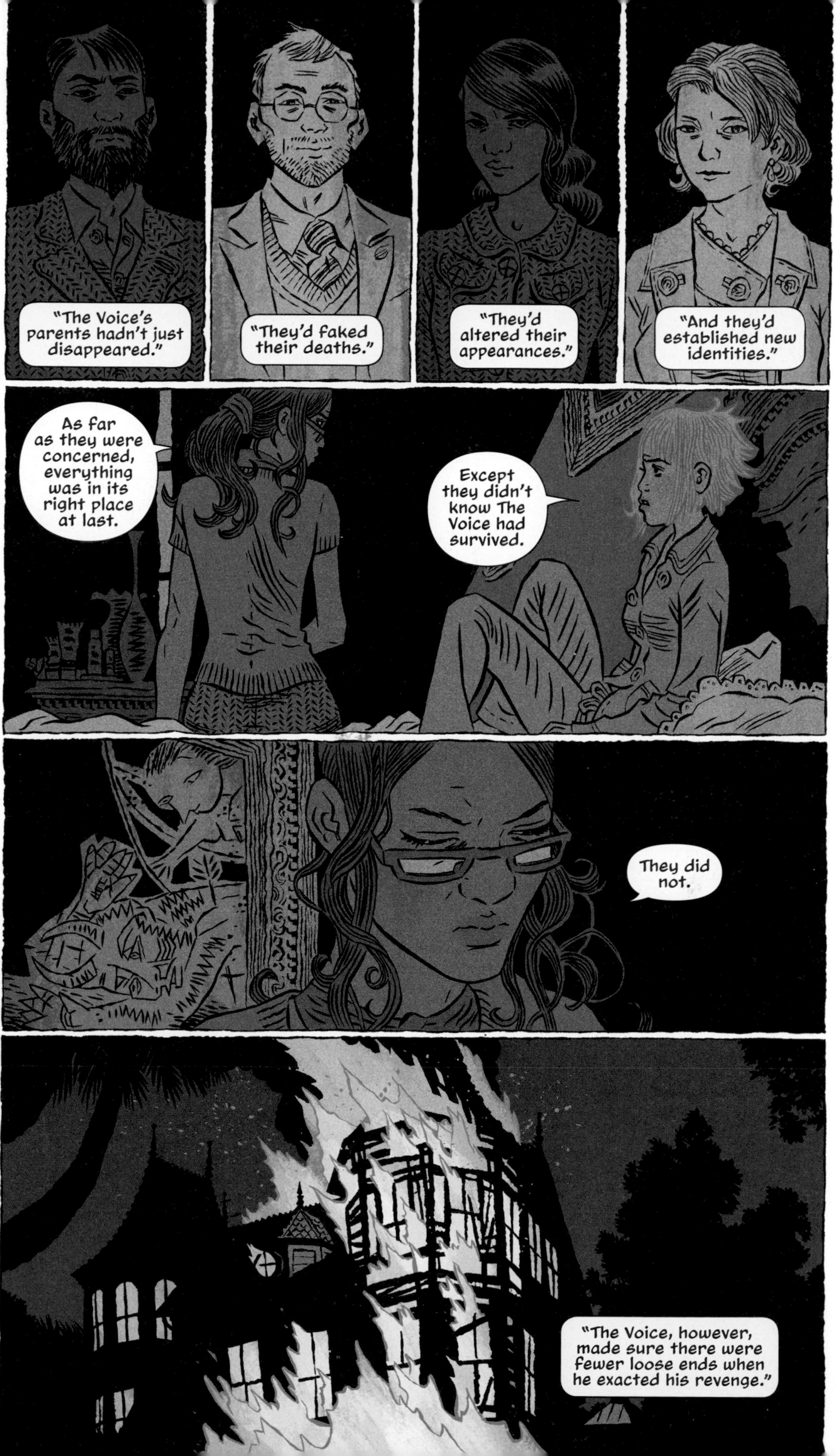
"The Voice's parents hadn't just disappeared."
"They'd faked their deaths."
"They'd altered their appearances."
"And they'd established new identities."
As far as they were concerned, everything was in its right place at last.
Except they didn't know The Voice had survived.
They did not.
"The Voice, however, made sure there were fewer loose ends when he exacted his revenge."

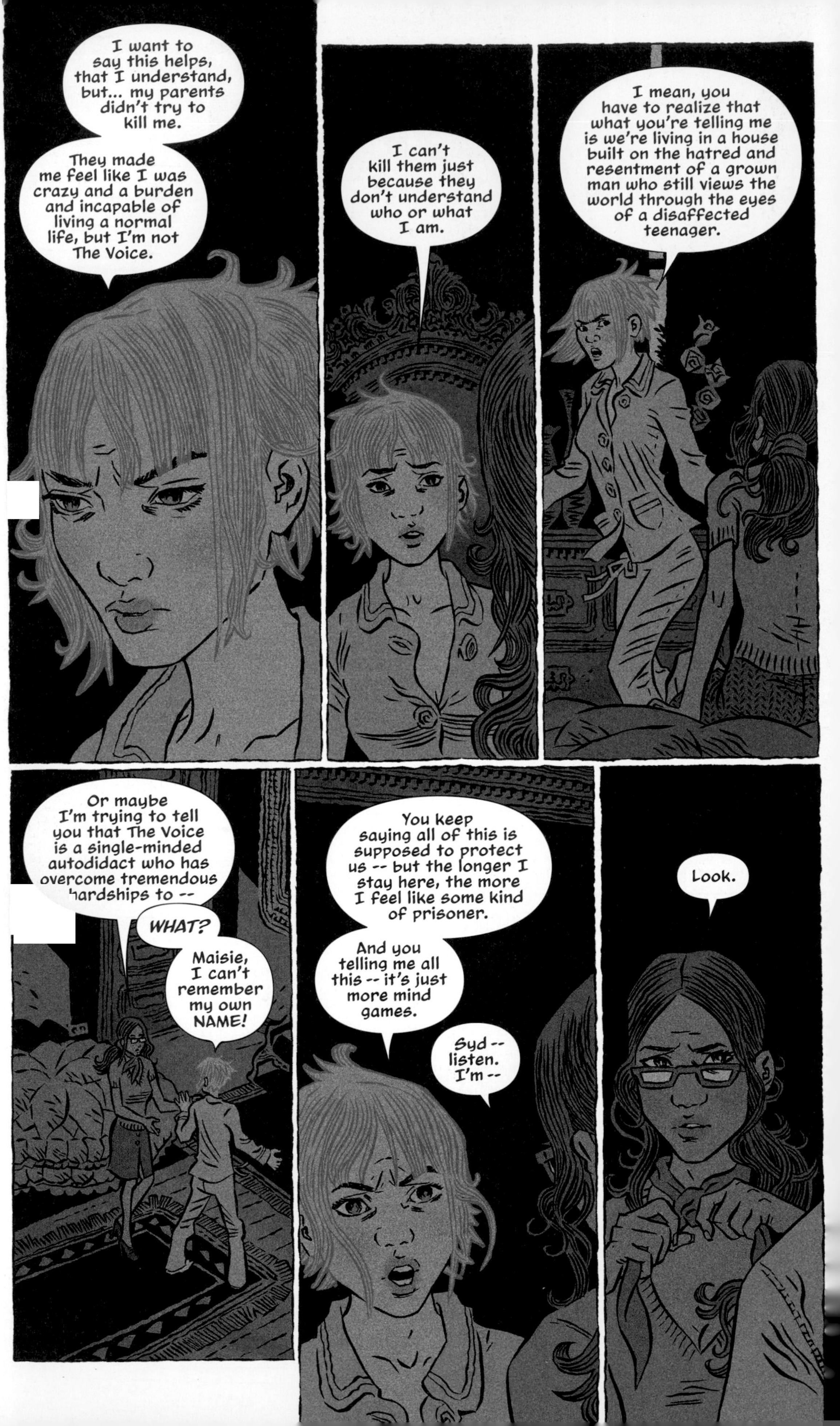
I want to say this helps, that I understand, but... my parents didn't try to kill me.
They made me feel like I was crazy and a burden and incapable of living a normal life, but I'm not The Voice.
I can't kill them just because they don't understand who or what I am.
I mean, you have to realize that what you're telling me is we're living in a house built on the hatred and resentment of a grown man who still views the world through the eyes of a disaffected teenager.
Or maybe I'm trying to tell you that The Voice is a single-minded autodidact who has overcome tremendous hardships to --
WHAT?
Maisie, I can't remember my own NAME!
You keep saying all of this is supposed to protect us -- but the longer I stay here, the more I feel like some kind of prisoner.
And you telling me all this -- it's just more mind games.
Syd -- listen. I'm --
Look.

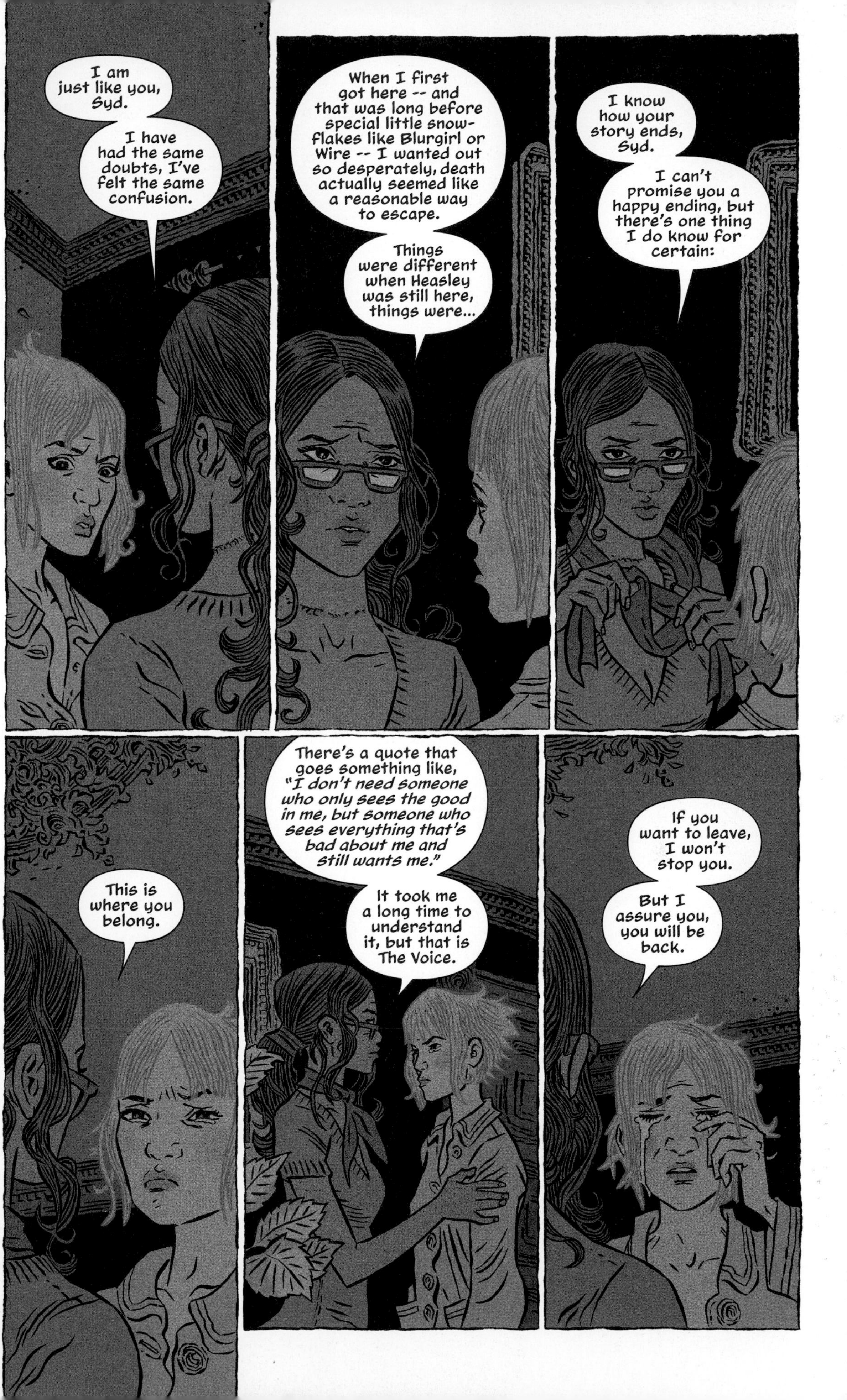
I am just like you, Syd.
I have had the same doubts, I've felt the same confusion.
When I first got here -- and that was long before special little snow-flakes like Blurgirl or Wire -- I wanted out so desperately, death actually seemed like a reasonable way to escape.
Things were different when Heasley was still here, things were...
I know how your story ends, Syd.
I can't promise you a happy ending, but there's one thing I do know for certain:
This is where you belong.
There's a quote that goes something like, "I don't need someone who only sees the good in me, but someone who sees everything that's bad about me and still wants me."
It took me a long time to understand it, but that is The Voice.
If you want to leave, I won't stop you.
But I assure you, you will be back.

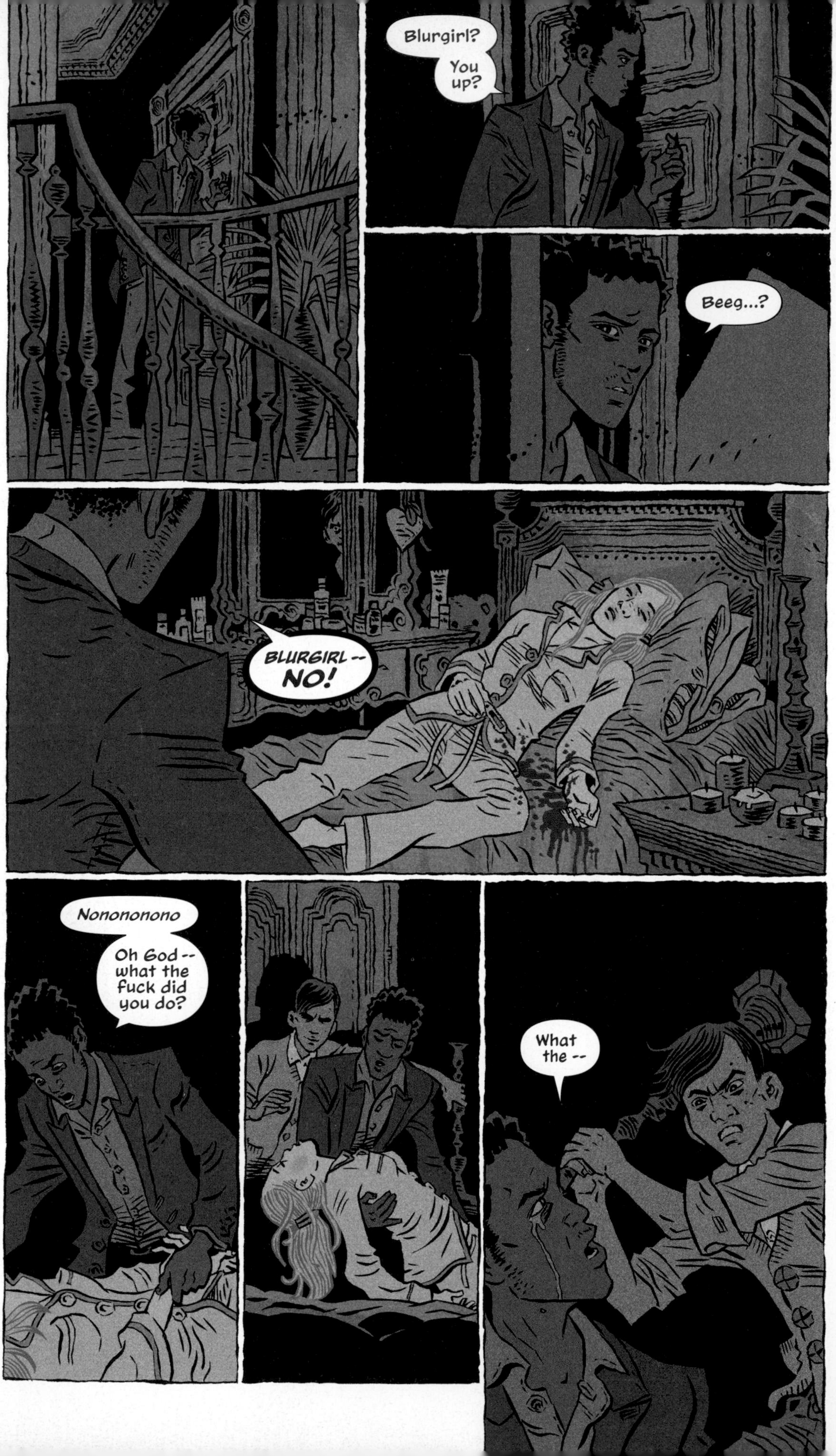
Blurgirl?
You up?
Beeg...?
BLURGIRL -- NO!
Nonononono
Oh God -- what the fuck did you do?
What the --

TO BETRAY,
YOU MUST
FIRST
BELONG

KIM PHILBY

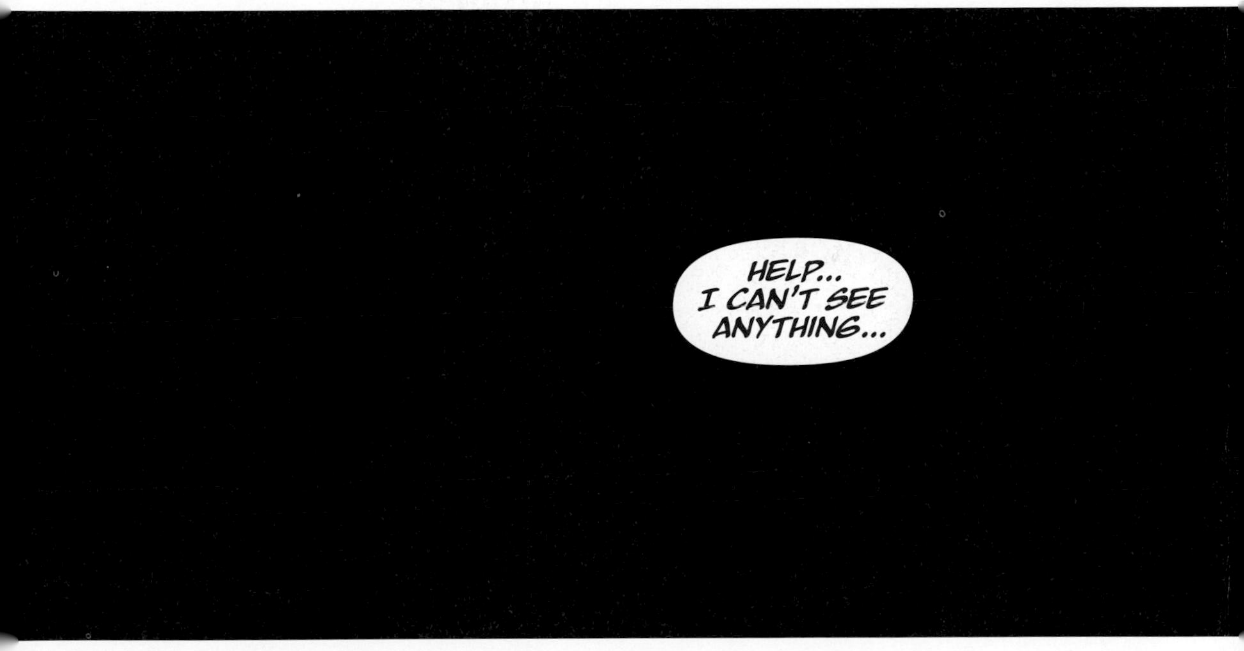
HELP...
I CAN'T SEE
ANYTHING...

6: ENGAGE WITH YOUR SHADOW

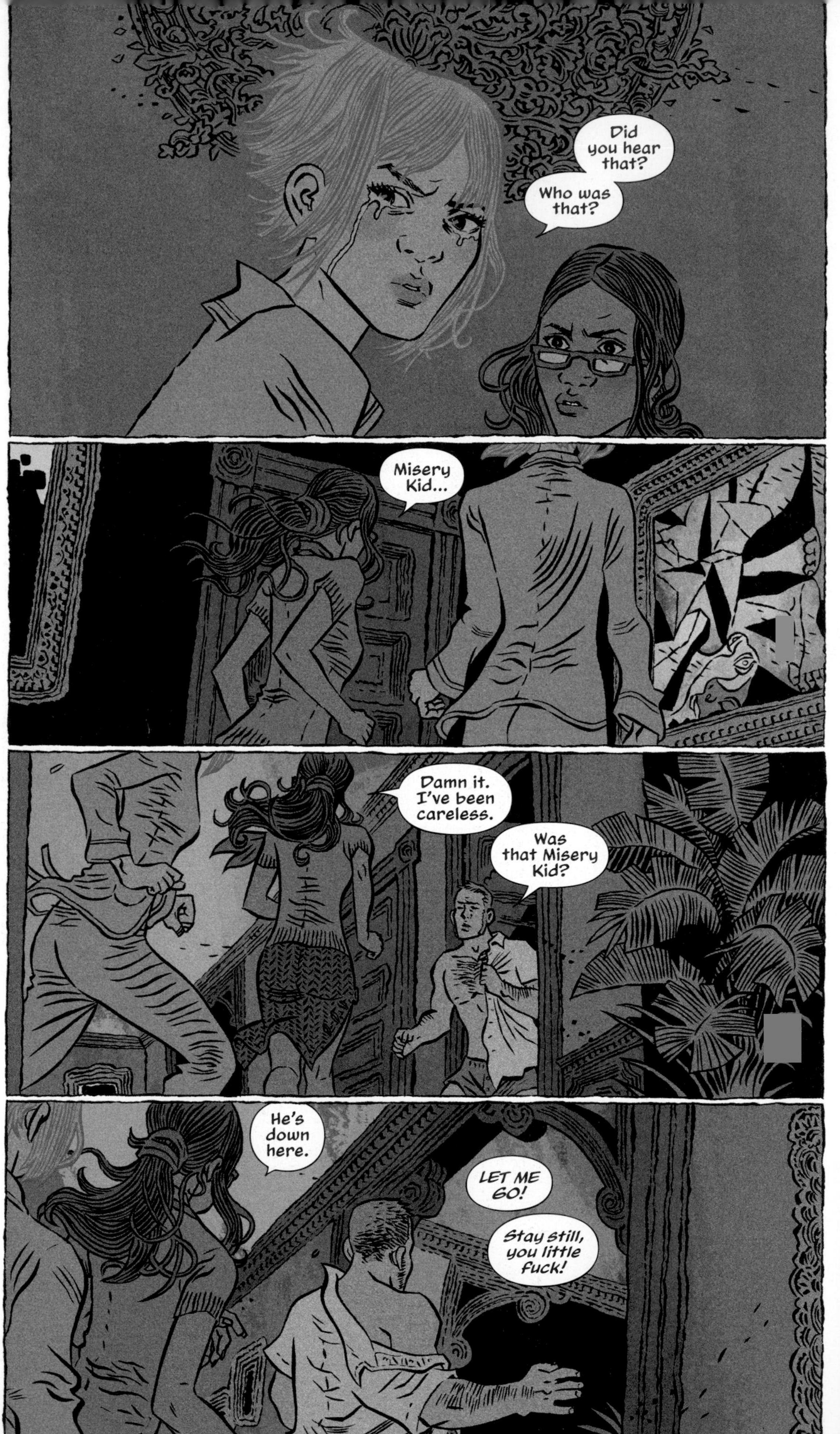
Did you hear that?
Who was that?
Misery Kid...
Damn it. I've been careless.
Was that Misery Kid?
He's down here.
LET ME GO!
Stay still, you little fuck!

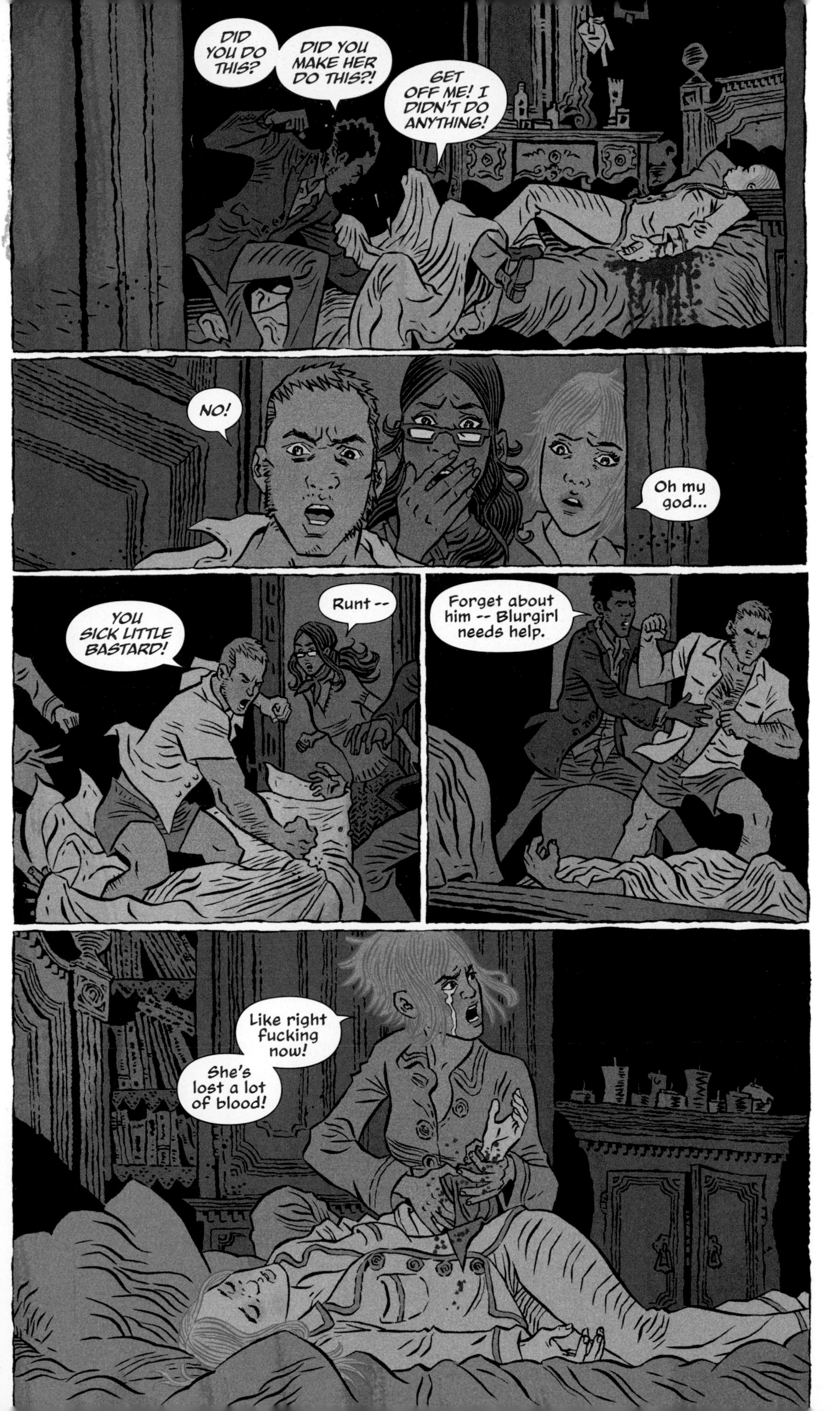
DID YOU DO THIS?
DID YOU MAKE HER DO THIS?!
GET OFF ME! I DIDN'T DO ANYTHING!
NO!
Oh my god...
YOU SICK LITTLE BASTARD!
Runt --
Forget about him -- Blurgirl needs help.
Like right fucking now!
She's lost a lot of blood!

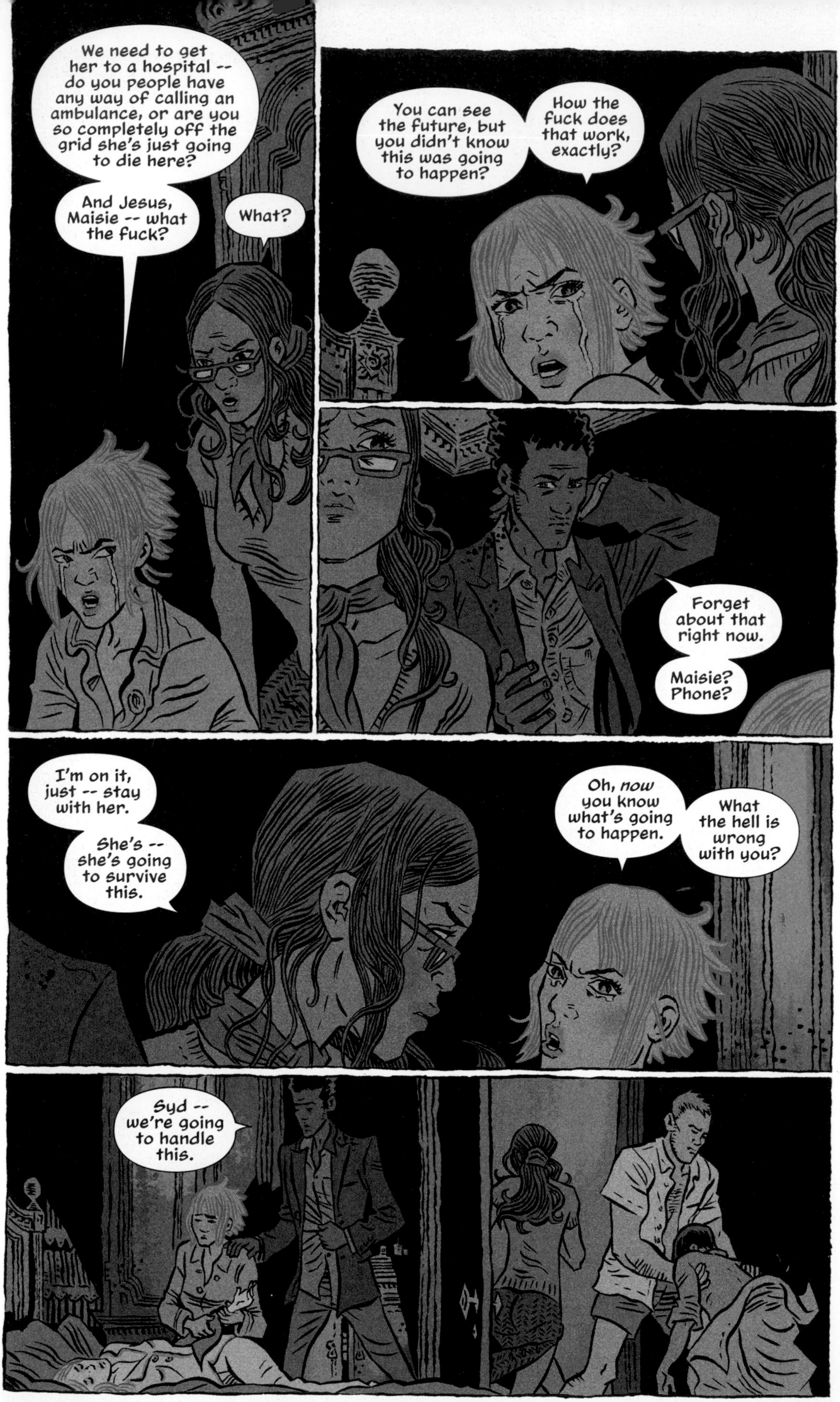
We need to get her to a hospital -- do you people have any way of calling an ambulance, or are you so completely off the grid she's just going to die here?
And Jesus, Maisie -- what the fuck?
What?
You can see the future, but you didn't know this was going to happen?
How the fuck does that work, exactly?
Forget about that right now.
Maisie? Phone?
I'm on it, just -- stay with her.
She's -- she's going to survive this.
Oh, *now* you know what's going to happen.
What the hell is wrong with you?
Syd -- we're going to handle this.

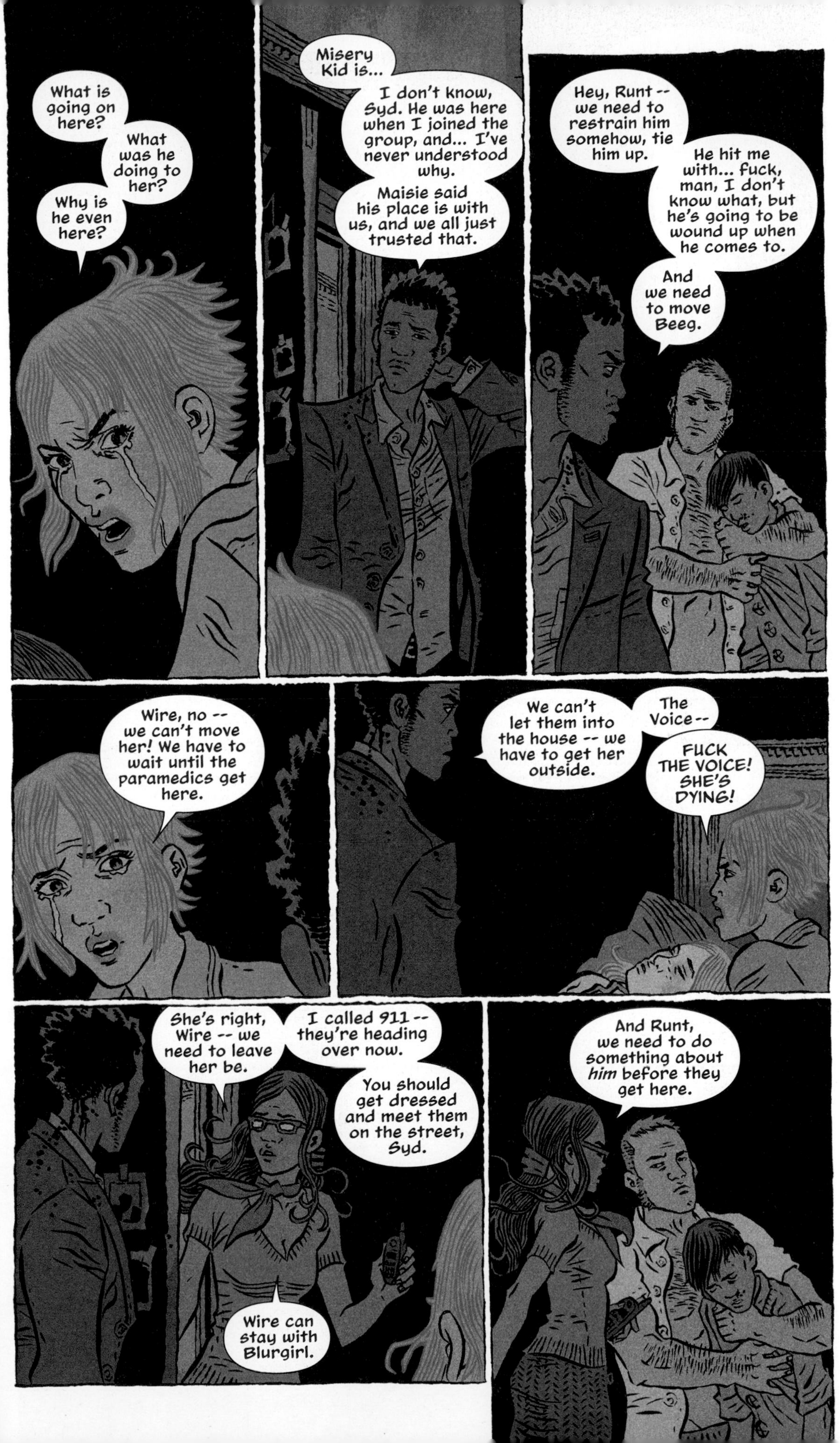
What is going on here?
What was he doing to her?
Why is he even here?
Misery Kid is...
I don't know, Syd. He was here when I joined the group, and... I've never understood why.
Maisie said his place is with us, and we all just trusted that.
Hey, Runt -- we need to restrain him somehow, tie him up.
He hit me with... fuck, man, I don't know what, but he's going to be wound up when he comes to.
And we need to move Beeg.
Wire, no -- we can't move her! We have to wait until the paramedics get here.
We can't let them into the house -- we have to get her outside.
The Voice --
FUCK THE VOICE! SHE'S DYING!
She's right, Wire -- we need to leave her be.
I called 911 -- they're heading over now.
You should get dressed and meet them on the street, Syd.
Wire can stay with Blurgirl.
And Runt, we need to do something about *him* before they get here.

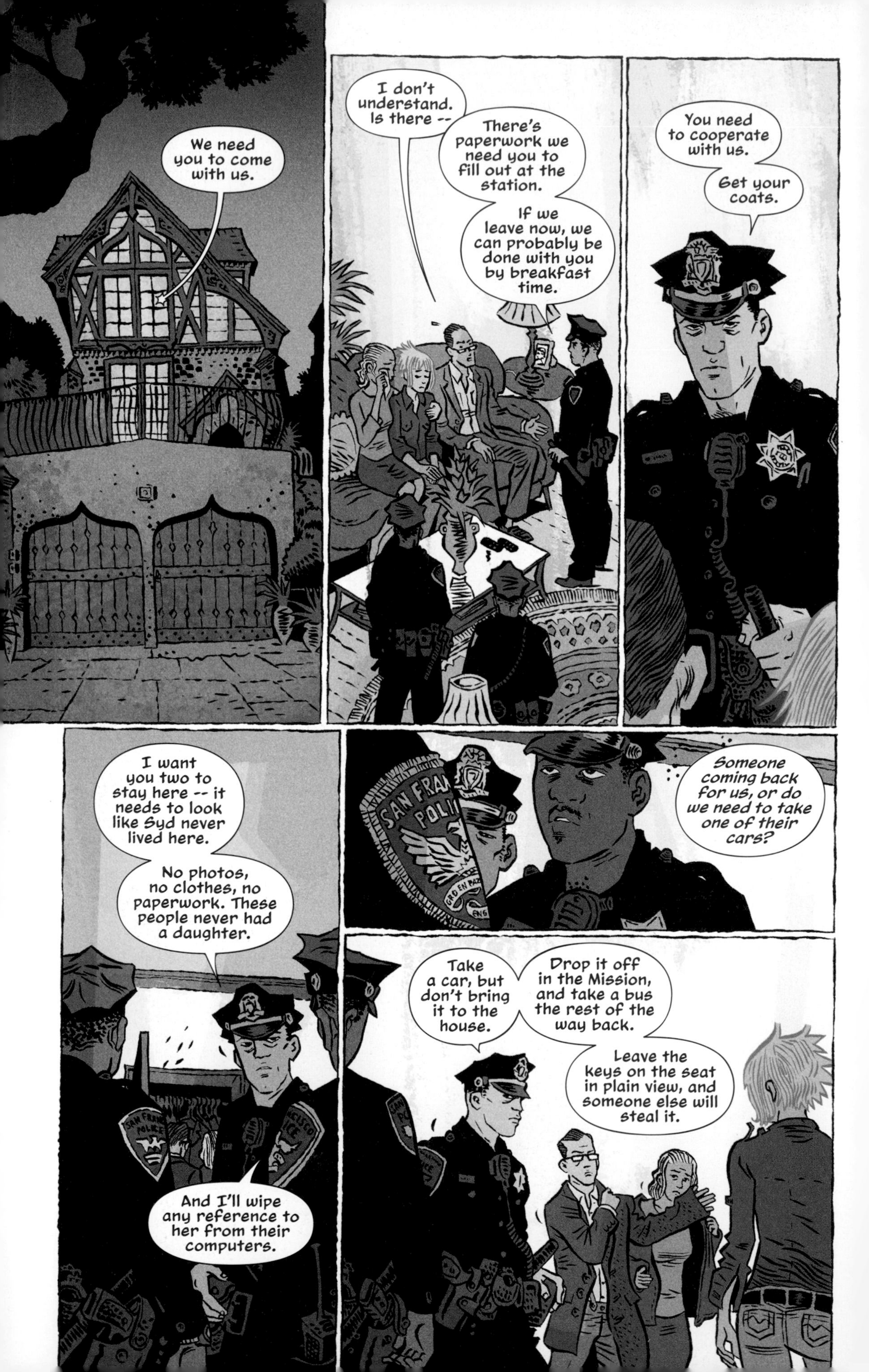
We need you to come with us.
I don't understand. Is there --
There's paperwork we need you to fill out at the station.
If we leave now, we can probably be done with you by breakfast time.
You need to cooperate with us.
Get your coats.
I want you two to stay here -- it needs to look like Syd never lived here.
No photos, no clothes, no paperwork. These people never had a daughter.
And I'll wipe any reference to her from their computers.
Someone coming back for us, or do we need to take one of their cars?
Take a car, but don't bring it to the house.
Drop it off in the Mission, and take a bus the rest of the way back.
Leave the keys on the seat in plain view, and someone else will steal it.

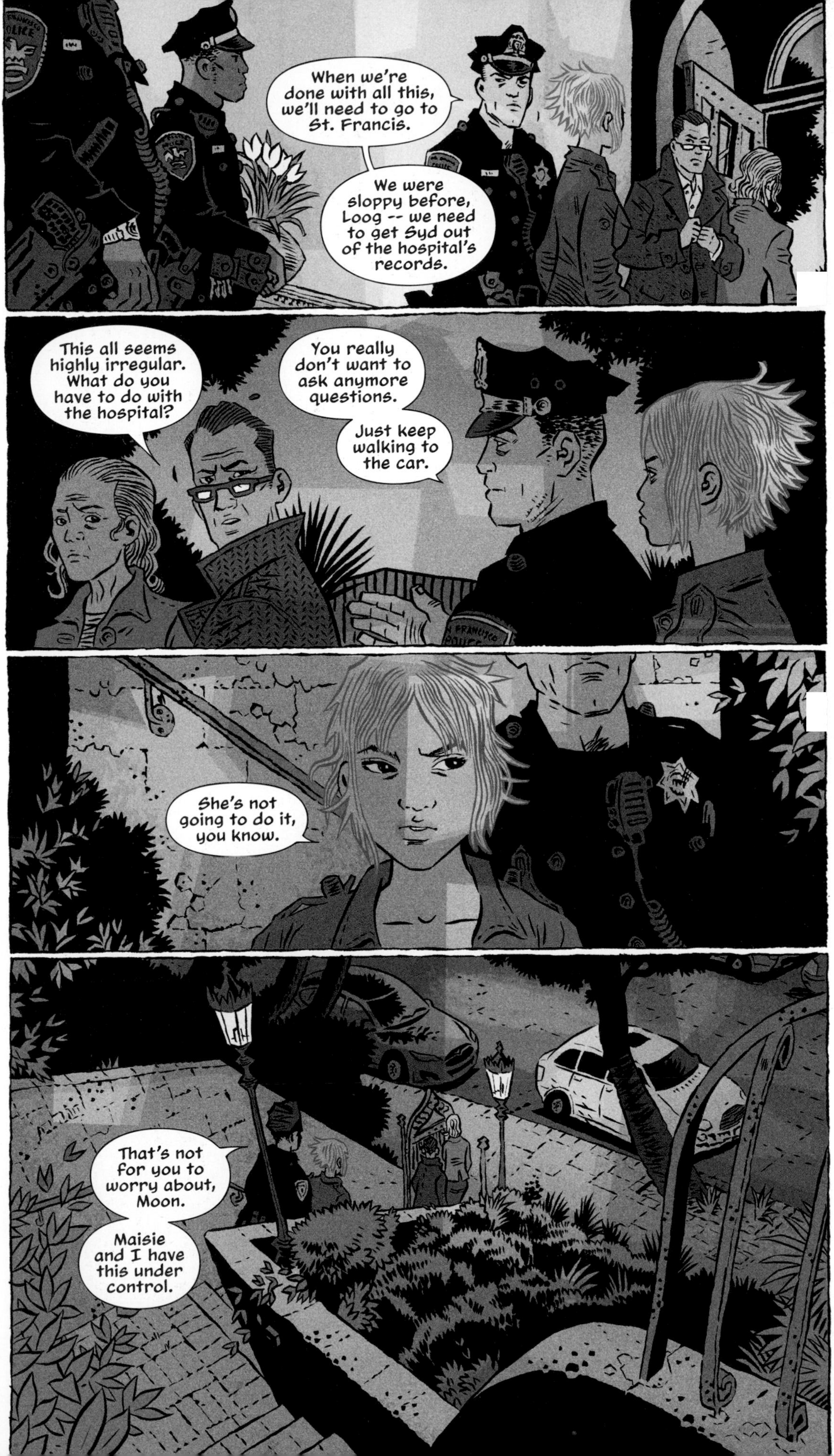
When we're done with all this, we'll need to go to St. Francis.
We were sloppy before, Loog -- we need to get Syd out of the hospital's records.
This all seems highly irregular. What do you have to do with the hospital?
You really don't want to ask anymore questions.
Just keep walking to the car.
She's not going to do it, you know.
That's not for you to worry about, Moon.
Maisie and I have this under control.

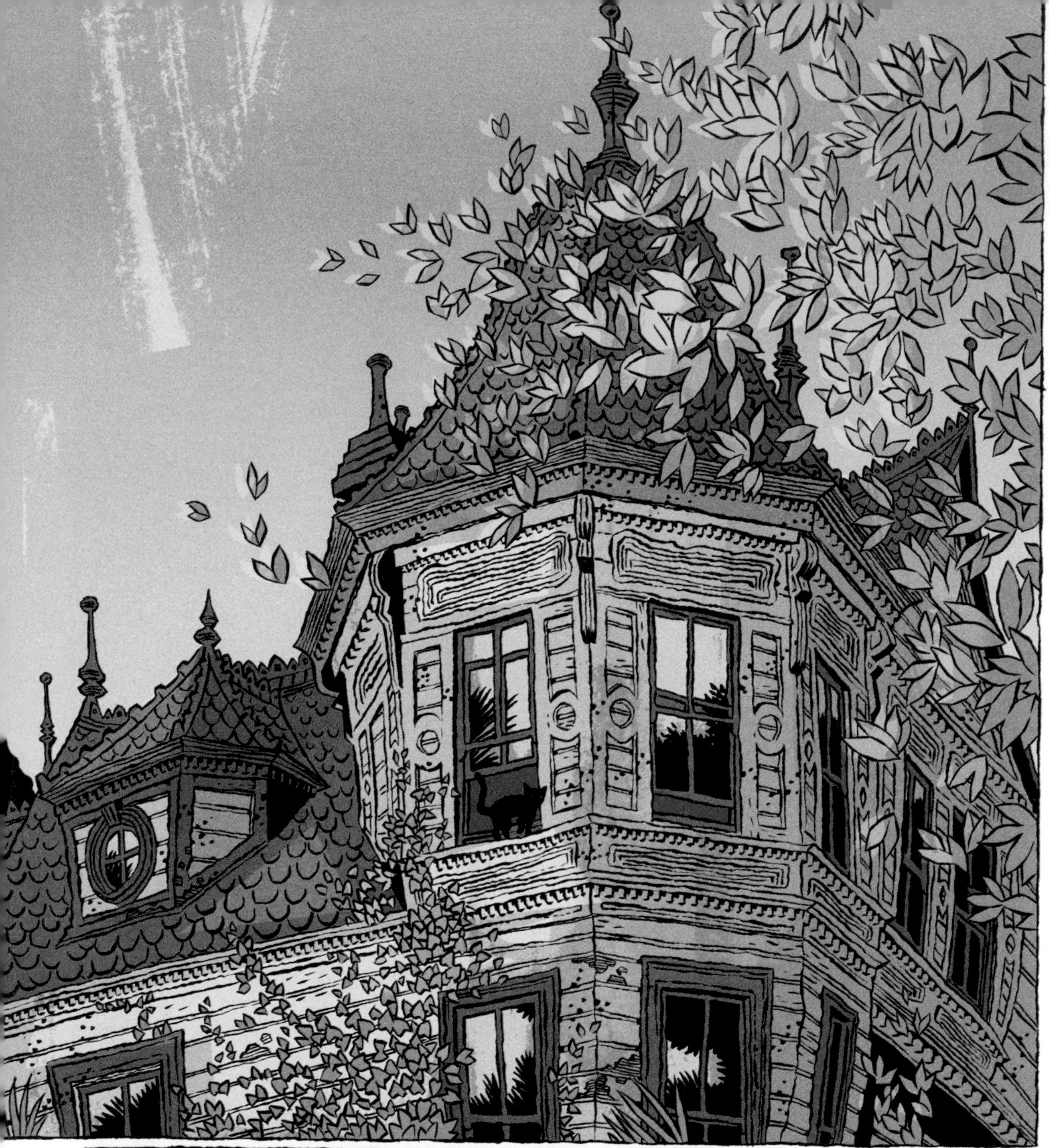

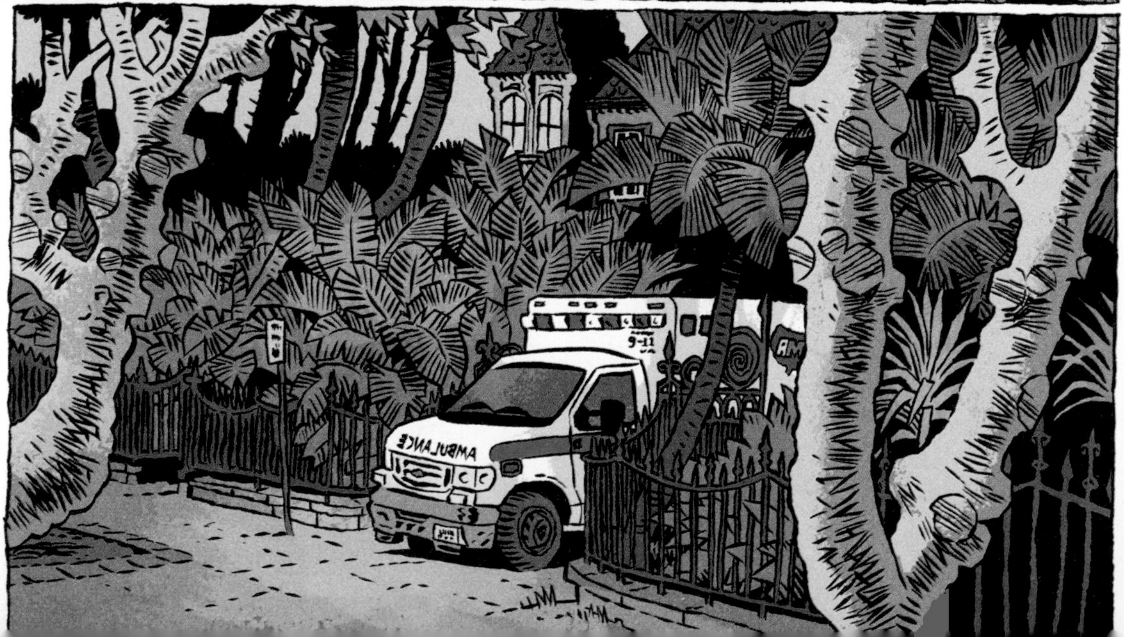
AMBULANCE
9-11

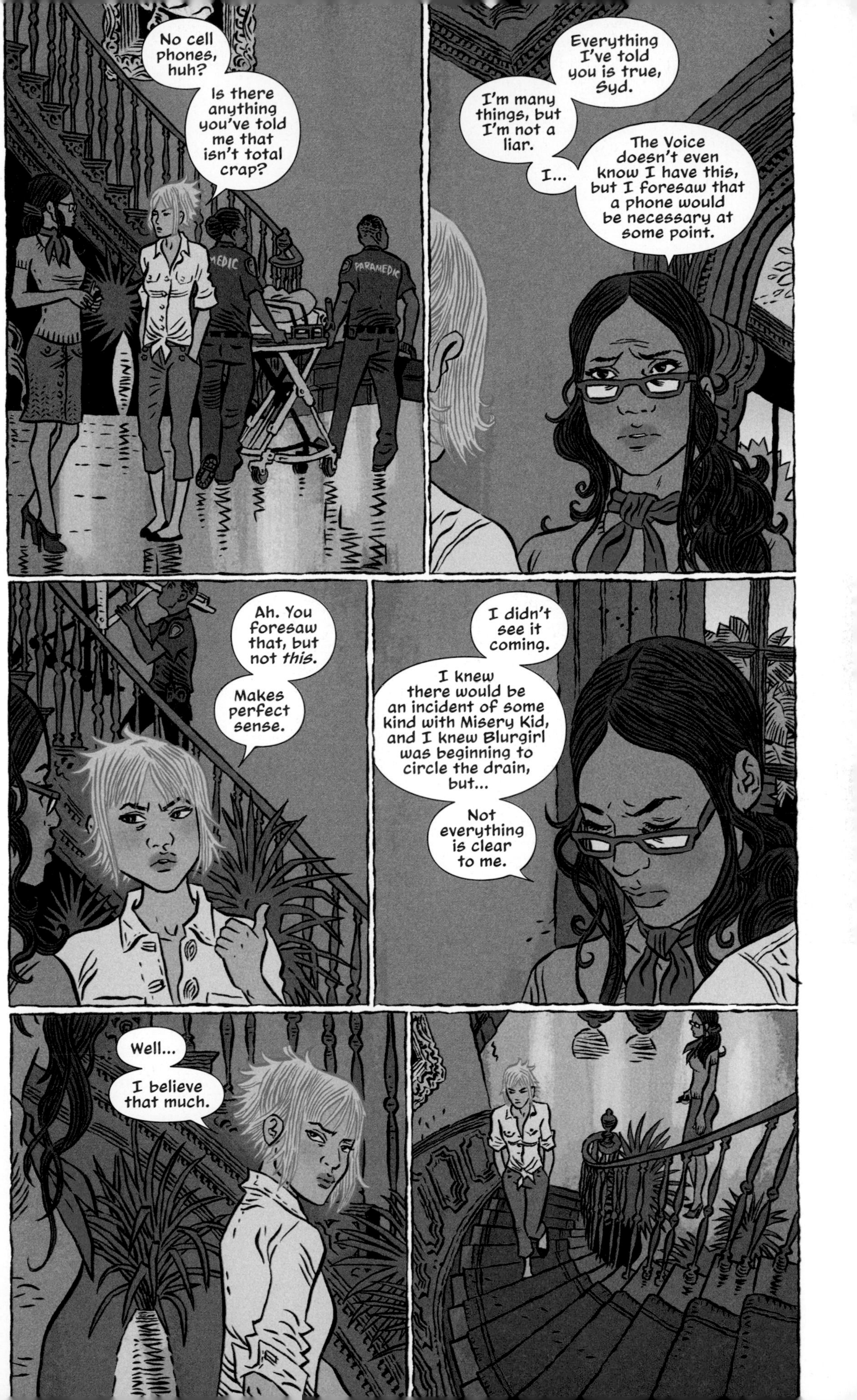
No cell phones, huh?
Is there anything you've told me that isn't total crap?
MEDIC
PARAMEDIC
Everything I've told you is true, Syd.
I'm many things, but I'm not a liar.
I...
The Voice doesn't even know I have this, but I foresaw that a phone would be necessary at some point.
Ah. You foresaw that, but not *this*.
Makes perfect sense.
I didn't see it coming.
I knew there would be an incident of some kind with Misery Kid, and I knew Blurgirl was beginning to circle the drain, but...
Not everything is clear to me.
Well...
I believe that much.

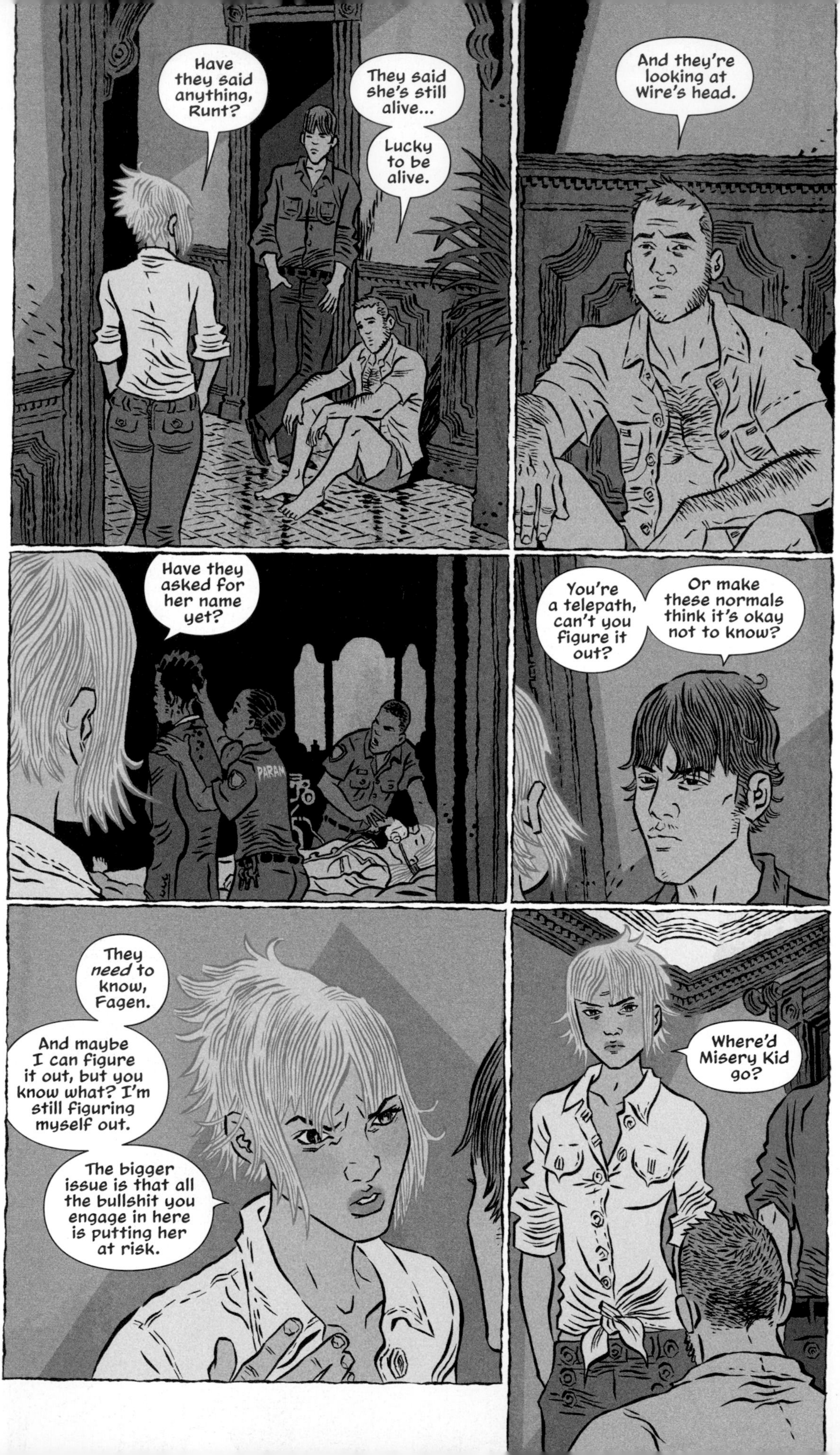

Have they said anything, Runt?
They said she's still alive...
Lucky to be alive.
And they're looking at Wire's head.
Have they asked for her name yet?
PARAM
You're a telepath, can't you figure it out?
Or make these normals think it's okay not to know?
They *need* to know, Fagen.
And maybe I can figure it out, but you know what? I'm still figuring myself out.
The bigger issue is that all the bullshit you engage in here is putting her at risk.
Where'd Misery Kid go?

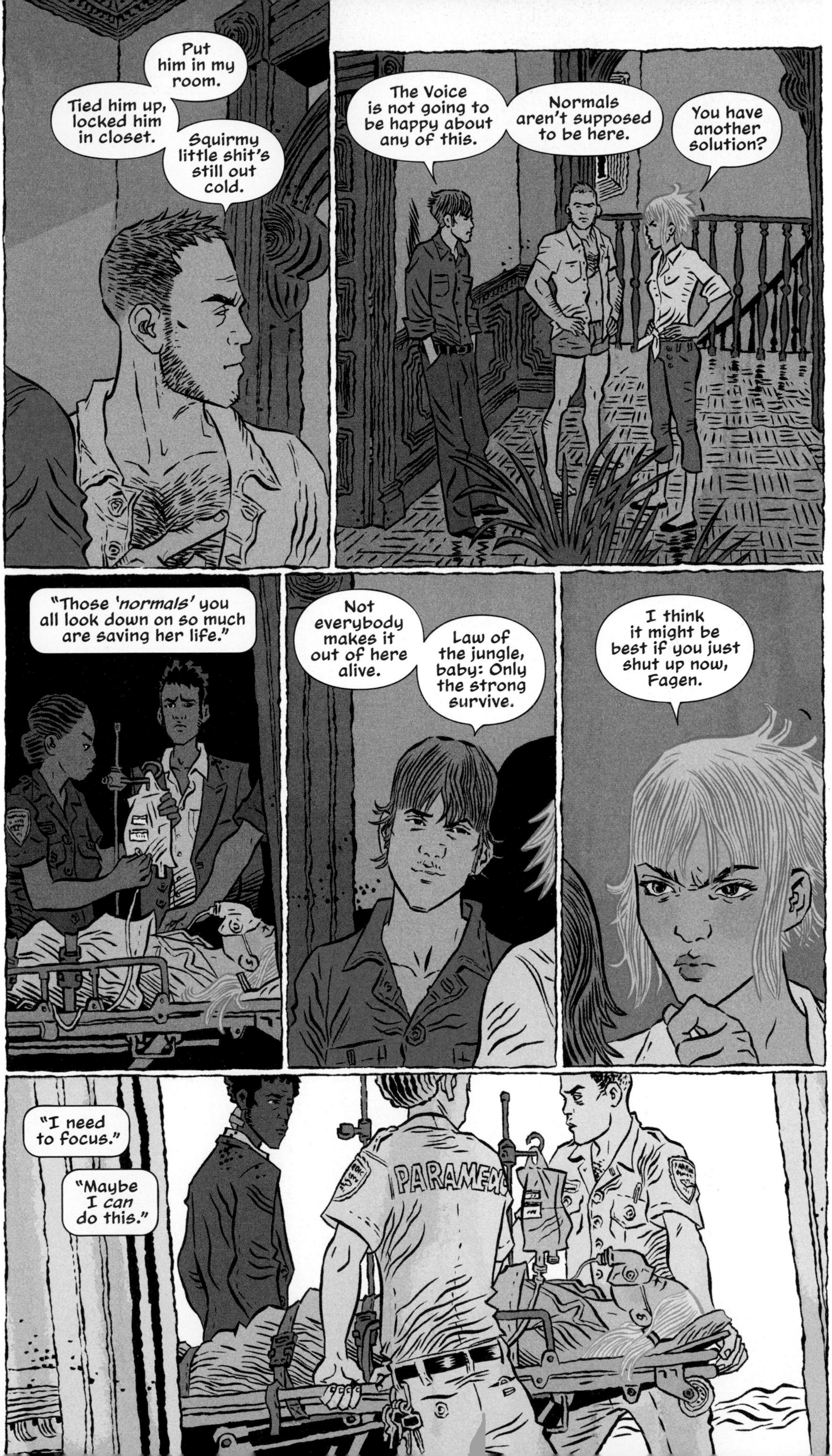
Put him in my room.
Tied him up, locked him in closet.
Squirmy little shit's still out cold.
The Voice is not going to be happy about any of this.
Normals aren't supposed to be here.
You have another solution?
"Those '*normals*' you all look down on so much are saving her life."
Not everybody makes it out of here alive.
Law of the jungle, baby: Only the strong survive.
I think it might be best if you just shut up now, Fagen.
"I need to focus."
"Maybe I *can* do this."
PARAMEDIC

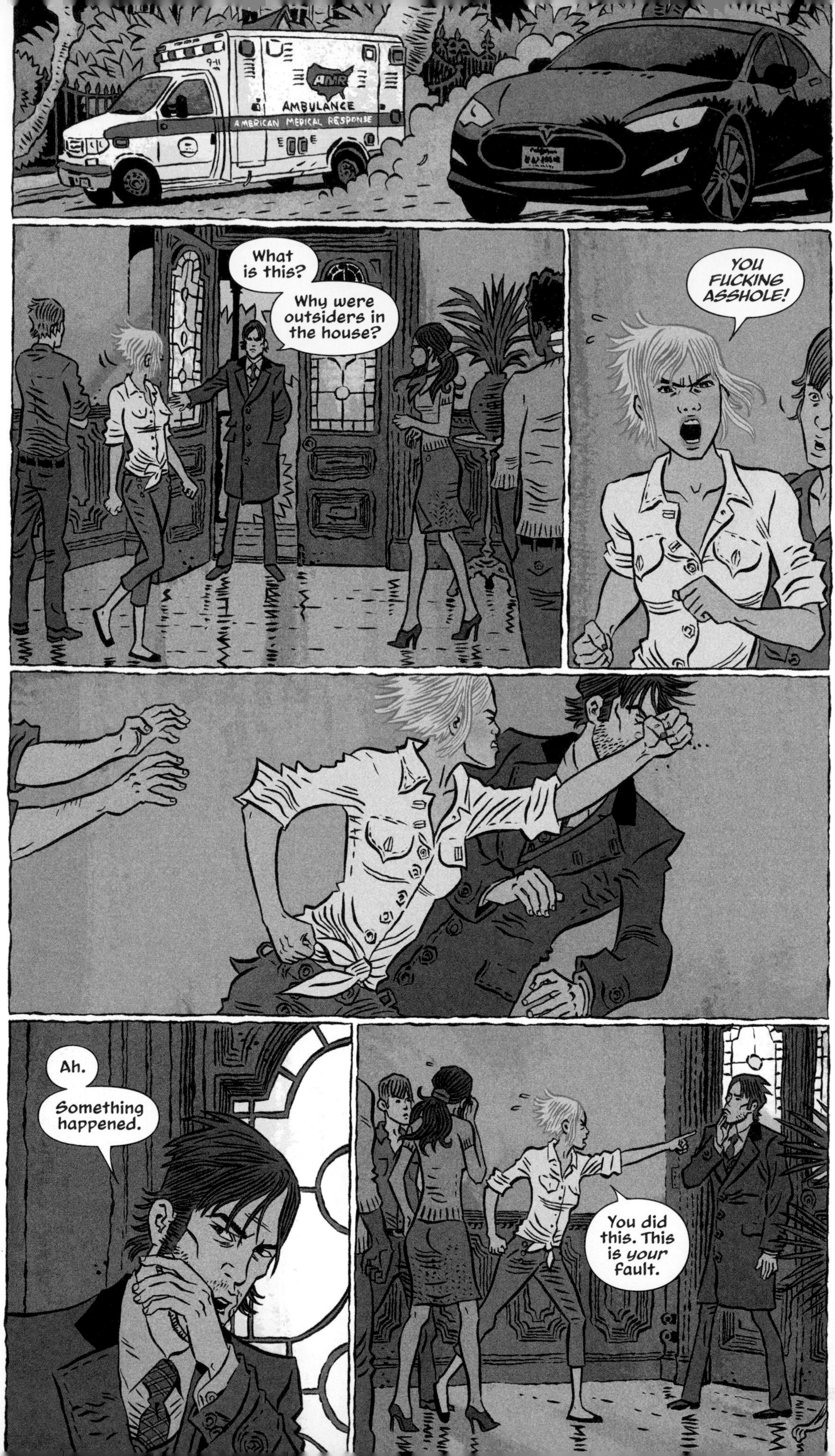
AMBULANCE
AMERICAN MEDICAL RESPONSE
What is this?
Why were outsiders in the house?
YOU FUCKING ASSHOLE!
Ah.
Something happened.
You did this. This is *your* fault.

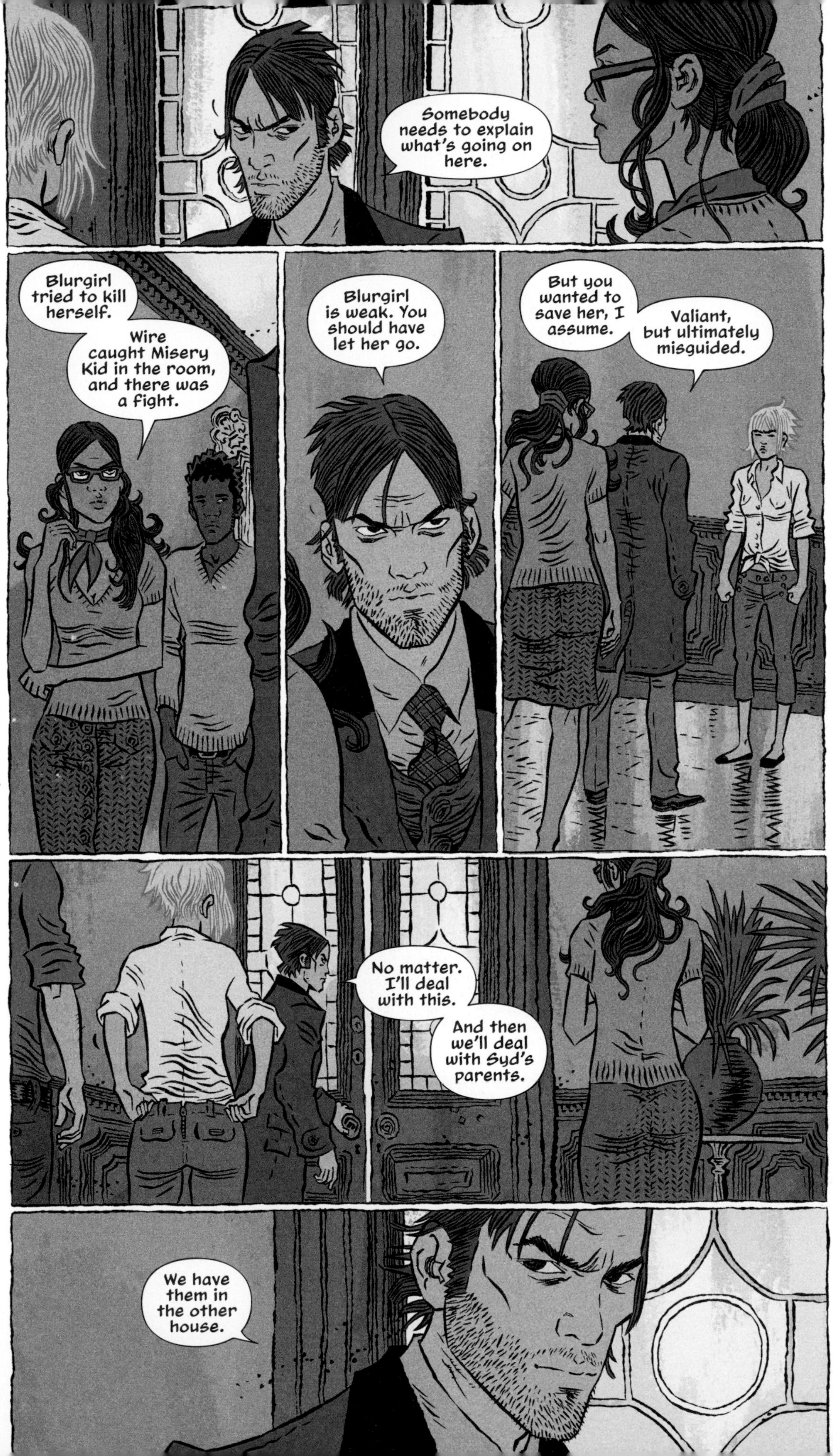
Somebody needs to explain what's going on here.
Blurgirl tried to kill herself.
Wire caught Misery Kid in the room, and there was a fight.
Blurgirl is weak. You should have let her go.
But you wanted to save her, I assume.
Valiant, but ultimately misguided.
No matter. I'll deal with this.
And then we'll deal with Syd's parents.
We have them in the other house.

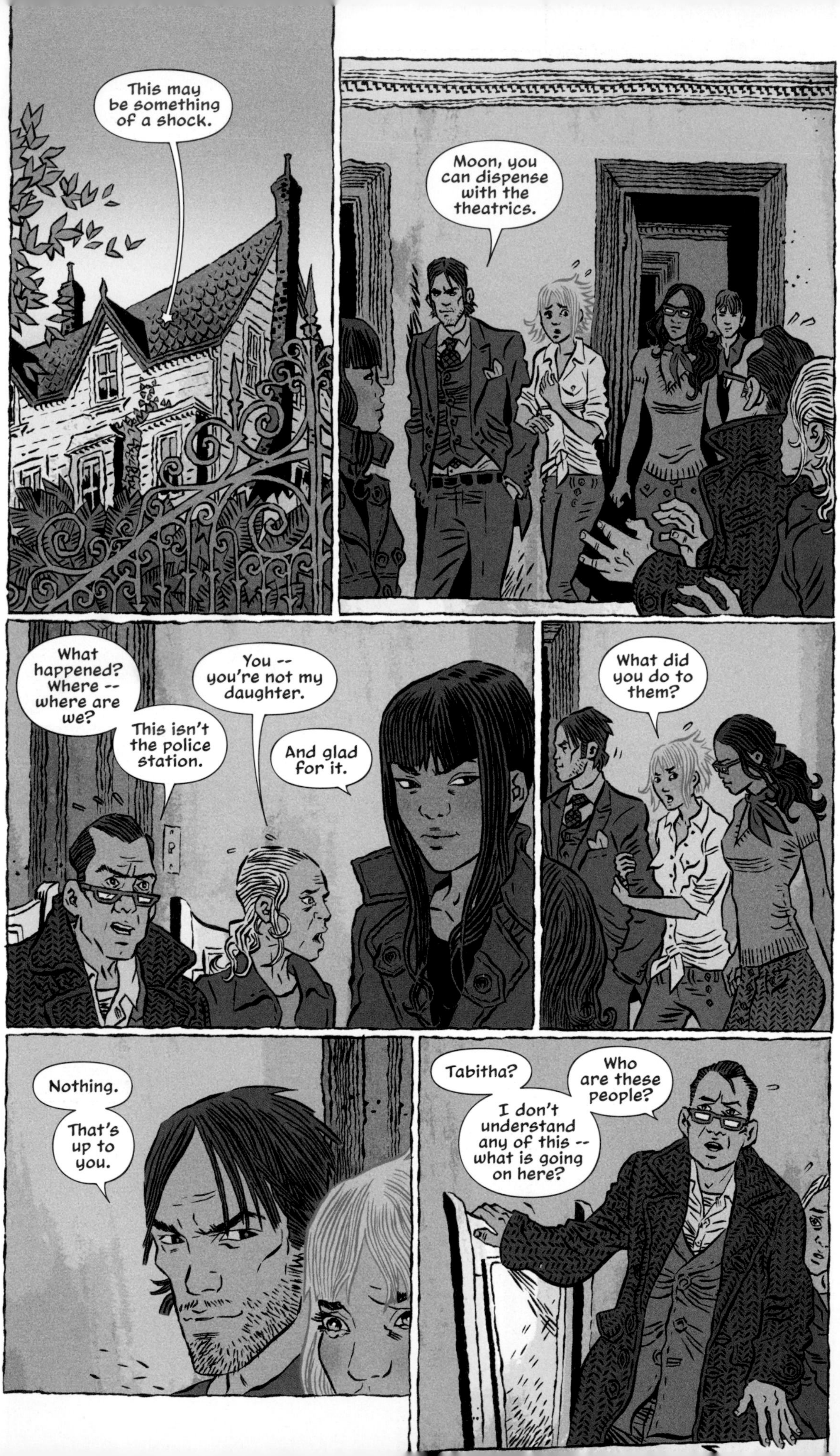
This may be something of a shock.
Moon, you can dispense with the theatrics.
What happened? Where -- where are we?
This isn't the police station.
You -- you're not my daughter.
And glad for it.
What did you do to them?
Nothing.
That's up to you.
Tabitha?
Who are these people?
I don't understand any of this -- what is going on here?

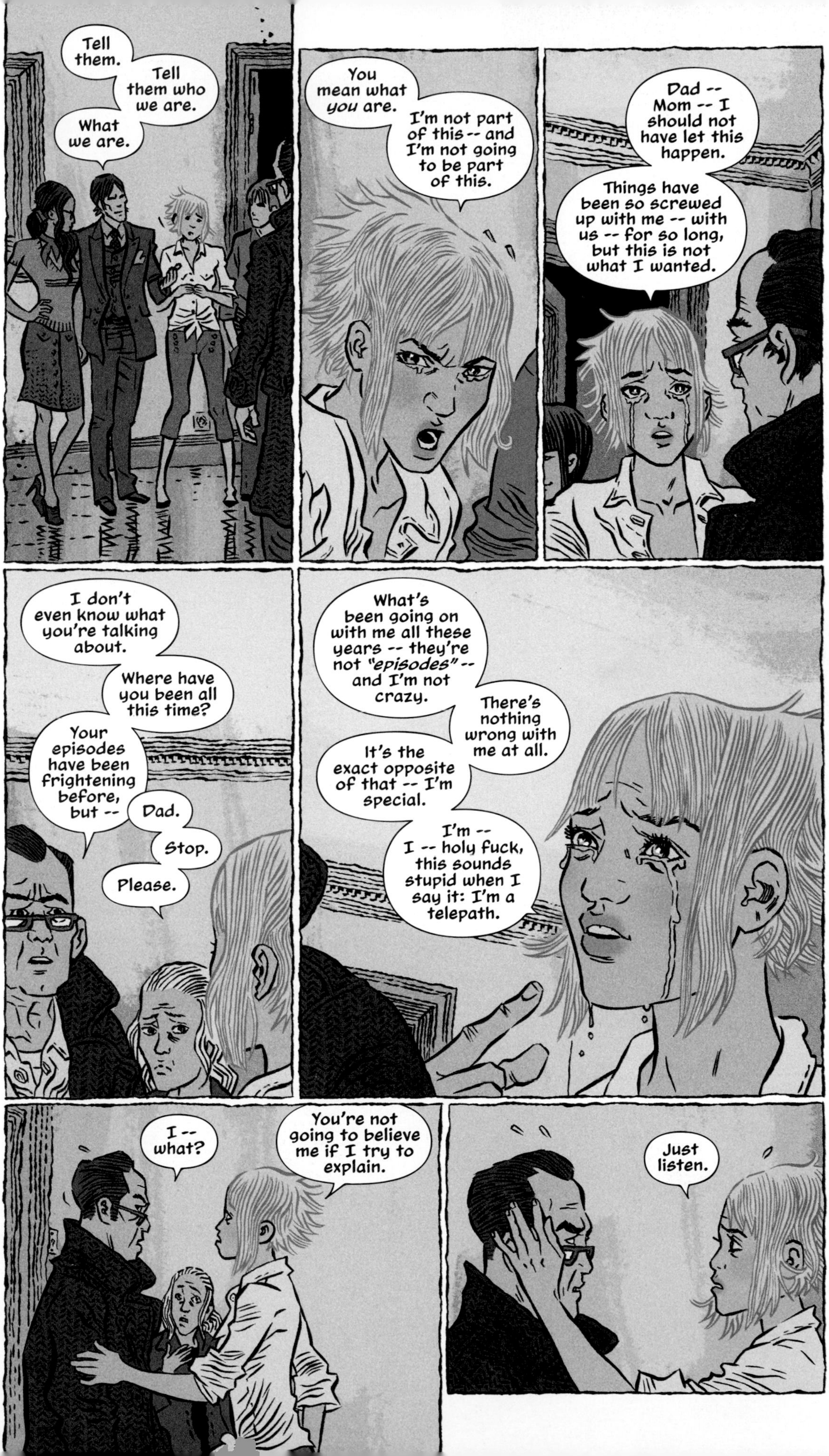
Tell them.
Tell them who we are.
What we are.
You mean what *you* are.
I'm not part of this -- and I'm not going to be part of this.
Dad -- Mom -- I should not have let this happen.
Things have been so screwed up with me -- with us -- for so long, but this is not what I wanted.
I don't even know what you're talking about.
Where have you been all this time?
Your episodes have been frightening before, but --
Dad.
Stop.
Please.
What's been going on with me all these years -- they're not *"episodes"* -- and I'm not crazy.
There's nothing wrong with me at all.
It's the exact opposite of that -- I'm special.
I'm -- I -- holy fuck, this sounds stupid when I say it: I'm a telepath.
I -- what?
You're not going to believe me if I try to explain.
Just listen.

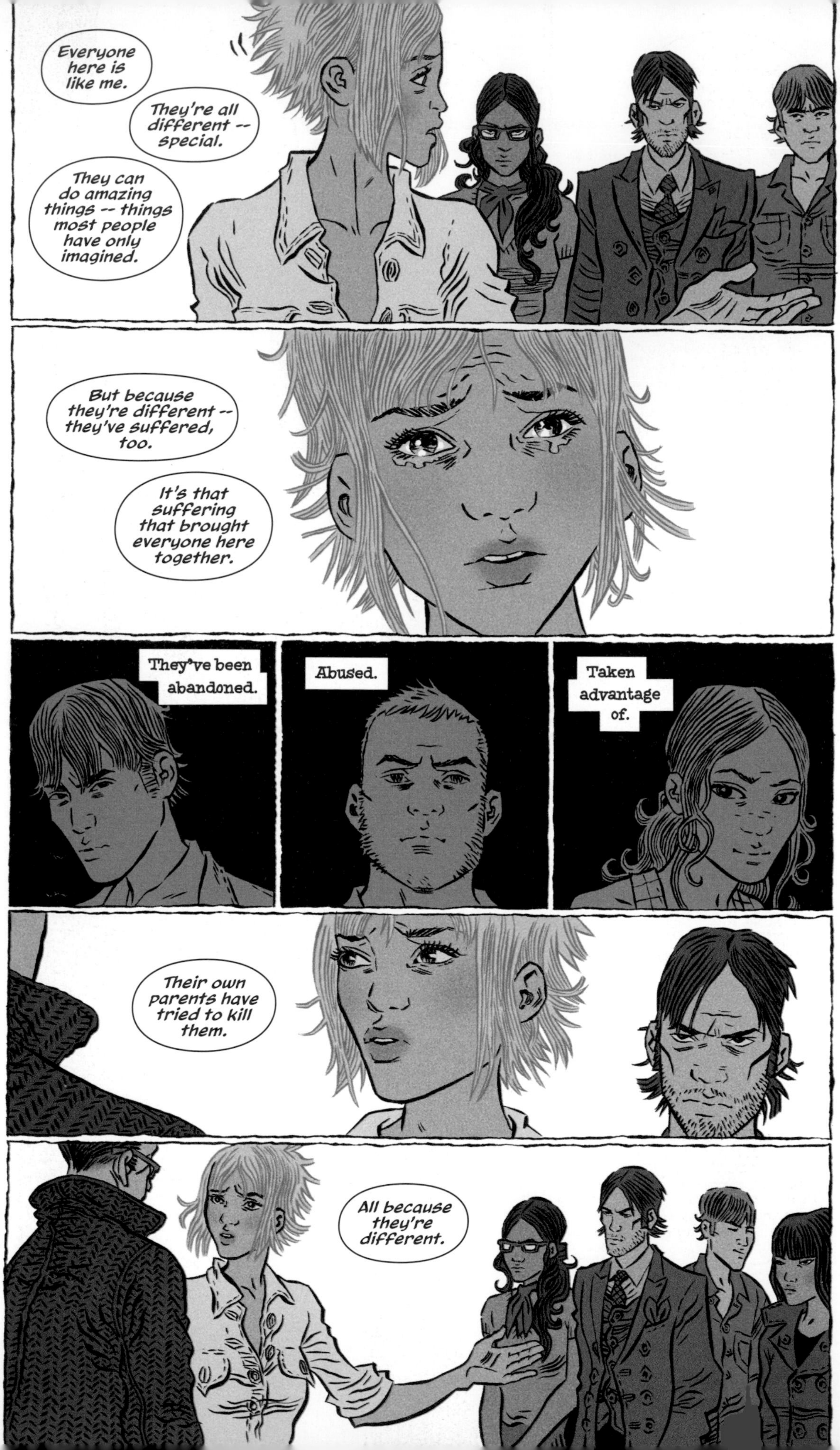
Everyone here is like me.
They're all different -- special.
They can do amazing things -- things most people have only imagined.
But because they're different -- they've suffered, too.
It's that suffering that brought everyone here together.
They've been abandoned.
Abused.
Taken advantage of.
Their own parents have tried to kill them.
All because they're different.

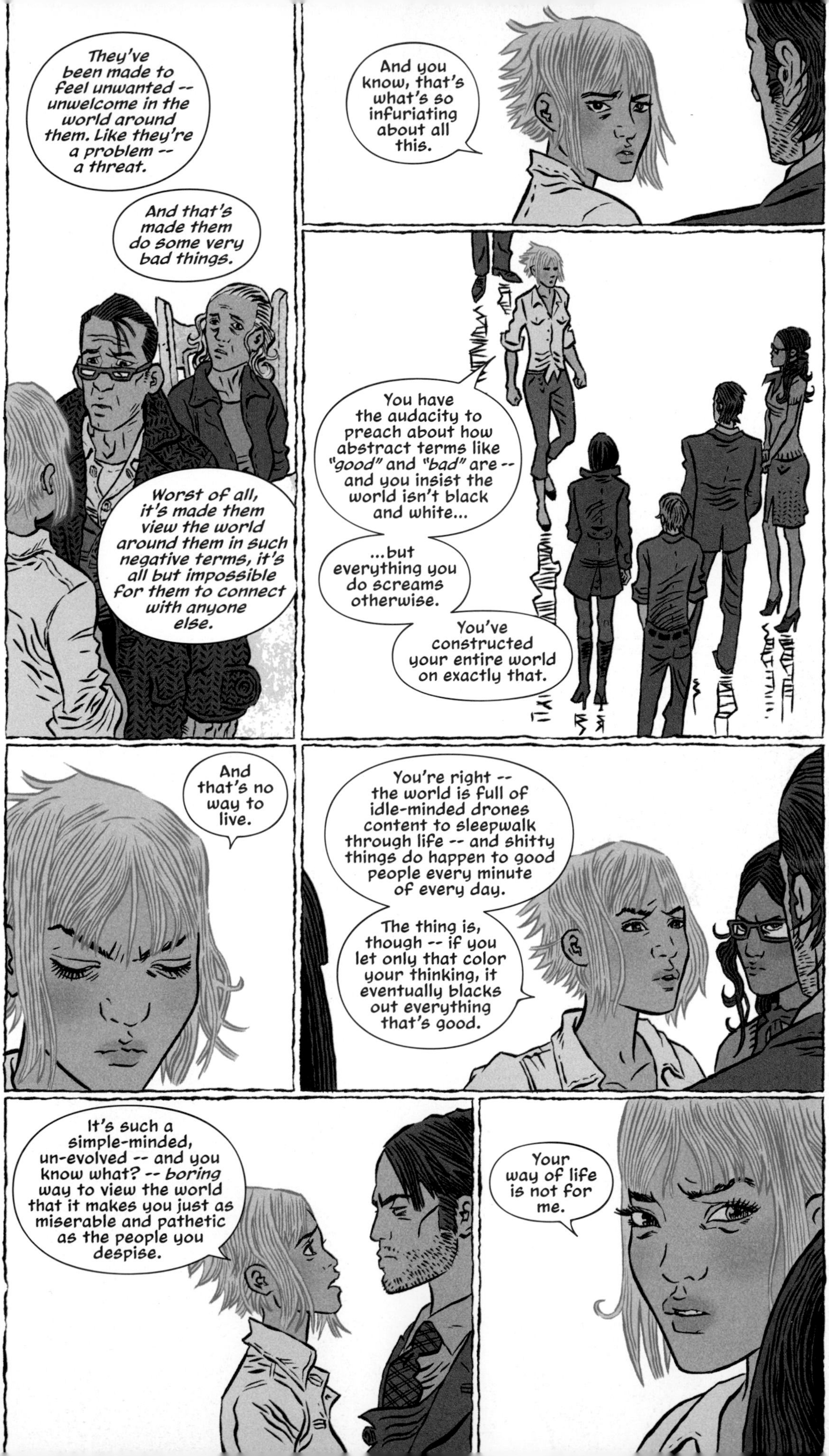
They've been made to feel unwanted -- unwelcome in the world around them. Like they're a problem -- a threat.
And that's made them do some very bad things.
Worst of all, it's made them view the world around them in such negative terms, it's all but impossible for them to connect with anyone else.
And you know, that's what's so infuriating about all this.
You have the audacity to preach about how abstract terms like "good" and "bad" are -- and you insist the world isn't black and white...
...but everything you do screams otherwise.
You've constructed your entire world on exactly that.
And that's no way to live.
You're right -- the world is full of idle-minded drones content to sleepwalk through life -- and shitty things do happen to good people every minute of every day.
The thing is, though -- if you let only that color your thinking, it eventually blacks out everything that's good.
It's such a simple-minded, un-evolved -- and you know what? -- boring way to view the world that it makes you just as miserable and pathetic as the people you despise.
Your way of life is not for me.

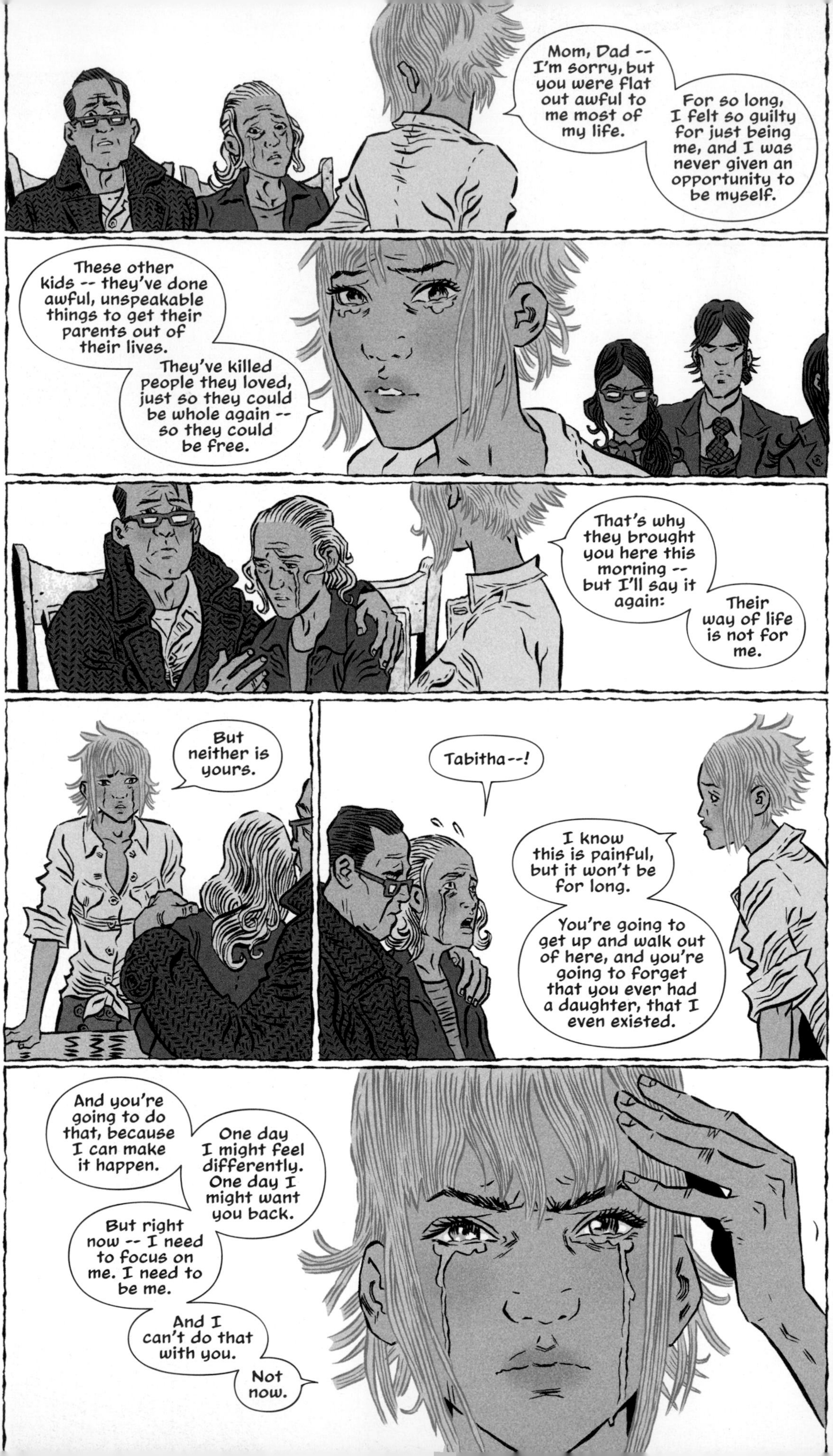
Mom, Dad -- I'm sorry, but you were flat out awful to me most of my life.
For so long, I felt so guilty for just being me, and I was never given an opportunity to be myself.
These other kids -- they've done awful, unspeakable things to get their parents out of their lives.
They've killed people they loved, just so they could be whole again -- so they could be free.
That's why they brought you here this morning -- but I'll say it again:
Their way of life is not for me.
But neither is yours.
Tabitha--!
I know this is painful, but it won't be for long.
You're going to get up and walk out of here, and you're going to forget that you ever had a daughter, that I even existed.
And you're going to do that, because I can make it happen.
One day I might feel differently. One day I might want you back.
But right now -- I need to focus on me. I need to be me.
And I can't do that with you.
Not now.

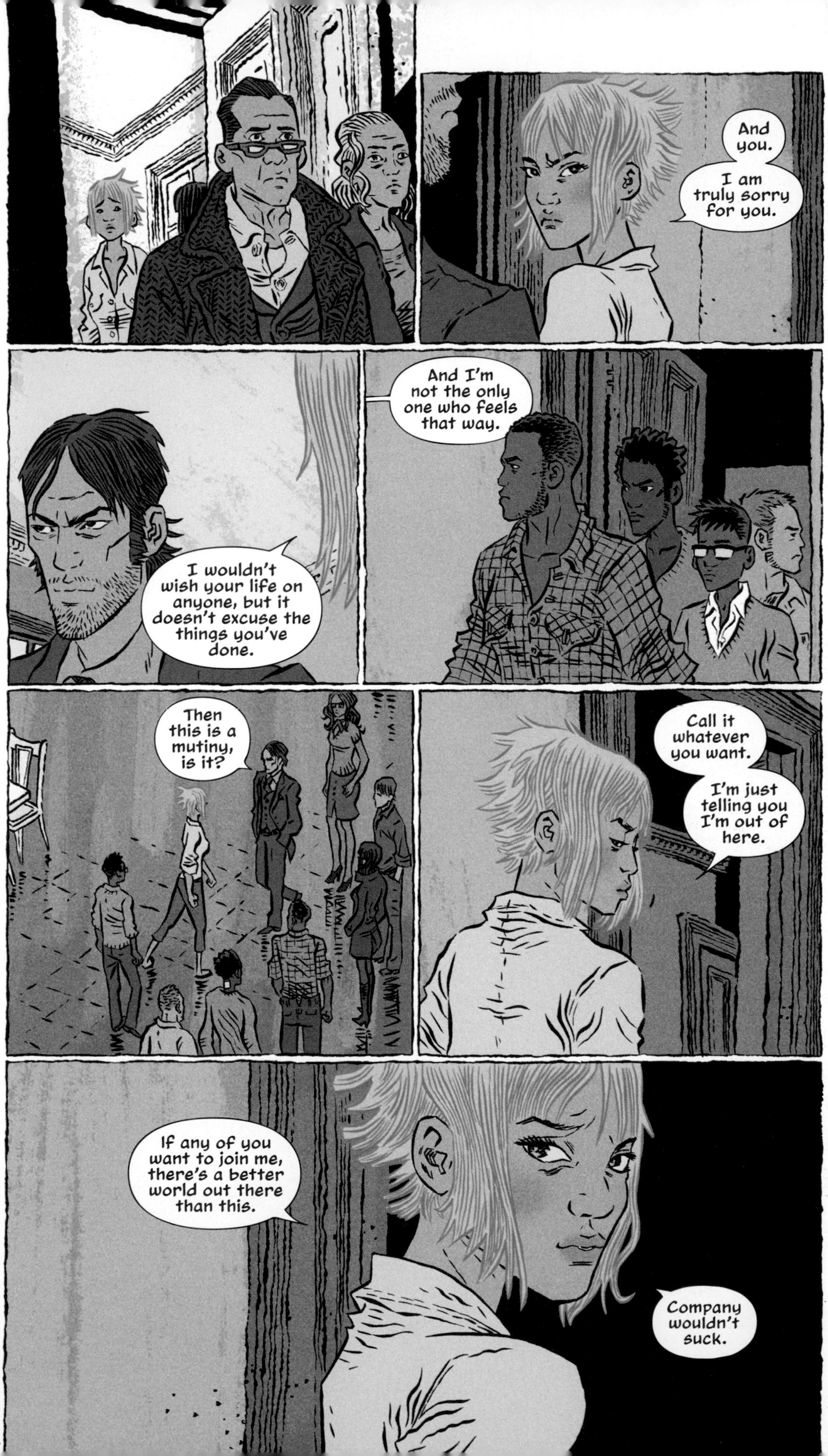
And you.
I am truly sorry for you.
I wouldn't wish your life on anyone, but it doesn't excuse the things you've done.
And I'm not the only one who feels that way.
Then this is a mutiny, is it?
Call it whatever you want.
I'm just telling you I'm out of here.
If any of you want to join me, there's a better world out there than this.
Company wouldn't suck.

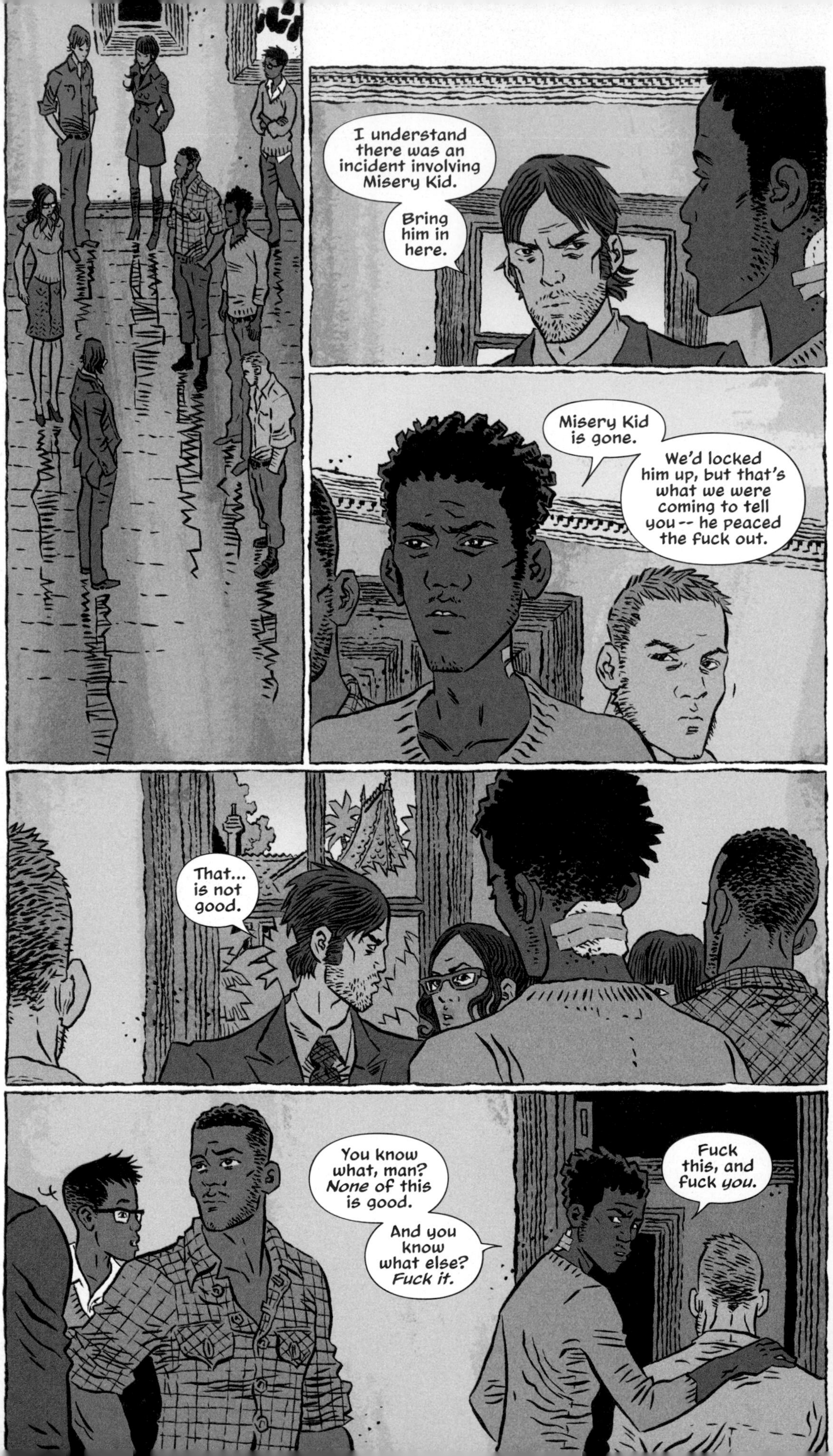
I understand there was an incident involving Misery Kid.
Bring him in here.
Misery Kid is gone.
We'd locked him up, but that's what we were coming to tell you -- he peaced the fuck out.
That... is not good.
You know what, man? *None* of this is good.
And you know what else? *Fuck it.*
Fuck this, and fuck *you.*

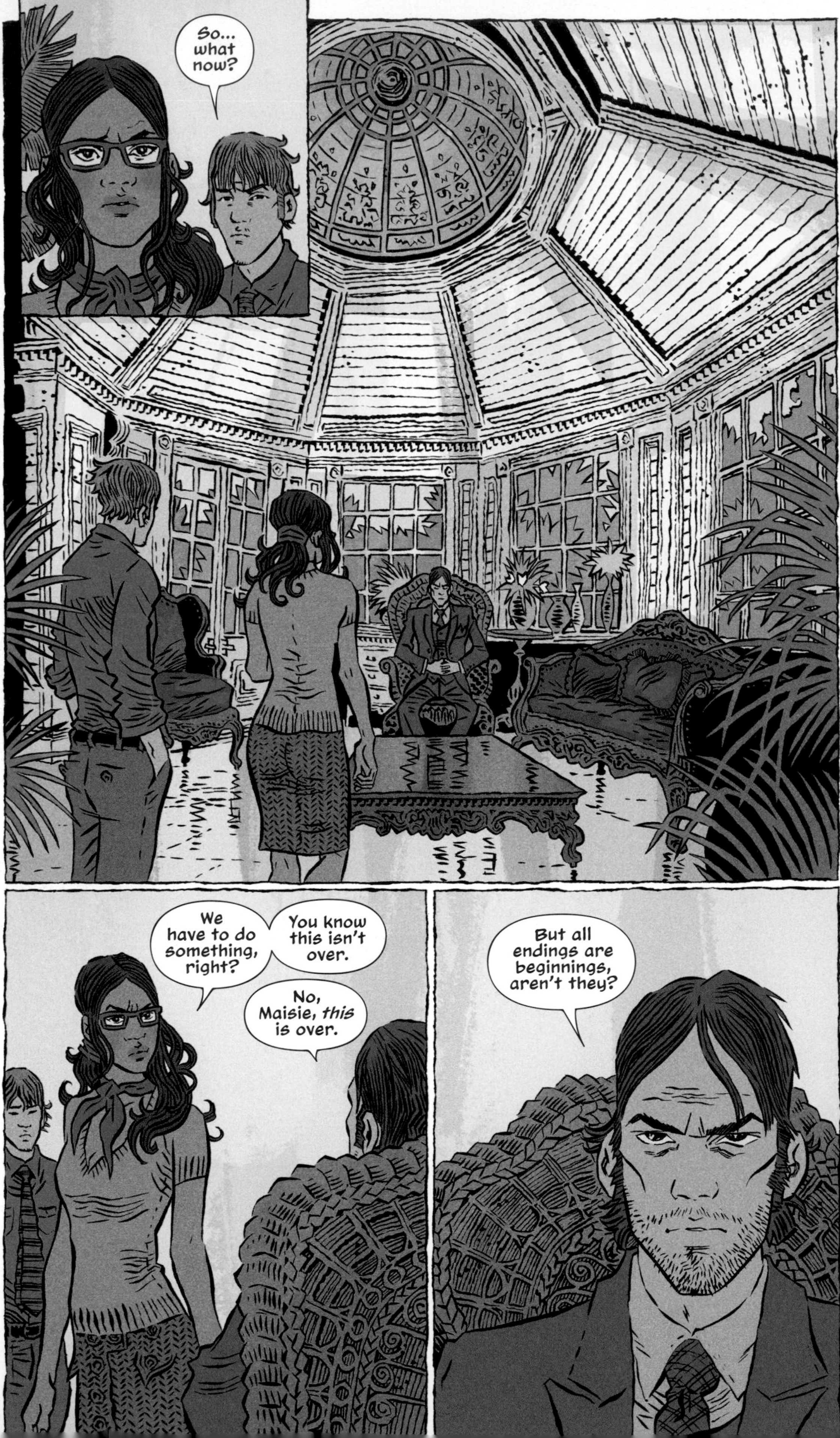
So... what now?
We have to do something, right?
You know this isn't over.
No, Maisie, *this* is over.
But all endings are beginnings, aren't they?

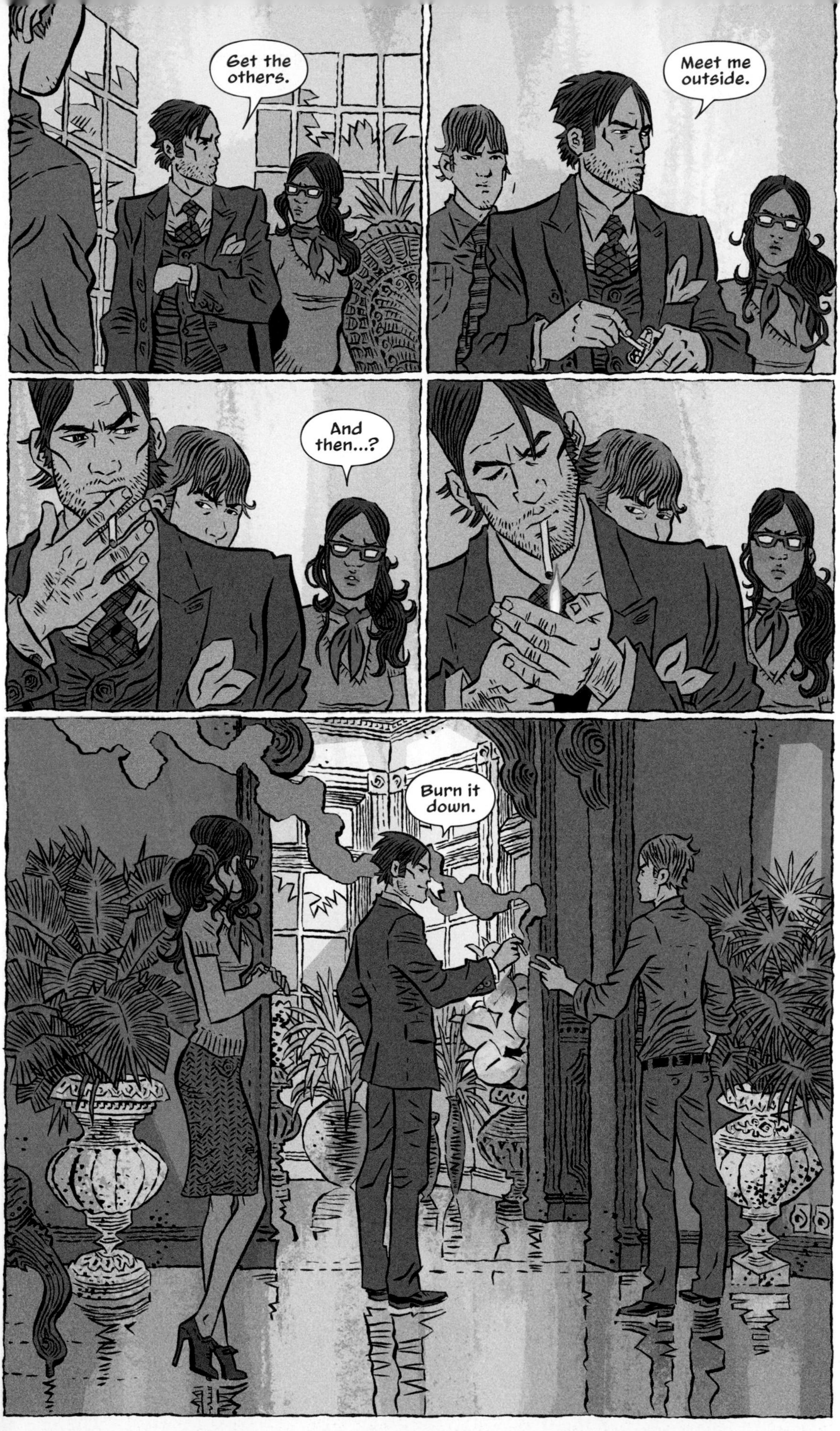
Get the others.
Meet me outside.
And then...?
Burn it down.

FIND YOUR TRUTH. FACE YOUR TRUTH. SPEAK YOUR TRUTH. BE YOUR TRUTH.

RICHARD JAMES EDWARDS

SIMON GANE
THE ARTIST

JORDIE BELLAIRE
THE COLORIST

Simon Gane draws things. Really, really well, as it turns out. The artist behind *Paris* and *The Vinyl Underground*, his other past credits include contributions to *Northlanders*, *Godzilla*, and *Graphic Classics*. Simon lives and works in Bristol, England, and when he's not drawing comics, he's basically on a never-ending quest to perfect a life of sheer awesomeness.

Jordie Bellaire is the world's most beloved Eisner-winning colorist. It would be easier to list the books she hasn't worked on than the ones she has colored, but some of the highlights include *Injection*, *Pretty Deadly*, *The Manhattan Projects*, and *Nowhere Men*. Jordie makes her home in Dublin, Ireland, but don't let the red hair fool you, she's 100% American.

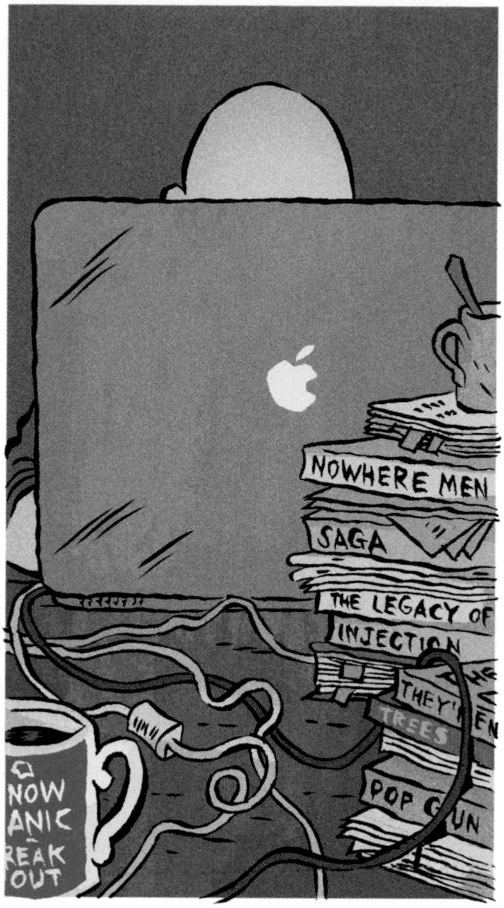
NOWHERE MEN
SAGA
THE LEGACY OF
INJECTION
TREES
NOW
ANIC
REAK
OUT

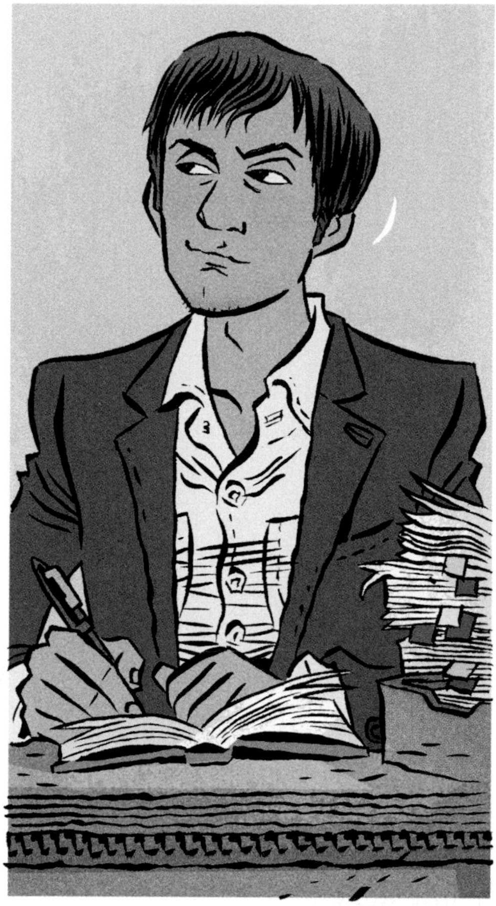

FONOGRAFIKS
THE DESIGNER

Fonografiks makes everything look its absolute best with some of the finest lettering and design in comics. From the *Luther Strode* trilogy to *Trees* to *Nowhere Men* to *Injection* to *Saga*, anything Fonografiks touches turns to, if not gold, something just as brilliant. The rich scenery of his native North East England is largely lost on him as he burns the midnight oil for his clients across the pond.

ERIC STEPHENSON
THE WRITER

Eric Stephenson has made a full-time occupation out of being utterly indebted to his beyond-amazing collaborators and eternally grateful for the tireless dedication of everyone at Image Comics. Eric is also writer and co-creator of the Eisner-nominated *Nowhere Men*, and generally speaking, he's fairly jealous of the rest of the *TNLU* team for living in the UK, even though Berkeley, California can be pretty nice, too.

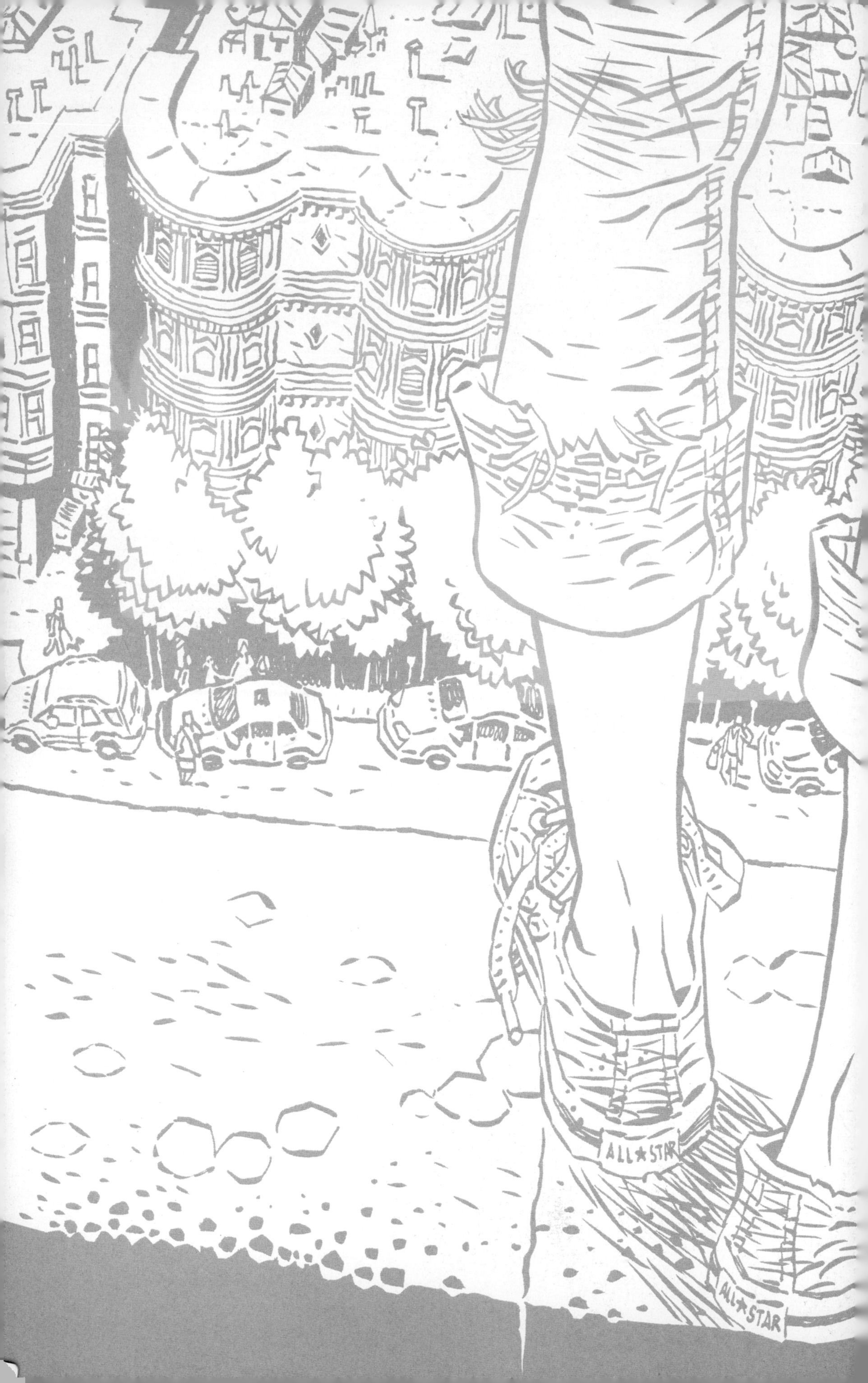
ALL★STAR
ALL★STAR